PSYKOSIS

WILHELMINA BAIRD

ACE BOOKS, NEW YORK

This book is an Ace original edition,
and has never been previously published.

PSYKOSIS

An Ace Book / published by arrangement with
the author

PRINTING HISTORY
Ace edition / September 1995

ISBN: 0-441-00238-2

ACE®
Ace Books are published by The Berkley Publishing Group,
200 Madison Avenue, New York, NY 10016.
ACE and the "A" design are trademarks
belonging to Charter Communications, Inc.

PRINTED IN THE UNITED STATES OF AMERICA

10 9 8 7 6 5 4 3 2 1

ACKNOWLEDGMENTS

Extra thanks and apologies to my editor, Laura Anne Gilman, who always works her head off but this time did it double coping with a truly fiendish manuscript, and the printers, who haven't yet sent me a time bomb, however deserved. (This is positively the last appearance of That Damned Computer.)

To Matt Bialer, who knows more than he says and keeps sending on the bacon, what more can I ask?

To Steve Hoffmann, for extremes of encouragement and constructive criticism (though he came in too late to educate Dribble)—in the hope there aren't any deer in the lake, and an assurance the music actually helps. If anyone else has the nous to go around turning my books face forward, do feel free.

To the kind people of ArmadilloCon 16 for letting me join in, particularly Casey Hamilton and Lori Wolfe, because if they hadn't raised it I'd have stayed home, never known Texas and been sorry ever after.

To Ellen Datlow, for selfless and totally undeserved kindness—in her place I'd have drunk the bastard.

And to James as always, who takes the heat.

The aliens went into Halfway third week of July when the Strip was sweltering. The temperature-inversion under the dome was getting so bad we'd run short of oxygen on the street corners and even the cool-suits were wearing smog-masks. Briefly, its whole seventy millions were in a bad temper. So aliens wouldn't have mattered, us having our own problems, if the Government hadn't decided it needed better battleships. Plus, natch, paying for the Navy, which expands on these occasions as they call in young Aris to play with their fighters, like the one that killed Sword when he was young and innocent. Which his armorer Hallway swears was once the case, though you have to take it on trust.

If you've met Governments you know expansion's a name for taxing the citizens. In our neck of the woods the 90% of the Unemployed who're Gooders and think they're normal live on Government handouts and haven't any money, and the real Strip economy doesn't believe in taxes, except maybe what they pay to Sword for keeping the peace.

This time tempers were so fragile even he couldn't do it. My stepfather Razor'd been swearing for over a year we'd have civil war someday. Someday showed up.

The riot started on one of the underground Floors where the kids go to dance. You lean on the dealers and they up their prices, the kids have to hustle harder for their switch and the paying citizens beat them up, having no money either. Then some fool calls in the cops. It was too hot for this nonsense anyway.

We'd spent ten months in our loft off-Strip behind Gordon's bakery, up to the eyes in parakeets and over-grown hollyhocks, which are Gordon things, pretend-ing it's natural for two guys to live with me, which mostly it ain't, making peaceable. It worked in general because the guys quite like each other and anyhow Sword's out all day and Moke commits sculpture at night. Don't ask about me, I'm just the bone here. I guess none of us expected it to last.

I wasn't on the Floor, pre-teens aren't my thing. But Moke and me were flashing our stuff in an eatery just off the drag when the firing started and the Honorable McLaren DeLorn, known professionally as Swordfish and mind your tailbone, dropped his iced tea in a clatter of plastic and disappeared like a bullet. Sword doesn't have to flash because everyone looks at him naturally, though his pants don't help. Since he's fully hyped, bullet's more realistic than you think, a trail of every-one else's crockery went swirling after him. I swear he left burn-marks on the floorboards. He wasn't even in a suit, I guess he was going to have to change in a phone-booth like Superman. Except you can't carry a coolsuit in one of these trick rings 'cause they're kind of bulkier, you can never nan the circuits entirely so long as they run off environment as well as bio. Question of batteries.

By the time Moke and I hit the scene at a human sprint there was nothing left but kid corpses, pooled water and drifting riot-gas. The noise had gone off down the block but we could still hear the screams fading like old bruises. The eldest kid decorating the paving could have been fifteen but it was hard to tell. She didn't have a head.

I said, "Jesus."

Moke didn't say anything. He likes kids, and was waiting for us to have one so he could civilize it. Anyhow he has a normal human stomach, which makes him unique Stripwise.

I ran to call the ambulance but the lines were blocked. By the time I got back Moke was sorting through heaps in case there was anything left alive underneath, and hysterical parents had started to arrive. An off-duty whore in a rainbow of spangles and cloned mink mini-shorts was cradling a bleeding carcass on her knees and trying to give it the kiss of life, which wasn't succeeding too well on account of you could see what was left of its heart between its ribs. A couple of local pushers were stuffing their wares into open mouths in the hope of stopping them screaming.

I went back into the eatery to throw up and had to come out again. The toilets were full. By the time the parameds arrived there wasn't much to do but arrange the bodies in rows under blankets.

Sword came back to the loft around dawn and shed his coolsuit on the bedroom floor, which made him visible. The view wasn't good. Then he stood a solid half-hour under the shower and damn the expense. Yell, our do-everything man who acts as nanny around the ranch, had made coffee and Sword fell in a chair and drank it, holding a scalding mug between both his hands as if he needed the heat.

"You'd think they wanted it," he said.

That was our personal beginning. Because if civil revolt was what the City wanted, which I personally doubt as stupidity's usually an adequate explanation, everyone got more than they bargained for. By the end of the week the entire population had been searching the attic and you'd be surprised what they found there. The fighting was working out toward the 'Burbs, the City fathers were threatening to nuke us and Sword had the choice of organizing the militia or losing control. There's only so much you can do with the help of a gene-mutated assault group, even one as well-trained as his Pack. Next thing was, he was drilling civilian squads on the drag and most of the bars had put up shutters.

If they hadn't they regretted it. Razor's officially retired as warlord, farming quietly, but quiet suits him like a blue mink coat and he thinks Sword's his son. He came roaring up to town in front of a pack of roughnecks like the Seventh Cavalry loaded with sonics, and the District Prote-Growers' Association roared in on his tail with rocket-launchers in their utilities. None of them got in because the Council had closed up the dome, so they spread out and dug themselves foxholes around the perimeter. They're kind of used to fending off pirates. After that everyone went deaf. Farmers don't go for having their crops requisitioned any more than most guys. And looking at the news, the scene was repeating itself all over the country. Who the hell had heard of Halfway?

It looked and sounded like a time-lapse version of Armageddon. Or maybe a bad acid trip. Covering the whole Eastern seaboard and propogating like a virus.

Before we got word Tokyo was burning, and that really scared them. Then the news of riots on Hampton-of-Argos and Federation flag-burning all over Virginity. Not to mention things out in farspace weren't so hot either, on the rare occasions you could capture a broadcast.

What got me involved was strictly the next thing and believe me, wars are not to where I run by nature. I normally head in the other direction, feet pumping. I guess I was tending a barrier or something or I'd at least have tried to talk Sword out of it.

The cops offered the truce-talks and it's true we were still losing children. But I don't know what possessed him to believe them, unless sex was clouding his judgment and I'd hate to think that. It might make it my fault. He'd been paying them serious bribery for the last eleven years, but any kid knows a guy who'll take it hasn't any morals.

Whatever, he went. Alone, which has to be a failure in the neural circuits, even if he *is* the personal equivalent of an ordinary Navy division. And I came home to a yell from our sane Luney Hallway, who doesn't yell, and left some marks on the floor myself, with Pack-boy Dribble dogging his mutant paws behind me and everything we could find on our united backs. Because Hall's word from the precinct was the morals were straight out of the police manual and that wasn't a conference, it was a gas-trap. Sword was dying of wrecked metabolism even before that and gas is one thing he can't swallow.

I shrieked for Razor, and got his advice. By fucking heliograph, they were jamming our radio. And found my father can't fix everything, though he really tries. I had two choices and I didn't like either. Sword hadn't spoken to his family since he was eighteen, when his daddy dumped him in a hospice and walked. If he couldn't live to kill me he'd sure as hell do his best to haunt me, but it was the best option. Or I was fucking Andromache, mourning a guy who was already dead. Except I've no stomach for lamenting on walls.

Takes a male man to die for his honor, I'd rather use the money for breakfast cereal. Worst thing about them is, they pull you in after them. Splash.

A flare traced celestial laterals across ink-blue cloud-cover and a wandering light-streak drifted to meet it. The mating lit the landscape with a glare like the opening of a shutter that outlined the trees in Japanese black and filled the sky with falling stars.

I stopped and flattened myself into a bush, cuddling my rifle. A coolsuit makes you invisible from most angles but its big disadvantage is its habit of turning black in strong changes of light. It makes silhouettes in vegetation that don't look like leaves.

The boys were lively tonight. It was the fifth or sixth volley in half an hour. Ashton was using its defenses, since you can't be sure what's in those babies, but I wished for once they'd trust the screen and let it soak them. The guys in the dugout weren't going to bombard their own side with major biologics and if this went on someone would notice the plantings looked funny.

The district was high Ari, the highest. Razor got me the sketch-map and a sneak way to the great outdoors but I didn't like the terrain. On missions like this I'm used to having Sword as back-up. This one I had me. And Dribble, who's eighteen.

The DeLorn dome rose up ahead, big as a village and completely polarized. Aris don't let anything so mere as a civil war disturb their sleep. I blinked after-images out of my eyes and darted another fifty yards.

Guard-post with parked copts and a glow in my scope that said electrics. Razor's word was the dogs were mechanical, which was always something. They're vicious but not normally psychotic.

Dribble drew level, belly to the ground. Another flare pinned us and we shrank. "I draw off guard, Cass-mama?"

"Stick around and guard my back, Fido. Leave the mechs alone, they bite."

"I got gun."

He quavered slightly. Sword's never used him for anything he couldn't sort out with his own teeth. I got to say they're shark country, genetic mutes are a local industry.

"Then use it. I need you alive."

The scope lined outer defenses at twenty yards. We eeled across and I nailed the edges with a Hall bypass. That got us a slit just about wide enough for two sets of abnormality, one undersized she, one oversized dog. We did it in turn. Sparks flashed off my suit fabric and raised my body-hair underneath. Dribble whimpered.

"You okay?"

"Yah-huh."

Meaning he wasn't.

"Want to stay here and hold off the mechs while I go talk?"

"I come. Got small burn foot."

Damn. He runs naked and his feet aren't insulated.

"There's a spray in my kang. Get it out yourself, I got my hands full."

Full meaning one brain-connected laser-rifle that was giving me vision, one heavy-duty res, an electrical cutter and some coils of this and that. If we needed even half of them we were meat. I glanced nervously at the outside corridor while he poked in my kangaroo.

Scorched grass tracked naked into dirt. Made by regular mech patrols, with or without armed people.

The spray hissed long enough for the burn to be a
big one. The red neural sightlines of my laser snapped
into focus and the shot took the mech in its control-
center before I'd finished seeing it. Dribble's disruptor
coughed at the same time. The two wrecks hit grass
less than six feet away. Ten feet up, completely silent
and they'd nearly bracketed us. Their people were elsewhere. Luckily.

"Good shooting, Drib. You set now?"

"Yeah, mama." Subdued. I wasn't sure he'd ever
even held a gun.

"Right. This here's the main shield, gonna take a
minute. Stand back, it'll probably spark."

Real serious material. Another line of electrics, a re-
pulsor-screen then the field of the dome. We'd get in
undetected when the moon fell in. That stuff needs
Sword and we didn't have him. So long as we made
it, it wouldn't matter. I fixed another bypass and
snapped on a drilling-disk to the cutter.

"Jump the line this time, huh? It's maybe eighteen
inches. My boots are protected."

"I learn that."

He passed back the spray and I zipped up my kang
and unslung the drill. I don't exactly have he-muscle
and I was sweating inside my coolsuit like a herd of
horses. Seemed to me if I unzipped it I could water the
garden. The disk spun like a catherine-wheel, slow
speeding to invisible. A smoke-ring of light spiraled
and expanded. A bright spot grew in front, reddened,
blossomed in a star of brilliance and irised out, leaving
a black hole that widened slowly. Not more than a
meter. And two feet off the ground.

"Skip, pup, fastmost. Big plant here. We don't have the power."

Jumping through hoops comes natural to Dribble, less so to me even when my belly doesn't hurt. Not to mention the gear. I could have got a prize in a contortion competition. I fell through the last bit and landed on my butt in damp earth, right on the pop of the closing flaw. You can't really hear it but I think I can. Every time.

"We go much longer?" Dribble whined.

"I sure hope not. Resonator should clear the main shield."

The drilling disk was dead, gray slag that frayed at the edges.

"How we get out?"

I let the whole rig drop in the dirt. "We don't, baby. If they won't help it isn't going to matter. Not to me."

He paused while I unhooked the res and set it for aperture. "Me neither."

"Here goes nothing."

Liberation, hah. I been working ten years on and off as a burglar and the guys do the heavy stuff. I'm the light brigade climbs skidline cliffs and brings the chips out. This one I got to do all myself. Wow-ee.

I levered the big barrel straight, steadied it with a knee and hit the button. The hum built for about an eon while I bust my gut stopping it from shaking. When Sword does it, it looks easy. Something moved on the edge of my eye and something else burped dimly. A metallic collapse was muffled in leaves. Dribble made a little lost wet private sound. Then the damn res caught and the screen opened, another small hole. *Big* power. We both fell through.

I glanced back and saw the broken mech-corpse maybe three feet from where I'd been standing. The slash across its control-bulb would have lost marks among the Navy, they like hairlines. I'm not particular. I stood up shakily.

Old, old, interplanetary money. Grass, trees that were tall when the moon was a virgin, flowers bleached by shadow that layered the lawn with heavy scent. Nothing new, nothing vulgar. The stepping-stones were crumbled from generations of gardeners, the earliest maybe even human.

"Okay, Rover, dump the shit. If you've social conversation, prepare to forget it."

His limpid eyes turned, luminous with reflections. A bright streak of tear was working down his cheek. He snuffled back snot. "We run?"

"We better."

A long terrace of lighted windows set with chaises, vased balustrade topped with urns. I stood behind a fountain of geraniums and looked along it both ways. No dogs, no guards, just a low containing wall. They believed in their security. Suckers.

I jerked my head to Dribble and stepped up. The window wasn't even locked. I kicked it open and we went through, to a frozen tableau.

Dinner chez the Aris.

One of these idyllic scenes. Papa Bear, Mama Bear and Baby arranged around a circular table in real wood I'd like to think was cloned but was probably cut whole from the trunk of the world's last giant redwood. You could have held a table-tennis championship on top. Instead they had antique silver, enough cut crystal to start a glacier and a moderate-sized orange tree in flower. Shiny chromed mechanicals fawned around them bearing trays with lids on.

The Bear family fit the décor except for Mama, who was a dwarf. Papa made the orange-tree look like a pot-plant and could have been a guy I knew, forty years

on. Except the guy hadn't forty years left. I don't know
if I mentioned, all the DeLorns average seven feet.
Sword claims it's genetic but I think it's natural arrogance. Baby, female, came up to his shoulder, which
probably made her six-six unfolded. I guess she was
self-conscious because she had that apologetic hump
tall people get when they wish they weren't. And
Mama had maybe four inches on me so she had to sit
on a cushion. They held three poised spoons, silver.
For the vichyssoise.

They all turned around when I made my entrance
and grounded the flatware. The women froze. Papa narrowed eyes like the weather on Pluto—some nearby
person who knew that look made gulping noises in my
throat—and pinned the piece of floorboard I had my
boots on. He was a foot too high but he couldn't know
that, he couldn't see me. I guess I'd made scratches in
his parquet.

What they could see of me was the rifle. Drib was
visible. Nobody screamed, which got them marks for
sand. Most people shriek their hearts out, it's the teeth
that do it. Among other things. I pointed the laser
vaguely in their direction, as a deterrent. I'm bad at
shooting guys but I also got a lead allergy. "Hi," I
whooped through my distorter. "Your name DeLorn?"

"Yes," Papa said. If he was impressed he was good
at hiding it. I could have been there to deliver their
pizza. "I suppose you want the silver."

"Thirty pieces, if you can spare it. To pay for your
son. Assuming you remember him."

His nose whitened in two straight lines, right down
to the edge of his jaw. I don't think Sword can do that
trick, but I never saw him crazy mad when he hadn't
a suit on. "I remember him clearly. What's it to you?"

"Just a ploy. I wanted to see if you could cry."

"Why?" His teeth snapped like a spring-trap.

" 'Cause you got around five minutes to do it. If you hurry."

"Before?"

"Christ. Before the City coppery tear his metabolism to pieces and run them through the sink-unit. He's a fucking hype and they got him in chemical restraint. His blood-balance was shot anyway, he's probably dead. You could have saved him yesterday. Or thirteen years ago when he was fucked. Drib and me's human. Well, I am. We ran as fast as we could but we ain't Sword so it took us too long. But you declared him dead and gave all he had to the Princess, and left his damned Techie mechanic to save him and look at you now. Eating freaking dead birds with their feet sticking up in velvet fal-lals while Sword rots and you care about the silver."

I was wailing, I could hear me. It sounded kind of eerie through the distorter. Like a banshee, whatever that is. "I fucking wish it was you."

"So do I," Pappy said promptly, trying to dissolve me. He was still too high and I'm used to vitriol. "What do you want?"

The girl pushed back her chair and the parquet took another beating. She was long, spindly and desolate like an abandoned lighthouse. At *least* six-six, her head was level with the chandelier. Her hair was pulled too tight and she gangled. She talked contralto which went with the ground but too fast. Like she was nervous. Not of guns or guys in coolsuits, but maybe of life. Of opening her mouth and making human sounds with it. Of being. I was willing to bet nobody loved her. "It's a mistake, I'm not the Princess. I was only standing in until Mac came back. We've kept thinking he would. He mustn't die. He can't. It *is* Mac you mean?"

"I don't know, Snow-White. Right now it's your old man's call. If he wants. But he ain't had his soup."

The dwarf pushed back her plate. She wasn't yesterday from kidhood but her face had once maybe launched ships. Probably not a thousand, but several. "I think we've finished dinner for tonight. If I leave the room, will you shoot me?"

I let the muzzle drop. "Hell. I came to you because there's nobody else. Sword's dying and you want the bathroom. Pull the chain for me."

"I'm going next door, to my office. To make some calls. They could do some good. Cameron, will you bully the City? Is it better in person or can you do it by phone? It's going to take me a little time, try to hold them."

"Time is what we don't have. They've got Sword at the Central Square Precinct. My stepfather could blast the copshop but that kills Sword. He can't get in, Drib and me got out because we're small. If Sword dies he'll blast it anyway. He'll do worse, he'll nuke the Council bunker and all who sail in her and believe me, he's one serious guy. And that's before we exchange biologics. Are you reading me? But it won't console me 'cause Sword'll be dead and he never did have his kid. Though I guess you wouldn't want a half-Ump bastard for a relative anyhow."

The old guy's eyes were flat as glass, his too-long fingers spread stiffly on the table. "You said you're on foot?"

"Since the boundary. You seen out there? They're blasting anything that moves. We're what's small enough to slide."

He nodded. "Go on, Anya, get started from here, I'll go in person and talk on the way." He gave me a gust of eye. "What are you, his stepbrothers? Get outside, there's a copt on the pad."

"His foot's hurt," the girl said, doubling over. Totally Snow-White.

"That ain't why he's crying."

Polar glare. "Then get outside. If my son had a child, I wouldn't care if its mother was madam in a symbiotic cathouse. Wait in the copt."

And he walked out the door like me and my gun were sugar icing. It's family. The whole pack are nuts.

"What happened?" he said as we zipped into fireworks.

Old man wasn't a bad pilot. Not up to the Navy but the kind of fast the rich young learn Ring-shooting and never forget. He ignored the sizzling flashes of warring computers that cut the sky into jigsaws and concentrated the first five minutes on voking through his throat-mike. I didn't get to hear the conversation but his jaw was rigid. It was condescension, limited vision or plain insanity. I'd met his son and I knew them all.

"He got riot-gassed under a truce-flag. For inciting revolution. Or so Hall says, and he's always right."

"I take it he's not guilty."

"You're kidding. He's guilty as hell. We all are. You could collect a fair packet on me. Don't know if Drib has a price-tag, not everyone thinks he's a person. They could maybe just want him in the pound."

Dribble behind made injured noises, little bastard's sensitive.

"I don't need money. You might unplug the gun, it's making me nervous."

He was as nervous as a grit tombstone.

"I'm using the night-sight to see with, I'm not hyped, no cero, no wetware. I just run fast."

"I heard Swordfish was hard to nail."

"He is. He's also crazy. Someone out-corrupted us."

"Someone always does."

Dribble was hunched in a miserable crouch with his jaw on my shoulder. He shivered steadily, a fine quiet vibration, without a sound. I held onto a hairy ear and stared ahead. My eyes were salty. I was fresh out of smart answers.

"Sounds to me as if the help we need's medical. I imagine the family doctor won't do."

I shook my head. Uselessly, since he couldn't see it. "He's a hype. Cero reinforcements and weird bio shit, it's specialist country. Kind's so rich he only takes the cases he feels like. Razor has one under contract." Or maybe in sight of a gun-barrel. "We're going to meet them."

"It had to be him."

"You betcha. He inherited the Strip, it don't run without him. We didn't ask them to kill our kids. We didn't volunteer our money for anti-Geek battleships."

"Neither did I. The last war took my son."

"This one's taking him again. From me. Why else would I come to you? He's spent his life avoiding you, if he knew about this he'd tear my head off. You're the only guys we know who could be big enough to pull it. For that, Razor's willing to talk to anyone. Even Aris. Welcome to Shitsville."

My voice was a twisted metallic squeal, maybe he couldn't tell I was howling. A salty pause. He was zigging reflexively between starbursts. "How long have you known?"

"That Swordfish was mine? From the first time I saw him on a newscast. Not to mention that abominable film." I knew the film, I even starred in it. It's luckily history. Sword starred too, though his part wasn't too flattering. "I know that boy. I saw him born."

"Oh," I said, small. It was probably lucky he couldn't see me, he maybe knew me too. Life's full of these nasty surprises.

"Is that thing human?"

"Why don't you ask it? He thinks Sword's his daddy."

"Sword boss," Dribble sobbed. "He want, I give. Sword raise me."

"Yeah. Where does human start, rich man?"

He turned his head, a cutout on the poled canopy. Reflections glittered off the whites of his eyes. "And what are you, besides a mouth and a gun?"

"His stepbrother, maybe. When he has time. We're his family." A flying slash made a tangent off his shield and the air filled with the stink of sulfur. The exchanges outside were nearer, reacting with the City shield in vast pulsations like sheet lightning. "Starboard three and hold it, I got to squirt down on the radio."

My ear-bead was on receive and I screwed my neck around trying for location. The short-burst transmitter at my throat ought to be spitting directions. Static cut my eardrum on every shot and sweat was crawling down my collar. A cool even voice spoke out of the middle of it. "*Cass. You're yelling.*"

"Why would that be? You see a gray copt someplace above you, private reg, company markings?"

"*Got you. Does your pilot know he has a police-copt riding herd? Tell him to lose it. They've spent the day trying to make my emplacement.*"

I twisted around. I don't have augmented vision but the next pulse showed a silhouette. "We have an escort, Judas. You yelled cop."

The cutout swiveled. "I don't have to, they probably

think they're trying to protect me. If you want weight, you also get Security.'' He switched in his mike. ''You there. I'm a Council representative and you're in my space. Move or start packing.''

''*Mr. DeLorn*?'' the panel said. ''*This area's on red alert. We've been ordered to see you in, sir.*''

''By whom?''

''*Zone Headquarters, sir.*''

''I outrank them. Stand off, I want to see your tail-fins.''

''*My captain . . .*''

The stone jaw tightened. ''Your captain just reverted to traffic. Leave.''

Did I know that voice. High Ari being aristocratic, or the Swordfish version of a tantrum. Hellish nasty but very convincing. The shadow hesitated, and swung away.

''They're looking for Razor,'' I said. ''There'll be at least one other, trying to triangulate. If they catch his beam there could be some shooting.''

''Surely not.'' He peered out at the thumping ground-batteries. The view below looked like a pinball machine. ''Do we go straight in?''

''There's no other way.''

He turned the copt's nose straight down. Orange dots streamed past. I hung onto my belt and leaned. ''Look for a pattern. Red flare, three-second pulses at five-second intervals. My father's coming up to join us, he'll follow you down. The doc's his business.''

''*On my way,*'' Razor said. ''*Took a detour, your other escort's walking home. The light-show's sight-lines, don't let the old guy panic. Just keep coming.*''

''He isn't panicking,'' I said, looking at the grave-stone profile. The edge of the lip lifted slightly.

''*Does he have an entry code?*''

I echoed aloud.

"Yes," DeLorn said. "So long as my party's still in government."

"*Okay*," Razor said amiably. "*Pass-or-fry time. Stand by for contact.*"

Near the ground was a *really* bad trip. Tracers cut up the dark like stamp-paper and the heavy intermittent poom of disruptors rattled the air around us. The nearest part of the City shield radiated off a violet halo. The defenses sounded nervy. The curfew was a bad joke. The cops had tried arresting the rioters, and caught so many they had to let most of them go again. Everyone's head was below the parapet while it hailed bottles.

A clear nose-light below us blinked upward, a blue fluo cross between its tip-beacons.

"Is this covered by the Geneva Convention?" DeLorn asked politely.

"The what? It ought to be, it's a fucking ambulance."

"*But not currently engaged in sexual activity*," Razor said in my ear. "*Ask your guy for his procedure.*"

"What's the drill?"

"They're expecting me." His throat moved. "Us. I've a six-minute window after mark, but I'd like to be nearer before we shoot it."

"*Tell him we copy*," Razor said. "*You get six minutes on mark from our side likewise, and if you fry we burn the cophouse. Maybe he'd like to pass that to his partners.*"

I passed it to DeLorn. "What about the ambulance?" was all he said. "Looks to me if we go, he goes with us."

"He's noticed," I told him. "He raised Sword."

"The hell he did."

"I expect it was hellish. He was kind of smashed up."

Silence. DeLorn swung into the field and strobing light spat over us. I hung on Dribble's ear and prayed. I've spent a lot of time in the company of lunatics.

Nothing happened. We slid through smoothly with the ambulance behind and a pair of police copts with whirling beacons fell in fore and aft and screamed us over the towers. The banging below was minor, the kind of handguns Gooders get from the attic probably kill more of the shooters than the shootees. It doesn't stop them. The lighted cross of the Police Headquarters roof swung below, and steadied. DeLorn dropped the copt in the middle.

"*Are you okay now, Mr. DeLorn?*" the trans cackled.

"I think I may manage." The escort wheeled away and the ambulance came down alongside, its door widening. "Where now?"

"Down. Get in there, I'm collecting the doc. Drib'll come with you, he'll find the place."

DeLorn looked at him with revulsion. "Do I have to?"

"Yes," Razor said briskly, jumping to the tarmac. "Nobody lies to his nose, it's why he has it. Move, dammit."

They went. I stayed. The wind was cold on the rooftop and the sweat was drying under my suit. Away from the fighting the City was dark and very still. Distant copt-engines whined out over the river and a couple of random searchlights quartered the sky. Hoping maybe there was somewhere with a lid off. There wasn't. Not with my stepfather's finger on the button.

A small sports copt came in with a hiss and dropped

almost on my feet. Real slick job, just the thing for
golf-trips. The guy slid out fast and smooth, tan elastic
shaped on a tennis-court, rich hair raked by the cut-
back jets.

"Blaine?"

"Here." I repoled my suit to black and stepped back
two. The shadow stretched the width of the roof with
me somewhere inside it. I wasn't sure I existed myself.
"Let's get down, he may be dead. If he isn't, we hope
his Daddy can work some miracles."

"Which Daddy had you in mind?" he asked dryly.

We started down the ramp.

They were in the downstairs squadroom. The cage
door was open and Sword was inside, his length doubled
on a screwed-down cot, wrists and ankles shackled to
the frame. If he'd been conscious he'd have tied them in
knots. He wasn't. They'd taken his suit off, which generally speaking's a mistake when the guy's in warpaint,
it damages your sense of esthetics. Cameron DeLorn
was holding the floor and Razor was listening with his
arms folded. He's fairly normal so DeLorn topped him
by head and shoulders but it's unhealthy to draw conclusions, he's as safe as a puff-adder.

"If you could just show me some paper," the
captain was saying. He sounded miserable. He had the
green uniform they wear and a lot of scrambled egg on
his hat and it wasn't helping him eight of his own men
were watching. His face was sweaty.

"I represent the Council," DeLorn said, like breaking glass. It sounded as if he'd said it before. "I hadn't
time for paper. I still haven't. Try your deck."

"The City's under martial law, the Council itself
can't do anything without the consent of Supreme Command." I guessed quite a bit of this conversation was

covering old ground. "I just don't have the orders . . ."

Sword's naked head was slumped to the side, the deformed bones glistening with a grayish sheen. His lips were the same color but dry. An artery pulsed in his throat. Hallway had told me a mechanical heart never stops, you can cut the guy to pieces and it carries on. Long after the corpse is garbage it'll be beating still, circulating nothing. His brain could be mush already. His chest rose and fell, lightly, once. The artery tripped and picked up.

"You're two steps behind," DeLorn said. "I *am* Supreme Command. Call them and see. And if you've a minute, check the spaceyards. If you can get an answer."

Razor lifted a brow. "There's a reason he shouldn't?"

"My wife owns them. She wants her son."

The doctor laughed abruptly, with appreciation. "Anya McLaren? United Space. What can she close, in wartime?"

DeLorn bared his teeth. "Enough. She owns merchant fleets operating out of Solar ports all the way through, plus Hampton-of-Argos and most major systems as far as Virginity. They trade a whole lot farther than that. Our labor-relations have always been good, the Guild finds it advantageous to work with us. Their captains are independent and this isn't their war. They see it as the Federation's private fuckup. Which in any case interferes with trade. You deal with me or tomorrow you're operating your ports with scab labor. Guild captains shoot them on sight. If you'd like a blockade we can close Solar by tomorrow morning, the place'll be locked as tight as an abbot's ass. Could take a little longer to call in the Outers. And I haven't started. Interplanetary Engineering."

"Solar mirrors," Razor said dreamily.

"The Government's already asked me to close down the City and I refused. I'm not in the business of wrecking civilization. That could change. I'm losing my temper. That's minor business, what I do is run dockyards. Superlunar, System, Outer Planets. They build battleships. I can be replaced, in maybe thirty years. If my son dies I could lose my motivation. You can use the same materials to can fruit."

"Nobody's going to speak to you again," I said with respect.

"Nobody speaks to me now. I outrank them all." In Sword's voice, his face despising the people who let him outrank them. Sword likes Moke because he doesn't impress him, Moke's never noticed rank. And I was wrong about Helen, her face had launched half the ships in the world.

Razor's polished eyes fastened on the captain. "You could do as he says, it would save time. Let the doctor past."

The captain looked around like he was drowning. "Mr. DeLorn, our situation's desperate . . ."

"So's mine. I have one son. The government owes me favors and we just got to payday. If you unlocked those chains, the doctor could work."

"After all," Razor said, "his class created the government."

For one moment those two vicious old men looked exactly alike. They made Swordfish look innocent. After all, he only runs a street-gang. I went and knelt by his folded side and tried to believe he was breathing.

They let us go under armed escort after a discussion that sounded like a disagreement in a yardful of pit-bulls. Cameron DeLorn was getting to be a hard man to hate. Razor and the doc loaded Sword in the ambulance with a braid of nasty gurgling tubes and took off leaving Drib and me standing on the roof-pad in the cold being disconsolate. DeLorn threw us both in the copt and lit out on their tailtubes. I sat beside him too depressed to insult anyone, cuddling my rifle like a teddybear and trying not to think of my belly. It felt like there was a hole in it. Drib lay behind with his nose on the floor and made like the tarbaby, though I heard gulps made me hope we arrived before he overflowed and we drowned.

"You can take that off," DeLorn said curtly. That was my suit. It was still blacked and I'd forgotten it.

"No, I can't. There's nothing under it but me."

23

Dammit, he was practically my father-in-law. It's probably incest.

"Then stick your head out. I won't go on riding with the Ghost of Christmas Past."

I did. He looked at me once, took in the face, and said, "Good God. You're the film-woman." Then we all shut up.

The hospital was outside the city under a private dome, well to the south and out of range of most of the fighting. It looked a bit like the Taj Mahal in cream ceramic with cathedral windows. I don't know much about architecture but I know what costs money.

Inside the Taj was very quiet. I'd never been in a clinic as a paying client, or even the friend of one. I've broken and entered, and you get a different feeling then. There were leather couches made from real dead animals and carpets like stretches of tundra and thickets of Swiss-cheese plants in china planters that probably had the corpses of the forty thieves manuring the roots. Smiley bims in mauve uniforms waded in and out carrying folders and looking like advertisements for eternal life. Razor disappeared with the doc and a gurney with Sword on it. The tubes had tendriled and had young but the blanket wasn't actually over his face. That's supposed to be good.

Cameron DeLorn looked around the way guys like him do when they're evaluating the enemy's bank-balance and the probable state of his defenses.

"Interesting," he said. "I've never been in an illegal clinic."

"Shame. If you had, you could've bought your kid some surgery and he wouldn't be Swordfish."

Then I thought if he had and he wasn't I'd never have met him and I shut up.

DeLorn looked at me like I'd crawled out of a bottle. "I once spent six months trying. Do you think it's easy to find this kind of service if you're someone like me?"

"Yes," I said. Then I thought maybe I was being unfair to him and shut up some more.

We sat around for roughly the length of the Upper Jurassic until Razor came back pinched around the nose.

"They're trying to clean up," he said. "Put some clothes on, Cass, you look like the Tin Man."

"Ain't got none."

"I'll ask around."

"I'm not coming out as a blackcurrant coughdrop," I yelled after him. He ignored me. After a while he came back with a faded blue jump that looked male and wasn't more than four sizes too big.

"You can roll the sleeves," he said.

I did. It looked terrific, if Sword was there and conscious he'd flip. Assuming he'd gotten lech a for bagladies since I last saw him.

"Whoop-hoo," I said. "I hope the boy doesn't have a crisis of lust and make like King Kong. I wouldn't like him to get a strain."

Razor looked at it. "He won't."

That's what I figured.

Someone took Dribble away to regen his foot after a bit and we worked our way through the Cretaceous. A year or two later he came back and lay in the carpet and leaked into the leg of my jump. It got pretty wet. We went on sitting.

By the time the doc came out it was daylight. Gray-yellow dawn with melancholy pink patches like scarlet fever the way it comes in glorious Ashton, but a sign the sun was lit and trying. I tried to remember from

the sitcoms what the proper thing is to say when you
want to ask if your best love's dead or not and couldn't
remember. My culture fails at vital moments. I said,
"Ulp?"

The doc was less smooth than he had been and his
hair was streaked over his eyes. He wiped his forehead
with the back of his hand. "Miss Blaine? You can see
him. Don't stay long, he's shaky."

I got up like a spring and spilled Dribble. He
woke up, whimpered and had to be trodden on by
Razor. He ain't sanitary. I ran slowly because Moke
keeps telling me you need dignity. I never worked
out why.

The room was rose-pink which isn't Sword's style
and half-full of orchids which made me sneeze and
had to be playing hell with his membranes. I put them
down to Helen. I sometimes wish I was a lady and
knew how to do it but not often. He was laid out
nicely in his civilian skin, the real one, with his hair
combed and his hands outside the blanket and he
wasn't any whiter than your ordinary dead fish which
said hard regen with no time for sunlamp, because he
was a cute bronze yesterday. He grinned at me, which
was cheating. I know when he's in grinning shape and
he wasn't.

I sat on the edge like it was fragile and took the
nearest hand. It was icy.

"You're a dogturd. You know I hate seeing you
dead."

"That's my Cass. Don't bust a gut looking for insults, I'll have forgotten them by tomorrow. My
head's hollow. Wait until I'm sane enough to kill
you."

Sword's voice has always been beautiful, it's the
smile that goes with it he's been hiding under a suit

all my life. He put his arm around me and I crawled into the space by his ribs. He wasn't in shape, he left bruises which he generally don't, but I didn't mind which is scary.

"Your daddy's outside."

"So Razor told me."

"He came running."

"You don't have to apologize, Cass. I want him."

"You do?" Sword and his old man haven't spoken since he was discharged from the Navy and he was eighteen then. He hit thirty-one a couple of months back and he hasn't changed in the ten years I've known him.

"Sure. Whistle."

I didn't have to. The old guy gave us precisely three minutes before he put his head around the door. And did a double-take.

"I'm having reality problems. This one died at eighteen."

Sword examined his spare hand to see what the makeup effects were, if any. "It's the indoor version, a bit rare for my taste. The other one's heavy-duty for talking to cops in."

"Face. If they'd any intelligence they'd have peeled it. They were too busy being scared of him."

"Face."

"Plastic. State of the art."

"Is there someone underneath?"

"Sure."

"How far down does it go?"

"To the core," Sword said. "Like an onion."

"They peeled him for surgery," I said. The old guy looked truly miserable, if granite tombstones get that way. "He had a tan and he's sulking. You ought to be happy, it's a sign of normality.''

''I'm glad to hear it.'' I wasn't clear if that meant
peeled, normal or both. ''You mean they don't know
what he looks like out of . . .''

''Face. I guess not. Does it matter?''

''Yes,'' said the old man.

''Yes,'' said the young one. Simultaneously.

''Oh,'' I said. ''Why?''

''Because I've got to show in public for a conference,'' Sword said. ''And I'd rather be McLaren
DeLorn.''

''Oh,'' I said again. Blank. Sword's sworn he
wouldn't take his father's money if it came with an
entry ticket to Paradise. ''That's all right, then.''

''Sure it is,'' he said. ''You look really cute in that
coverall, Cass. Which penitentiary do I have to break
into to kill the guy?''

''Ask your stepfather,'' I snarled. The bruises were
deepening. I didn't want to mention it but he noticed
and stopped. ''The one taught you sadism. He said I
was the Tin Man.''

He looked me over. ''He was mistaken. You're a
dead ringer for the Cowardly Scarecrow.''

The Strip had taken to war like a rat to garbage. We
were short of tourist cars but the sidewalks were crawling with white Navy uniforms, every one surrounded
by a clump of floral decals on bare buttocks, mostly
male, and a frilling of boas, mostly female. In feather
on the whole though the real thing does happen. The
owners were all three sexes but their merchandise was
the same. They looked like something you get in your
blood that gangs up and kills you.

Somebody'd set up a sweet stall at an intersection
and was hawking cutesies in pink pokes to a set of

guys mostly so dermed-up already I hoped they were conscious enough to know they were about to hit space. A couple of Brothers of Mercy leaned on the side of a salvage-copt right across looking bored and waiting to pick up survivors. There were several layers of customers laid out in cold-racks already and a couple of borderlines propped on the curb.

Somebody's pimp in a glitter overall and thigh-boots was varnishing his nails puce under a streetlamp and applying kalei treeds to the surface. Some of the positions he was advertising weren't just unknown to the Kama Sutra, they'd need a disarticulated skeleton. He probably had a few. Jetskaters zoomed in and out trailing rainbow streamers and leaving scarves of smoke that marked their route in fluorescent vapor for blocks behind.

The dome was still pulsing and the violet wave-patterns did things to the streetlights and turned the darlings' paint putrescent but no one was taking any notice. The ordinary neon colors are so indistinguishable from death you tend to assume if the guy's still standing he must be alive. It's usually true. A heap of old copt-skids and what looked like skirts from a couple of tour buses were burning in front of the Spacers' Mission, pouring black stink into the higher ranges of girders. A set of ratchety coughs and swinging hams said a pack of Tarzan punks were doing their thing, which in the present case was throwing bottles, with and without explosives. They could have been yodeling but if they were you couldn't hear for the noise. Maybe they weren't. When they want to be heard they use a bullhorn.

A guy in a green colorchange cloak edged up as I passed and said, "Psst."

"Fuck off," I said. "Next time I want to psst I'll

use a public lavatory. My friends call me Jane the Ripper.'' And I gave him a look at my ya.

"Hey-hey,'' he said, hurt. His cloak went abruptly dark blue. "You don't wanna buy some guaranteed Navy surplus exercise slings, genuine leadlined with certificate of authenticity? Your old guy's gonna love them.''

"My old guy's Swordfish,'' I said. "Apart from that, do you want a one-word answer or do I have to get definite?''

"Okay,'' he said, letting the cloak drop. It had blackened. "No need to be nasty. Ain't got his size, anyhow.''

"How would you know?''

"I wouldn't, but this ain't it. How about a complete set of platinum pube-rings with pearl fringes, give you a price?''

"Tell you, mec, you don't hear good. How about I cut your ears off and see if it sharpens 'em?''

"I said okay,'' he said, withdrawing in haste. The cloak flared. "No offense, I got a living to make.''

"Don't see the need myself,'' I growled, and turned my back. He got his first eyeful of Drib as I walked away and ten paces down I could still hear him running. He was the fourth in two blocks, the place was as full of them as weeviled cheese. If this fight lasted, everyone who was still living was going to be a millionaire, unless they swallowed each other and vanished first. But I guess the money and the merchandise were both from the Navy and their pockets have no bottoms. So long as we've guys who pay taxes.

With us I was surprised they bothered. Drib and I limped wearily and I was still wearing Razor's coverall. Most people would think as Sword did, the last owner was lifting weights for the government and cons' bims got stay-off labels. But maybe my fulsome charm shows through. Razor had dumped us at the southern walkway terminus and we'd fastlaned in but our loft's off-Strip and it's a long way when you're creased in half. Dribble edged up and took my hand. His nails are hardened steel and you can lose your fingers but he was too depressed to squeeze.

"Sword truly okay?" he fluted. "You sure?"

"No, catsmeat, I'm not. I'm not sure this is a pavement or you aren't a nightmare. I'm taking everything on trust until further notice. You wanna hotdog?"

He shook his shark head.

"Yes, you do. I'm going to buy you one. Mokey'll ask me. If you come back with a rumbling belly he won't let me in."

"Your belly rumble too."

"No, it don't, Rin Tin Tin. My belly burned clear out about five hours ago and there's nothing left but a hole. I eat whatever, it's going to fall out on the pavement. You want mustard as well as onions?"

"And ketchup," he said gloomily. He had three. It ain't surprising, he's not full-grown yet.

Gordon's windows were taped against sonics, which wouldn't help if we actually got them in force but it looked good. It being gray daylight when the screen wasn't convulsing he was open and working on a breadline. The bread was real, it's what he makes, but the line had an angst problem on account of flour supplies got hit by transport cuts. The first fifty guys get it, then there's an invisible Packer to slug people try to bulldoze. We get ours at the back door because we're tenants, plus the Moke charm. And the loan of the Packer, since Sword does have other uses for them. I shoved through the line, collecting a new lot of swear-words, and said hi to Gordon. He gave me his sad beagle smile.

"Yell's taken yours across. Is Lorn coming? His man here's getting scratchy."

"She's a bim," I said. "Lorn's detained but I don't see that stops 'em changing the guard. I'll call Hilt."

"Waste a time," the bim said sadly out of the air. "Boss-guy's inside."

That was bad news. I adore Hilt unconditionally but he weighs three tons and if he was upstairs we needed a new staircase. Drib and I threaded the tulips and a clamor of parakeets (it wasn't the hollyhock season) and I found the staircase in place. Maybe he levitated. Then I got inside and found Wings, bare, sitting opposite Moke at the table and eating our eggs like he'd never seen fruit before. He probably ranks Hilt and he weighs normal which explained the stairs but I like Hilt better.

"Hi," I said. "He's alive, you can stop fasting with grief."

"I know," he said with his mouth full. "Razor called in."

"Your guard's getting pissed."

"Tough. We're stretched. House trouble in the west burbs."

Bastards. They've a nose. It probably wears a green uniform and inhabits the heights of the police department.

"Which is why you're out there managing."

"Lay off, Cass, I just got in. Sword left me to mind the store, not direct it. He really okay?"

I slumped into one of the spare chairs.

"I dunno. Sure hope so, he looks like hell. You guys

got some food left? Kid here's starving."

"What happened to his foot?" Moke asked. He has
an eye like a gimlet.

"He stepped on a live net-junction. Gimme a break,
Mokey, it was dark. They fixed it at the hospital."

"It's more than they did you," he said, stretching
a blunt scarred hand. "You want eggs or flapjacks?"

I took the hand. It was hard, warm and friendly. He
squeezed. "Not hungry, guy. Thanks. I kind of burned
out waiting. You got coffee?"

"No," he said. "Coffee's what causes burnout. Yell,
how about milk? And flapjacks. Hans-Bjorn's sent us
honey, I was keeping it to celebrate."

"Celebrate what, Martin?"

"Dunno. You coming home, maybe. We'll keep
some to do it again when we get Sword."

"Not if he gets in there first," I said, scowling at
Wings. His romantic brown eyes had lit up.

He threw his hands in the air. Mokey patted me.
"It's a big jar. Come on, Cass, don't be nasty. Have
some nice honey. You can cry on me right after you've
finished."

Sweet Moke. "Can I cry now?"

"Not until you've eaten. You get sick when you're
hungry. Drib, sit on a chair. You're a person."

He even believes that.

Wings has Valentino bones and a vicious little mus-
tache. He got the kind of smile on his face gives the
Strip whores nightmares and dug his spoon like Winnie
the Pooh. The effect was gruesome. I decided not to
bite him until tomorrow, it might be bad luck. I leaned
on Moke's shoulder which doesn't get less bony and
nibbled about seventeen flapjacks since he turned out
to be right again. Then I moved on to Yell's franks.

"It's lucky we haven't a food shortage," Yell said. He showed me his nice teeth so I wouldn't think he was sore. He was. His girlfriend Issa'd gotten caught ex-Jove when the fight started and she was probably blockading. I told him so.

"Great," he said. "We've a food shortage."

"You could make Cass give some of hers back," Wings said innocently. He doesn't snarl these days, not when he isn't wearing his suit. I worked on laughing at him.

"Don't even think it," Yell said, and went back to the kitchen.

He was doing okay, he has contacts. When you've Sword and Drib in the same house you need them. If we got a food inspection we were in trouble but only he knows where he's cached the freezer. Yell was brought up a spacer and what they use for morals you could boil for glue.

Wings switched in the holovid while we caught up and we got the standard smoothie with sideways hair over a Doomsday face and that little wrinkle they get holding back elation. The media's first cousin to Countess Bathory, they stay young on the blood of virgins.

The war was still on, there'd been a major battle near Henrietta in which the aliens had suffered estimated losses compiled by the friendly neighborhood downtown fortuneteller and the Navy had taken out three more of their own stringers. Civic disturbances in Ashton center were being firmly repressed by the civil authorities and the area was now calm.

A couple of matched sonic vibrations from something a lot bigger than we'd had to date came in on cue to show how right they were. A little plaster fell from the ceiling and got in the gravy. Then the guy switched faces for the upping-morale one that let him

show all ninety of his teeth openly and we had a society
wedding, excerpts from the latest spaceball game in
which I was glad to see the Sabertooths were two
points ahead of the Bootleggers and a funny story in-
volving a cuddly blond child of indefinite sex and a
dog belonging to someone who told long stories. Then
they brought on the commercials.

"My God," Wings said, and left.

Yell extracted Dribble from the icebox and kicked
his behind, which probably satisfied some deep inner
need. We'd all been too busy to do it since last night.
He went right on munching, and Yell isn't a weakling.
Mokey put him back on his chair. He's the only guy
in the world doesn't feel the desire to kick.

"Go to bed, Cassandra," he said.

"Only if you come with me. I need someone to lean
on."

"That's me."

"Okay. In a minute."

I took the great circle route to the inside stairs, and
barefooted down to the workshop. The place was cold,
sad and dead. A dark teepee of heavy-duty plastic covered something columnar in the middle and I tugged
at it. I needed uplift. Six polished meters of stainless
steel with a lot of smoothed-off angles and holes above
its pelvis, between its ribs and between what was left
of the bones of its skull. It still managed to look like
Sword. The child it held in its bony hands was slender,
beautiful and dead. Their identical faces were turned to
the ceiling. It would have been the sky of Hampton-
of-Argos but we had a problem.

"Guess no one wants war memorials in wartime,"
Moke said behind me. "I should have finished him
sooner."

"They'll want him in time. Took five years for the

aliens to back off last cycle.''

''I can't sit on my hands that long. You think the Navy wants an unemployed sculptor? I could sweep flight-decks.''

''They got mechanicals, mec, they don't trust people to do it right. And only Aris have Sword's luck and get to kill themselves in hopships. Why don't you go build something?''

''The only thing I could build right now would be a tower of dead kids, Cassie.''

''Then maybe it's what they deserve. Make it.''

''Maybe I will. Later. But not today, they'd call it sedition and lock me up forever.''

They just might. Looking truth in the face isn't a prime activity of governments.

''If you really want penance, Razor could use someone to run his soy houses while he shoots up the city. He said the Umps would reach the end of the dark-brown brick road one day. Five years to go, and the Aris are mauling each other already. We're going down the tubes.''

''I know. And Gordon pays for it.''

''Gordon?''

''Generically speaking. Come to bed, girl, you're gray with pink patches. If Sword comes back and sees you he'll have my hide. Or a relapse. Or both.''

''He won't. He's out for a day or two.''

''Then we better get some sleep. If I know the man we haven't as long as you think.''

We hadn't as long as I thought at all. We climbed back up to the loft, or crawled in my case, and found Yell whacking deep-freeze prote in the skillet. He shoved his head around the door.

''If we got to have a corpse in here, will you make him lie down before he falls through the floorboards?''

"Hi, Sword," Moke said. "We were talking about you. Why don't you do as the guy says?"

He was the color of a wartime sky and his clothes looked like a spare pair of engineering jeans from the copt and one of Razor's undershirts. His hair was lank with sweat. He combed it back with his fingers and stretched in an overstrained basket-chair.

"Lying down's what you do in hospital. Why I left. If I do I may never get up again. All I need's food."

"That's not all you need," Moke said, narrow-eyed. "What are you doing here?"

"Apart from being normally obnoxious?" I added. I was sick mad. I'd taken against the orchids myself but a few hours back he was dying.

"Got work to do." He reached for a fork and stretched a yard of arm to spear fries from the pan. "Can't think in there, pink gives me migraine."

"So what's Wings for? Can't he kill people single-handed for a couple of days?"

"Sure," Sword said. "In fact he's going to have to. I've some guys to talk to, then I'm spacing."

Yell stood still. "Need somebody to fly your jumper?"

"Let you know. I'm looking in on the family estates tomorrow. See what we can pull."

"From what, big man?"

"Two wars, Martin. If there's anything left. Who's the woman with pink eyes? You bringing bims in off the street now?"

"I tried to make her go to bed," Moke said. "She wanted to look at you in steel."

"Then she's seen me." Sword gave me a cold gray look. "You got fifteen seconds before I beat you."

But I went, if only to stop him getting up to do it.

He'd feel he had to. Blackmail isn't one of the things that's beneath him.

I meant to wait them out but I guess I fell asleep because when I half-woke up a lot later Moke was draped all over me and Sword was sleeping on his belly on the other side with Dribble curled on his feet. We looked like a hard night in the Ark. Sword was still the color of the early moments of the universe but nobody's ever succeeded in arguing except Razor and I guess this time he sold the pass.

When I turned over Moke groaned and got a scissor on my left thigh and Sword opened one thoroughly alive eye and gave me a lewd wink. When we finally came around it was another violet-shaded morning and Yeller was walking through the parakeets with bread in his hands.

It looked like a great day for quarreling with Aris. The big sonics had taken up seriously and the ceiling was looking like a map of the Moon. The light pulsed blue and yellow—it's a visual effect of heavy discharges—and the tulips responded in purple and black. There were three dead pigeons in the yard and a couple of heaps of colored feathers behind Gordon's mesh. He was going to be real upset, they're his family since his son left.

Down in the cellar Sword's steel statue sang in sweet harmonics under its tarp and the cutlery rattled on the table. I wondered how long it was going to take before the crystal towers began to shatter.

It was sure as hell time someone did something. I just don't know why it has to be us, or why Sword should think he's a one-man substitute for the Navy. This war was doing funny things. He used to be content to be a street gunman. I felt like Mighty Mouse, less zoom. Small, bright and overrated.

Another dead pigeon fell on the roof while we ate and Moke went out to advise Gordon on insulating cages. The steel Sword sang like a demon under our feet, like the war-spear of Lugh that had to be kept in a cauldron of blood to stop it killing by itself. I had a feeling the cauldron was coming, and there mightn't be that much blood in the world.

The pigeons went on falling.

Sword got up the color of bone and vanished into his closet. He came out in quiet black pants, plain shirt and a bulky jacket that minimized his height to one-and-a-half human. The boots came from the kind of arcade we don't patronize.

I said, "My God," and went on hauling at the bits of my wetlook jump that don't go on without violence, such as all of it.

He pinched up his nostrils. "You can't wear that."

"Try me."

"Didn't know she was," Yell said.

"Parts of it," Moke said, judicious.

"It probably passes as smart in Hampton-of-Argos where their notion of propriety's nose-paint, but my family's old-fashioned."

"Last time I saw them I was wearing the latest light-weight self-sighter. Maybe I should try a bazooka. The rifle didn't impress them."

"We're going to meet nice people. Like my mother and sister."

"Helen and the lighthouse. Helen doesn't care, she sneers at bazookas. The lighthouse is too shy to notice. You think Moke and me don't know nice people."

"You and Moke know Hans-Bjorn Eklund. He's a liberal-minded guy who likes lunatics. Dress."

"If they're real class they'll swallow me. Like Hans-Bjorn and your old man do. Your sissy liked Drib."

The pinched look got thinner. "Relia's one of a kind. To start with, she's two meters tall."

"That's about where I'd put it."

"She's spent her life peering down at suitors. Who were many, she's very rich. Until she found one only three inches shorter who swore he loved her for herself alone."

"She should've known better. They all say that. If you're lucky they pull your string as well, to see if you say Mama."

"She didn't and wasn't. He left her holding up a wall at their engagement party and she found him in the conservatory. Where he was having sex with her best friend and discussing what they'd do with the loot."

"I hate guys who chatter during the action."

"So does she. She broke off and he told the world he'd been jilted. There was a scandal. No one speaks to her."

"I'd call that a plus."

"Her feelings are normal unluckily, like a human. I agree she's shy. Not like you."

"Too true. I'd have carved my name on him."

"That may have been one of her mistakes. She also didn't tell my old man, so he didn't kill the guy. By the time my mother found out, he was married to someone else.''

''I bet it wasn't the best friend.''

''No. But I've heard they're very happy on his new wife's money. Aurelia happened to be in love with him.''

''Then I'm surprised he's present tense. Never known you let details stop you.''

''Relia didn't want it,'' he said, like a knifeblade.

''Never known that stop you either.''

Moke was glooming over what looked like a gooseneck barnacle in wet clay. He straightened up, smearing gloop over his cheek, and wiped his hand on his pants. Nice people wouldn't be impressed. But it's marvelous what they pay for his sculpture.

''Be kind, Cass, the guy needs help. Maybe his sister does too. I made you a present.''

''Don't know if I'm going to like it. Do I get a yacht to put underneath?''

''This isn't it. This is the Tower of Babylon. When it's finished it'll be fifty feet high. No one's going to want it, even me.''

I looked closer. It was a kind of crematorium chimney made from dead children. There was a hole in the middle for smoke to come out. Someone was going to want it, I'm his business manager and I know.

''Yech. If my present's a deathmask I promise to wear it. It'll go with the bazooka.''

Sword made patient, like something left over from Easter Island. Moke dug in his jeans and fished out silver with a scatter of moonstones. If you really tried you could put your finger through. It may have featured a guy and a bim having unnatural congress among a constellation. In four dimensions, which is Moke-normal.

"Gee, thank you, Mokey, it's beautiful. They'll see I'm the ideal partner for their little boy right away. Will you put your left foot behind your right ear, Sword? I've never tried this."

"Why don't I just kill her?"

"She loves you." Moke was born a peacemaker and he's never learned better. "Tell her how glamorous she is in black and she'll put her other jump on."

I growled at him. Pulling my string's his specialty. I say Mama every time.

Flying in advanced sonics is like inhabiting a microwave in an egg-cup. We rang and jittered and I watched the rivets anxiously to see if they held. In their place I wouldn't have. The climate was Snow-Queen at the downtown highrises. The bronze mirror windows were fractured into jigsaws and their debris littered the sidewalk. They sounded like a china-cabinet in a hurricane.

"Haven't we got baffles?" I yelled, above the singing in my sinuses.

"Sure. We're using them. If we weren't we'd have damage."

I watched another pigeon thump off the canopy and plunge roofwards in a spray of feathers.

"Uh-huh. I wouldn't like that. Am I wrong, or do we have to cross country?"

"Don't worry, I'm in contact."

"Radical."

Razor's had ninety years to practice. As we shot the screen the sonics cut and a buzzing silence closed over us. I looked below and saw earthworks. A moonscape of mud cheesed with craters, fractured rock, drifts of glittery shale. A small dome was shorted to a burn-ring with dust-devils at the center. Sand. There were ghosts of shapes that could have been garden. Silicon archeology. I wondered about the people.

"Razor gave them time to relocate."

"Sure." They don't, of course. It's called war.

The DeLorn compound looked bigger in daylight. Its force-screen glowed with blue highlights and the triple defenses circled out of sight. Their electrics lit red LEDs on our canopy-display. I wondered what had made me think I could get in.

"You must have been crazy," Sword said, looking down.

"Learned it from you." I stared across velvet acres. "What's them?"

"Horses. You've seen them."

"In vidshows. It's indecent. Those is zoo animals. Where's the tigers?"

"My mother rides. Relia used to. Now they're too small for her."

Aris. What did it cost them to have horses? And they sat on them. When you can get a good scooter for eight hundred bucks and it doesn't eat a thing.

"You got brontosauruses too?"

"No," he said.

The mess of copts was primped with badges saying people with egg on their heads. There were also a couple of long sleek ones with blacked-out windows with sulky guys leaning on the fairings wishing their boots weren't so tight. A stand of oleanders hid a battered human job.

"Who's the lowlife?"

"Hall, at a guess."

I'd forgotten his armorer was ex-Navy. Razor's utility with yellow stencils was a calculated insult, nose to nose with something so starred-over I'd have put it at Admiral. One of them was going to have to back up and I bet I knew who it wasn't.

The gang were five miles inland in what I suppose was the library. The Reference Foundation in Ashton Central's smaller but the idea's the same. We were being cozy because you could almost talk without a loudhailer and mechanicals were carrying trays around. Canapés were laid out on a sidetable. The guys divided into the Navy, a matched set of suits, several thumby gonzos in old fatigues wondering what you did with the canapés, and Razor. I sat beside him. "Hi. How we doing?"

"It's been noisier. Right now we're talking the aliens in the attic."

"We have them all the time. Don't we?"

"Every fourteen or fifteen years. And there's stuff the Government's been sitting on. Situation can't last, it's why Sword's here."

"He's going to solve it single-handed."

"He's going to try. He wants to be Ambassador."

"To Geeks?" The guy was hitting new highs in nuttiness.

"Yeah." He looked at me sadly. "Can you think of something better?"

I snarled. "Yeah. They killed him once. He could let someone else do it."

"That's exactly why he wants to do it himself."

Helen drifted over in a cleavage was an insult to nurture and handed out flutes. My reaction-dyed mailbag sniffed her perfume and turned magenta. Her old man stood by a mantel supported by Gog and Magog and leaned his elbow on their heads. "Could we come to order?"

We could. Hallway was fixated by a bust on a column but he has a permanent interest in electronic entomology. The bust might have been Caesar, though I wouldn't bet on it. What was more interesting was what was behind. When he and she straightened they were looking into each other's eyes. Hall's from Luna and seven-three so his look sloped down and the light-house's sloped up and the shockwave rattled the windows. My bag went blue. Aurelia's face changed like a stoplight. Hall had his back to me, but his spine froze. Sword's eye was glacially un-innocent. They scurried for seats with their heads ducked and counted their fingers but they both kept peeking. It was cute.

Razor'd collected a weathered blonde with an eggy collar, Admiral's boots and a haircut by Dimitri. She cased my seven feet of trouble, McLaren DeLorn's lashes veiling cold Swordfish eyes.

"Hi, Meany. Hoped you'd grown out of bad jokes."

"Hi, Brand, pleased you could make it. I'm still serious."

"It's what I was afraid of."

They grinned like old buddies.

"Admiral of the Fleet," Razor murmured. "Federated Planets. Sound like business?"

"Complete waste of time," a meaty type in a turtleneck said. His fingernails were blue and he had lowercase boom. The line of his jaw was rounded and hard at the same time, like a pumpkin. His eyes could have been glass. "We have paid diplomats."

"There's nothing there, Councilman. How can they talk to smears? Meany's fought Geeks. They could want him."

"Deep-fried," Sword said. "How's the fight coming?"

"Right question. Badly."

"Worse than last time?"

"Not good."

The pumpkin inflated. "Is there something we should know?"

"Several things. Can I pass you my Head of Intelligence?"

An old high-ultra in a spangled cap. Gray enough to be Brand's father and she was no chickie. "We're talking people. Last war cost us a million and a half fighting personnel, a third of them sixteen or under. We lost four inhabited planets, maybe seventy million more. Plus the reparable damage. They were frontier posts so the people were ground-breakers. That was War Three. I date back to One. My mother, my sister and I got away from Unity in the first wave forty-three years ago, my father sent us to Argos. He and my uncle farmed kelp. They aimed to defend their territory with shotguns. Unity isn't there any more. I went back two wars later in a radiation-suit and I knew it from the chart. They were far out back then. They're coming closer."

"Which has us worried on Argos," Brand said. "We're nearer the warzone and we're conscious superlight means just that. We're holding a front, and it could get too long. When we go, you follow."

"Ashton's running out of control," Razor said. "And I don't mean street clashes. Two different House groups in the 'burbs have shown up with abandoned stocks of obsolete nucleonics. Up to date we've stopped them. We had a long-time agreement with the police, which was broken without notice by your side yesterday. I hope you know where the nukes are. And it's spreading world-wide. We can't keep hold on all of them. Our society's imploding."

"We've already apologized," a silver guy in a suit said wearily. "It was a mistake, we admit it. Imploding's a strong word. We won't help ourselves by . . ."

"Panic?" Razor suggested softly. "What word would you like? Fission?"

"Still fussing over a street gunman?" Pumpkin-face

snorted. "The police seemed to me entirely correct. Factional rumbles can't be tolerated. Given adequate backup our law-enforcement agencies . . ."

"Such as what? Should we call on the Navy?"

"Surely the point is . . ."

"Gentlemen," said the silvery type. "Of course you're both right. We can't have internal fighting in time of war, and the war's more serious than you realize. Our local troubles relate directly to the Admiral's concerns. But the police—"

"The cops are tied in reef-knots," a sharp-faced redhead in pale suiting cut in. "There are renegade Families involved. Obsolete nucleonics don't get abandoned. People with strings are using House sheikdoms and certain Heads are willing to sacrifice almost anything. If House gets access—"

"Thank you, Madam Vice-President. It's getting nasty and we daren't have it spill over. Mr. Morland's concerned with more than his class, or even the legitimacy of their aspirations. Wandering warheads are urgent. A backfire here could destroy our rear. I admit a conference is a slight hope but I'm willing to try. The Diplomatic Service can be consulted. But Major DeLorn could be our key to the door. If the aliens value their kind. His kill-record's unequaled."

"They could want to look at me," Sword said. "Without the gunsight. We're old acquaintance."

"We need keys here too," the elder DeLorn said. "Somebody's got to start talking. The Families don't want to, but when it hurts enough they'll find voices. The question's what we're willing to accept. We began by murdering children. Do we nuke our own cities next? It's too late to buy out, even with concessions. We've gone too far. People no longer want bribes, they want freedom. We're talking access to government."

"For illiterates?" Pumpkin-Jaw said, his jaw swelling.

"I don't exclude education," DeLorn said dryly. "I hear some Family juniors need a domestic to count their change."

Someone snickered. It could have been the redhead.

"So we need agreements," the silver guy said. "Time's pressing. We want ideas, please. Feel free to discuss things. Call in your principals . . ."

I slid an eye to Sword. His arms were crossed and his gaze absent. I'd once thought he'd no feelings. He had a good coolsuit. The boy was sitting on tension. His fingers were white.

Helen smoothed what threads there were around the edge of her cleavage and smiled like burning towers. Clumps of heads argued around her and slates chattered in code among the bindings. "There's one good maxim in war: keep your eye on the commissariat. Another drink?"

It came in long-necked bottles in an icebucket with caviar on the side. I could get to like her.

We spent the discussion looking at horses, Sword thought it was educational. They were a lot like animals, big and smelly with teeth. You can take herbivore and set it to music, I know what teeth are for. I offered one sugar and it bit me like I expected. Hall and Aurelia stood around looking superior but they're too big to be put on top. I'm small and Sword's spent years not listening, we could've had bloodshed. A domestic saved us by calling us in. Animals are like gardens, overrated. They both make me sneeze.

The guys had reached agreement, with bruises. A couple were breathing down their noses and the pumpkin was purple. Sword had become symbolic, an Ari prince who fought for Umpdom, someone cared. Like, Sword did. But something'd got 'em going. Looked more and more like stuff we ought to know. Hall could come, to show Techs were welcome, and Razor was Ump advisor with three thumbs. Daddy DeLorn was reporting to the Council and the Right Honorable McLaren was Ambassador to Geeks. The lucky suckers.

And we could go home. The delegations did, with a lot of rich mechanical whistling, and Razor and the Admiral had a contest in gallantry and he let her win. Silence fell except for the smash of domestics collecting glassware. Those of us left poured the last of the bottle and looked like a party, God knew why. I smelled dying.

"Congratulations."

"Big fucking deal." I hadn't forgiven those horses. "When do we go?"

"When I have Mokey."

"That's my line. You took a left turn lately?"

"Don't be dumb, Cass, he thinks form. If we've got to interpret smears I'll take Moke every time, he intuits things. We've never seen Geeks, they don't leave traces."

"And what'll I do, knit socks for soldiers?"

"Hold my hand."

"Apart from that, you macho pig."

"Hold my hand, Cass. It's all the comfort I need."

"Dammit, you bum, I been holding it all afternoon."

"Licking the skin off. I thought it was starvation, I'm short three fingers. That gives you two days to pack. When Brand moves she's a flier."

"Goody. Can I have a lot of new dinner-overalls from Shcherbatsky?"

"Yes, you female demon. Anything that stops you

eating me. If you don't behave I'll buy you a tiara."

"You sure know how to terrify a woman."

"And me," the lighthouse said from the corner. She was behind a stand of palms being invisible, it was a family habit. Sword bucked. To stay with horses.

"No."

"I can help." She made a DeLorn jaw, sized down for female. "You'll need a social secretary. I've worked with Mother."

"I said no." He sounded the way he did when I was fourteen, I used to kick him. "It's dangerous."

"Not for Cassandra."

"Cass is a nogood street burglar with an evil nature and if anyone gets fresh with her she knifes him."

"He taught me how himself."

"And you care for her." Pathetic.

"Don't take it personal, Moke and me've spent years fighting it. His macho protective bit. He means you're the female of the species and younger so he'll have to look after you. Look after means escort to the bathroom, he doesn't believe we can do it alone."

"Thank you, Cassandra."

"He thinks I'm no good."

"He's thought that about me for years. I jump on him."

"Oh." She peeped timidly past me. What was past me was Hall, and apart from being male and single he's red-haired, freckled, intellectual and sweet. "You've all been friends for such ages."

"Cass is three years younger than you," Sword said, falling for it. You should always beware of pathetic girls with little timid voices.

"Oh, is she?" Aurelia said with innocence.

"I think you need a secretary," Hallway said. He's

had practice avoiding riots with Swordfish in them. "Let Cass prowl."

Sword looked from one to the other with a flaring eye. "As you like. But I won't be responsible."

"Oh, no, Mac," Aurelia said with humble gratitude. "I wouldn't want you to at all."

Hallway didn't say anything. He was looking at his clean surgeon's fingertips. They must have been interesting, he looked at them for minutes and minutes.

We'd family dinner around the giant redwood and the old man and Helen made jokes about their friends and rivals. Late, I should think. Sword talked about Wittgenstein. Hall and Aurelia made spaces of silence at each end of the table like bookends. Helen's latest dress showed more bellybutton than the last which hadn't seemed possible, proving money buys anything. Naturally I wasn't jealous at all.

At the end they drifted off so the lighthouse could show Hallway something important like a pre-Noah duckpress, and Sword and I were left alone. I grinned to let him know I forgave him.

"Your old guys are okay for Aris. And their caviar's galactic."

"Beluga." His voice was far away. His face scared me. Like a crystal skull, every bone showing through.

"You shouldn't be fucking here, you were in hospital last night."

He draped an arm around my neck. "I find my old guys okay myself. But I'm like the man in the song, Cass, I'm sick in my heart and I fain would lie down. Take me home."

"Okay, guy. Lean."

Sword's bones are enhanced cerosteel but he has the muscles to match and he moves like a shadow. He gave me a grin like the return of the vampire and faked dropping it all on my shoulder. Somewhere in the middle his face went out and his eyes turned blank like a switched-off light. His whole reinforced weight came crashing on my arm and I felt tendons tear and bones rip apart as my knees folded.

Cameron DeLorn crossed the floor like a bullet just before my back broke. He slid an arm under, caught the weight on his chest and held him up long enough for me to crumple and roll out from under. By the time he'd lowered him to the floor Sword had blinked and his face was alive again. He stretched out an uncertain hand, propped himself up and glanced around, shaking his head. Then his face drew up all its intelligence like a searchlight and flung it in my eyes.

"Cassandra?"

"I slipped." My voice was quaky. "Think I sprained me."

"I'll see to it," his father said. "Let's get some pain-killers on and I'll call a medic." He hauled on Sword's wrist and got him upright. "You okay, son?"

"Cass is right, I just left the hospital. Where's the damned doctor? The girl's hurt."

But while the Bones operated with a hand-regenerator he loomed above me with his jaw-muscles lumpy.

"Cass, don't ever let me do that again. I can't lose you."

"Hey, mec, you're kidding. You want me on top for the rest of your life?"

"Yes. That's exactly what I want."

I almost thought he meant it.

Moke gloomed down the chimney of his crematorium. I understood that, it would have given nervous
quivers to a vampire bat. The dead children were getting
deader and bits were dropping off. Looked to me it was
returning to dust the hard way before he'd even made it.

"You were right, Mokey, it's horrible."

"I told you it was," he said. Deep depression in the
Moke-weather. It's lack of hard labor, he's usually too
busy to notice.

"Do you have to make it in radioactive mud?"

"I thought bronze," he said, with deeper gloom. He
isn't against bronze but he prefers it to bong. That
wasn't going to bong, it was going to sit there being
shat on by everything in sight with a snitch of good
taste, including dogs and little children.

"You wouldn't rather do it in blue china or
something and convert it to a candlestick?"

"Um," he said.

"I got good news, we're packing."

In his state any news had to be good. He looked pained. "There's a war on, Cassandra."

"I know. That's why we're packing. Sword's going to makeum big pow-wow with the fucking aliens."

"Then he doesn't need me. I've promised to redesign Gordon's birdhouse."

"We do exactly need you, Martin," Sword said. "Gordon doesn't want his birdhouse redesigned, he only says so to make you happy. He and his son did it themselves to their total satisfaction. I need someone knows form."

Moke reoriented his head the necessary five feet and considered. "The Navy's got them. They're called exobiologists and they do beautiful things with ugly cubic microscopes."

"Gorgeous. What they've told us to date is it's organic with silicon base, a little silicon to a lot of organic, and the whole thing's reduced to a smudge. I hoped your ideas would be more dynamic."

"I'd have to see one."

"So would the exobs. What we've seen in forty-three years comes down to shreds and broken spicules. Space doesn't seem to agree with them. I can tell you from personal experience they're right in there and fighting like bastards. Jelly doughnuts they ain't. Since what we know's zilch, anyone can play. The exobs'll tell you how they breathe and what they eat, supposing they do either. You can tell me what they are."

"Um," Moke said. He smeared his thumb over the clay and misshaped a row of skulls. They'd been hideous before. "I'm thinking of smoke signals."

"Spelling SOS, I hope. Are you going to have a little man with a blanket, or something sophisticated like a bellows? Come downstairs and pick your tools, I'd get it wrong. I ain't artistic.''

Mokey watched him recede down the steps. When Sword gets ideas he has this habit of carrying them through. If it kills us all, which it often does. When clanging sounds started floating on the breeze he got up and threw a wet cloth on the crematorium.

''Shit,'' he said. ''You know what that cutter cost?''

The answer is you bet he does. Sword checks the accounts, I guess it's an inherited talent. But when he wants to be annoying no expense is spared. Moke galloped down three steps at a time, and not too early. I heard them yelling at each other in the distance.

I propped my feet on the table. ''How's the beer?''

Yell's head appeared. ''Cold and wet. Am I tools?''

''Lonely?''

''What do you think?''

Issa hadn't been home in a month.

''Hell, the way Moke's imagination's running if you don't take an end he'll wind up with a hernia. Anyhow Hall tells me there's room on battleships.''

''Not room, countryside. Greck country. *Greck* greck,''

Yeller started as a spacer, the sort go around in ships where you can see both ends at once with the naked eye. It makes him snobbish. Issa's the same; tough, competent and tends to throw intrusive bims over her shoulder and tread on them. She wears spike heels. She'd screwed a bank into a downpayment lately, on an old ship of the kind you walk onto, sniff and run about looking for a place to throw up in, and promoted herself Captain. She was running it with two other bims and a guy. The guy was gay which would complicate life for humans but they seemed happy. Sword says spacers are psychotic which is probably true, he gets along with them.

"Unless you'd rather stay home and fix Gordon's birdhouse."

"Nah. Sword's right, Gordon likes it the way it is, he gets upset seeing Moke mooch. Should I go down maybe and separate 'em?"

"Not worth it. With Sword you can't and with Moke it ain't necessary. The boys will return when they've finished breaking things. I'll get the bill in time. Put the jug on the table and if they take much longer we can probably get totaled before they come back."

We sat peaceably listening to the clatter. A couple of glasses later Moke and Sword came up, in that order, with a kitbag each, Moke's containing tools, Sword's the big cutter for serious metal. I could see the Naval captain was going to fall all over us. If we ever got out of the brig we'd be able to talk to the aliens or dice them, whichever came first.

"Nice to see you. We've had the beer."

"Then you'd better have another jug or you're both about to have short lives." Sword dumped the bag and reached for my glass with an arm like a leadline.

Moke let his drop heavily, which ain't usual. He turned me hard shiny eyes like I hadn't seen since the day Dosh lay down and couldn't get up, before things changed forever.

"I changed my mind."

"Great."

"I'm going to turn it into a candle. In pale ceramic. Translucent, I think. And I got to redo the figures, I want them intertwined. I need to work out how to run a permanent flame up the middle. In a fifty-foot pipe."

"Rocket exhaust country," Yell said.

"It's what I've been telling him. If he wants to study

the behavior of refractories, Naval ships are built in ceramic.''

"Um," I said. If anyone really wanted to study the behavior of refractories they could start with Swordfish.

"You got time, Yell? Or you waiting for Issa?"

"She's running machine-parts around the edge of the battlezone. I'd rather be someplace I don't have to think about it."

"Hard," Moke said. He sounded vague. Yeller looked at him sharply. "Can we take the power-rasp apart? I'm going to need it for curves."

That's roughly what I mean. And it had taken fifteen minutes.

"I hope you remembered to pack your tomahawk," I said to my seven feet of incandescence, much of it ceramic.

"I buried it. This round's peace-pipe."

"Ugh," I said.

Because if I know Sitting Bull, and I've had ten years to learn, what he does with peace-pipes is smash them on people's heads. Assuming they have heads to smash them on. If they haven't he's apt to improvise. It was going to be one interesting truce-talk.

The ship came as advertised but in realspace. Wall to wall. You couldn't see it from the ground because of the cloud-cover but once you got out of atmosphere it swung behind the Moon like a small planet, glimmering. A shoal of shuttles and hopships swam around its flanks like brit. It sucked them in from time to time and spat them back out like it was breathing.

Close up its flanks widened to fill the sky. A horizontal plane, dulled and cratered, splashed with trails where meteorites had melted, patched with green and brown like it was arable. Rust, dust, magnetized particles. You expected to see huts down there and bare-foot guys in tunics driving plows. Except it was in vacuum. The entry-port was as big as Ashton International Spaceport with much the same traffic. The shuttles and tenders weren't brit-sized. Most of them were bigger than we were.

We'd taken Razor's lighter to Lunaport with enough junk to fill a destroyer and done the circular worm-jive in and out the subways to Liberty while six sets of guys checked our papers and stuck derms all over us like Christmas garlands. The docs put Sword under a scanner and it shorted out. Admiral Brand had a brief sharp conference and they let him go. I think she told them he was a military secret.

Then they repacked our gear onto a Naval tender and everything got covered with multicolored decals and stencils in algebra. I used to wonder where the taxpayers' money went. It goes on paint. Liberty's like Ashton Internat upside down. A lot of glare, a lot of noise and people rushing wildly around not getting anywhere. You spend hours belted up wondering when this sucker's going to take off then you wake up and find it already has. Since we were at war they livened our wait by checking our papers every fifteen minutes. It passes time.

We joined a stream falling into the crater, which had lights around the edge that didn't help and a set of landing grids so far down you needed binoculars. Most of the fry don't land, they take up temporary moorings and a squad of automatic deloaders guts them and drags the stuff away into the bowels. It gets covered in flight, it's upsetting to have micrometeorites drift into your cargo-space and vaporize the water-supply.

We settled down the rabbithole. Rows of lights went on past and the riding-spots of unloading merchanters blinked at the sides of the well. Our nose-spot was pointed into darkness and the pencil faded and got lost in the depths.

"Can they maneuver this potato?" I asked. Yeller snorted.

"No," Sword said from underneath me. He was in designer leather and faking being crushed. My fanny. The shuttle was full of diplomats who didn't know us yet and the lady in the sacque across the aisle was wearing a face went with backed-up drains. His eyes were dreamy.

"She's a battle-platform," Hall said. "What she does is travel. She has hunter-killers and pickaback assault-ships to do the maneuvering. Most of the crew are Marines from the picks, the mother-ship's own are Tech. Engineering, hospital, briefing and tracking, science. She has homes and leisure centers. She's a city. People live here."

"You heard how to tell them from spacers?" Yell asked, innocent.

"No, but I'm going to."

"If we've an engineroom fire, the nearest guy grabs an extinguisher and puts it out. If they do, they call the head of section who tells the officer of the watch, who informs the Exec who reports to the Captain who orders his Safety Officer to shout up the fire-detail. Then they go get it, after kit-inspection. It's why the Navy's full of young men and the Guild's full of old ones."

"There's also the smell," Sword said.

"Right," Yell retorted. "You guys smell like roses."

"And you guys smell like what they grow them in."

"Whereas genetic mutes—"

"Don't smell, they stink. Like this thing's air-supply," Moke said. "Which one of you's extincting?"

Sword did the snorting. "Don't be unreasonable,

Mokey, if we cut power we could drift here for months and we'd all smell. Is this bim yours? It's like nursing a litter of hyenas. Hot, squirmy and given to yowling.''

''What day is it?''

''Wednesday.''

''Then the answer's no. You've got to be strong, I'd say wild horses.''

''How about you boys come to mama and I smash both your heads in?''

The lady in the sacque turned the back of her fifty-credit hairdo and looked out the port like she meant to write a paper on rabbits. She'd a lace hanky to her nostrils. It could have been the air-supply, it had an eggy stench. The lighthouse was up front with Dribble, who had the window because it stopped people seeing him. Her nice jump with flowers was wet at the knees. She turned to her brother. I thought for a minute we were going to be buddies, she wanted to kill him too. I was wrong. Her eyes were radiant with adoration.

''Feels like we've been here from Monday to Saturday,'' I said. ''Does somebody know that we're here?''

Mokey peered out. ''Maybe fifty feet isn't enough. Should I make it a hundred?''

''If it's going to spew flame, I recommend it,'' Sword said. ''Have you thought of light-effects?''

''He did that last time.''

Moke had another stare at the well. ''It wouldn't be a chimney with lights. How about blue and green flames?''

Dribble whimpered and was sick, it was what I'd been waiting for. Aurelia gave him her own lace hanky without a quaver. Tough people, the DeLorns.

•   •   •

After we'd done the moving ramp, the bullet-train, several high-speed walkways and a maze of corridors with neon arrows, Sword got commandeered by a steward and the rest of us were sheepdogged into a nasty gray ratrun with doors down the sides, proving Alice was right about the inside of rabbitholes.

My cabin was eight feet square with a closet engineered into one corner where jets of water hit you in the face when you opened the door and another in another where you could hang your spare uniform for when this happened. I dumped my soaked coverall in the laundry slot and put on a modest transparent jump while I went to see what the stew had done with Sword. Several people stared in the corridor but it could have been my ya. I usually carry it up my sleeve but it looks stupid when your sleeves are glassite so I'd hung it on a hip-chain to dangle. I found him in a stretch of scenery the size of *The Field of the Cloth of Gold* with matching decor, calf-deep, looking like an abandoned windmill.

"Hi, mec. Got a compass?"

"No, but I've filed a requisition." He inspected me. "You look every inch the Ambassador's lady. Especially around the middle."

"Not my fault, I think they misread 'Ambassador's Suite' as 'Ambassador's Suitcases.' Now I got my duffle in my cabin I'm gonna have to sleep in the passage. Could you requisition me a pup-tent at the same time?"

"Sure. Pitch it anywhere. If you meet Moke or Hall in the grass while you're doing it give me a shout, I want to talk to them."

I dropped on a bed as wide as the Great Mongolian Desert and as deep as the San Andreas Fault and peered up at him. "They ain't in here."

"That's okay, then. Eliminate a couple more places while I lay out some flags."

"Golf?"

"Survey."

"Uh-huh." I rolled back out on the floor. "You get the feeling the Dips and the Navy ain't totally stuck on us?"

"No, why?" He found a bell among the curlicues near the fireplace, which was real. The stew took ten minutes to answer and showed up in a white uniform with peaky boots and gloves like Mickey Mouse. Maybe it'd been working on its pipeclay.

"Could you bring Miss Blaine's things across? She'll be staying. And I need Mr. Faber next door and the rest of my group near us. I haven't time to take a train when I want to consult them."

"The cabins are allotted by the Captain. Sir," she said. Mickey-Mouse gloves down the seams of her pants but a look in her eye I'd have slapped off sharpish if we'd been elsewhere.

"Garbage," Sword said equably. "Captains never allot cabins, they've better things to do. The baggage, please."

"I thought it just came," I said, not too inaudible.

"Don't waste your time, Cass. This isn't a democracy, it's a battleship and that's a Naval rating. You point it, paint it or salute it but you don't exchange insults with it."

"I'd rather carve it into cutlets. Why should I get used to their nasty ways?"

"Because I've got to live with them. And with the Diplomatic Corps, unluckily. Have you another dress?"

I made do with glowering.

Dinner was stiffer than a celluloid collar. Mr. Ambassador DeLorn shared the Captain's table, with companion. They didn't say which but I got taken. I'd

personally rather have eaten with the crew who looked
as if they were having a better time but nobody asked
me.

The place was thick with sacques and my black
Schcherbatsky all-over evening skin with three diamond tears and gold mouth-grille caused a drop in temperature of roughly nine point three on the Richter
scale. When I get heated it raises to violet and if
sacques arch their eyebrows it's been known to develop
lambent flickers. Annoy me enough and the whole
damned thing melts and leaves me in a gilt figleaf. On
the Strip it makes them die laughing, especially if
Sword's around when it happens.

Only he wasn't. I'd Aurelia on one side in white like
a shy snow-post and a guy in a puce cravat on the
other, and if I wanted him it was going to take a tele-
gram. Sis gazed sadly into the distance where Hallway
was a diminished peak among a pack of grunts and the
cravat lectured me on zinnias. Don't know why I bring
out the garden in guys but one day I'll get it seen to.
The Captain was a tired high-ultra with startling blue
eyes and a pinch between the brows, who might have
been cute a mile nearer. He'd got Sword tied down and
I heard them in fragments between dwarf conifers.

"Chances they'll answer?"

"If they speak. Do we know?"

The Captain raised a brow at a uniform at the end
of the table. I'd have said bim, in the shortage of evidence.

"They use sonics, above our range but patterned.
We've sent messages and we may have got answers.
Unintelligible. Comm Section's working but the results
are ambiguous."

"Can we meet face to face or is it a suit job?"

"We believe they're oxy-nitros," the Exec said. She

was taller than Aurelia and possibly Luney but no light-house. More a solar flare. "The planets we've fought over have been human-habitable."

"And inhabited."

"I'm afraid so. It doesn't mean we can necessarily share atmosphere."

"We propose Resurrection," the Captain said. "Old Earth settlement, radically destroyed fifteen years back. Early re-terraform. It's neutral. We're not quite living on it and they spent a few months there before we drove them out last."

"There's a small colony," said a long type with a spaniel face. "The terraforming team, of course, and an alien research-group. Since they're close to the bat-tlezone they get specimens. It should be safe to take families, the dome's environmentally stable. They've been there several years."

I sat up suddenly. Families? I'd seen a "Crèche" sign on a side-corridor but the Navy's so full of labels I'd thought it had to be code for something. Seemed it was code for crèche. Dips aren't normal. If I'd a kid I wouldn't want to take it to meet a pack of guys smeared down to jello under pressure. They were tougher than I was, even in cravats.

We gathered on the prairie after the service and thought about a campfire but Hallway talked us out of it. He said he and Sword tried when they were kids and the sprinklers messed your electrics.

"How're the heights of power?" he asked, stretch-ing his Lunar length over a lot of floor.

"Full of little pine-trees."

"Chilly," Sword agreed. "The Navy'll cooperate if we aren't in their way. The Dips think it's a joke but they want to be around in case chestnuts are cooking.

And they've brought their children. I don't like that."

"Nor do I," Hall said. "Geeks as I knew them weren't into nurture."

"Crew think the same," Moke said. "Me and Yell talked with the guys. I think he's still out drinking. They'd experiences in common."

Sword grinned. "What's the scuttle with the sailors?"

"They think we're nuts," Hall said. He didn't look crushed.

"Worse," Moke said. "They think this'll be short and bloody or long and bloody but bloody anyhow and aliens have the habits of rabid wolverines."

"Means they've been there," Sword murmured. "Nurture, okay, it was war, they couldn't know we were children. But they'd a nice line in comeons. Rebroadcast distress calls were among the cute ones, but they've done human screams from booby-trapped wrecks and once they convinced High Command their prime was going under so they hared off to save it, when the Geeks had a blitz on elsewhere. They could be forward in translation. They can cut tapes up, anyhow."

"Were there really people on the wrecks?"

Hallway looked at me. "We don't know. If you went in to see you went up in radiation."

Oh.

"We weren't the Knights of the Round Table ourselves, Cass," Sword said. "But then I doubt if the Knights of the Round Table were either."

Yeah. So did I. "Okay. I'm going to bed, but seeing it's Wednesday I haven't any theories about who's coming with me. If anyone. Is it lace nightshirt weather or shall I unpack my teddybear?"

Silence. Moke and I looked at Sword, who owned the bed. He was lying back, head on the tilted pillow,

his face perfectly blank. His eyes were fixed on the
wall like gray marbles. I leaned over and shook him.

"Hey, Killer, it's you, Moke or my teddybear.
You've got thirty seconds before I settle for Yogi.
Speak now or get left with the décor."

His wrist was icy and as stiff as a tombstone.

"Sword?" I looked at Hallway with terror. "He did
this at home, the time he fell on me . . ."

"What?" Swordfish sat up and reached for my hand.
"I'm going to bed and since Moke says it's Wednesday
I'm keeping Cassandra. The rest of you guys can do
as you like, only don't wake me, diplomacy's exhaust-
ing. If you don't like your quarters bribe the steward
if she will, charm her if you can or torture her if all
else fails. I recommend the latter, I've tried charm and
bribery already. See you later. Much later."

Hall got up and stretched. "Take it easy, Mean."

"Check. Get some sleep, guy."

Moke hesitated unhappily. "You okay?"

"Sure," Sword said with serenity.

I believed every word. Or would have if I hadn't
known him.

I guess Moke thought the same because sometime in
the night he migrated in. Sword moved over, or so I
suppose, because in the morning he'd an arm over both
of us. I tried sneaking out and leaving them together
but they both woke up at the same moment and raced
me for the shower.

Sword got there first and I had to nearly drown him
to get my natural rights. I figured he was normal.

But he's fooled me before.

Big ships move with deliberate speed, like an elephant getting up impetus to jump through a hoop. We went into warp the second night shortly after clearing Pluto and I nearly did Moke damage.

"We did this regularly for years, Cass," he said reproachfully.

"I know. I always hated it. The bigger they are the more they discoordinate your inside."

"Have a trank."

"It's too late. I think I'll go roam corridors. Maybe there's a wild party in the Sergeants' Mess."

There wasn't. There were sergeants coming on or off shift with coffee and doughnuts and a couple of diplomats watching their kids play video-games. The Navy runs thirty-hour days and if you aren't used to it it plays hell with your metabolism. If you are it plays hell with your metabolism every time you land anywhere. A second look located Aurelia in a corner with

Dribble at her feet looking soulful. I went over.

"Hi. Looked up any good skirts lately, dogmeat?"

He used his large hurt look. "I not get chance he-ship, Cass-Mama. All the ladies wear draggy things."

I'd noticed. "You've leaked on Sister's knee again."

"Relia not mind leak, Relia like me," he said smugly. That was impossible. Nobody likes being dripped on.

"You got to kick him," I explained. "Otherwise he goes on doing it. He don't have to talk like that neither, it's something he does to be annoying."

"It's all right," she told me, shining like a beacon. "I don't mind at all. I like children."

"That's okay then. Sword'll be happy, he likes it too."

"Why do you call McLaren 'Sword'?" she asked innocently.

Drib and I looked at each other.

"It's a long story. Why'n't you ask McLaren about it sometime?"

I figure he's more inventive than I am.

I left them leaning together like a memorial to the Motherland and went up on the observation deck. It's closed to civilians but since half the Diplomatic Service spends its time up there drinking coffee with its pinky in the air and seeing the universe minds its manners I figured nobody would notice another one.

There were guys strolling around okay. Jump disturbs a lot of people's stomachs. An elegant Oriental dip in a cheong sam was doing some kind of intricate puzzle in a corner and another pair, possibly crew, were playing cards by a set of keyboards. The cheong sam smiled at me inscrutably, which was more diplomatic than most of them.

I leaned on the rail a bit and looked out of the screen

at the corrected image they holo up to give you an idea
of where you'd be if you were anywhere really. Every
so often you pass through the corona of a star out there
in realtime and the gravity-dimple makes flaring rainbows around the images and twists the surface of reality like a wrung dishcloth. You get to watch the
constellations swell and burst and fall back into their
places like fireworks as the ship rips through. I watched
it a bit, then I strolled around a bit, then I sat in a chair
under a set of chart-screens that were muttering quiet
streams of figures and wished I was in bed and hadn't
the energy to go.

Sword snuck up in my rear and sat on the arm and
breathed on me. It's something he's been doing for
years. I think being visible bothers him sometimes, he
used to be able to do it and hope I wouldn't guess.

"It's you and you can't sleep either."

"It's me and I always look at stars on Moke-nights.
Why've you abandoned Moke?"

"Jump upsets me," I said.

"After all those cruise-liners?"

"They have wild parties on cruise-liners while
everyone gets over it."

"Okay, let's constitute ourselves a wild party,"
Sword proposed.

"Your sister's having a wild party already with
Dribble in the Sergeants' Mess. She's sitting and he's
leaking on her. We could go join them and I could
drool on your knee."

"Or we could go and dig Hall out and drink some
beer." He looked wistful.

"Or Yeller? He's got friends among the engineers."

"Or both." A glimmer. "Hup."

We ran Yell to earth in a cabin full of oil-stained
types in scattered bits of uniform where Hallway was

folded in a corner. There seemed to be plenty of beer and not much discipline. They cheered when they saw us and fell about when they sized Sword. He told them with dignity he was the Federation Ambassador and they fell about some more. It seemed he'd known a couple when he and Hall were fifteen-year-old tiddlers of six-eight and seven feet respectively and when they saw them, the guys couldn't stop laughing. We reminisced half the night and I got my hair raised and finished up drunk as a skunk and Sword had to carry me back to Mokey, who was mildly surprised but amiable. He'd have been nasty about the party because he likes parties only he was busy planning hundred-foot chimneys on his slate and he'd forgotten me. It happens. It's kind of humiliating not to hold a candle to a chimney.

In the morning I met a diplomatic lady at breakfast who said, ''My dear, the women of the crew take their tone from the Ambassador's lady. One has to be careful to give the right impression.''

''I think they got it.'' Three of the engineers were bims and they'd been even drunker than I was.

After that the dips looked around me. It worked. Aurelia fell into place as social secretary, proving she was right, and the only person exasperated was Sword. His noblesse obliged him to eat with the Captain and it griped him to death. The nice people found out too late Moke was a celebrity and tried to get him into velvet but by that time he and Yell were dug into a lighter-bay with their heavy equipment and a hundred and fifty tons of weapons-grade ceramic and they couldn't have moved him with dynamite.

We were a disappointment. Except Aurelia, who even made it in a sacque. She manifested every afternoon at the coffee-hour and sat in the officers' lounge with her lovely legs spread over two or three yards of carpet like a widescreen gazelle and gazed into the distance with melancholy sweetness. A lot of guys watched her with stunned expressions but I guess she was rich for their blood because they didn't come nearer. The DeLorn money had a lot to answer for.

While the dips dippled, Hallway made dutiful rounds of the tech sections with a notepad. But after a bit his patterns of movement began looking like iron filings. They kept coming back to where they started in elegant curves. Maybe it was fellow-feeling for her length of leg. Anyhow he spent a lot of time sitting around watching her wistfully. But not as wistfully as she watched him. Unluckily they each did it when the other wasn't looking, which didn't get them far. Life's like that.

Two weeks out Sword put on his Ambassador's pants, the decent ones, and went up on the bridge. He'd been before but to gossip with the navigators, you could tell from the fit of his jeans. One of the navigators was a sultry black mama with beads in her hair who looked bedrooms at him in six hearts so I kept a suspicious eye open but what they really shared was a love of astrogation. Or so he told me. With those jeans he deserved whatever she gave him and I hoped it had teeth in it.

Bridge was an exact description and I wouldn't be surprised if they used the damn thing to join Cape Horn to the mainland when it wasn't in service. You needed a telescope to see the far end and it was full of guys in white uniforms with and without egg, some sitting around looking occupied and a lot more scurrying. They glared at us to let us know we were disturbing something very important that wouldn't happen without them, such as continuing to mess up the coronas of theoretical stars.

We walked a mile or two to the far end, passing the black navigator who was busy navigating but not too busy to pinch Sword's backside as he edged past her—he had to, there wasn't more than twenty feet between her and the next guy—and finished up at a lighted hookup with about fifteen holoscreens in different states of disturbance gyrating madly into a common image of mind-numbing complexity. Three worried techs were trying to synchronize it.

"Pretty," I said. "When's Signis?"

Sword said, "Shut up, you ignorant bim, we're talking to Geeks."

The black navigator smirked to let me know he didn't speak to her like that and if he did she'd slug him. If she'd known him as long as I have she'd know slugging him's no good, you bust your knuckles.

"That's nice. Are they listening?"

"That seems to be the problem," the youngest and best-looking of the guy guys said. There were two on the rig, one blond, C-plus, one brown, A-minus. "We're trying to raise them but we can't be sure if we're getting an answer or rhythmic static. Happens if there's a neutron-star around."

"Is there?"

"Usually," he said. The image went on twirling.

"How do you know when it's them?"

"Characteristic speech-pattern." The Captain leaned over the bim-guy's shoulder. "Or maybe it's a call-sign. About all we know is they aren't human."

Spicules and smear. "Uh-huh." I know some pretty smeary people myself but it's true they tend to also have meat. "What's the purple line?"

"Paydirt." A-minus played frantic scales on a pad.

"Shall we switch in the translator, sir?" That's the Navy. He already had since that's what they were there for but you can't let the Captain feel redundant.

"Mr. DeLorn?" The Captain sounded more than usually tired. Maybe he'd had alien conversations before.

Sword ran his eye over the rig, nodded and pointed his profile. Crazy Horse in spades. It came to me he needed a blanket. To cross his arms in.

"This is the carrier-ship *Hercules* out of Argos. McLaren DeLorn, Ambassador to the Federated Planets. My Government suggests we should talk truce-terms. We propose the planet of Resurrection as a meeting place, at any time that suits you."

White man wasn't wasting words. A longish pause. Then the nearest four screens spat rainbow zigzags and the image somersaulted lengthways several times before it settled into a slowly turning spindle. A shrill keen rattled the mikes. We all grabbed our ears and the bim-guy played games with row of switches. The hum of the rig came down an octave and we got noises like human speech as uttered by an oldfashioned fairground automaton with a dime in its slot. The cute guy with neutron-star trouble made more adjustments and a crystalline chime rang across the deck. The instruments shivered.

Maybe they were range-finding. The chime repeated several times at lowering wavelengths and ended with a singing hum. Then voices. A lot of overlapping speakers chanting on top of each other in close harmony. It took me a minute to figure out they were human. They could have been the angel choir out of the school Nativity play, wrung up so high they sounded like children.

"**Federated** PLANET *I do not read you* **do not**
copy *red leader* DO NOT READ end of engagement
unforeseen **abort mission** NO WAY JOSE
get up you lazy bums *repeat*
DO NOT READ YOU
what is your position THIS MISSION
don't see the need
RENDEZVOUS get up you lazy bums *repeat*
what the hell are you guys doing REQUESTED

message ends message ends message ends."

Which it did. The silence was even more ringing
than the transmission. The Captain reeled out the transcript, which wasn't much different, and read it with a
ridged brow.

"It's the same crap we get every time. What do you
want to do with it?"

"We'll call you back," Sword said swiftly. It looked
like a good decision. The spindle spired, swiveled and
died.

"Whew," said the elderly bim in silver coveralls
who was managing the switches. "You've aroused
their interest. That's about the clearest we've had."

"Glad you think so," the Captain said sourly.
"Don't suppose you know what it means?"

She grinned, tired. "Not right now. Suppose Mr.
Ambassador and I get together."

"Sure," said Sword.

"Mem Evander's our comm expert."

"Spent forty years on it. Shows, huh? We've been
collecting and collating all the material we've picked
up since the beginning of the first alien war and trying
to organize it into a comm-program. The thing you're
talking into's the result. It's not much of an art but

that's the state of it. I'm sorry to say what they're receiving probably sounds pretty like what you just
heard.''

"So I figured," Sword said. "The voices are human.''

"Adult, in spite of the pitch. They've taken words
and phrases from recorded transmissions they think
they've understood and they're repeating them back to
us. It's much what we're doing ourselves. You've been
told our exobs think they probably don't use oral communication much so the material's thin?''

"Your Science Officer said so.''

"It works both ways, unluckily. If they don't use
oral communication much, it isn't a method that tells
them a lot so they have as much trouble constructing
a message as we do understanding it. The vocabulary
just isn't there. There's a grammar of sorts but it's basic. For transmitting orders, perhaps? It seems to have
very little tonality and no emotional charge. We don't
know how they normally communicate but this doesn't
seem to be it.''

"How do you handle it?''

"We have to take phrases at face-value, I guess. Assuming this is actually an answer to your message,
which they may or may not have understood, we ask
what the original human communicators were saying
and how it might relate to a reply.''

Hoo. "That's gotta be fun. How do you join the
party?''

"Help yourself. Any number can play. Why don't
we go down to the mess and screw our brains over
coffee?''

The two guys fell in, grinning. They weren't bad.
But Sword gets straight As when he isn't playing foot-
sie with navigators. We processed to the mess, took

over a corner among the philodendrons and spread the transcript over the table.

" 'Federated' and 'planet' is a clear reply—why 'do not read you'?''

"Means either 'can't hear' or 'don't understand'?'' I said helpfully.

"Which could mean 'won't hear'?''

"And 'Do not copy' would mean 'Don't agree,' maybe?''

"If it's one phrase,'' the blond said doubtfully.

"It was two voices but run together. So, 'Federation don't understand, don't agree'—what? Does that go with 'red leader'? Why 'red leader'?''

"Sword said he was Ambassador who's a sort of leader, I suppose. Why not red? It's the kind of dumb thing pilots say on the radio.''

"Thank you, Cassandra. In my hunter-killing days I was Red Leader for my wing. So let's say it's me. Okay, they don't understand the Federation—why should they, we don't know what they call themselves or even how it translated—and they don't agree—don't accept, don't want?—an Earth ambassador. What about 'do not read' again and 'end of engagement'?''

"Does that match up with 'unforeseen'?'' the cute one asked. "You proposed talking truce terms, that would be the end of the engagement.''

"Right,'' Evander said. "They don't foresee an end to the war. That follows on okay with 'abort mission,' 'no way Jose.' No way do they propose to end the engagement.''

Sword made a sour face. "Nice little things. Do you think they're abusive on purpose?''

"I doubt it,'' Evander said. "I don't think they've an adequate grasp of language. I can always be wrong. It does sound that way.''

"No, it don't. I was trying to figure how you'd say 'Resurrection' if you were an alien. Do they know it's just a name? It means 'getting up again.' They say 'get up you lazy bums'—I guess your high-class pilots aren't big on literary education—and 'repeat.' Equals 'getting up again.' "

"Plus 'do not read you,' again, which sounds like 'don't understand.' Mem Blaine could be right. They don't understand Federation, they don't understand Resurrection—proper names are among the hardest things to translate—and they aren't interested in ending the war or talking to an ambassador. 'What is your position' sounds like a plain question. I mean, 'why do you want it,' or something like that."

"Could be. 'This mission,' 'don't see the need' seems a repetition."

"Except ''rendezvous,' " Evander said. "Which actually repeats Blaine's 'get up you lazy bums repeat' meaning Resurrection. They don't see the need for a rendezvous on Resurrection, which after all is what Mr. DeLorn asked for."

"If I'm Blaine, call him Meany. The engineers do."

"It's a question of protocol," she said, with a sly glint. She was old enough to be either of our grandmother.

"He's been ambassing just fine as Swordfish for generations. He don't answer to anything else."

"Which does he prefer?"

"Ask your sexy navigator."

"What navigator?" Sword said with irritation. "Guess I can't blame her education on anyone but myself. What's next?"

"Then they repeat the question, 'what the hell are you guys doing,' " A-minus said, quashing an interested look. "Which leaving out the routine expletives, gets us 'What do you want,' like Leroy suggested.''

"Plus 'requested,' which does suggest they want information. And the message ends there."

"Okay," Sword said, doing a fast edit. "In summary, they don't understand the label 'Federated Planets,' they aren't enthusiastic about meeting an ambassador, they don't mean to end the war and they don't know what we mean by Resurrection, or maybe just which planet Resurrection is, and they want more information. They don't know what we want exactly, don't see the need for a meeting but they want to know what we're up to. They haven't slammed the door."

"We think. But it figures," Evander said. "We'd like to look at them. They're going to be suspicious, naturally. We should be too. But don't you think they might really like a look at us?"

"Goes for our side," Sword said. "I'd like to see them."

"Brand hoped they'd want to see you."

"Fried."

"If that's really what it means," blond Leroy said. "We break our heads for weeks over this stuff sometimes."

"Not like this," Evander said. "We listen in and try to make sense. Since we don't know what the subject is and who's talking to whom and why, I agree we can spend weeks just trying to correlate sounds with groups we've heard before. This is the first time they've tried to answer something specific. Maybe they wanted to try out their translator as badly as we did. And Mr. DeLorn doesn't have weeks, he's here to stop the shooting. If we're likely to meet these guys face to face we'd better learn to translate quickly. We can't have a conference if there's a two-hour break between civilities while we decipher each other. We have to speed up, guys."

"I dunno. It could solve the war. If we could get a cease-fire while the guys were talking we could all just sit around and wait for them to finish. By the time they had, we'd have died of old age. No more problem."

"Her mind's like that," Sword growled. "Let's get back there. Can't wait for Act Two."

The techs got through faster second time. Maybe the Geeks were waiting. Anyhow we raised the spindle, red and green rings playing up and down its length in braids and coils. There was something right-angled in it that hurt your mind looking. Down-home not.

"Contact," said Evander. The Captain got back to leaning on her shoulder and Sword took his stand at the trans.

"The Federated Planets is our group of human-occupied systems and I'm official representative of its government. During the last war I personally killed over five thousand of your people. You killed almost everyone I knew. That seems to me a reason to talk. There's plenty of space in the Galaxy without us destroying each other for this bit."

Another long pause. Then a preliminary squeal that made everyone in range cower. The turning spindle flipped a couple of times and the dime-robot voice spat some garbled phrases and got back to crystal. The glass choir took up.

> "YOU GUYS **gotta be kidding**
> *last mission* **NO SURVIVORS** *repeat* no survivors
> **so who cares** *high command* **REQUIRES**
> *control* **THIS SECTOR** *mission headquarters*
> **coming from everywhere** LISTEN
> *we need this equipment*

NO QUESTION abort mission
what's the matter with you guys
oh come on MAKING SPACE
ain't as easy as that
LISTEN YOU BUM I'M NOT STANDING FOR
any more of your garbage **I'm telling you**
MISSION COMMAND *got it all* **what are you guys**
asking for here what is this **SURRENDER**
surrender SURRENDER **you asshole**
what are you *scared or something*
YOUR REPORT IS AWAITED *repeat*
answer **answer** *answer*

message ends message ends message ends."

"That isn't difficult," Sword said, in a voice like grit in the gears.

"It isn't?" A-minus asked innocently. According to Leroy he was called Scotty and had a devoted wife with sharp claws who worked in Engineering. I probably knew her. A shame, with Sword out there fascinating the astrogators whatever he pretended.

"I don't think so either," Evander agreed. "Back to the coffee-machine?"

We got a provisional translation a lot faster this time. Scotty said all Evander's translations were provisional, which wasn't surprising when you heard the material. She read it out anyway.

"They don't believe you're a survivor of the last war. That's interesting. Why shouldn't you be? But they don't care a lot either way. They don't agree the Galaxy's that big and they want it all. I wonder why? I'm not sure they even believe your offer to talk can be serious but if it is, the only reason they can think of is we want to surrender. What an interesting way to think. A rigid mind-set, would you say?''

"Moderately," Sword agreed. "Let's go back and twist their little arms again."

"I can hear them howling from here," I said.

"I'd like to," Leroy said morosely. It was the earlier hours of a thirty-hour morning and we'd been on the job fourteen hours straight. The guys probably longer. His eyes were blood-colored.

"Ever onward," Evander said tiredly. "Let's do it."

We went back and did. Fairly fast contact, we all seemed to be getting the habit. This spindle was doing blue and ycllow braids with sparkles. All the better to eat you with. Sword sounded somewhere between Cochise on a bad day and trouble in the subway. His voice could have been canned and used to quell riots.

"You're mistaken, surrender wasn't one of our options. We wanted to talk about a ceasefire and some kind of territorial agreement. Let's at least meet. We may have something useful to say to each other."

Very long pause. The spindle broadened, ran down the color-scale into the ultra-violet and disappeared. Then it shot back thin and high in yellow-greens that clawed at the retina. The answer took so long I thought they'd given up on us and gone. Evander played over her pad, scanning the net. Nothing. The Captain scowled at the luminous spirals that ran up and down the spindle. It multiplied and distorted from time to time in interlocking spires. We were all collecting headaches.

When even Evander was wondering about switching off another agonizing squeal woke us. It dropped swiftly toward crystal angels.

"I'LL HAVE TO TAKE THAT
on advisement LOOKY

here baby HOW ABOUT *that date* I'd
REALLY LIKE to see each other *one of these days*
where the hell are you THINKING ABOUT **going**
how'm I supposed to **FIND**
get up you lazy bums *repeat* DO YOU COPY
estimated **ETA** *how long do you* make it
DATA REQUESTED

message ends message ends message ends.''

Sword looked across at Evander. "Do you read what I do?"

"Agreement? Cautious, but yes."

"Plus request for data. Time and place."

"I'll handle it. Procedures we got."

He spoke into the trans. "Stand by for a time-count. We'll give directions for Resurrection. You'll recognize it, we fought there. Look forward to seeing you."

The spindle turned into a top and spun twisted ribbons.

"HERE'S LOOKING *at you* kid *YOU ASSHOLE*

message ends message ends message ends.''

Sword raised his brows. "You're sure they don't understand insults?"

"No," said Evander. "I'm not sure what day it is."

That wasn't surprising. It had been tomorrow for a while.

"What's procedures, when they aren't out grazing?" I asked Sword's elbow, which was nearest.

"Praxis," Evander said, running arpeggios over her pad. "Slow and boring, but we're short of solutions. Our measurements are arbitrary, based on our bodies or our home planet. So must theirs be. Maybe they locate the center of the universe on the Great Goddess Meathook who's hovering three degrees northwest spinwise of the Horse's Head. So we give them our standard time, space and direction marks so they can match them with their own system, then tell them how many x we'd measure to Resurrection. They should be able to get a fix. As Mean says, they've fought there.''

''They killed half my unit there sixteen years ago.'' He was making like he hadn't heard the promotion. I figured that's what it was. Evander had just elected him serious. ''They have to remember.''

''Want to bet?'' I asked.

''No,'' he said after a pause.

''Do we trust them?''

''No.'' No pause. ''They agreed too fast. Took too long to think first and not long enough second. In their place I'd have wanted days to consult High Command. They took twenty-seven minutes.''

The Captain nodded. ''My lower gut says the same. Evander named it. Rigid thinkers. But yes, too fast. It doesn't add somewhere.''

''Any nineteen things,'' Evander sighed. ''Let's hope nineteen's the limit, the math gets complex.''

''What do they want?''

''God knows,'' Sword said. ''I need Mokey. Knew I would.''

''Um,'' I said.

Evander was flummoxed and she's a paid-up comm artist. Moke's merely a genius and he was in the middle of a hundred-foot ceramic tower in one of the lighter-bays so we didn't even have all his attention. I wasn't sure he'd be enough. If this lot looked half the way they sounded we were in for major nose-filters and those purple zigzags on the trans said severe problems in the frontal lobes, assuming they had any.

I can smell catastrophe, and I was sneezing already.

Resurrection showed up as a glaring disk with high reflecting atmosphere patterned in grainy swirls. UV and IR made it heavily cratered, rift valleys edged with trenches zigging along the edges where continental shelves had been. It had a nice display of plate tectonics and some real hot hotspots around the craters. The whole issue was awash in torrential floods that evaporated before they hit and steamed back up into the cloud-cover. I'd heard the Government was terraforming. You could have fooled me.

"What hit it?" I asked.

"We did," Sword said. "Then they did. Then we did again."

"Oh. What was it like before?"

"Better-looking."

"When does the water settle?"

"It has in parts. There's a bit of cold dew in the trenches. The way the geology's been shook it's still seismic but there's a plant-growth program. If you look at the northern continent there are hazy cool spots. It's mainly lichen but they've tailored bacteria working on the rocks recycling oxygen into the atmosphere. It'll be habitable in a century or two. If nobody bombs it.''

"Remind me to stake places for my great-grandchildren."

"Only if they're going to be miners. Though they might just farm algae. Last lot were ranchers."

"Guess they're retraining."

"The ones who survived."

"I meant those ones. Haven't we planets that are habitable?"

"At your age, and raised on the Strip." Sword shook his head. "Yes. What's here is no population can be held to ransom, nothing worth killing for and a permanent reminder of the pleasures of war. You can't walk around much outside the domes, though. It's a drawback."

"I bet the nightspots are lousy too."

"I'll take you dancing in the mess after dinner."

"If you promise your high-ultra squeeze won't claw my eyes out."

"If she does I'll buy you new ones with gold splatters like the Exec has. They're the latest wow."

"Vulgar. You wouldn't ask your sister to wear that stuff."

"True. But Aurelia doesn't fight other bims and need new eyeballs. And if she did, I wouldn't be matching spangled frills with no front. Could you put on panties for dinner? The Captain's getting the idea we live in sin. Or do something with sin in it, anyhow."

"How right he is."

He laughed. Evilly.

●　　　●　　　●

We fought hurricane-force winds all the way to ground-level through cloud like soiled cotton and listened to the lighter's skin abrade across the force-screens. Our fuselage gave an ugly red glow to the outside vapor and the temperature got high enough to be nasty. My neighbor was a sacqueless dip in a businesslike jump with a baby around her neck in a sling and she spent the ride sponging its face from an ice-jug. The bits on show were scarlet but its lungs were okay.

"Does he go everywhere?" I screamed over the banshee whine of skin-resistance, howling winds and the baby.

"She. You bet. It's the only way she'll grow up knowing who I am."

"How about Daddy?"

"He's got Bubba. We take turns. With luck they'll each remember one of us."

"Wish you joy."

"Just wish me a water-supply," she yelled back. Her daughter seconded with a shriek of rage that outscreamed the airstream.

"Want me to hold her?" Moke shouted. He got her and made male noises. She shut up. He doesn't intend to make you feel inferior.

We came in on a beacon. It stayed dark and the turbulence lasted right to the skin of the dome. We cut the force-screen like a cheeseknife and near-silence and a fading whistle smacked us in the ears. We'd hit grid near the edge of a bubble the size of a ballpark, where the sky was a mess of dark suds that washed around the screen and the streets were lighted with pylons that threw yellow circles on brown twilight. It was the middle of dayside so things never got brighter.

The place looked sci-station, geodesic constructs for

stuff like people and a central cube without windows
for things that mattered. Guys eat sand but decks don't.
I sometimes think we're too adaptable. One of the geodesics had animal cutouts around the facets saying
school, a garland of stars burned above the chapel and
a bigger geodesic off-center had pink and mauve neons
saying *Happy Hour*. All the things the heart can sigh
for. So long's you don't get unnatural urges to jog in
the open.

The Oriental dip was standing next to me looking
around with her eyes narrowed. She came to my shoulder which made her clothes nice stuff for Kids and
Babywear. Unless she had them made special.

"Primitive, huh?"

"I've seen worse. Lot of half-developed worlds here.
The plumbing tells all."

"What's it tell?" She had me worried.

"I've six packs of wipes, if you need to share them.
There are no green tents."

"That good?"

"Means they either got indoor toilets or you dig your
own hole. I see no holes." Triangular smile. "Let's
keep hoping. I've two kids in tow."

Jesus. "Gonna be wiping."

"Seven and nine, they wipe themselves. Need to
look at the school, though, they've had too much vacation. Time they learned something, if only the theory
of wind-systems."

"There's opportunity."

"Seems so. What I do for my sins. And my son."

"He the seven or the nine?"

"The forty. He's the kid-owner."

Re-Jesus. "You're Grandma?"

"Better believe it. Also head of mission, being senior dip, supposed to keep Mr. DeLorn in line. Name's Chan.''

"Enchanted. Blaine. Don't think it's ever been done. Except by Moke, maybe."

"Also charmed. And my conclusion. If all else fails I'll appeal to Moke. Meanwhile if the guys don't like the plumbing, I get the bellyaches."

"Great vacation."

"You said it. Jen's grubbing fossils, he's an exarcheologist. Marywolf's stayed home so several times it got to be Gran's turn. Who didn't know she was getting sent on an exo. Kids are in paradise. Jen knew, he'd have hysterics."

"You ain't told him. Diplomatic."

"My life's work."

"Your old man nursing elsewhere?"

"A suicide commando found Kai's posting impure. Political or religious, I forget. Jen was a year old. He's stayed only."

"I might have quit."

"What for? It's too late now. Sometimes we're useful. Like the plumbing. What's else to do?"

The ambassadorial geo had Earth's linked circles in Sword's honor and was otherwise standard plastic, scratched-up on the floor where somebody'd dragged square things with edges. Cheap bazaar rugs covered bits of the damage. That stuff's imported and loved by someone so Moke hung them up before they got trod on, and since the walls sloped like all geodesics they made sinister flappings like spies behind the arras. Hall shelled those out before we sat. Having your sexlife on film's a specialized taste, even in the wilds where they're short on amusement.

That was the living-space. Apart from plastiles with

square-object marks where the rugs had been and a couple of low-tech mobiles that tinkled in the draft there were blownup chairs not made with Sword in mind, a table so low you had to lie down to drink off it and a breakfast-nook with high stools and an auto-chef. Yell snarled because he cooks better than it with an old-fashioned cuisomat but this was science country. And all the crockery had buttercups on the edges.

"Hello, cold prote," he said. "Do you guys want leather chicken or leather steak? Don't rack your brains, you won't be able to tell the difference."

"Swordfish, I hope you're going to talk a lot of sense to these guys very quickly. I suppose the furniture's an aid to concentration, like hot craters."

"Standard issue. Guys live like this for years at a time."

"I bet their teeth drop out."

"Possibly. If they do, they don't notice."

"It was built for Mokey," I said, enlightened.

Moke looked at me with red-green eyes. He'd been working like a dog nailing up rugs. "The plastic's okay." That's a Moke philosophy called fidelity to materials. "It's the air-currents bring sand in, I guess the rim's eroded. Inevitable in the climate. I'll fill it and maybe tape the rugs down and it'll be okay. The bedroom's decent, standard bedpads and double for Sword."

"Thick ones or thin ones?"

"The shower works," he said. Confirming my suspicions. "Of course you have to get in one at a time . . ."

"Oh, Yell. But you wouldn't really want to bring that blonde Tech-Two back, if Hall's missed a cam Issa might see."

"Cassandra, your prote's going to be particularly cold."

"You're getting nasty with old age."

"And it's going to have kelp sauce on it."

"See?"

"Don't panic, there has to be a commissary," Sword said. "You'll find the whole station eats there. How d'you think Hall and I survived five years in the Navy?"

"With difficulty," Hallway said. "Where's Dribble?"

"Sniffing Romeo's sister's skirts. Poor girl's got to have a laundry-bill like the State of the Union."

"It's time someone killed that kid."

"He's done it to me for four years and you've never objected."

"There's a reason for that," Swordfish said coldly. "Let's go look at the commissary."

He was right. It was down the snuffy-smelling street under the arcs right next to the sign saying *Happy Hour*. The door-sill had scraped a ledge in the dirt that sifted in with every gust of air. The screen was doing a lot of opening and closing with the Naval lighters and the dome seemed to generate its own drafts. Partly the cooling-plant, but just air-conditioners and breathing and atmospheric convection. A film had crept over our scarred floor already and made trails of footprints wherever we went. We had a dustmouse but it was disheartened, you could tell. It made small anxious forays now and then buzzing dismally, stirred the stuff around a bit and went back to its hole.

The joint was run by a redfaced guy with arms like Popeye and an old-fashioned broom, and it was so crowded you couldn't see the floor so the dust didn't matter. The tables and chairs were plastic in public-service red and there were he-and-she guys in bits of work-dress down to the indecent sprawled all over them. The Fed Ambassador impressed the hell out of them. They gave him a lackluster eye and went on doing what they were doing before.

Sword sighed. He has a strong sense of order and a fancy for chairs. He looked around, grabbed a handful of male collars, and put them in a pile by the wall. One of them turned out to be a bim though anyone could have made the same mistake. She bit him and screeched like a fire-alarm. I've made that error myself in my youth. His muscles are cerosteel all the way through. That cleared us a table and we sat at it. The wildlife considered us sideways and decided we had diplomatic immunity.

Red-face gave us the cold eye and got His Excellency's Number Two look in exchange, the one you can cut steel with if you run out of laser. Number One's radioactive. He did a fast take and learned what runners of eateries all over the Strip have known for years. Sword just ain't worth the aggro. He handed out a couple of handwritten menus looked written by the hand of a failing mechanical with a finger dipped in grease and Sword located steak by what I took to be X-ray vision and ordered five with, plus coffee. It came on clean plates. Surprisingly I've had worse prote in places with a cabaret. Unless some of the local zoology was the cabaret, it was hard to tell. There were a couple of leftover Christmas garlands by the bar if that meant anything.

Chan the China dip came in in a khaki coverall while we were eating and ghosted over to inspect the food. We made OK signs and she whistled the grandchildren, who spindled heads over her, and got a table by osmosis. The nearest louts set to work spoiling them. Daddy was bound to find out in the end. But I wasn't too worried for Grandma, she was cast in asbestos.

Evander arrived even later with her guys and flopped. She looked beat. I reckoned she always looked beat but that time she looked beater. Leroy had eyes like an albino hamster but Scotty was the lucky kind who gets romantic dark circles. He was alone for once but so was Sword, so heavy moves would be a waste of talent. Anyhow Moke had his eyes narrowed. He's much stronger than he looks, sculpture's a physical job.

"I'm getting too old for this," Evander groaned. "These punks think I can get three loads of high-precision equipment into one geo and load my staff on top. I've spent two hours exchanging insults with the Head of Station. I swear I'm going to retire next trip."

"She keeps saying that," Leroy said. "She knows Scotty and me are both waiting to leap into her shoes so she's too damn mean to actually do it."

"You wouldn't know what to do with my shoes if you had them."

"Right," Scotty said. "They're four sizes too small, especially for the two of us. Are we going to do something revolutionary like sleep tonight, or do you want us to set up the rig as usual?"

"They're so unreasonable," she complained. "When I was young it was an honor to be allowed to die of exhaustion in the service of your elders. This pack of degenerates expects to sleep."

"As often as twice a week sometimes," Leroy agreed sadly.

"Are you going to pander to them?" Sword asked, stretching. He had romantic dark circles himself but he hadn't noticeably slept lately. He maybe didn't like space.

"I suppose I'm going to have to, they're getting mutinous. But if you aren't headed for bed I know guys want to talk to you. We've the best exobs in the Service and there's stuff they're busting to tell."

I'd thought the exobs were grieving over gel and spicules but even Hall can be wrong. We were headed for a long night.

"I'm busting to hear them," Sword said.

"Fine. We'd love to ask you to coffee, but . . ."

"She means Scotty and me got our hammocks in the gaps between the generators," Leroy explained. "We can sleep there or stand there but not both. I think they've a luxurious geo of their own, filled with glassware."

"And smells," Scotty said helpfully.

Inevitably. "That's nice. Why don't they come to our place? If they got the rotgut we'll show them our autochef. I bet it makes kelp canapés."

The guys all gave me guy-type looks.

"We'll go around right away," Sword said.

Sometimes even the bright ones are suckers.

The exob geo was by the sci-block, which I guess was forming terra. It throbbed. They had a lab, a lot of circuitry and a bedroom in back but they were sprawling among the benches on random slob and sag furniture, cooking up coffee in beakers. Hall does that too but with strange biologists I'd rather know who died in there last.

The up side was an icebox with a live-in bottle-opener. Yell's eyes brightened. Scotty was right about the glassware and also the smell, though part of that was maybe Resurrection. It smelled heavily of something, and not what you'd put behind your ears. They'd a dust-lock but it hadn't kept the sand out.

Only three of the bodies lived there, a guy and paired bims who were either twins or married. They held hands. The rest were two space scientists and a statistician from the terraform team. One pure sweetie, one pure bastard and the most beautiful bim I've ever seen, with raven locks to her hips and the kind of eye goes with flamenco guitars. I looked at Sword nastily and he looked nastily back.

"Coffee or coffee?"

"Beer in a bottle. Doesn't the wind drive you guys crazy?"

"Yes," the beauty said. "They tell you you get used to it but don't believe them."

"It explains how we are," the guy said. He was a medium redhead with a friendly grin, bleached-out by the climate. "Excuse us if we stop now and then to rip each other's throats out."

"Don't mind us, we're used to it." This isn't strictly true, Moke jumps on violence, but I like to encourage people.

"Okay," Sword said, admiring beer. Some dumbo had put it in a beaker but the alky might distract bacteria. "We're listening."

"Ah-huh," said the taller of the married bims. She was thunderously dark but not as splendid as the spaceist. They were in station grays, which do nothing for anyone who ain't the star of a space epic. Except Flamenco, who was the mold the stars come in. "We wanted to show you."

Sword's ears stood up. Not that he was expecting them to tell, we were waiting for the drum-roll.

"Half the doctoral dissertations for forty years have been alien morphology," the guy said. "Material from space-wrecks."

"Spicules and smear."

"Which produce conclusions. Light fragile form, supported by air or maybe water. Prefer E-type planets where there'd be both. Partly gelatinous. No skeleton though the spicules suggest support, a stiffening or framework. The obvious work is genetic reconstruction—"

"Which we've been trying," the second bim, the small light one, put in. "Like everyone."

"And you got something."

"Yeah. A whole lot of goo," the dark one said. "Like everyone." A slap. They wanted to finish their patter.

"Which wasn't intelligent," Sword said.

"No, it wasn't," the light one agreed. "Didn't develop spicules. Or anything much. Sort of sat there."

"In water or air?"

"Water. Collapsed in air. No skeleton."

"It was living, though," the guy said. "Like cloned meat. Living but not alive, if you see what I mean."

"They're water-forms?"

"We thought so. Then recently we tried something. A hunch. Dumb, but Retta got it so we tried."

Ta-ra-ta ta-TA. Retta rose like a trapezist about to do four-and-half rolls and posed by a glass bell on a bench. It was covered by a tarp. It should have had stars and spangles on it but I guess they ran out.

"Some totally dumb thing I read in highschool, happened to stick. Bio-archeology, extinct Earth-animal, called sponges. Guys did really gross stuff with them, bath-pets or something."

"Yech," Beauty and I said in close harmony.

"They lived in water, sea-animals. Rooted. Not intelligent."

"Like our goo," her mate said.

"Put 'em through a centrifuge, they'd turn out as

mush. Jelly and spicules. Stuff you could pass through a filter. But if you poured the whole mess back into seawater—''

Tara-ra ta-TING. She whipped the cloth off.

A circle of round mouths. The jar had a layer of muddy sand in the bottom with a mushroom-shaped lump of gray-translucent jelly, rooted. It was standing on matted tendrils that humped through the mud and their pale tips splayed against the glass. There was something alert about them, as if they were paying attention. The cap was smooth and droopy, maybe eighteen inches across, with a fringe of beady stuff around the edge. The stem looked too fragile to hold it up. It swayed slightly like there was a breeze, though there wasn't, and the beads swung in short arcs. It was maybe two feet tall, almost touching the pierced cover. If it got any bigger they'd have to transplant it. I didn't envy them. Nothing would have made me touch that gray blind thing with its wise tendrils.

"That's it?" Sword said explosively.

"Well, not exactly," the guy said.

"It's not intelligent," Retta said. "We've tried every test we know. It doesn't think because it hasn't anything to think with. It's sensitive like maybe an amoeba, it recognizes heat and light and it reacts to food. It's looking for prote."

"But it's not an amoeba," Moke said, lit up with interest. It's a look he usually saves for face-to-faces with tortured metal. "It's pretty complex. What's the fringe for?"

"We don't know. Maybe only cilia, it uses it to herd prote-flakes. They look complex, yeah. But it hasn't a central nervous system or sense-organs we can identify. There's a generalized response that maybe comes from a skin-reaction. It doesn't feel pain but it avoids heat.

It could be an idiot. Or something from hydroponics, if they had any. Or a form of fetus. We keep watching.''

"Is it in water or air?''

"Air. It can spend an couple of hours underwater without harm but it's basically an air-breather. Not as fragile as it looks. Gelatin backed by silicious spicules with a tough integument holding it together. It's light, full of bubbles. It breathes by exchanging the contents, there's a slow circulation from the outside. The stored oxygen supports it underwater. It doesn't use much since it's not lively.''

"It may extract dissolved oxygen too,'' the guy said. "But it's slow, maybe vestigial. Leave it too long under, it hibernates.''

"Shuts down, anyhow. Kind of closes like an umbrella. Fish it out and warm it and it comes back to what you see.''

"How did you get it?''

"Retta's archy-sponges,'' the pale bim said. "We found a lump looked like one organism, vacuum-dried whole. Centrifuged it, put the mess in saline. Then we gened and it took. It used the material to re-form.''

"It's grown,'' Retta said. "We regened about three months back. It started around eight inches but it eats its weight in prote every couple of days. We don't know what the adult size is, or if it has one. Some seabeasts go on growing. The limit could be determined by gravity.''

"So Geeks could be bigger?'' Sword said. "Maybe a lot?''

"Can't tell,'' the guy said. "Our specimen looked whole but we could be wrong. It could be partial or even dead. The central nervous system might have decayed before we got it.''

"A brain-damaged jellyfish."

"Something like that."

"But it acts healthy," Retta said. "It's symmetrical, it eats protein, it gets bigger. It formed in the saline and crawled out."

"Crawled?" Sword said with sudden attention.

"It has primitive capacities for movement," her shadow said. "Or had. When it formed, the base was stubbier with pseudo-feet and it scuttled. Clumsy but mobile. When it settled they lengthened to real roots. Seems fixed now."

"We need to experiment," the guy said. "But it's the only whole specimen we've found. Right now we're watching it grow."

"There's nothing you've missed?" Moke asked. "Odd senses?" Apologetic. "The ship guys are intelligent."

Retta shrugged. "When it formed we hoped for more. We keep testing. But our job's all mysteries. This is the tissue alien ships are full of. There isn't any other. Either the others, the intellects, evaporated, every hide and hair and left their dinner behind, or this is one. An idiot, or a throwback, or a juvenile. But them."

Whoo-hoo. I looked at Swordfish. His skin had that pale translucent look, the bones of his skull coming through at the cheekbones and jaw. His eyes were black holes, singularities that took in and gave nothing back.

"How d'you feel about discussing peace with smart-aleck sponges, guy?"

"Or even dumb ones?" Yeller said. He didn't look healthy either. None of us had been getting much sleep.

"I'll talk to anything," Sword said. "Singing jelly if I have to. Whatever it takes. What else do we know?"

"Ask these guys," the pale bim said. "Grad and Strina've mapped distribution."

"How would they breed?" Moke asked quickly.

Retta noticed him carefully. People do when they've heard him speak. "Good question. We don't know. Could be offshoots, seeds, even division, though that would be unusual with a form as complex as this. But I'd make a bet."

"Yeah?"

"If I've met this shape before, they do a lot of it."

"They are alien," the guy said.

"Yeah," Sword said. "But I'd bet they do a lot too."

"Why?"

"They want the whole of space for themselves. If they practice safe sex it's going to surprise me."

Strina was Naval for Beauty. Her male half lacked the looks but they were a perfect song-and-dance act.

"Our data's the same way. And Whitney's done math for it." That was the stat, who scowled at us blackly. "They're established over a lot of the Outer Arm and the charts show them spreading. If we don't watch our tails we could wake up encircled. How was it again, Whit?"

"Expansion every fourteen or fifteen years," the stat growled. Her voice was deep, almost bass, and it went with her face. "In all dimensions. We're holding this front. They're exploding back towards the Rim, east and west along the Arm and inwards around our flanks. It'll take a couple of centuries but they're moving to pincer us. Signs say runaway population-growth with no natural bounds, expanding wherever there's a supportive environment. They outnumber us already, counting major centers, and their numbers are increasing exponentially. They could overrun the area within three hundred years.''

So that's what Brand wasn't telling the Council. Sword's face had tightened. ''Makes it plainer why they aren't great talkers. How long to saturation once a colony's founded?''

''Depends on the planet,'' Grad said. ''With oxygen and water they could outgrow an Earth-type in a couple hundred years. Their growth's wild. And the bad news is they're adaptable. They like pure Es but our reports say they've colonized places we'd have to terraform. Water and cold don't faze them. They dislike heat and they're sensitive to some forms of radiation—blue stars. But they adapt.''

''It could be form,'' the pale bim said. ''The integument may thicken with cold and they don't have to maintain blood-circulation. This one passes out underwater, but it's adapted just fine to our prote. And we know absolutely nothing about their culture. We can't tell what their technology's like.''

''Their battleships function,'' Sword said. ''Believe me.''

''Yes and no,'' Grad said. ''There are things they're good at. Advanced weapons, sophisticated drive and grav units. But they're odd. Take battle-computers. Highly specialized, do the job, but limited. Engineered for attack, maximum damage and quit. They barely try defense, like they find it easier to die than program ways out. They're nil on the things we have in our pockets. Pads, slates, timers. Primitive comm-links, no equivalent for holo. I don't mean gear we don't recognize, I mean blanko. Unless they read pictures off the hull-plates. Hardly any tools. Nothing looks like cryo, or hospital equipment, or kitchen gear. Lockers are for arms storage. Some micro-appliances we haven't figured out yet, we think medical. Honeycombs of open bulkheads radiating from a shaft system, and not a thing in them but organic remains. Place plastered with dried gloop but nobody home, not even their baggage. If they had any.''

''They communicate good for guys without commlinks.''

''Yeah,'' Grad said glumly. ''Some things complex, the rest too simple. We're missing something.''

''Maybe they don't need tools,'' Moke observed. ''Retta's specimen remade itself and takes raw prote. If they all do, they could eat anything and put themselves together if they got hurt.''

Oh, great. For me jelly's permanent bad news but self-regenerating jelly's the end. I thought maybe I'd just go home. Until I looked at Sword's ivory face and Moke's red-veined eyes.

Whatever the Geeks were, our hands were full of them.

The alien ships showed up suddenly in the morning like a sprouting of poison mushrooms and drifted around the orbit winking at us.

"Weird," I said.

I'd been having dreams featuring the thing in Retta's jar and it wasn't quietly tethered and fishing for crumbs. It had grown five times to almost fill our loft and it scuttled around on the tips of its tentacles and whatever it touched smoked and burned up. It had finished the table and chairs and I knew it had killed Gordon's parakeets and maybe Gordon. It had touched Moke's six-meter statue and dissolved it to slag and floated up the stairs like a dancing spindle and started in on the living-room. Sword was trying to grasp it by its glittery fringe and I was shrieking at him to stop, or trying to. It was one of those dreams where nobody hears you, or if they do they don't take any notice. Then at last he succeeded and I saw the smoke begin to rise from his hands, and I woke up dug into Mokey's armpit crying like a maniac.

Moke cuddled me and made coffee and Sword, who has telepathic tendencies, looked in and spent half an hour proving he hadn't burned. I passed the rest of the night shivering between them and trying to remember it wasn't even intelligent. Retta ought to know. I don't know why it gave me the cosmic shivers but it did. I was practically glued to Sword's neck, he had to peel me off to shower.

"The whole idea of alien intelligence is prickly," Moke said. "I mean real alienness. It's inhuman. We don't deal with it well."

"I don't know about that," Chan said. "They give me the squirms and I've seen plenty of planets with alien flor and faun. I suppose you're right, it's the idea it's thinking at you. Judging, maybe."

"Thinking we're ugly." But it wasn't ugly, or I didn't think so. I just hated it.

"Do you get used to them?"

"No," Hallway said.

"Yes," Sword said simultaneously. "Well, not exactly. It's war, you recognize them, you kill them. If they don't kill you first. It's a relationship. I know they're smart. People. Retta's thing gives me creeps, but not because it's intelligent, because it isn't. Too mobile for a vegetable, swaying as if it was looking for something. I didn't like it either."

"Looking for food," Hall said.

"Of course. That's not what's wrong."

"It was empty," Moke said, a wrinkle between his brows. "Pete said a partial or an imbecile. Not what it should be."

"Ugly fucker," Yeller said cheerfully. "Ships are the same shape, did you see that? Radial symmetry."

"That bother you?"

"Nope. But our ships aren't people-shaped. Are they?"

"Perhaps they are," Chan said. "I mean, our symmetry's lateral. We have a back and a front and we look out the front. We look at our aft screens second like over our shoulders. Or I do. Heads and tails. Bowels and belly."

"Pretty idea," the Head of Station said. He was called Hunt, it was his screen and he was letting us share it. "I've waited for this. They killed my son."

"A lot of sons," Hall said somberly.

"And we killed a lot of them." Sword was gimlet-eyed. "I hope it isn't a problem, Commander."

"I'm not going to hose the place down with a laser. I want to look at the murdering suckers, that's all."

"We all do."

"It's as well they have their own compound," Chan remarked as we walked back to breakfast. She stopped to pick a small child in what had been a yellow jumper out of a dust-hole. It wiped its mouth on its sleeve and shot off to take another dive, among a pack that all looked like mud-monsters. "Horrors. Kids, I mean. I bet mine are the same."

She dusted off her hands. "I'm not sure we were right to bring them, Mr. Ambassador. Too many people feel that way. I don't think Commander Hunt's likely to lose his mind, but wherever humans gather you find irrationality . . ."

"Agreed. But what's the alternative? This is as neutral as we can get. And it has to be our place because theirs is half-finished, it barely has habitat. The only place big enough for a meeting-hall's the sci-block auditorium. There's a desert between us."

"I hope it's enough," Chan said.

"So do I."

"Those ships twirl. I suppose for gravity? It's stupid to feel scratchy but Mr. Faber's right. We don't deal well with the alien. They seem—not quite couth."

There were swirling spindles in the comm-net. Radial symmetry.

"Nose-filter country," Sword said in a neat echo.

"It's subjective," Mokey said. "I've got to see them. How different's different?" He sounded hungry. People and Moke don't see things the same. It's why he's a genius.

We looked up reflexively, to scudding cloud. Above, the alien spindles were twirling, looking down. I wondered what they thought about us, if thinking was what they did. And what kind of nightmares I was going to have afterwards.

We didn't see them come but we felt the tremor that rattled our crockery and the level of twilight got a shade or two darker as swells of dust gusted around us. Then silence. As far as it was ever silent with the screaming wind that filtered through the screen. The whole place was on pause, like everyone was standing with their ears stretched waiting to hear movement from the alien compound. But there wasn't any.

"How're they getting here?"

"Delicate question. Military security both sides. We've agreed half-and-half. Their own transport to the dome edge and our ground-cars to the sci-block."

"Don't they get a better look at us than we get at them?"

"We'll be scoping their vehicles like crazy. And they're here. The right guy could take advantage."

"No," I said. "No, no and no."

"Cassandra, I didn't ask you. I don't want you, I wish you hadn't come. Remember? Our Marines are paid to take risks."

But they hadn't my experience. I bit my nails. "Are they out there cooled? Invisible? Or are they going to go up to the door and knock?"

"Guess. We'll have a team out reccing their perimeter. Equipment's secret."

"Then coolsuits exist."

"What do you think?"

"I think your exobs don't know enough about their senses to tell if we can cool our suits out against them or not."

"So why ask?"

"I like to hear your cute little voice."

He snarled, but not with conviction. It's also true.

"There's something I should have asked," Moke said, tugging his ear. "How many genetic forms they've identified."

"As many as there are bits of guys, I should think."

"Not what I mean, Cass. Human tissue comes male and female. You can identify sex from the genetic code."

"You mean they could be guy-toadstools and bim-toadstools. Radical."

"Not as simple. There could be six sorts, or forty. Just wondered."

"Ask," Sword said. "The exobs are in there. If these guys even breathe we'll be collecting genotypes off every surface near them."

"I bet they aren't sitting on their hands either. What do you lay everyone's in a force-suit?"

"Not a thing. And I'm not telling you the scuttle I've heard on ways of getting at genotype through a lattice."

"I love diplomacy. It's full of mutual love and trust."

"It's a way of doing things. We came to look. So did they."

"I wonder if they're cultivating us in a glass jar."

Even the thought turned me over.

There was martial law on the base in the morning. Everything battened down tighter than a vacuum-packed pickle. Aurelia disappeared in the school with a stream of kids and an armful of educational wood-block, Dribble snuffling at her heels. He wasn't happy, the dust was getting to his nose and giving him sinusitis. Everyone else had the choice of home or work-place, turn and stick. It left a lot of frustrated people, but the Commander had a face like a tank-trap and the settlement lockup was on vid for inspection. Cold prote and cero benches. The day started to the sound of doors clicking.

"Hard-hard," Chan said, fiddling with her lattice. "My pair of Martians are breaking their hearts for little green men. I've told 'em it ain't so, but who listens to Granny? This thing's as bad as a spacesuit."

"You've never been jogging in vacuum."

"Heaven forbid. It's against my religion."

"Mine too, but I haven't had the choice." That's a lie, the weirder it is the better Sword likes it. "Let's go, I want to see them arrive. Movement in the open's revealing."

What you could see outside the dome was dust blowing, the roiling mess punctuated by an ozonous crackle as grit-particles burned off the screen. The wind-wail was louder, like a pack of steam-whistles holding a caucus just out of vision. The whole surface could have been full of little men, green or any other color, and we wouldn't have known. We only had scopes to say there was nothing there but the normal atmospheric load of dust, water-vapor and mud, some blowing, some steaming and some just puddling about.

A blast of huge drops spattered over and frizzled, with a noise like frying fat. Lightnings flickered through the force-field and the cloud layers lit with a monstrous pulsation of brilliance under a rumbling crash that shook the ground from west to east and rolled into the distance.

"Nice weather they brought," Hunt said.

"I hope their drive-units aren't interacting with the atmosphere," a tech said nervously. "We don't know how their space-grids function. If their field clashes with our terraform batteries we could have seismic problems."

"Don't shit your panties," Retta jeered. "It's like this five days out of five. You guys never come out of the commissary. We drive through it twice a week."

Another crash, with a blue-white pulse and a fresh sizzle of bullets. The tech with the scope pointed and lurching shapes loomed almost on top of us, vapor streaming around their bubbles, grav-cushions spurting bow-waves of mud.

"Open up," Hunt ordered. "But keep it short. Mem Evander, tell your clients they've thirty seconds. Even that'll give us a month of clearing the filters."

"They know. Haven't you a canopy?"

"Online. They're already in the tunnel. Our drivers do it in ten, and then we've to clean."

"I've got them on comm. They're coming in."

The bubbles had slowed and closed up. Four, maybe twelve feet across, with radial symmetry. They weren't twirling, maybe because they were ranked for entry. Two waves of two. The controller opened the flaw and a hurricane of wind-driven sand and liquid clay drooled around us. Sword grabbed me on one side and Chan on the other just before we vanished into the scenery. I flew from his belt like a flag and met Chan's hand in midair. We hugged frantically with stupid grins.

It took them twelve seconds and a half. The screen snapped to and quiet fell. A tornado of dust swirled to the summit of the dome, crackled in the field and sifted back down in coils. The bubbles sank, into four saucers of cleared ground. Minor dust-devils died on their canopies. They'd been twirling, they'd dug themselves a hollow each to rest in. They sighed down to ground-level and stood still.

A tense silence. Then something transparent, a long trailing ribbon, flowed from one of the bubbles and blew in the air-currents. A bunch more followed, carnival streamers in colored glass. The canopy parted and re-formed.

Not a jelly toadstool. Bigger and brighter, something too real to be real, a vaudeville fairy. Taller than Hallway on the tips of its tendrils, pirouetting slowly. Long clear filaments waved under the cap and spread like it was tasting the air. It had a fringe of glassy beads like Retta's Thing but they looked the same like me and an aardvark. I mean you might say same planet. The shape was toadstool but this was wide, light and floated as if it was weightless. The glass umbrella was balanced on tendrils as thick as a finger that scarcely tickled the ground. Pearly colors ran through, pink and mauve and green, pulsing in waves. A sprinkle of gold flecks rose from the middle and dissipated to the edge. It moved like a Disney ballerina, a cartoon flower with wafting skirts that fluffed up and down in exaggerated curves. And it twirled. In a spindle. Without stopping, its hanging fringe swinging.

The human people reacted as one. Those who hadn't sunk filters did, fast. Those who had, such as me, switched to full cutout. It stank like a ripe tomcat in a heatwave. Worse, ammoniac and sweet at the same time. Like rancid marshmallow. Like syrup of black tulips gone bad.

Chan and I let go each other and gulped.

"Uh-oh. Told you so."

"We were both right," Sword whispered. "Not a person. But it's sure as hell a mind."

It was wrapped in a glassine envelope you could just see as an outline in the arclight. It rustled faintly. Or maybe the thing rustled. A soft whisper that could have been jelly or plastic. They looked alike.

The others came after it like the bubbles that birthed them, their caps and canopies so alike the one could have reshaped into the other. Eight, two Geeks per bubble. Ugly they weren't. They looked like Thanksgiving, bright as carnival ribbons, stinking like the Valley of Death.

They moved silently but in rhythm, like they were dancing. They spent a minute skating in circles while they touched tendrils, then three peeled off and settled by the cars and the other five constituted a *corps de ballet* with prima ballerina. They fouettéed toward us.

Evander had the transmitter for her geoful of rig cached in a palm. She and Sword juggled and he took over.

"Hi. Pleased to meet you. McLaren DeLorn."

There was the kind of timelag you get on a long-distance radio that isn't subbed. Prima B lifted its ribbons in a spire and made noises. It was weird. You could hear its whine, thin as a mosquito, and a choir of human babble a few seconds later to a different beat.

"CALLSIGN *recognized* **RED LEADER**
pickabacks *running protection*
OUR FUCKING SHIPS
you asshole WHICH OF YOU GUYS evander."

"They recognize you, they're leaving guards, they want to know me," Evander said rapidly. She grinned. "I haven't managed to eradicate 'asshole.' "

"I think there could be a reason for that." Sword looked them over. "I said they were smart. This is Mem Evander. You can leave your guards and vehicles safely, we've told our people to stay clear. Our own guards are also staying, for your protection. They won't harm you."

Another spaced-out pause. Ripples of color ran over the caps and a couple of the *corps de ballet* reached out ribbons to Prima Ballerina. They looked like a blissed gymnastic team. PB shrugged its tutu and went back to whining.

"I copy **EVANDER**
FEDERATED PLANET *red leader*
mechanical **YOU BITCH** *I DO NOT COPY.*"

Evander scratched the back of her neck. "Oh. Would you like speculations?"

"No need. They've been scoping us and I'm heavily hyped, full of cerosteel. Their vision's different, anyway."

"In that case, they note that I'm me but they think you aren't human and they want to know why we're represented by—excuse me—a mechanical."

The ballet went on twirling. Sometimes they twirled in place and sometimes in circles with PB in the center. PB itself spired on its axis placidly, like a humming top with an infuriating hum. I got an itchy feeling, like a ghostly nail scratching between my shoulderblades. I hitched my lattice and tried to rub through it. You can't. Other people were wriggling. Chan made a face.

"I'm human, I happen to be technologically enhanced. Necessities of war. It doesn't affect my competence." Except to make him a one-man howitzer. "If you'll risk our ground-cars we'll take you to the auditorium. They may not be comfortable, they were designed for us. Sorry. This way."

More ribbon gymnastics. These guys weren't cowards, they had to feel exposed. A very fast color-ripple rose in the caps and welled back down in blue and purple so maybe they were nervous. PB came on net.

> "**I DON'T** *need this garbage RED LEADER*
> **garbage** *repeat ALL I WANT*
> *FROM YOU BABY won't*
> *YOU GUYS* for godssakes **TALK TO ME**."

"I'm afraid they don't believe you."

"So am I. It isn't the first time. Got to say, I don't see them with cerosteel skeletons. The alien's hard to cope with."

"You're telling me? But a limited imagination, right? Not what you'd call open-minded. They came to talk and they want to get on with it."

"Check. Your disbelief's a pity, but it's your problem. We're also here to talk. Let's go."

Brilliant color-displays and rippling ribbons. They came back with their tints cooled.

> "**Message received** RENDEZVOUS *awaited*
> **TALK TO ME**
> ten four."

"Well, they concur on starting."

"Suits me. Commander?"

"Cars, people. Don't press too close, we don't know their range of action. Drivers, stay cool and move easy. Their balance looks good but I don't want them thinking we're trying to kill them."

"However much we want to," someone said from the crowd. Hunt glared.

"And cut the shit."

I didn't feel good either. These guys reminded me of stinging jellyfish. Maybe they were calm because they knew any one of them could wipe out any nine humans anytime with its tentacles tied behind its back. The drivers were Naval marines in full body-armor, so somebody else had thought so too.

We let them on sandwagons, one to each. Since nobody had known how many or how big they were, Hunt had laid on a dozen. The rest of us piled in heaps on the spares and tailed the procession. The itch in my shoulders had gotten worse and a string of tension joined my temples. Sword was rubbing his forehead through the lattice. The aliens swayed gracefully, turning in spirals. They had no trouble with their balance at all. It was everyone else was going to have a migraine.

The sci-block auditorium had chairs for people and a pile of hopeful garbage meant for alien backsides. That problem had kept the Quartermaster up all night. They solved it by not having any. They twirled majestically in and took up formation on the dais.

I wondered if they rested and how. Maybe they spent their lives upright like horses. They were so light it must take almost no energy to stay in the air. Did they twirl in their sleep? Did they sleep? What did I know?

We twolegs shuffled in with human creaks and the *corps de ballet* waited courteously. Maybe. They could have been watching the way we moved in the open, which is revealing. Sword rose to his full seven feet. He doesn't stoop like his sister, he's spent too much of his life invisible to be selfconscious, but even he had to look up. Though it wasn't fair, he can't levitate. He ran a hand over his forehead again, grinding the heel into his shield.

"Okay, let's talk. Why don't we start by sorting out your difficulty over war-survivors? There are several here, I'm fairly recent. Mem Evander's been through two conflicts—"

"Three. This is the fourth."

"Commander Hunt here's on his third and our Head of Intelligence remembers the bombing of Unity before most of us were born. A lot of people also died and that's why we've come. I'll say it again. The Galaxy's full of planets that can be made habitable, there's room for us both. My people are good at terraforming. We could help each other."

The ballet stank quietly in circles until he'd finished. They might be listening, though since they hadn't any faces it was hard to be sure. You couldn't tell what kind of sense-organs they had or where they kept them. Maybe the fringes did something. They didn't seem to mind which side was forwards but they obviously recognized shapes somehow. They were neat movers. Their caps changed color and their long filaments floated, sometimes drifting, sometimes gathering together in braided spires. They looked festive. My head ached worse and worse.

A humming pause. Sword had the tran in his hand but none of them carried anything. They stayed still maybe half a minute in identical attitudes, a bunch of

ribbons knotted at the center of their caps. The way PB
stood when it first spoke. Maybe it was a ritual. Maybe
their backs itched. Mine sure as hell did. The mosquito
began again.

"WE'RE *no way* sharing our space."

In a high-pitched echo of Sword's voice, an ethereal
baby Sword talking back to himself. I wondered if it
upset people. I wondered if they knew it. I'd the same
suspicions he did about the way they used insults.

"FUCKING IMPOSSIBLE
we do not copy *proposal*
IT MAKES NO GODDAM SENSE **asshole**
the whole frigging world KNOWS we gotta win
I WANT IT ALL those are regulations *in this service*
one of us **HAS GOT TO GO** you guys
are out of your *EVERLOVING* minds
you can't just GO HOME half way *help to terraform*
BE DAMNED we got *MY OWN WAY* **baby doll**
how's that again *SURVIVOR FROM
THE LAST WAR alive*
we do not copy SHOW ME baby **SHOW ME."**

Evander raised her eyebrows. "Improving fast. Do
you need translation?"

"For the record. My proposal doesn't suit them."

"And you've got to be crazy even to think it. They
spit on your help and they still don't believe you."

"Or you. They want proof." he sighed. "I don't
understand. Have you no records? Some of you must
remember, I fought you here sixteen years ago. There
was slaughter on both sides but we destroyed your
prime and ended the battle. I was one of the pilots who

led the raid. The debris's still circling. Hall here saw
it from the platform.''

"Right," Hallway said. "I saw the battle and I saw
your assault-ships cut to pieces. I saw you withdraw
when you lost the prime. The whole area was full of
corpses.''

That got vivid displays and a high buzz that could
have been distress. Or not. Another yoga-session. PB
answered again.

> "**all this stuff** *IS ANCIENT HISTORY I know you*
> SAY ANYTHING *I doubt* that was *YOU*
> *you stupid prick* YOU THINK
> I'M DUMB OR SOMETHING.''

Sword didn't wait for translation. "Why should we
lie?''

Evander grabbed the tran. "I've been in the Navy
forty years. Pilot in the first war, where I was wounded.
Second, I was a tech and my young son died. In the
last I lost my granddaughter. What proof do you
need?''

A swelling and fading like a firework fountain and
the Bali pose. A long time. Maybe seven or eight
minutes. Then PB spoke. I was beginning to recognize
voices. Some was Sword, quite a lot Evander, a bit
Leroy and Scotty. But most were anonymous human
pilots, men and women, talking to each other or their
controller, not knowing they were being recorded.
Probably most of them were dead.

> "*WE DO NOT COPY* we *KNOW IT HAPPENED*
> *the same way you do* WHAT D'YOU *gain* LYING
> *CHILDREN* lie YOU GUYS *are not CHILDREN*
> *you say* you say MY SON *my granddaughter YOU*

have got to be **LIARS** *repeat*
WHAT ARE YOU GUYS PLAYING AT
you kill *the enemy*
if you can I ASK **are you** *afraid* **RED LEADER**
I say no SO ASK is it TREACHERY *your*
PRIME is in orbit *THIS IS THE NAVY* **SO ASK**
what do you guys THINK **you want**
WE DO NOT COPY ask *ARE YOU* **people**
IN YOUR RIGHT *heads.*''

Evander made a ''Whew'' mouth. ''My little friends are whispering sweet nothings, more nothing than sweet. Ouch. I'll remember that, Lieutenant Scott. They still don't believe us. I don't understand them either. It's something about children, they expect lies from children but we're claiming to be grown up? 'Son,' 'granddaughter' 's a real block, I don't see it at all.''

''Maybe they don't either, that could be the trouble?''

''Perhaps. Then my little mates think, the idea of war's to kill the enemy, you claim to be a fighter so they don't get why you don't want to unless you're a coward, which you don't seem to be. We aren't sure about the treachery. Leroy thinks they're asking if we're just bad soldiers. Only our prime with Navy markings is waiting for us. So they're wondering if our race is sane.''

''Don't even ask. Jump to conclusions, don't they?''

''I said a rigid mind-set. Goes with arrogance. Only one way to see things.''

''Okay.'' Sword turned back to PB. ''You puzzle us too. There must be common ground among sentient races. Why do you fight? What are you looking for?''

I call that optimistic. My experience of one supposedly sentient race is common ground's less common than you think. But I guess Ambassadors are dedicated to optimism. Maybe the ballet were shaken too because they circled the dais completely several times with a couple of entrechats and thirty-two fouettées. Then they went to Bali. It took five minutes this time, looked like they'd shaken hands with themselves over our sanity.

"WE DO NOT COPY *most of THIS GARBAGE* why evander **one thing** DAUGHTER *one thing* hunt *OTHER* **we do not copy.**"

That raised everyone's brows. "What the hell?"

"Damned if I know. Why are some of us one thing and some another? What sort of thing?"

"No idea. Let's try. We have different names, it helps us to identify each other. What do you do?"

"A little direct, Mr. Ambassador. They won't tell you."

"Didn't really think they would. Headache I've got it's a wonder I'm lucid. If I'm lucid. Damn them."

"A natural sentiment, but undiplomatic," Chan murmured from behind.

"Thank you, chief. I'll control myself no matter how fungicidal my instincts."

"Hey, you guys, watch it. I think they're listening even without tran. I don't trust them."

There was something alert about their pirouetting. If they'd had any sign of a scope I'd have sworn they were scoping. They spired briefly.

"You guys **TALK** *worse than children* WHY *one half of* you guys *HE* **like** HUNT *one half* she **like** *EVANDER* *it's the same* ON THE RADIO *what is* **SON** what is *GRANDDAUGHTER* **are you**

OFFICER *we do not copy* **ARE YOU** he *are you*
she **red leader**."

"Christ. What do I tell them, Mem Chan?"

"The truth? We're trying to understand, after all.
What can it matter?"

"Check. It's a question of breeding-habits, we come
two flavors. I'm 'he,' Evander's 'she' because she's the
other sex. Either sex can be of any rank."

Bali was brief.

"***HE*** *she* SEX *we do not copy* what do you guys
mean DEMAND *answer*
DEMAND *answer* ANSWER."

"Oh, God. You wouldn't like to do this?"

"Certainly not, Mr. DeLorn. Ambassador's privilege
of rank. Which, as you rightly remark, can belong to
either sex."

Sword groaned. "Heartless woman. Half of us are
'he' and make seed, the other half are 'she' and make
young. We're born that way."

That hit like a ripe tomato. The whole group spun
and their cap-colors welled purple and orange. They
spent several minutes in a huddle with quivering tendrils. After they settled the color-flow went on being
hectic.

"**can** *RED LEADER* make seed **WITH**
evander CAN *evander MAKE YOUNG*
of ***RED LEADER*** demand ANSWER."

"I knew it," Sword said bitterly. "I'm giving sex-
instruction to jellyfish. Technically, yes. Since Evander's a long way my chronological senior she wouldn't

appreciate the attention. Neither would my mate.''

The dance was turning into a jig and threatening to become a reel.

> "WHERE'S **my mate** *if not* **EVANDER** how
> ***can it* APPRECIATE** demand *answer*."

Sword growled. "I suppose it would be undiplomatic—? Yes, I see it would. My mate's here beside me. She has a fine sense of appreciation and a mean uppercut and she resents guys who horn in. Respect's advisable."

"Now, now, Mr. Ambassador. Mustn't give way to temper." Chan sounded like she was laughing her white felt socks off inside the lattice.

"You're a nasty lady."

It was the first time I'd heard Sword in Swordfish mode being plaintive. The toadstools weren't showing delight either unless I was gravely mistaken about delight-signals among toadstools, which is possible. The purples had deepened to bruise-color and the orange broke through in flaming streaks. Their filaments rustled like dry leaves.

> "*we do not copy* YOU ARE lying **repeat**
> ***THAT IS* children *though* IT IS**
> **pretend** *ONE OF YOU it's too much man*
> *garbage* REPEAT *GARBAGE*."

Sword had blood under his skin over a fleshless pallor. It looked to me like his headache was reaching escape velocity. I spiked the rude stinking spindle with a redhot glare.

"Garbage yourself, you ever been told you smell like a dunghill?''

Sword grabbed back the tran too late. There was a bubble of laughter behind.

"Oh, Cassandra." But she didn't sound like her heart was breaking. Even dips have trouble with prurient jellyfish.

Sword closed his fingers on the tran and tried to unsort us. He's had practice in thirteen years of Strip.

"There are no children here. Cassandra happens to be small for a woman and I happen to be tall for a man. We're both within human limits. I don't see . . ."

The ballet was gyrating like a school of small fish that's noticed a shark, their caps flashing on and off like beacons. They didn't even stop to hold hands.

"*WE DO NOT COPY* we've got to THINK THIS *mess over* we have NO MORE *to say* I GOTTA *leave you baby* when WILL WE SEE each other *again* *ASK* tomorrow *demand* AGREEMENT ten four out."

And the entire water-ballet swirled its skirts up to its ears, if it had any, and left us baby. Right like that, faster than they'd come, as if they had the Wild Hunt on their tails. The Marine drivers had to run to the wagons and the Commander did the two hundred meter hurdles to see them out.

Sword sank onto the nearest chair and put his head in his hands. "Jesus. Did I ask for this job? God, my brain's coming out my ears. Anybody got a really serious derm before the worst happens?"

Moke was on his knees and working at lattice. "Get the doc, Cass, the guy's sick. And give Yell a shout, he isn't getting home alone."

We took him back half-conscious in the rear of a

sandwagon with his head on Moke's knees, a line of derms up one arm and sweat pearling from a transparent forehead.

"Is he often nervy?" Chan asked, concerned.

"As a stone wall. It's something else."

"I've a headache myself." She paused, her head turned like a pointer. "Sacred heavens. What are they—?"

The whole eight aliens were posied into a circle close to their vehicles, whirling like dervishes, tendrils joined in a single high spire. Somewhere in the middle a dark mound made up of huddled shapes crouched with hands over their ears. I saw a flash of black hair and a colored jumper before Chan was on the sand and running.

She didn't get there. A white fury was pelting from the direction of the school and it covered ground like a racehorse. Long legs thrashed under a double handful of lifted silk. Taller than the average bim and driving to the Ride of the Valkyries.

Aurelia flung toadstools aside with a powerful sweep like a swimmer and caught up a child in each arm. The toadstools didn't like the touch. They spun away, bursting into broken patterns, and their dance staggered. When she galloped towards us she was white as her sacque. Which was tripping her up now she'd no hands to hold it.

"I'm so sorry, Mem Chan. It was my fault, I should have watched them. But they wanted to see the Martians and the guard had gone away. I think they're more frightened than . . ."

She caught sight of her brother's gray face and stopped, letting the children slide.

"Mac?"

"I'm fine," he said with irritation, sitting up. And was violently sick.

End of the perfect day.

We held the post-mortem in our place where Sword could flop in a blowup we knew was strong enough and Yell's in charge of the beer supply. I've never enquired into Yell's private practices but he may have been a pirate in a previous life. That's good news so long as it's you he works for. In our case he does.

"Two," Retta said, answering Moke. "I wouldn't like to say girls and boys, they could be chocolate and vanilla or chalk and cheese. But two."

"Get any traces off the platform?" Sword asked.

"Gimme a break, we only just parted. But frankly, it'd surprise me. I don't think those suckers touched surface beginning to end. They were genuinely floating. We've taken air-samples, I'll have a result later. There could have been exhaust gases."

"Remembering our jar specimen can spend periods underwater," the ginger guy said.

"It's gotta breathe out just the same. And these were talking."

"One was. The others didn't make a sound."

"Careful bastards."

"I wonder if they were sampling us. I had a feeling they were but I wondered how. They hadn't any instruments."

Moke gave me the narrow green eye. "Uh-huh. Got a headache, Retta?"

She looked blank. "Me? I never get headaches. They did stink, though. Makes 'em carnivores, I guess. Vegetation just doesn't do that."

"What about the thing in your lab?"

"Is it carnivorous? Never tried. Been feeding it prote flakes which are basic soy. We could try it on meat. You think that could make the difference?"

"No idea. I meant has anyone in the lab had funny feelings off it?"

"No," Pete-With-Freckles said. Definite. "No way at all. It's harmless. Hard to imagine what the relation is. Maybe you're right and it's a food animal. I get a feeling it's lonely in a dumb insentient way but it's never made me itch. Those big suckers did. Had to come back and slap a derm."

So did I. "Less an itch than a saw-cut. Through the front of my skull."

"You can say that again," Sword said, rubbing his temples. "I still ache. They'd a small delegation compared with ours. I'd expected a crowd of specialists."

"They're telepaths," Moke said. We all looked at him. The boy's brilliant but rarely fey. Sword raised an eyebrow. "They have to be. No instruments. And all those silent pauses."

"I've identified tentacle-movement and color-change as means of communication," Retta objected.

"And Evander's got through with sonics. If she hadn't we couldn't talk."

"I know. I saw that. But Cass complains about Sword's mind-reading and he has the worst headache. Apart from being nearest and the one they were concentrating on. My head aches, but Hall's and Evander's don't. If you go by med bay there's a queue waiting, migraine and bilious attacks. Especially the kids. Chan's are throwing their guts up. Doctor says shock and pheromones but other people who were near aren't sick at all. Aurelia actually touched them and she's fine. Shaken, but not ill. Kids are more sensitive than adults. I don't know why they've several comm methods but they have. If their base was in mental contact they wouldn't need a big group. Work being done elsewhere, like Evander's rig. But biological."

"Doc could be right about the pheromones. It's more complex than just smell."

"I know. It could be with Chan's kids, they got a scare and they'd no filters. Though Aurelia hadn't either."

"People's resistance varies. Maybe Miss DeLorn's tough."

"Sure she is," her brother said. "Toughest egg in the nest, you have to say Boo in quite a loud whisper."

"That's not what I mean."

"It's what I mean," Moke said. "They were so well suited you're scratching for traces. So how did the pheromones spread? And it's not nervous, I've never seen Sword so sick. An egg he ain't. Hall and Evander are emotionally sensitive but neither of them's unwell. There's a Marine Master-Sergeant with a reputation for eating live salamanders and he's flat on his back. And he was guarding the batteries in an inner room. People didn't notice the stink until they got outside. A lot were sick before. Some have been sick since ten this morning when the aliens arrived. The only one who smelled them in an inside room was our kid Dribble who has a hyped nose. The scent made him nauseous but his head doesn't ache. If anyone can nail a pheromone he can. He says they stank. He says they're carnivores, like Retta, and he says—listen—they eat each other. He said it was the only way he could think of the smell could get that strong.''

''How does he know?'' Retta asked sharply.

''He gets the same smell off the thing in the jar, but fainter. Theirs is the same, magnified.''

''Uh-oh. You're getting out of my league, I do science. How do you test for telepathy?''

''Stars and wavy lines,'' Sword said lightly. ''You want me to requisition a pack?''

''That's garbage.''

''Sure it is. Humans aren't very telepathic.''

''Get me a test,'' she said stubbornly.

''Okay. We'll put you as close to one as I was, in a hard-vacuum force-suit and a good pair of filters, and see how long it takes you to throw up. A day, two days, two weeks, two years. A genuine experiment.''

''Sadistic brute. It's still garbage.''

''But he could be right,'' Pete said, thinking hard. ''If something in their—what, electrical auras?—disturbs human brain-function, there would be degrees of sensitivity but almost everyone should react sooner or later. Probably sooner under those conditions. We'll do it. You can really be in the front row tomorrow, Retta, and tell us what you find.''

''Thanks. I'm betting on nothing. But even if my head aches it won't prove telepathy.''

''True,'' Sword agreed. ''And if I say their guards were in the bubbles and waiting before the delegates came out and that all eight homed in on those kids like one, you'll say supersonics. Maybe they have supersonics too. But I brought Moke because he's a synthesizer. He puts things together and gets six. He just did. Now I'm listening."

"What for?"

"The sound of toadstools thinking."

"You know a group of Marines went walking while we were catching skull-pains?" Yell said lazily.

Sword turned him a sharp eye. "I thought they might. What did they find?"

"Story is, a lot of prickly perimeter defenses and enough alarms to start a penal colony. They didn't see anything, the weather was too bad."

"Pity. We were hoping for enlightenment."

"Hum," I said.

"What does 'Hum' mean, prophetess?"

"I thought yesterday our Navy weren't professionals."

"Try telling them that."

"They're professional Marines. I'm a professional burglar."

"With a weak stomach. And a strong partner. I could just chain you to the floor."

"Hum. Did the coolsuits work?"

"What coolsuits?"

"The ones that don't exist."

"Between ourselves, hard to say," Yell said. "They didn't get close enough to try. The whole place went off like a Chinese carnival and they scarpered before the residents caught them and declared war."

"You'd have to be waiting when the jellyfish left. They've got to open the screens to get in and out. Someone could get in while they're open."

"Passing the exit party on the way. And staying inside until the wanderers returned.''

"Right. It could just be done. If the suits worked.''

"But we don't know they do,'' Moke said.

"Pete's done stuff on them,'' Retta said. "Changed a few things.''

Sword whistled. "To what frequency?''

"In the blue.'' Pete sketched an outline. "We believe the aliens have IR oriented vision. But we can't guarantee anything. These suits show to us, they could be visible to mushrooms as well.''

"It's a nasty effect, whatever,'' Retta said. "Standing there in plain sight and they're supposed not to see you.''

"It's a pity we didn't try it.''

"But we did. Pete was wearing one all through the meeting. Didn't you see him? He looked as blue as Saint James's Infirmary.''

"Christ. Did they notice?''

"We honestly can't tell,'' she said with regret. "He did all he could to attract their attention but it's hard to be sure they didn't see him. They may just have been concentrating on their chat-show.''

"I went right to the edge of the platform and waggled my fingers. It's why I've such a beastly headache. They didn't blink. Or anything. But if anyone means to try I recommend a load of derms in advance.''

"And a coffin,'' Sword said. "I suppose I've got to be there tomorrow . . .''

"Yes,'' Moke and I said simultaneously.

"Sorry, mec,'' I said. "Talk to the doc about anti-heave stuff. But you're the one person who has to, you're the damned Ambassador. Stand farther away, they can't object.''

"That's not what I was thinking.''

"Hum," I said for the third time. I knew what he was thinking.

I was meditating on it myself.

I found Evander in her geo listening to hums and buzzes on tape while Leroy and Scotty leaned over her. All of them had red eyes and they all looked snipey.

"I need help."

"I know you, Blaine. You're planning something the Ambassador isn't going to like."

"Sword would do it himself if he could. He's missing his damned mutant assault-group, this is their kind of country."

"Didn't think it was anyone's kind of country for the next three hundred years," Leroy said with distaste.

"The Pack would cope, especially if they'd Sword on their backs. The Navy should try genetic mutes, it's snobbery. Drib's helped Retta already."

She sighed. "What do you want?"

"A coolsuit. One of the ones the Marines were testing this afternoon."

"For God's sake, Blaine, they're experimental. Nobody even knows if they work."

"Red Pete says maybe. He wore one and they didn't seem to notice."

"He thinks. Damned if I'd risk my neck on that evidence."

"Believe me, I don't want to. But now I've seen these guys I think we need a closer look and the Marines didn't make it. I'm a professional burglar. Sword and me are the guys who're used to working cooled, the Marines ain't. He can't go so I must. That's all."

Scotty scratched his head. "Can we assume all their senses work in the same range, like ours? I mean, we've cracked the auditories. We're generally medium-wave, they're short. If that was true as a whole those suits need cooled out further towards the blue, but they could work.''

"Could," Evander growled.

"I don't like them being so visible to us," Leroy said.

"No, that's okay. Sword's always been able to see people in suits, his vision's specialized. All it means is with them we all can. Could you do it? Or I mean, could your Techs?''

"Go away, Blaine. DeLorn's going to kill me if I help you."

"Only if you tell him. He's been threatening to kill me every day for ten years.''

"One of the Marines was small," Scotty said. "The suit would be biggish for Cass but she could belt it . . .''

"No," said Evander.

I smiled at them nicely. "I got to be out there before they leave in the morning. I'll need transport and some briefing on the alarms. I'm relying on you guys.''

"Get lost."

I did. But not very. Evander had a look in her eye.

The report on the alarms came with supper. A small dark Marine with a crewcut and bare dermed arms slid the chip into my hand as I stood at the bar.

"Derm up, kid," she said in passing. "Those bugs make your head ache.''

"Did they smell you?''

"Shouldn't have. Maybe. We crossed their tracks, was enough.''

"Thanks.''

I spent an hour in the evening washing down until Sword came crashing in to ask if I'd drowned, which time I had to palm the chip fast before we got into our water-act. The shower might not be big enough for two but some guys keep trying. In the morning I slid out quietly and found the reason I'd been alone was Moke was sitting at the breakfast shelf wearing jeans.

"Starting work early, mec?"

"Same time you are." He looked at me earnestly. "Cass, please don't. If you get caught Sword's got nothing."

"Caught at what? Pass me some prote, I need fueling."

"You're not strong enough to manage a sandwagon single-handed in this wind. The Marines had to spell each other."

"What you talking about?"

He raised his hands. "Okay. When are we going?"

"Evander told you."

"Yes. She wants the stuff, they all do. But she worries about Sword."

"So she should. You aren't used to this garbage, Mokey."

"Then I'm about to get used to it. You need backup. That's me. Backup Faber. Shut up and eat or I'll wake the guy and tell him." His hatchet face was implacable. "That's the deal. It stinks, but I've got to stick with one of you or the other. Maybe I can synthesize. Since Sword wants it."

"I wish you wouldn't."

"It's the deal. Take it or leave it."

Two coolsuits were waiting in the sci-block and a car was outside with a load of humps shielded in back.

"Hey, I'm not a Marine. Hope you don't think I'm going to backpack that."

"Recording stuff, the transmitters are miniaturized," the charge-tech said. "Everything you need to record goes over the suit-radio. All you got to carry is yourself.''

''Even a bead can stink in a sharp nose, mec, ask Drib.''

''Whole lot's sterile. I guarantee nobody's smelling anything. Suits ditto. Your biggest worry's if they see or hear you.''

''Name of the game.'' I looked the suit over. It was blue okay, damned blue. Like a midsummer sky, veering to violet at the zenith. It had a silky sheen that reflected the light. It would have looked good in the middle of a trapeze act. ''It's lucky I trust you.''

''Don't,'' he said. ''I wouldn't guarantee you five minutes.''

''Thanks a lot.''

Moke said nothing. We suited up in silence and slid into the car. The tech ran a hand-sterilizer over our outsides with attention to bootsoles and leaned in.

''Don't forget lattices. You're going to need them outside.''

''Got that. Evander got any theories on how far these guys can see?''

''We've all got *theories*,'' he said, sinister. ''Remember their vision's IR, heat shows up most to them. Heat from the car, heat from lattice exhausts. Heat from you if you crack your suits. They can pretty certainly see farther than we can through duststorms. What you've got on your side's the ambient temperature, they could find it hazy. Use the hotspots and pray for a lava-flow.''

''You're kidding.''

''Why d'you think we built their dome on a fault-line?'' he asked with an evil grin. ''Luck, guys. See you.''

''I hope so.''

• • •

The blast that hit us in the face as we cleared the screen almost dynamited us back to our breakfast-bar. I wrestled the power steering and headed into it. I was beginning to think I might be damned glad to have Moke. Hell, I'm always damned glad to have Moke but this wasn't sculpture country.

"Be better outside the tunnel," the tech's voice said in my ear. *"Blows straight in. Keep your heading, the instruments work. You got to know or you'll think they don't. But watch it, if you overshoot we could have trouble helping you."*

"Check. It's okay, I done instrument flying."

"You haven't done this," he said.

I hadn't. The twilight was dun shading to brown and the canopy drummed under the blast like it was going to fly off. The wagon was heavy but I still had to keep correcting for wind-drift. Every so often our radar showed a mudflow and we had to detour not to dig our nose in and disappear. I had the Marines' charts but in this chaos the topography changed every day. They'd annotated yesterday's changes and Moke annotated to-day's.

We traded places once, on the move. We were plow-ing through an area of dust-desert and I was scared to stop in case we sank in and never came up. It was all instruments, what you could see outside the canopy was zickory. Once we'd changed, Moke's stronger arms coped with the steering, but I hung over the scope like Van Leeuwenhoek discovering mouth-flora, watch-ing for crevices. The damned desert was full of them, a mile deep and filled with dust. Most were narrow enough for the car's extensors to bridge but there were a couple marked where the technique was fly and hop if you didn't want to go twelve miles around. Even one was a major effort.

I hurt all over already. Moke handled the bar with his hood tilted grimly and said nothing but I could hear the rasp edging into his breathing.

"Want to change again, guy?"

"Nope. Scared me bad enough last time. How do such fragile organisms survive this terrain?"

"Force-screen, I guess. And we don't know how fragile they really are. It's one of the things we'd like to."

"Don't they ask why we've put them so far away?"

"Probably not. If it separates them from us it also separates us from them. It's only eight miles anyhow. Just feels longer."

"If I were them I'd find that volcanic fault sinister."

"If they're as smart as Sword says they know damned well why it's there. Heading two starboard, I think I got it."

It was on the scope, a brilliant line with an aura of radiance that said heat and a lot of it. Not exactly a lava-flow but a deep crevasse down to the magma. The dome was marked a quarter-mile southeast.

"We're going to miss."

"We got to. We're going around north and coming in from the fault side so as to screen our emissions. Only way they won't see us coming."

"We hope."

"We hope. Then we walk it."

"Uh-huh. How far did you mean to trek?"

"Marines tried three hundred yards and set the screens off. They recommend five. It's the mean between what we can do and what they're going to notice."

"Sword—"

"Would do a kilometer and be certain. You see those belt-weights?"

"Had an ambition to be a diver."

"Right. But they tell me they're the only way we won't blow away. We leave 'em outside when we go in."

He grunted. The wind screamed like a million voices and the dust tried to abrade through the canopy and chew us to bone-meal. We took another detour for a mudflow the Marines had marked yesterday and found it had widened. Moke turned upstream looking for a bridge-point. It cost us country and I began to panic. If we didn't move we'd miss the dome-opening and lose the whole exercise. Sword would kill me before he'd let us try again.

Finally the nose rose under the extensors and we humped clumsily over. It was wide and wet. Our rear curtain came down on the edge and for a moment we teetered, the cushion smashing useless holes in the mud, the drive rising to a whine. Then we skidded over and moved forward.

"Can you give us more power, Moke? Time's running out."

"Doing all I can. I think we're going to have to risk something and go in closer."

I stepped on the laugh that rose behind my mask. "Let's be careful. I wouldn't like to risk anything serious."

His blue goggled face turned. I wished I could see him, Mokey's good for me. "My sentiments entirely."

The fault glared in the scope and I could see the outline of the dome on our right, fragile against the storm. Our tech was right, the ambient heat gave everything a cloudy unreality.

"We got to get close up and crawl with the glare

behind us. No reason their scopes aren't at least as good as ours.''

"I got the idea. Stick with it.''

He took a long curve towards the flaw and we crept narrowly along the edge. You didn't need a scope to see it from here, the red glow lit the vapor and shone back dully from the blowing dust. Our skin-temperature was rising and the inside air was getting hot and dry.

"Damn," I said. "We should've started in lattices, this could get nasty. The Marines didn't come so close to the flow but recommended it, they thought their route was too far from the heatsource.''

"You're one of those guys who avoids the sun-room.''

"I just got a taste for Arctic exploration.''

We bumped over broken ground. The border of the crack was heaved and lumpy, scattered with pumice, showing the glassy rays of old lava-flows. Red and yellow flashes roared up on our left and something heavy and burning splashed across the canopy leaving a sooted trail.

"Ouch.''

"Going to get more," Moke said. "You want to go inland?''

"Not yet. Few hundred yards more.''

He was right. By the time we were almost level with the dome shadow we'd a criss-crossing of slashes like a badly-barbecued steak. Every time they hit the shield sparkled and the engine-note rose to an alarming keen while the wagon paused in its tracks. Every time the field threw the stuff off and we came back on course. I hung on as long as I dared but it was beginning to scare me. Moke didn't say a thing. He just kept steering.

"What a Marine you'd have made."

"I'm a pacifist," he said thinly, hauling on the bar. "This is a peace mission."

"Sure it is. There's a hollow out there according to the chart. If we get in it the car's out of sightline."

"What are those hatch-marks?"

"I wish you hadn't asked that. It means they *think* it's a hollow."

"Then I'll go down slowly. It could be a branch of the big fault and I'd rather come up. Sooner or later."

"Me too. I hate overcooked steak."

The nose dipped and we slid into murk. I still couldn't see anything but wind. The scope showed surface, scoured bare under dust. The glare of the flaw cut off abruptly and the temperature eased.

"Right, mec. Lattices and belt-weights. And check your comm, we're gonna get static."

We writhed in our seats, trying to keep elbows out of each other's faces. Then I opened a slit of canopy. Dust shrieked past the screen with a noise like a vacuum-cleaner played through a seashell.

"Dive fast, we got to break through without letting grit in or the whole damned place'll fill. Go."

I took off feet-first through a wall of sparks and found out why the screen was itchy. The surface beneath was hard and smooth but the wagon was up to its canopy in a dust-pool that buried me over my head. Moke shot out behind, I knew because the blackness roiled. I'd as much vision as if I'd been blind. It was lucky we were hard-latticed, it was Suffocation Alley. His square competent hand found mine and we dragged ourselves out towards brown light.

I did what I could about closing the canopy but I couldn't see if the remote had functioned. If it hadn't we were going to have to dig our way in and liable to be going home without a shield. I didn't tell Moke. From the sound of the silence he'd figured it anyhow.

Upslope we came out in the full blast of wind. I was lucky to have him. Without his weight I'd have soared like a kite. We put our heads down and breasted it, clinging to each other like Scott of the Antarctic in negative. In five seconds our lattices were blanketed in dust and I had to keep wiping a glove over my face-plate to see out. One plus for us, it made for total cover.

We staggered in the gusts, dragging weight. It was like walking in water. Violent, muddy disturbed water. I wiped the scope on my cuff and took a look.

"Mudflow ahead. Wade or jump? I don't think we've time to go around."

"You can do as you like," he said. "I'm wading. I haven't practiced long-jump carrying a smelting-plant."

We waded. It was no worse than the dust except it clung like glue. We sucked and splodged, disappearing to our waists in the holes. That made it shallow for the locality. I only went in once over my helmet and Moke pulled me out. Neither of us remarked on it.

It was the first of several, one rather deeper that al-most buried both of us. It was horribly hot and I'd visions of what would happen if the lattice failed. Fea-turing as lobster on an alien menu's never been a hot ambition. The five hundred yards must have taken forty minutes. Which made four hours for the trip. Two miles an hour. There's no limit to human advancement.

Then the wind slackened a moment and we both stood still. We were twenty yards from the dome.

I grabbed Moke's sleeve and held on. "Christ, we're on top of them. If alarms were going off they already have. The Marines raised hell before they got this far."

"Maybe it worked."

"We've only one vehicle which makes less of a target, and only us which is two guys. It's the burglary principle, you stay small. But if their screens detect life they must have noticed."

"Be optimistic, Cass. Maybe the suits work."

"It's our only hope, mec. Let's hope Toad don't keep us waiting."

"Or didn't leave early."

"Now you're starting to sound like Sword."

We flattened ourselves into the rock with the hurricane gusting over our backs. The dome was smaller than our base-camp but it was thrown up in a hurry of what the marines had to-hand. We could hear the spluttering-fat sound of electrical disturbance from our twenty yards. Sparks flared and blew on the wind.

"Is this the front?"

"The Marines thought so. It was built this way."

"They haven't another door?"

It was worth checking. I tried the scope and found wall. Belly-crawling wasn't attractive but it was the only way. I wiggled off far enough to get an angle. Clever Moke. The bastards had modified it, the tunnel was at the back.

"Sword said they were bright. Let's move, guy, they may have done for us."

We shuffled under a layer of horizontal dirt that streamed from the flaw and poured down-wind. It was as hot as a foundry. It might be screening our body-heat but it did damn all for my breathing. The weights dragged painfully, catching on rough spots, and the crawl took forever. We made it to the tunnel and lay gasping, as close as we could without being inside.

"Get some breath, hero, we going to have to move. Don't know how fast these guys travel in the open."

"They were fairly stately yesterday."

"Don't prove nothing, they're sneaky."

"Can we get farther in?"

"Daren't. If they've any sense they've a motion-detector."

"With this wind?"

"No telling. Can't risk it. Watch it, they're coming."

I was damned glad to see them. I'd begun to think they might have left while we were crossing country, we wouldn't have known. But there was a glint of movement behind the screen and it looked like bubbles.

"We go in as soon as they open the field. The fucking tunnel's narrow, they got to come out one at a time. Gives us more time but damned little room. Pull in your belly."

"Already did," he said.

The tunnel like the dome was outlined in sparks. It didn't make me happy, our dusted lattices were liable to show. But if we crawled slowly we just weren't getting there. The moment the dome opened I flipped around the corner, bending low. It wasn't hard. With our weights the problem was standing. Moke's hand was on the back of my belt.

We were lucky. The opening dome did exactly what it had done back at base, the cool inside air sucked a blast of gas and dirt in and flung it at the bubbles. Moke pushed and we fell into a staggering run, helped on by the gush from behind.

The Geek cars breasted the wind with stately grace, tail to tail. As the first came level its skirts almost brushed me and all my hair stood up. I could smell it singeing. Moke beside me gave a sharp gasp. And there were three more. I jerked his hand and we dived at them, concentrating on getting to the entry before it closed. If they were going to see us, now was the time. The lattices showed nothing but dirt with cooled suits below. We were visible or we weren't.

We rolled inside with a clatter of metal like the day of judgment as the last passed through and the closing field snapped on our backs, and lay with our heads down waiting for something to fall. It didn't. In the tunnel the last of the cars rolled out and they spun smoothly into cruising mode. We watched them flow off into the dust.

"Boy," Moke whispered. "You do this often?"

"No. It's the absolutely first time. Shed lattice, mec, this is a suit job."

If there'd been a committee waving handkerchiefs we'd have had trouble. The light was brown-dark, like the base without arcs, and I could see grouped humps looked habitation but nothing that moved. There were no lamps. Maybe with their sight they didn't need them. It helped us. We dropped our lattices by the portway with the weights beneath, switched in recyclers and stood up with caution.

It was hard to see anything in the twilight but Moke's skinny form looked solid and very blue. I pulled my visual filters down and saw him beside me, nose directed inwards. The camp burned with a ghostly brightness that gave everything brilliant edges and lit surfaces with even gray light. It had to be hot, the only place I've seen that stuff before's in burning buildings.

"Now what?"

"Lions' den. We go look for the lions. And don't forget to report what you see, Evander's straining her ears."

I wished I felt bright-eyed. Burglary was never like this. Moke nodded briefly and set out first, with a free careless stride. He was right, if the suits didn't work there was no place to hide. I trotted after him.

The dominant shape was a coin-shaped cylinder big as a swimming-pool under the vault that had to be ship. The Navy would give their molars for a blueprint but it wasn't my job, and if there was a guard that's where they'd have it. A cluster of humped domes loomed near us. We had to get among them to see they were laid out like the ballet-group, a big one in the middle surrounded by four smaller at the cardinal points. A kraal.

They weren't geodomes as advertised, they'd been retailored too. They'd reshaped our structural members into high pointed huts with an elevation that was almost an arch, like exaggerated haystacks. They had their backs to us. Nothing moved around them.

"Guards?" Moke whispered.

"Maybe not. If they didn't see us come in they may

be enjoying domesticity. Let's take a look.''

We crept to the nearest. I didn't see an entrance but that was around the other side too, facing inwards to the center of the circle. It was high, wide and open. I couldn't believe it.

"There has to be a force-screen. Nobody lives with no door.''

"As a matter of fact, I think early Earth societies often did. Our own bit dates back to winters. I don't exclude a screen, what does your scope say?''

"Nothing. Want to risk it?''

"I think we got to. If we're getting anything out of this.''

Practical Moke. If it'd been a lion he'd probably have approached it the same way.

I sidled to the arch and poked my hand through. It wouldn't have surprised me if it had burned off at the wrist. Nothing. Not even the shiver of an electrical field. I stretched my ears for noise and peered into the scope for signs of movement. Still nothing.

"Do you think this one's empty?''

"No telling. Let's look.''

We stepped over the sill like cats in the meatsafe. The geos had been laid on concrete bases but this was built on sand. Looked like they'd dissolved the concrete out of their way and erected their hut on the plain soil. The sand was tracked over, in and out the door, with faint wandering trails. Such as might have been braided by twirling tentacles that didn't quite touch ground.

The first thing hit me was a blaze of brilliance that made me pull the filters off fast and the second was a wave of stifling heat. Moke had flinched too. He raised his head to look at the ceiling.

"IR sensers?''

"You said it."

Retta thought her jelly didn't like heat but I thought these guys hadn't our eyesight. Maybe it just didn't like our light. Because the domes, like our own geos, had no windows and the place was lit. With infra-red lamps. The ceiling-bars shone with a red glow that heated the air without light. The temperature had to be in the low hundreds.

"Bastards. They found a way to blind us twice over. It's too bright with filters and too dark without. I'm keeping some thoughts for our Navy techs."

"Keep a thought for me," Mokey said. "Is there anyone in here, that's the question."

"Not right here, no. Unless it's playing statues."

"Scope?"

"That's my evidence."

"Right. Keep in mind they'll see this as a blue-white glare."

Boy got to've been an Eagle-Scout in a previous existence. He fished in his kang and brought out a common hand-lamp with a heavy mesh mask glued over the lens. It might be a blue-white glare for them but for us it gave a dim small beam could be directed in front. He played it around.

The hut was divided like a pie. We were standing in the hall, a triangular segment with doorway each side. A construction stood in the angle in what might have been plastic, or vegetable fiber, or twisted glass. It was a kind of tree with muddled stems knotted into a snaky mess, at least two meters high and balanced in midair about a meter off the ground. Color was difficult in the subdued light but it had an opaque sheen suggesting pink or mauve. The ghostly trail-marks spiraled in front as if the guys lived there stopped to admire it every time they passed. Moke hissed and shoved the lamp at me.

"Hold it, Cass, I got to slate this."

I stood while he did. It occurred to me it was kind of dumb to stand in the middle of an alien camp that might be crawling with pulsating mushrooms holding a blue-white glare while an earnest sculptor slated their artifacts, but I'm kind of old-fashioned. It was probably as useful as anything else. Besides, if you've met Moke you know you can't stop him.

"Which side?"

"Nearest."

Which was left, so we took it. Another doorway was just a doorway, no surprises. Braided trails led through the middle. Apart from doors and constructs the hall was empty. The next room was empty too. Another piece of pie for a greedier eater. A big construction in the far corner, another doorway in the opposite wall and a wide shallow saucer in sand in the middle. More IR bars lighted it to what was probably a cheery blaze and the inner walls had an eggshell sheen as if they were coated with ceramic. If they were mine I'd have found them over-shiny.

"What's that?" Moke was drifting across.

"Careful, Mokey, we're leaving footprints. Clever devils, these. Don't tread on the hollow."

He swore. "We'd better look standing. Is there a way to disguise it?"

"Only the traditional. Brushing. I've a nitro-blower'll do the job if they don't look too closely, but if we break the tracks or change the shapes I wouldn't like to remake them. Unless we hole the dome as we leave and create a cyclone."

"That might look obvious. Okay, you're Page. Put your feet where I do."

"Thanks. Why's it the guy always gets to be King? Don't stride, I'm doing the splits."

"You can lead if you like," he said mildly. "I wanted to slate this."

"Of course you did, Mokey. Slate the bastard."

I held up the lamp. Another mess of twisted whatever, more complex and twice as big. It looked like a coil of snakes heaped into a beehive, balanced in the middle of a field of turnips. The turnips closely-planted and sticking up. The colors were pale but complicated, veined and splotched all over like marble.

"Fascinating," Moke breathed.

"Like a spitting cobra. What is it?"

"Dunno. Got to look properly when we get back. Let me get it recorded."

He took a long stride around and caught the hind view. Then took a breath.

"What?"

Pause. Then his voice came back, muffled. "It's okay, it just startled me. Light's so bad. Thought I'd been dumb and it was alive. But it's plastic. It's turning."

"The hell." I peered. He was right. The turnip-field was fixed but the beehive wasn't planted in it. It floated an inch or two above and it was spinning on its axis, slowly.

"That settles it. It's one of them."

"Doesn't look like them," I said doubtfully. "Too many filaments."

"No way of knowing how they look to themselves. What's through the door?"

"One way to find out."

I took the step since I was nearer. And bit on a yelp.

"Cass?"

I'd frozen from reflex. I slowly ungummed myself. "Come on through."

He stepped right behind and leaned on my shoulder. I could hear the hiss of his recycler through my mask.

"They're like Retta's," he whispered at last. "Juveniles?"

"If they are, these guys are as nutty as our dips. Dozens. What is this, a nursery?"

"Or a garden?"

"Then Retta's is a vegetable after all."

The inner doorway of the compartment was smaller. Or looked it because the floor was two-thirds full. The point of the pie was jammed with a mess of pale-green caps. They swayed as Retta's did, like there was a breeze you couldn't see. Their too-sensitive tendrils were twisted into a mat that anchored them to the sand and spread out over the floor. The tallest were at the back and must have been three feet high and four across. Rows of smaller ones scaled down in front to nubbles an inch or so wide in the corners.

The littlest weren't much more than bumps of jelly but the big ones were fringed like Retta's Thing. They showed stages between, from nicks in the edge to long strings looked ready to break up and roll in handfuls of beads. The biggest had necklaces long enough to touch the floor that lifted on the air-currents like floating hair. Bits of fleshy stuff were slopped around over them as if someone had slung in a handful of scraps and didn't much care if they missed. The far wall was blank.

"Have we come all the way around?"

"Never. Can't have. Anyhow there was a door across the hall, it's got to go to somewhere if only to a store-room."

"Yeah. They're kind of short of *things*, aren't they?"

"The Navy said so. What d'you suppose the hollow's for?"

"Sleeping in?" he suggested. "I mean, it's the only private room, the place isn't much more than a tent. There isn't space in here for one of the big guys."

"Then what's this place for? What d'they do with Things? Someone's moved around a lot, there are tracks all over."

"They've got to eat them. You can see where they've been picked."

There were broken ends that looked fresh, dribbling jelly. Breakfast. We hadn't seen anything like dishes, anything like equipment, anything like cookery. I guess they picked their food and munched.

"Dribble said they ate each other."

"Based on stench. He must be mistaken." His hands worked steadily on the slate.

I fished for sample-pouches and started collecting, stepping in Moke's footprints wherever I could. Jelly from broken stems, floor. sand, a separate scoop from the saucer-shaped hollow, a shaving of plasticky stuff the constructs were made of. One from each. Labeled. I looked in corners in the hope we'd missed an artefact. If we had we weren't finding it without a microscope. A whistle told me the shapes man was finished and worrying.

"Come on out, Moke, I'll try to fix footprints. Maybe you better do next door if it's clear, don't want us to tread all over. Get some samples while you're there, huh?"

"We only got one torch. I'll have to hold it."

"Uh-uh. I get the torch, you do the looking. There's just enough glow, been using it myself. I'm cleaning up. If there's something different, shout and we'll look together.''

''Okay,'' he said morosely. ''Hope Sword's keeping 'em occupied.''

''If he knows we're here he'll talk until sundown.''

''Sundown here's twenty hours off.''

''I know.''

I spent the next half-hour squatted, wiping out tracks, the gentle gas-flow of the nitro-brush rearranging sand in smooth random drifts. If they'd senses like the Devil they'd know. If they were just guys they wouldn't. Moke was silent and nothing moved outside. The blinding blue glare hadn't attracted a lot of attention. Of course there weren't any windows and the door faced a wall. I crossed my fingers and Paged across the hall. Three giant steps, he was being careful.

''Got your samples,'' he said, coming to meet me. ''Been labeling. It's identical, even the big spinner. I'll come back and slate it but it looks the same. Garden, broken stalks, everything. Will you turn me the torch here?''

I did. It looked the same to me too, even the color. He'd trodden like a stork, there wasn't much clearing, though I had to straddle the gaps. Guys' legs are longer, it's an unfairness of nature. Wherever you go bims have farther to walk.

''Next?''

He sighed. ''It's what we came for. How do we know if they're in?''

I didn't think I wanted to answer.

The next hut was almost the same. Empty, divided in two, hall, construct, inner rooms, constructs, closets, gardens. Eaten. Saucers in the dirt in the middle of each half. The only thing different was the construct in the hall, which was the same size as the last but a fuzzy S standing on its tail. In midair, naturally. Greenish.

"Gee. An individualist."

Moke slated it without speaking. We took samples, brushed footsteps, went on.

"This is creepy. We got to meet someone."

His blank mask turned. "Only if there's someone to meet. You felt the place is too quiet for a camp? Suppose those eight guys are all there are?"

It felt empty to me, too. But I feel humans. "I wouldn't like to be mistaken and come face-to-face with some guy catching down-time. You mean when the Marines came and woke all the alarms and ran for their little lives there was nobody home?"

"You got a headache?"

"No."

"Neither have I. Maybe that's exactly what they did. Maybe they were supposed to."

"Demonic."

"And careless. I'm not leaving a phosphor bomb, but how can they know that? Would we take the risk?"

"Maybe they're scoping."

"If they are it's a scope you haven't met yet."

"I ain't Hallway, mec."

"You're the state of Sword's art, as last seen. Satisfies me."

We finished the round. Five huts, four in a circle and one by itself in the center still to be explored. One of the four was bigger with a single round room. The big construct by the door was a spiked sphere with bristles, in golden yellow. A curved screen at the back protected its garden, very thickly planted with big ripe caps that floated their necklaces. The owner must have been hungry, there was a swathe of chewed stems. The beehive-in-a-turnip-field was in front of the screen. All the others were duplex. The hall-thingummies were different but the rest was the same. The big hut had a saucer-shaped hollow in the main room, the others had one in each half.

"Eight guys in the group," Moke said. "We've accounted for seven. Three pairs and a single."

"Which makes Prima Ballerina the man in the middle. Retta identified two gene-types so allowing they don't have to be married, do raspberry and vanilla play housey?"

"Can't tell. Let's look at PB."

PB had the kingpin. It was wide and tall with a doorway big enough to garage a hopship. We poked our noses in with care. This was top brass so if there was trouble he had it. The door was as doorless as the rest but shaded by a screen, maybe for dust. They didn't seem to need to keep their private lives private. A thingummy all of three meters high blazed out scarlet in our torch, reflected in ceramic, five feet of space underneath. A seven-bladed propeller with radial symmetry and a starburst front and back. It was the brightest thing we'd seen. The screen was open both ends so we took one each. Thick braids of trail decorated both like the whole camp went in and out.

The room behind was wide and lit red. A screen at the back hid the garden and the beehive-and-turnips was jumbo to stay in proportion. Otherwise it was like everyone else's. But this had a whole set of saucer hollows, one large and deep and seven shallower gathered around it.

"Symmetry's not radial—" Moke had begun when I let out a yip and charged his shoulder. He staggered and sat down. Not in a hollow or I'd never have got rid of the marks. "What . . . ?"

I hadn't expected a trans. We hadn't seen a sign of technology at all. I'd started to think what they had was on the ship. Foolish me. A clumsy ceramic box halfway up the left-hand wall was lit with a faint glow. A thready mosquito hum came out. Colors of sorts moved across the screen but the images didn't say a thing to me. A semicircle of hollows was opposite, maybe where they got their orders after session. PB had to sit in the middle in front. Moke was right, though. It was hellish symmetrical but only half a radius.

"Are they on net?"

"Don't know. You want to sample this guy's garden?"

"Yes. But take it careful, let's creep underneath the trees. Right below we'll be under sightline."

We crept in giant fairy-steps, like amateurs playing monster. We had to do it in infra, we'd risked the torch enough. The guys receiving this could have seen the glare from over the door-screen. For all I knew the hum was them yelling their hearts out. We moused around the wall, snipping sand from each saucer, and took refuge in the garden behind the wall.

"Wow," Moke said.

It was wow country. This garden was bigger than a whole small hut and the ripe caps clustered in heaps were tossing their fringes like trees in a gale. They'd a private wind, and it wasn't small. We couldn't feel a thing. Crystal beads shot off the ends and scattered over the floor, rolling among interlocked roots. A couple of handfuls had spilled out of the bed onto the sand. Moke fell on them with a pantomime whoop and scooped them into a pouch. "Seeds."

"I bet he misses them, that's fourteen lettuces he ain't having for breakfast. Hey, mec, we're spending time. Gotta go, the Navy'll die if we don't scope the ship. We should've gone aboard if it's not guarded. Too late now . . .''

''They've seen ships. Houses they haven't, even if these are temporary. There's a lot of hierarchy, you can see from what we've got. The exobs'll go crazy over the samples . . .''

''So long's we get back. Let's make country.''

The trans was bugging me. PB was likely to be snipiest of all and we didn't dare use the torch while I was cleaning up. We felt our way back on the line of our steps while I scoped every inch of floor and nitroed it to death. It took forever.

When we sneaked around the door Moke was itchy. ''Come on, Cass, we've been here all day. I've sent back a lot of stuff for Evander but the atmosphere's bad. Time we slapped lattice. Apart from wanting to stay alive, if we don't take seeds back they don't get 'em.''

''Too true. I just gotta scope this ship. From the outside. Come on, man, take five minutes.''

''I know your five minuteses. I'm lining up gear. If you aren't back in quarter of an hour I'm coming to drag you.''

I ran a quick survey from on the ground. No question of trying to get in and like he said, the Navy'd seen ships. I stuck the tools back in my kang. Then I got a look at my wrist-didge and made like a rabbit.

Moke was latticed himself and waving mine, as near to hopping as he ever gets. ''Come on, get this on, it's a wonder they aren't here already.''

''Sword's likely got 'em chained down. Damn, the dust's gone. Guess the lats lost charge.''

''Got to risk it. Stand still.'' He fitted connections

and whacked it into mode. ''Get into your belt-weights. Jesus.''

Mokey's not usually profane. I looked past and saw movement in the dirty washtub Resurrection uses for an atmosphere. Sandcars outside, in formation, whirling. They were coming up like ships in full sail, cyclones of dust streaming from under their drive-units.

''Okay, let's move. We gotta be in the tunnel as soon as the screen splits or we won't make it through. Same routine, suck in your belly. Now.''

He got my last link snapped just before the port opened and the leading car was on top of us. It was swirling fast, the other three behind. The dome parted and a wall of grit hit us in the face and frosted our lattices head to foot in a crust of dirt that stuck like glue.

We forged through, sucking gut, and I felt my body-hair stand up and fry for the second time. I guess Moke had it even harder between the thighs but I hadn't time to ask. And zoop, zoop, zoop, three more times. Pushing against the in-draft, dragging weight, buffeted by wind and blinded by dust, we hung on each other's hands and crawled for our lives.

Then the dome closed, the eddy slacked and we lay on our bellies just outside with the storm screaming over our heads.

''Come on,'' Moke gasped after a moment. ''Let's walk. Before they get their alarms back up.''

We walked.

I'd rather not think about the journey back. We were tired already, we'd done four hours in a wagon before we started and the wind was against us. Without Moke I'd never have made it. There were a couple of moments I thought neither of us would. We found the hollow with the dust-pool and fell into it—our muscular control was long gone—and rather to my surprise the canopy was closed and the screen still in action, burning dust patiently underground.

Moke took the remote from my wavering mitt, opened up and shoved me through. By the time he got in himself the cabin floor was a foot deep but neither of us cared. He grabbed the stick without waiting to argue and headed out into the gale.

Two hours later a row of ranked dots showed up on the scope and a team of Marines loomed out of the murk and hauled us out of our car and into one of theirs. It was as well, if we'd met one more mudflow we were never coming up. We were both still latticed, which helped. I got dumped through a canopy onto hard knees and angry rough hands started stripping.

"The next time," Swordfish said in a voice like ammonia ice, "you pull something like this I'm going to kill you. Both of you. If I don't do it now. I'm still thinking about it."

I wiggled into an armpit and barnacled onto his ribcage, shivering. "We scoped toads all over and Mokey's got some gorgeous seeds, Retta'll love them. I hope you brought sandwiches. I'm starving."

"That's the least of your troubles," he snarled.

But a friendly Marine was dealing out coffee from a lavish basket full of parcels. It was an act of charity. It stopped me eating Swordfish.

Night was sandy-eyed and crowded. Half the camp was gathered in our quarters, including Hall and Aurelia side by side with Dribble drooling on Aurelia's ankles, all three trying to look as if they'd met by accident. In another couple of decades they might start talking.

"I'm glad we got you back," Evander said. "That was a cute dust-pool, we were getting nothing but static with snatches of Cass talking about footprints."

"I'm glad you got us back too. You'd have done better to get Moke, he'd more interesting things to say."

"I've been listening. We got the complete transcript out of the recorder. It's fascinating that's the whole group."

"And no guards." I'd say the Marines were miffed. "What are they playing at?"

"I think they're dispensable." Sword sounded

dreamy. He'd got over the rage, he usually does, and settled for hugging what was left over, which wasn't much. "I used to wonder, when we were fighting. They're kamikazes. Fight until there are too few left to run the battle-comp then blow it if they can. It's why we've never had prisoners. Every time you take a ship the locks are open and there's nothing left but dried tissue. The top cops thought it was strategy but I wondered if it was suicide. It was universal."

"Still is," the small dark Marine said. "Don't know about too few, though. There's always lots of tissue."

"It was an impression. Transmissions falling off to nothing, then boom."

"The left-over garden-stuff maybe," Retta said. "There was a lot of garden compared to the eight guys, from the tapes. If they eat it they maybe take it with them. It explains how we got one in our jar."

"Lots of beautiful material," Pete said. "Constructs are marvelous."

"Place was unbelievably empty. We wondered if it was because it was a camp. But they build real solid tents."

"It's all evidence," Evander said. "Like your trans. Only piece of technology on the base apart from any gear they have in the ship. I suppose they must have used something from there to reshape the screen and the geos?"

"Unless they've talents we don't know about. That plastic's worth analysing. It isn't a breed we've met."

"Anyhow. I don't think you need worry about having attracted attention, it seemed in routine receive-mode. All the stuff was normal with familiar groups, we'd say everyday chatter. They may call in when they've something to say. No sign of panic. I'm interested in their visuals. If that's what they are."

"I like the spinner. If that's really how they see themselves their vision's very different. What do you think it is? Portrait of the President?"

"Why don't you guys stick to communications?" Jean the blonde exob complained.

"Conventional wisdom is things divide into cult objects, read religious, conventional forms which could include portraits of the President, personal decoration, or None of the Above," Retta said. "In this case they could be any one. The big one isn't personal, that's all we can say. The others aren't quite identical, there are small differences of color and detail, but there's no doubt they're the same form."

"Surprising such minimalist people have a taste for art," Evander remarked. "Especially in a temporary camp. Those things must be a pest to transport."

"You can't assume it's art," Pete said. "That's the trouble with our job, you can't assume anything. Maybe they do something we haven't thought of."

"Well, we're happy," the Marine said. "Our gimmick worked with the lattices, Sarge is doing hornpipes. He thought if we made them dust-attractive it would act as camouflage."

"I wish he'd done a better job on the wagon," Sword growled. "If we hadn't gone after them I'd still be digging up mudflows."

"Yeep?" I asked squeakily.

"Damned field was a hair off failing, you're lucky we got to you. Being parked in a pool probably didn't help but the first thing the Marine driver had to do was get out and start fixing it. Not funny in a dust-storm. Next time I come."

"I hoped that was the last."

"It probably will be. Our discussions got nowhere. Mulberry bush territory."

"They want something," Evander said.

"They may well. Peace it ain't."

"You're not giving up, Mr. Ambassador?"

"Not while we're talking. But I've a little red blinker says they're making signals to fill time. They've something in mind. If it's tactics I'm not going to play."

"To be fair, we were doing the same."

"Some of us had reasons. I have to save this goony's tail some way. But we've got all we're getting for now. Maybe they have, too. Won't surprise me if they don't come back."

"How's your headache?" I asked. He wasn't green and he sounded sweet.

"This smart guy fixed it." He nodded at Evander. "Or mostly. She made me a mcguffin."

"Thank little Leroy. The boy's good for something at long intervals. We began to accept half the camp had migraine and he'd said something clever about electrical auras affecting brain-function. So we thought if we could run electrical interference, disrupt the signal, it might help the headache. Since Mr. DeLorn was the sickest we gave him the prototype. If meetings go on we can at least equip the people nearest."

"Give the comm guys a medal. How was camp today?"

"Mem Chan's children have recovered," Aurelia said. "They're back to normal."

"But they stayed in school this time," Evander said grimly. "Though I believe they're boasting of their adventures to anyone who'll listen."

"Brats," Sword said. "Don't suppose they saw anything the rest of us missed?"

"No. They said the Martians were hot. Their eyes were hot. And they saw your bones. Kid thoughts."

"Part-true, maybe. Their lighting works in the IR."
"Well, we'll see tomorrow."
But we didn't.

Moke and I flopped on separate pads, we both hurt
too much to want to touch. I suspected Sword of being
protective six inches behind my sorest bits but every
time I turned I was wrong, he was miles away sleeping
like a log. After I hadn't caught him for the fourth time
he opened an eye. "Suppose I get you a derm and we
start over. All this skipping's keeping me awake."

I grunted and he got up to dig in the locker. So we
were both upright when the dome flexed and stirred on
its platform and a shriek like a demon cavalry-charge
howled down on us trying to tear the walls off. The
lights flickered and went out. Something rough and evil
caught my throat and began to strangle me and a flight
of hot stinging points made holes in my skin. Moke,
passed-out across the room, woke with a volley of
lung-rending coughs and I could hear Yell swearing
among clattering cookware from the kitchen where
he'd laid out his pad alongside the freezer.

Sword's forearm hit mine in the dark like a jackham-
mer and carried me backward on the rucked bedpad in
a tangle of covers.

"Stay there," he rasped. "Cover your head."

It sounded like he was doing it again to Mokey.
Yeller was staggering towards us, also coughing. I
heard him fall over the table.

"Where you put 'em?" he wheezed between chokes.

"Here," Sword said. His voice was suddenly normal
and oddly echoed. "Have this for Moke, I'll fix Cassandra."

It took me a second to work out he wasn't strangling
me, just trying to drag a lattice over my head. I sat up,

groggy, getting another faceful of live sandpaper, and waved my arms. Since I can't see in the dark and he can he shoved me aside and got the mask on first. The rest I managed myself when my lungs had cooled. I still felt as if I'd breathed in hot coals.

"Okay, stay there. Don't whatever you do go outside. Stay close to the guys and hold something solid."

And he was gone.

"What is it?" I croaked into the inter.

"Dome's breached," Yell's voice wheezed in my ear, rough but breathing. "Wait'll I fix this . . ."

Moke's croakings died and gave way to rasping breaths. He cleared his throat in the dark. "Nitro?"

"And carbon dioxide, with a heavy load of sand. The good air of Resurrection. It's not actually corrosive but it ain't made for people. Keep your head down and sit still."

"Christ. This place is full of dips with children. Where's . . ."

"Sword's gone to help them, fastest way's locate the gap and get the field back. Then we can fix damage. You couldn't stand up out there. Neither could I, it's going to need body-armor. Except for Sword, maybe. We got a full company of Marines, they're trained for it . . ."

A scream like a diving jet swooped down on us as the dome-roof gave with a hideous tearing noise and split like a pumpkin. I could feel sand ripping at my lattice. Things bumped and smashed in the dark and the bedpad scraped across the floor with me rolled up in it like Cleopatra. I thought I was going all the way into the roaring blackness when it hit a stanchion with a bruising jolt and stuck hard. I felt like I'd been steamrollered. But I'd stopped moving.

"Mokey?" I croaked.

"Over here." He sounded breathless, his voice still raw from untreated gases. "I think it's the kitchen, or used to be. Yell and me're tangled together. I think.."

He stopped.

"We're lying on the china," Yell said. "You don't like buttercups?"

" 'S right."

"They died. You got holda something?"

"Yeah, don't know what but it feels solid . . ."

"Keep holding. If they don't get this under control the rest of the place is going. These weren't built as externals."

"Resurrection has a fifty-hour rotation."

"Right. And we're the beginning of nightside, it's going to be hot and dark for a long time. Hang in."

"And civilians with us."

"You may not have noticed, but you're a civilian."

He's mistaken. I haven't been a civilian since I was fourteen and got mixed up with Razor and Swordfish.

"Is there anywhere safe?"

"Probably sci-block. They got heavy equipment needs reinforced walls and I'd expect their own oxy and lighting. Leave it to the Marines, you're going to blow away into the desert. And if you do Sword kills me this time for definite. It takes min twenty minutes to strangle terminally, even with sand. We got facilities. Don't add problems."

"We been here four hours already."

"Eleven and a half minutes by my chron," he said. "They're still alive, Cass."

The wind-shriek hesitated, hicced and broke off like somebody'd caught it by the throat. It dwindled to a mosquito whine, far and wee. We lay still in silence. Frangible things sifted to the floor and franged on it. My bedpad came unglued from its stanchion and unrolled, spilling me in a layer of splintered joists and broken concrete. I yelped. Somewhere in my ear Moke bit on a moan. The lattice whispered intermittently as swirls of sand sifted down, repelled by the field. Something in the distance had begun to thud in an earth-shaking rhythm.

"They got the pumps in," Yell said. "Stick with the suit, it'll take a few minutes to restore atmosphere even with pure oxy. Don't strike matches."

"I think my granny left them to my cousin Louisa."

The ceiling-plates flickered and came back up, or the one did that was hanging by enough cable to make a connection. The other sputtered and shot sparks.

"Did you say matches . . . ?"

"It'll be okay, air's almost pure nitro," Moke said. "So long as nothing's sparking by the pump-outlets. We got arcs?"

More uncertain flickers ran up and down as the kliegs made circles in sepia fog. We could see the street fine, the roof disappeared six feet above the floor. Our own air was fuzzy, though the water in my eyes maybe helped.

The dome was more of a ringwall. My stanchion was one of the structural members and it had broken off five feet above ground, a bent-in jagged end pointed down and glinting like a pike. I must have been hanging on it just below. Everything we had was in shards. Bits of gear and furnishings were in ragged bundles swept into corners, piled in a drift against what was left of the leeward wall.

Moke and Yell were humped by the side of the freezer, one of the few things too heavy to blow away. They'd been lucky, after a fashion. The floor was scattered with pieces of buttercup and a lot of garbage that used to be our shower and all that went with it. A squeezed squeeze-bottle of bath-oil was frothing bubbles on the icebox that once had our beer-supply and my birthday perfume was flavoring prote. The tiles were gone and a muddy trickle out of the cabinet said the shower had quit showering for this incarnation.

And there are things I'm never wrong about. Like what goes on inside Moke. Yell was hauling himself up in sections, hanging on the rim where the washer had been, and Moke was doubled over a wrong-shaped leg with his head down.

"Yell, Mokey's hurt."

"I know. Let's see what's left of the medkit." He made a wry mouth behind his faceplate. "It's gotta be me for now, the doc could take time. I've done it before. Lay out a pad like a good kid while I find derms."

Sword came back about the time we'd got Moke laid on most of my pad, the one I'd been rolled in, and stripped his lattice except the recycler. Mokey was gray all over except where he was blue and his leg was black around a puffed swelling. Yell had found the kit under the garbage in mostly one piece. He'd gutted it out like he knew the routine and lined a rank of derms up Mokey's thigh. He was prodding gently looking for the place and Moke was inspecting the ceiling. I held his cold hand and dripped on his chest.

Sword looked us over, knelt rapidly astride Moke's belly and moved his hands once. It made a sickening crunch but when he stood up the leg was straight.

"Thanks, Yell. Spray a cast and feed him anti-shock, I'll tell the doc. Take it easy, Genius, someone'll be here before you get gangrene. Could be a while, though, they're over their heads. You guys got blankets?"

I crawled away sniveling and pawed through my

wardrobe. I'd a beautiful blanket with head-hole I used to wear with my bullfighter pants. It wasn't very dusty and the rips were quite small. The pants had joined the Great Corrida anyhow. We wrapped it around Moke and he tried to look grateful because he's cute. It didn't work well because the blanket clashed with his complexion, green ain't its color. We put a Shcherbatsky cape under his head and he fell asleep.

Sword did a circular count-around. "Three and a half."

"What happened?"

He looked at me bleakly. "I acted like a fool. I didn't bring my own guards, and we had a failure of security."

"Meaning what?" Yell said, tense.

"Meaning this wasn't an accident. Our dome was breached by a heavyweight disruptor as soon as it was dark, and a gang of invaders got in through the flaw while we panicked."

"Alien?"

Sword nodded.

"The eight?"

"More than eight. They'd reinforcements."

"What did they want?"

He took a grating breath. "What we did. Specimens. A bit of everything. Food, furnishings, equipment. And there are dead people."

"Many?"

"We don't know yet. But I've still got three and a half. You and Cass whole, Moke hurt. And Hall, who was in sci-block and so's in better shape than most. He's working on electrics with the techs."

"Drib and Aurelia?"

"We're looking. There are a lot of huts down, we're digging in the wreckage. Most of them were lightweight, there's every chance there are survivors. I came back to check on you." His face was tight. "Keep Mokey warm and if a doc doesn't get around soon catch one and torture him. Make yourselves chocolate or if you can't work the autochef try the commissary, they're doing hot food. I'll be back when we're through."

"I'm an old spacer," Yell said. "Damn the autochef, I carry a portable. Don't kill yourself, we could need you."

Sword nodded curtly.

"Guy?" He turned. "I do need you." I wiped my nose on the back of my hand. "Moke suggested a phosphor grenade."

"But he didn't do it."

"We hadn't one. Anyhow he's a pacifist."

His mouth turned up slightly. "So he is. Pity it ain't catching."

He closed the door behind him. To keep out the draft, I suppose.

Hallway came around later to fix our light-plates and coincided with the doctor who replaced derms and did a neater repair job with fewer bruises. Moke didn't notice either one. Hall brought a plastic sheet issued by the Navy to repair our roof until they could fly in fresh parts and I could see we were about to eat a lot of dust. There was no way they were getting there tomorrow, or the day after. Or probably the month after next.

His freckles stared under lank hair and there was oil on his hands. I've never seen Hallway less than immaculate. He said they thought Aurelia was under the school and if she was her brother would get to her. Tight as a tourniquet. I didn't know what she was doing in the school at the start of a twenty-hour night but insanity comes all sizes. What she and Sword have in common is they're both unnatural.

Moke was flaked, Yell and Hall were up to their ears in pale-blue plastic and I'd ants in my thigh-muscles. I couldn't lie down without twitching. So I left them to it and went to help Swordfish dig. Assuming it *was* Swordfish.

The base was a mess. The attack had come from the east, which made sense because that was where the Geek camp was, and they'd opened up a flaw between nodes and just floated through. With their cars, no doubt. The gale and dirt had been enough to flatten everything near it like broken eggshell, half-bury the outer buildings and damage everything else right to the boundary. Our geo was one of the wholer ones, there was some left. Only the reinforced sci-block and a couple of domes in its shadow had stood and the gas had got everyone.

The Marines, like us, slept with their lattices—we're that sort of civilian—so they were in shape and digging mole-holes. When Sword said commissary he meant the late, the only thing left was the frame of *Happy Hour*. The aliens either had taste or were total abstainers, the glass was gone. Someone had cleared enough roof to make a floor and Popeye was in the middle with a functional stove, which had to rate a medal.

He'd a ladle in his hand and a recycler around his neck and he sipped from each alternately. His face was bluish among the red but the soup was going around and no one was complaining. The clients sat on bits of reconstituted plastic with masks in one hand and spoons in the other and the place was the only piece of camp that smelled like home.

The exob geo was one the gale passed over so you might think they'd got away, but when I got to the front I met Jean and Retta pitching glass into a skip.

"Got you too, huh?"

Retta gave me a black brow. "I was looking for one of you. I suppose Mr. Ambassador's busy."

"His sister's under the school. What's the gripe?"

"Come see."

I followed them in and found Pete in the lab restacking specimen cases. The place looked like the receiving end of a wrecking-ball.

"That was a hard wind. And local."

"Very."

It didn't take heavy deduction. The smell had had time to evaporate but it would still make a cat upchuck at five paces. I grabbed my mask.

"Yeah," Pete said, muffled by his filter. "Them."

"In force," Jean said. "We sleep in back. First the wind, then the lights went out. We were staggering around choking looking for masks when we heard things smashing."

"We were lucky," Retta said. "We use recyclers to work, a lot of our material's ripe. So we had them. We put our noses out one inch and took them in fast."

"They didn't come after us," Jean said. "I don't know if they knew we were here."

"What did they want?" A bad feeling swelled like a bubble under my belt.

"This, by the look of it." Retta pointed to the wreck of a bench, the one that had had the big jar on top. There was nothing left but splinters and slime.

"They came to rescue it?"

If they had they'd climbed half a step in my esteem. It's one sole reason I'd just about allow for wrecking a camp full of civilians and babies, even if they aren't your own. Though they could always have asked us. If they knew it was there. But they must've, maybe they'd smelled it. I didn't think I believed in telepathic lettuce, even for Moke.

Retta looked at me. "Guess again. That's it, all that's left. The wet isn't water, it's pulverized jelly. They pounded it flat. It and its jar and the bench it stood on. We heard them. There was no light and we were afraid to show but they were all in here and they went on and on. I'd say they took turns, two or three at a time. They were like crazy."

Fairy mushrooms, cartoon ballerinas. "They don't look that strong."

"They're that strong."

"What about the other stuff?"

"That you brought in last night? Didn't raise a spark. Pete's found most of it already among the garbage, including seeds and jelly. We'll find the rest. They were in sealed cases, they maybe didn't sense them. It was this they wanted."

"It could have been revenge. For Moke and me."

"Forget it, Blaine. If they knew about the raid their specimens would be the first thing they'd want. And Evander has stuff too and they didn't go near her. It was this. They wrecked the lab to get it."

I looked at the destruction and shivered. That bench had been solid steel and it was hammered through the floor, some of the blows leaving holes in the surface. Kamikazes. Their savagery was frightening.

"Nice guys. And so pretty with it."

"Sure. Pass me a friendly alien. Something with bug eyes and warts, preferably green."

She scooped an armful of glass into a trashbag.

The school was a collapsed circus tent with its painted animals scraped and eroded. A little crowd stood by with the stricken faces of bereaved parents.

A crew of Marines was throwing sections delicately onto heaps, careful not to put weight on anything beneath. Sword was with them, lifting steel sheet like paper. His cerosteel muscles stood out in cables under his shirt, moving with a steady directive motion as if they were being pulled by a puppetmaster. But with him the master's inside.

Chan was one of the lookers, her arms folded over her cheong sam so tightly it was pinched into folds, the mask of a recycler almost covering her face. She was as small as a child. I got a twitch as if she'd tried to smile.

"Jen's never going to let me touch them again. After what they did the other day. They boasted amazingly, they're total monsters. Don't know what they'll make of this, I'm waiting for them to stand up and come out. Boasting." Tears stood in her eyes. "Any minute now."

I didn't know what to say. Hugging would be an impertinence. I tried to smile back.

"Any minute."

Sword caught my eye and looked at me with a set white face, his steel-wire muscles not wasting a second, as if they worked on their own. He didn't pause. Aurelia thought he was God. And Dribble was with her.

"How long's it going to take?" I asked a passing Marine. She looked at me with contempt.

"Isn't much left, is there? You seen the chapel? Sister Mary Margaret was taking evensong."

I followed her nod. The chapel had been almost next door. I hadn't noticed the smashed lights and broken star. It was a flattened tent too, but a tent slashed open. Not by careful Marines but by something violent that had thrown whole sections end-over-end and ripped the door off its hinges so it pinwheeled away down the street and lay at the bottom slanting on a wall like a blown leaf. The bulk of the sci-block should have protected it. Like the school. A line of flat humps lay shrouded in front, a Marine with disruptor posted each end.

A second look showed the stains. They were everywhere in spite of the dust, puddling into mud, splattered over the walls, smeared on the leaning door.

"They tore them apart," she said. "All of them. Those they left behind."

It took a few seconds for that to get through. "They took people?"

"Yes. You wouldn't think you could tell but you can. Four of my platoon came to service, two guys I know well. It was a good operation, we were pleased. Three of them are here. The fourth's missing. There are more, ask around. Three we're sure of, four maybe."

She glanced at the school. And I understood those tense faces and Sword's white mask. They weren't waiting for their kids to be brought out, they were waiting for them not to be.

By morning we knew. Fourteen children and a teacher had been ripped to pieces where they sat, reading poetry at their desks while Aurelia spoke it aloud. Seemed she had a nice voice. Four more and the other teacher were missing, including Chan's grandchildren. Dribble and Aurelia were gone.

Sword came home with the dawn, hit what was left of his pad without looking to see if there was foam there to catch him and lay on it like a dead man, his eyes blank as glass.

The rest of us sat in a circle feeling like orphans.

It was barely light—as light as it got—before we
had the Navy, in force and worried. A small fleet of
lifeboats touched down on our pad and kicked fresh
dirt on floors people had just got clean. I thought Hunt
must've sent for them but he hadn't needed to, they'd
been on their way. They came from a pair of pickabacks up in orbit, sent to ask why the aliens were running in circles and why our comm-link had been out
all night.

"We saw them flurrying about and a couple of extra
ships go down, then they came back up and the whole
pack streamed off and jumped for another system like
their tails were burning," the Lieutenant in charge explained. "We tried to raise you and couldn't. So the
old man thought we'd better come check."

Hunt grunted. It was the first I'd known the comm
was down. He was maybe fending off panic.

"We've had a problem," he said.

"We still have," Sword said, a methane glacier. He'd known. If there'd been a functional radio he'd already be gone. I didn't know why he was still here now there was.

Hunt turned him a red stare. "I'm sorry, Ambassador. I know how you must feel about your sister. I've friends and their children among the dead. Sister Mary Margaret—"

I'd heard that already from the Marines. The Order of Stella Maris aren't celibate and they'd known each other a long time. Her eight-year-old daughter had died in the school. He passed a shaky hand over his eyes.

"Let's say I'm bitter too. I think *Hercules* has the solution."

"A final solution, I take it." The tone was so steely I figured he was talking to Swordfish, whether he knew it or not.

"What else? Mr Ambassador, we have to face facts. The chances are the—specimens—were dead before they were taken. Let's hope so. But even if they weren't, there's nothing we can do. Except end their ordeal. And trying to distance myself from my personal feelings, hard though that is, it's clear to me we can't let the aliens get away with this. Humanity can't let them. We need to show them how this behavior's dealt with so it doesn't happen again."

"I see." Sword was still coldly calm. "Does *Hercules* carry planet-busters?"

Hunt and the Lieutenant looked at each other unhappily. I'd have said they weren't enjoying it, but few people have a great time in the same space as an upset Swordfish.

"Very well, she does," he concluded. "And I take it you believe you know where they were going." His icy glance swept their faces. "Or were you going to bombard the nearest alien base on principle?''

"We've as many principles as other people," the Lieutenant said, flushing. "This business has gotten beyond the Diplomatic Corps. The decision's for the Navy—"

"Which includes me," Sword said grimly. "My term as Ambassador just ran out. You may assume the hostages are dead and hope if they aren't they soon will be. To begin with, I doubt it. They wanted specimens and they wanted what we'd have wanted ourselves, live ones. The chances are at least some of them have survived. My sister could be one, and I'm not going to stand by hoping she dies soon and easy. I've seen these things act. So have you. Do you believe it's likely?''

"What do you think you can do?" Hunt asked, raising his arms.

"I know what I can do. Take me up to *Hercules*, Lieutenant, or give me a ship and I'll take myself."

The Lieutenant's eye had a sideways roll, like a nervous horse. It's a common Swordfish effect. "I don't see—"

"You don't have to. I'll discuss it with the Captain."

"Major DeLorn's a trained pilot with functional implants," Hallway said from beside him. "I've been his tech for eighteen years. The equipment's advanced since the last campaign, but so have we. We'll handle it."

"Hunter-killing's a boy's job," Hunt snapped.

"I've never thought so. It's the old story, speed versus experience. I'd bet myself now against any kid in the force, I know tricks he hasn't thought of." Swordfish has a certain cold gray truthfulness, it was in his face. "In any case, the decision isn't yours. I want one ship, the smallest and latest. If necessary my father'll pay. It's his daughter.'' And that was the DeLorns. I'd never seen him be both at once. The combination was nastier than you'd believe. ''And I want it now. If I fail, you can explode the planet behind me. But I mean to go catch them first.''

They did try to argue. They didn't stand a chance. I think he'd have flown up on the sheer force of his rage if nothing else had offered. Or at least the nearest lighter he could break into. They compromised on agreeing to take him to the prime. I think they hoped the Captain might talk him out of it. They didn't know him.

''I'm coming with you,'' Hallway said with poised calm.

I wondered why I hadn't guessed. It wasn't worth asking if it was for the brother or the sister, he'd have gone with either. After all, he gave up his career for Sword when the Geeks got him thirteen years back. He believed it was his fault. Maybe in his Lunar mind the debt still wasn't paid. Maybe while Swordfish lived it never would be.

''And me. And Moke,'' I said. A little piccolo after those brazen trumpets.

They looked on me as from a great height. I thought Sword had already forgotten who I was.

''You can come back to the ship,'' he said. ''I expect you're safer there.''

And turned away to do things that mattered.

Hercules' landing-deck was a gray plain that stretched into distance, laid out with war-matériel like ranked chess-pieces. It was alive with activity like a maggoty cheese and everybody there was playing *Through the Looking-Glass*, running as hard as they could to stay in the same place. We stood in the Chief

Tech Sergeant's office above the activity, with a broad bay looking down on the board, examining equipment.

"We've worked on the coolsuits," the CTS said, laying them out on his table. "There are improvements based on Miss Blaine's and Mr. Faber's tapes . . ." He looked uneasily at Moke and me as if he couldn't connect us with tapes of coolsuits. "Though you've got to realize we can't guarantee them. These are the first real field-trials. We're monitoring, we're anxious to know ourselves how they perform." That brought another uneasy glance. He was remembering Moke and me'd already tried them.

"Fine. How about brain-flow resonators?"

"Mem Evander and her team have done what they can. They haven't had much time, but you should find they help."

"It's chiefly me. We don't know how Hall may react to prolonged exposure but he's been immune over short periods. I'll make do if I have to. If this isn't done fast it won't be worth it. We've got to get there before them and act at once."

The Captain raised thick bluish brows. "You don't think they'll start experiments on board?"

"I can't bet on it, but we wouldn't. We'd wait to get full-time scientists and proper labs. Let's hope."

"What about their prime?"

"I'm not convinced this gang's from a prime. If the base-planet's close they may be operating directly from land. Hall and I've dealt with them before. They don't like being in large groups on a single ship. Maybe they learned from the loss of *Top Gun*."

"Maybe they give each other headaches," Moke said. He was perfectly grave. The officers smiled politely as if the cat had just spoken. Alice used to have the same trouble.

"And nose-filters," the CTS added, laying them out. "We believe the atmosphere's breathable. There may be trace gases with disagreeable side-effects, but you don't mean to stay long. The smell's likely to be the main problem short-term."

"Living-materials?"

"Tents, water-purifiers, insect-repellent. Packaged rations. I don't advise you to eat their protein."

"I'm not sure we like the look of it. Of course the planet isn't their own, the local prote may be different."

"No telling. We don't know what they'd call terra-forming. They may or may not convert flora and fauna. We'd import whatever grew well."

"So long as our scopes are adequate."

"They are. As far as we can make them."

"And there are weapons in the armory," the Captain finished. "We can give you the latest lightweight hand-arms, but if you're taking a hunter-killer you have to choose between weight and speed."

No sonic cannon. Tough shit for both sides.

"And there's the problem of getting back. You're the pilot. If you should be—um—disabled, Mr. Hall-weg hasn't the training . . ."

Guys sometimes piss me off in spades. They all knew their chances of coming back were nil to invisible so none of it mattered a damn. They just had to go on playing the game. The Game. As modified for Scout troops.

"Unimportant," Sword said coolly. "Hall can handle anything I can. He built half of it. And we need good comm-links. It isn't going to help my sister if we get them out and you drop planet-busters on our heads."

"We'll be right behind. I think as you do, if you

can't help at once you can't help at all. If you rescue anyone, you won't be able to bring them out in your ship and we're going to have to send in a lighter. That means running interference while she picks you up. We'll handle that, we have the materials. If not—'' He hesitated and coughed. The other thing guys in uniforms hate is looking human, they think it shrinks them. ''If you can't do anything, save yourselves. Let us know so we don't fire on you.''

He'd a hope. Maybe it's why they hate showing humanity, they all know how mule-headed the others are.

''Of course,'' Swordfish said politely. ''We'll remember.''

In a pig's eye. If I may say so.

I looked down at the chessboard. It was all hell impressive to be so useless. All the might of modern technology, and it didn't have what it took to pick up five guys, a girl, four kids and a dog from a foreign planet without killing everyone on it including the interested parties. If they were still alive.

Real big deal. Hipooray. I just don't know how we she-people stand the glamour. Except large numbers of us were down there flying them. And there's a rumor the race is intelligent.

I hadn't seen Sword to speak to since he straightened Moke's leg forty-eight hours and a couple of geological epochs ago. In fact I hadn't seen Sword to speak to since he was last Lorn, and he'd forgotten that. I sat on Moke's knee in the shuttle and I shared Moke's pad in the ship. We got squirted on by the corner shower together. It was better than the muddy trickle we'd left behind, but not much. We waked around in the walk of the great men, or vice versa, and kept our proletarian mouths shut. The one time Moke opened his I've recorded.

When they'd inspected the armory and chosen their variety of packaged death in this week's flavors they processed back to their cabins and closed the doors.

"Excuse me," I said to Moke. "I got a guy to reason with."

"Be my guest," he said wearily. They'd reset and regenerated his leg and he looked like bad Brie. "I'd come along and help, only . . ."

Only his estimate of my chances was the same as mine and he hates to see me disappointed. I waggled my fingers and left.

Terminated or not, Sword was in the Ambassadorial suite. I didn't knock, it's never done any good. He didn't seem to have taken measures to keep people out, maybe so his steward could bring him the occasional lavish glass of water he lives on when he's stuff on his mind. I got in, anyhow. It still looked like it was meant for the King's Whore and he went with it like a live shark in the swimming-pool.

"Hi. You won't remember me, I'm one of the various perverse bitches you've laid on your way through this dark world of sin."

"Cass," he said tiredly. I was bringing out exhaustion in the males of the species. "I wanted to see you."

You could have fooled me.

"You should have telegraphed, I'd have come running."

"I'm leaving tonight."

"You surprise me."

He turned the most skeletal face I've seen on him, even in his Strip days.

"Please, Cass, don't make it harder."

"Why not? I'm still waiting for you to make it easy."

"There's no way to make it easy, Cassandra."

"Yes, there is. I'm coming. I'm never going to be buddies with the lighthouse, I ain't a lady. But she's okay and she didn't deserve to get caught in your lifestyle. Plus my favorite dog-boy's down beside her. I can't leave Drib to the cannibals. Move over. If you can carry seven different handarms you can carry me, I weigh less."

"Cassie."

"Don't Cassie me. What am I supposed to do, stand by and watch? And don't try the I'll-have-to-shoot-you-if-they-get-you line, it works for us both. Why do I have to dream about you being dissected?"

"Because I'm already dead."

"No. No, no and no. You got away with that once. Second time it don't run."

"It has to, Cass, because it's true. When I said it last I'd as long as ten or twelve years, maybe. It's down to nothing. That session in the Precinct House?"

It seemed a very long time ago. My stomach clenched. "So?"

"They killed me. The doc managed to patch what was left, for a while. He couldn't say how long. Three months at the most, but it could be days or hours. My metabolism's trashed. I've been blacking out at intervals ever since and they're getting closer. It'll soon be permanent. Ask Moke, I had to tell him to make him come. So he could look after you. It's why I wanted this mission, why they let me have it. It was a way to get rid of me. I was a nuisance back on Earth. My father's money helped, but mostly they didn't need a loose cannon. It's why he made it stick. He knows too, there was no way to hide it. It was the last thing he could do for me and he did it. It cost him. It might have worked.''

He sighed, a long bitter breath. "I didn't want Relia to come. I didn't want you to come but I've had ten years to learn I can't stop you. Bringing Moke to protect you was the best I could do. Now Relia's paying for my pride, and Drib with her. He loved her for herself, but he loved her for me too. My sister. It was pride. There was no reason I could do what nobody's done, nothing but arrogance. I thought one fighting man might be able to talk to another. It was seeing them as people and they aren't. Not my kind. But I had to try. For my kids. Or yours. Your and Moke's kids.''

"What about your and my kids?"

"It's too late. If I had a child now it could have two heads. You'd have to draw on the gene bank. I've never believed in it. If a guy can't have kids when he's alive I don't see a reason for him to have them when he's dead. The world's full of good people. Moke's good people.''

"He's the best. I can't live without him. He isn't you.''

"I'd have liked to raise my own brats.''

"And give them your own complexes.''

He smiled. "We all do that.''

"You could have told me.''

"It was a choice, Cass. I could have watched you cry every last day of my life. Now you get to yell at me.''

"And I get to cry every last day of your death. Thinking of things I've wanted to say to you and never have.''

"Like what?''

"Swordfish, you're a shit.''

"You've said that before.''

"But never with such conviction. You'd have gone without saying goodbye."

"You're wrong. I know you better. It's why I left the door open."

They have to have the last word.

I didn't cry until Sword had latticed and gone. I hugged Hall in silence, didn't look in Sword's eyes and avoided breaking Moke's hands until they'd got into their ceramic dart and shot straight into red-shift like a bullet. Then I spent five minutes leaning on Mokey's shoulder while I chewed my lips to shreds and made a wet patch on his shirt.

He rubbed my neck and said nothing until I'd stopped. Then he said, "Do we ask Yell now?"

"Yes. Please, Moke."

We were clinging together forlornly on the edge of the chessboard when a comm-tech in a crisp uniform strode confidently up. She checked a moment when she saw my eyes, and recollected herself.

"You're Blaine?"

"Correct."

"Call from Mem Evander. Urgent. She'd hoped to catch DeLorn but he's gone. Will you take it?"

"Sure. What else am I good for?"

"Blaine?" Evander eyed me doubtfully. "You don't look good."

"Ignore it. Just call me Andromache. What's the scuttle?"

"Hector's left, I take it."

"You just missed him. He wouldn't have stopped for you, he's got guys to kill."

"I know the feeling. This might have helped."

"It still could. Give."

"Your specimens. We've been analyzing genotypes. We're trying accelerated growth but we haven't results yet. Call me again in twenty-four hours."

"What do you have?"

"Raspberry and vanilla. You're right and wrong about them sharing their huts. They do, but they aren't all big guys. The big guys are all, let's say, raspberry."

"All of them? Even from the pair-huts?"

"Every one. Pete and Retta like your idea of the saucers as resting-holes, they've found genotype traces in the sand from each. Five individuals. All raspberry."

"Only five?"

"Only five. The sand from the pair-huts shows a single genotype in each."

"I don't understand. We sampled them all."

"I believe it. Stick around. All eight are raspberry, I think you can accept that."

"Then what's vanilla, for God's sake?"

"The gardens. Each of them. Again, five genotypes, but all the same flavor. Un-raspberry. And a conclusion. We're dealing with clone-groups. You and Moke sampled sand and jelly from different individuals at each site. The pairs are identical."

"Plants *and* pairs?"

"Both."

"Is it normal for plants?"

"Depends on their methods of reproduction," she said cautiously. "Retta's clear they're five different clone-groups, two individuals, three pairs, each with matching garden. Same for the seeds. They're all from one garden and the two we've sampled are identical to the mother-group. We're trying to grow the others. We expect more clones but we'll let you know. Since they're seeds their genetic makeup just could be different. Depends if they're vegetative or if they've been fertilized. In Earth-veg, seeds imply cross-pollination.''

"Right. So in spite of the clones, we got basically guys and their food-supply. Raspberry's people, vanilla's dinner.''

"Possibly.'' She was sounding more and more cautious. "There's something peculiar. If they're people and dinner, their genes are very closely related.''

"Well, I guess Earth mammals are genetically similar too?''

"That's not quite what we mean. These genotypes are alien and we can't be definite. But Peter believes they're as closely related as yours and Hector's. Think about it, Andromache. I hope he's going to drag them around the camp by their heels, the bastards. I'll call you back, my dear.''

"Yes,'' I said. "Pray none of them's called Achilles. But thanks.'' I looked at Moke, stunned. "Drib said they ate each other.''

"That's what he said.''

"But it's maybe their sisters.''

"Yes,'' he said. "I've been wondering that. The shapes are so similar.''

That's my Moke.

Yell was propping up a beer-bottle and looking discontented. There were three dead soldiers on the floor so he'd been doing a lot of it.

"I'm getting lonely. None of you guys has broken anything recently. Except your hearts, and I can manage without that. Can we go home and smash something like in the old days?''

"No. We're going to smash a lot of things right here.''

He dropped the bottle and sat up. "Like what?''

"Naval regulations. How good are you at avoiding friendly fire?"

He grinned like a wolf. "I'm a spacer. Try me."

"Then let's get going before we lose the angle."

The chessboard was as usual, full of brisk guys being busy. Sufficiently to not notice three extra sets of blues. Yell's friends had paid off in diamonds. Nobody had actually shown him where the coolsuits were or how to get around the quartermaster or which shuttle big enough for three guys and a tent was likely to be un-padlocked, but the information had somehow oozed across the membrane. The reputations of Teeny and Meany maybe helped. Just before we left a bim I'd never seen walked past and slipped me a she-sized cov-erall wrapped around a laser. She whispered, "Give 'em hell, kid."

It was an old-model iron and I had to roll the legs and sleeves of the jumper but I appreciated all three; the thought, the camouflage and the artillery. The one thing you can't liberate on a Naval ship's hand-tools, they count them like bank-bills. What we had instead was Moke's heavy equipment. Considering what it does, there ain't that much difference. I wouldn't like to be on the wrong end of either.

We strolled across roughly five miles of plates, avoiding crew where we could, jingling tools and whis-tling. Not too loudly, there's an ordinance against it. I had a bad case of prickly-neck for a mile or so until we got out of range of the big bay in case someone was looking, but I guess the CTS had other things to think about. After that I quit worrying. Nobody rec-ognizes people at five miles.

The important question was whether there was a guard on the shuttle. Our crimes up to date were limited to fraud, theft and miscegenation but if we had to slug someone they could get serious.

There wasn't. A sleepy-looking tech laid down his tools and took off on a stroll just as we arrived, whistling nearly as elaborately as we were. Yell picked them up with a businesslike air and set about putting back the drive-casing. Moke and I stood by looking earnest.

"Why don't you kids get in there and check out the gidget on the fizzgig?" he said. "Lattice up while you're at it, they're in the aft locker. Then strap in good. We could get turbulence."

We took the second and third pieces of advice and found ourselves places. There wasn't much room for anything and even less to strap ourselves. She was a battlefield liftship with seats for pilot and medic, a couple of stretchers and a section for cryo-pods with our gear in it. We did our best, leaving the pilot-space for Yeller. A few minutes later he hauled himself up looking particularly cheerful and started connecting lattice. He must've really missed moving, I hadn't noticed how much he'd dimmed over ten months of quiet.

"Okay, kids, hold on. Why don't we take Baby outside and see if she flies?"

I seem to have spent quite a lot of my life being flown about, in space and out of it, by lunatics. Swordfish is prizewinner but any number can play. I took a firmer grip of my seat.

"Okay, why don't we?"

He put the ship on warm-up and we moved slowly across the near bit of chessboard. Other people were warming too, like three work-sleds meant for hull-inspection, preparing to inspect hull. Yell smiled whitely.

"If we wait a minute the nice man's going to open the field for us."

"You're a marvel, Yell."

"Wait until we get there. It all depends on reliable intelligence, ask Sword. You won't mention my source to Issa."

"That blonde Tech-Two? Never."

"I knew I could depend on you."

The three sleds gathered speed. We kept pace a half-mile behind. Yell made engine-testing noises, keeping an eye on the panel. The lights stayed green. We passed a pressure-iris and another and the vast funnel of the entry was in front of us, marked out with lights and gantries at each layer of the ports and engineering bays that lined it. Even in flight there was traffic, transporting people and goods from one level to another.

The trio of sleds arrowed up the middle, rising towards the glow of the field in the far distance, and we puttered aimlessly behind. Yell tried another little power-jolt and made a couple of minor zigzags.

"How's the gidget on the fizzgig?" I asked anxiously.

"Functional. I think. I hope these guys don't mean to take forever or someone's going to ask questions."

The well narrowed beneath us, a black pit. A sharp beep sounded on the panel and Yell glanced down. "Uh-oh. I'm about to have trouble with my trans. Let's not hear him for a bit. We need farther up."

The sleds went on proceeding in a quiet triangle. Yell zigzagged some more and got into the shadow of a gantry. The beep of the callsign cut out for a few seconds.

"Fuck 'em. What they going to, a burial in space? We're getting cops any minute, I can feel 'em in the seat of my pants."

He was right. Down in the deeps I could see a couple of beacons flashing up out of the narrows. They weren't attending a burial. Unless it was ours.

"Can't we move, Yell?"

"Not until they open the screen, lovely. If we run now they'll lock it on us. If we keep on piddling I can maybe make them think I'm just incompetent. I need these three bastards to get a move on. They're the only guys going out, but being maintenance they aren't in a hurry. If they'll get their asses up there I'll move us, I promise."

The top of the funnel looked a million miles away. We wandered vaguely, getting among a flock of lighters loading at a cargo-bay, then drifting to the other side where a personnel carrier was picking up a pack of watch officers on their way off-shift. The beacons flashed bigger in our aft plate, from points to specks, from sparks to fireflies. They were going to catch up any minute and turn into wasps.

Yell's trans went on beeping intermittently as we moved in and out of radio shadow. He switched it on and off a couple of times and made garbling noises. It did the same.

"... *identify* ... *at once, I repeat* ... *Return at* ..."

He switched it out and wiggled the toggle up and down a few times. It sputtered.

The triangle had speeded. The pale glow of the field was brighter with cold stars shining behind the veil. The beacons were visibly cop blue below, whirling lights rising fast. Yeller did another aimless drift, headed for a string of water-barges. I made nail-holes in the upholstery.

And the field opened. One moment it was there, the next a clear black ring widened at our nose and irised out. A stutter of dust scattered the gap, and bare starlight glittered. The three sleds swanned serenely through and Yell jammed his finger on the drive-button.

"Hold on, kids, we're moving."

He was right to get us latticed. The acceleration nearly blasted me through the floor. Moke grunted on his stretcher. I'd a one-second vision of blurred light-chains and a blue veil arcing towards us, then we were in sparkling blackness as the field snapped shut behind. The whole open universe stared down.

"Fifteen minutes to warp," Yell said.

We were out.

Over moderate distance a powerful small ship travels faster than a big one. It was Sword's hope and ours. Our prime with her enormous mass had to clear system before she could warp. The aliens had been relying on that when they ran in their medium-sized pickabacks. Our small light hopships could outfly them too, with a bit of luck. Maybe even enough to make up for their start. While we were trying we got to sleep on stretchers and eat out of packets.

There's a nasty disadvantage in doing a long haul hyper in a hopship. If you lose drive you disintegrate. Sword, naturally, was too lunatic to care. So was Yell. So why should it bother me?

It took us forty-eight hours to make system and another seven coming in cautiously to catch up the orbit. There was nothing in sight, no insane hunter-killers, no alien patrols. That was careless. If they'd had even a sniff of Swordfish they should have known better.

195

The sun was a cool red star that made rose-colored reflections on the coils of cloud and washed the lakes with bloody light. Crusts of glitter at either pole said ice-fields fringed with blackish tundra, paling out north and south to cold steppe and glinting marshland. Dark vegetation, possibly jungle, girdled the equator.

Most of the planet was landmass, probably damp, studded with the overgrown lakes it used for seas and carved with thin steely lines of wandering river. It looked warm, wet and feverish. Half a dozen low-slung moonlets weren't likely to make its nights more joyful. The terminator was a dark-blue bruise smeared with smudges of crimson. There was no sign of life.

We hung in the shade of one of the little moons while Yell used his instruments and looked at the results dismally.

"No radioactivity outside natural norms, no industrial emissions, no visible settlements, no agglomerations of metal."

"They're not technological by our standards," Moke said. "We're not going to see kraals, if they're villages without industry."

"We would if they were on the steppe, so I guess they aren't. It's an outpost planet so there probably isn't a large population and the climate's not too lovable. I'd say insect-bites and marsh fever."

"If they're there at all they gotta have a spaceport," I objected. " 'Specially if they're bringing in prisoners for experting. There's gotta be at least a sci-base."

"Could be underground, there's rock under the mud. Would screen their emissions. If they've a city it ain't showing, though."

"They didn't look underground animals," Moke said. "All that fragile translucent stuff. Underwater?"

"We weren't made to be underground animals either

but we dig in when we got to. And someone said this lot were adaptable. Seas are pretty shallow and being landlocked they gotta be salty as hell. Bet you can practically walk on them. I'd pick jungle. It's in the warm latitudes and settlements would be screened by trees. I still say if there was a major city we'd see heat-streams. They emit a lot.''

"Hot and wet says things suck blood. Yech. Hope those fucking derms gonna work.''

"Real vampire country,'' Yell said grinning. "Shoulda brought garlic. We going down?''

"Have to. But where? Helluva lot of land down there.''

"That's planets, kid. And Sword's done exactly what I'm gonna do, he's made one real discreet landing. I been looking for exhaust trace and I'd call it dubious. Could be something down there, could be background radiation. Let's go look. What we got the Geeks haven't's a human-band trans, they don't hear at our frequencies. I say we go down, dig ourselves a hole and scope our boys out. If we're lucky we maybe fall over some Geeks doing it.''

"Fantz. That's what I was waiting for, meet a real live Geek face-to-face. But I always wanted to say hello to Tarzan.''

"Sorry, princess, you ain't gonna do it here 'less he considerable shrunk, that jungle ain't more'n six feet deep. But you can always hope.''

And he moved us into a shallow glide for dayside center.

We came down quietly in a flurry of sap and water and burrowed ourselves a dugout in the soft earth. When there was nothing above ground but our nose and upper hatch, both chameleoned, Yell switched in the forward sensors and we got a look around.

He was right about the jungle. Leathery-leaved whippy stuff barely covered the hump of our nose-assembly. Big yard-wide triangles paved the surface and they writhed and bent towards the space we'd cleared more like animals than plants, shouldering each other for the sky. The zenith was purple shading to violet with a near moon showing as a pale star. Plum-colored rays slanted out of cloud in the west. South-wards a huge storm filled the vapor with flashes that looked unnaturally steel-blue and a gust of rain hissed off our canopy. Low crests smothered in vegetation made a black line on the horizon. To the north a chain of saw-edged mountains curved across the sky.

The dripping leaves roofed us in so completely we were almost in darkness. The floor was covered with bleached spongy stuff like pale sphagnum that crawled out over the disturbed mud towards us. It moved much too fast, with the same animal speed as the leaves. Its rootlets felt for the ship and frizzled on our screen. It didn't stop them. Waves of curly white tangle piled up in a squirming ridge and ringed backward into the jungle.

Among the fuzz tall white-yellow stems stuck up. They seemed rooted but the swollen tips poked about like they were looking. Maybe for us. The glaze of slime that covered them was too much like live intestine. Vampire country. Even Dracula might have chosen not to rise from the grave here. And there were insects okay. The plate shimmered with specks as if the image had gone grainy. The slime-tips blackened over like they were charring until they were sooted all over. Then they abruptly plopped inside out. The new surface glazed right over and started again. A reversible stomach. Cute. Ingenious. Revolting.

I watched something segmented with too many legs wiggling towards us flirting moss and insect-eaters out of its way and decided not to be an exobiologist when I grew up. "Turn it off for the love of God, Yell, before I add to it."

"Okay, Beauty," he said peaceably. "You don't have to go out until I've raised the guys. How about dinner?"

Spacers as a race have strong stomachs. I could see how it happened.

"We got a frequency for Sword?" Moke asked.

"Yup. Don't bet he'll answer."

"I bet he does, if we can raise him."

"Could be difficult," Yell said. "Unless they're close, and there's no reason they should be. We could ask *Hercules* for coordinates."

"She's going to have warm little thoughts for us."

"Cassie. You getting old, woman. Never known it bother you."

"It don't. Don't want to squirt if we aren't sure of an answer, it's thready here. I got prickles in the neck-line."

"Normal," Yell said. "Alien forests got foreign vibes. Squirt 'em."

I tried the subspace. It beeped thin static for a long time before it spat me a pip. I tuned long-play and got what I expected, the senior comm-tech being uncivilized.

"Blaine? What the hell are you playing at? This isn't a kiddy-game, we've civilians in danger. We've enough trouble without you. I've a message from the old man. You got yourselves down there, you get yourselves back up. If we come in on a bombing-run he's not stopping."

"Tell him Happy Christmas from me too," I said. "Where's Swordfish?"

"Who?"

"Major fucking DeLorn and company. I need co-ordinates, dammit."

She snarled and there was a long silence while they decided if it was a military secret. I guess it wasn't because finally they gave. Yell nodded.

"Could be worse. They're on the high ground to the north, couple hundred miles northwest. Anything on the Geek fleet?"

"Not right now. Probably still spacing."

"Let's hope."

"Blaine?" the trans said. *"There's a message from Evander. Urgent. Stand by."*

"Cassandra? Latest on your samples. Retta's finished growing. Raspberry and vanilla are the same species. Vanilla are seed-bearers, the eggs they scatter are fertilized and come both flavors. Our first two just happened to be vanilla too, ratio we have here is six to one against raspberry. The others have a different cycle. They root briefly in the mother-garden and grow into towers. When they're mature at around six inches they break apart into disks, twenty to a hundred per tower. Each tower's a raspberry clone-group. They start feeding and growing filaments right away but they aren't viable until they've reached maybe eighteen inches. At that point they've developed a nervous system and minimal sentience, which goes on developing. Pete's calculated growth to useful size would take fourteen or fifteen years."

Nice. Exactly our delay between wars.

"The vanillas have a primitive mobility at eight inches or so that lets them find favorable places, then they go vegetable. They're insentient, or possibly bor-

derline. Retta thinks they've a residual telepathic aura. We've tested their electrical fields and they both react, mobiles strong, vegetatives weak. The guys aren't clear on fertilization but they suggest airborne spores, maybe at long intervals. Generations have to attain adulthood in waves, in the circumstances. And we're being careful, the mobiles are dangerous. Quite a small one can punch holes in plate. Maybe they have to be tough, the wastage at each stage is enormous. The exobs are keeping them in cerosteel. They're waiting to see how long it takes before they punch holes in that too."

There's nothing makes me happier than an optimist.

"The plastic your sculptures were made of's a secretion, though we're not clear whose, there are traces of both. It's certainly art or something, the material's been worked and there are minerals and vegetable cells mixed in as coloring. That's all for now but the message is, be careful. Specimens older than fourteen or fifteen could grow to any size at all, Jean's hypothesized their upper limit's either gravitational collapse or probably death, if a lot are so small it's probably because they're so aggressive they don't live long. Dribble's right, they fight on sight and they eat each other. Luck, children, and don't turn your backs. Love to Hector when you see him."

Nice Evander. I sent our love back and an absolute promise never to turn my back on a raspberry. Or a vanilla either, come to that. The hair that blew where there wasn't a wind. Maybe they stayed rooted. Maybe when they were real old ladies they got up and went walkabout, eating whoever they met. I decided not to be there.

"Sword was right," Moke said. "They've got to outgrow their environment fast, especially if they've solved predators. Have the exobs any idea what those might be?''

"I'll ask, though I don't see how they can. And let's tell Sword we're here. He'll lose his mind, but he's used to it.''

"Lucky guy," Yell said. "What would he have done without you?''

"Died at twenty-one, probably," Moke said. "Let's eat, I need coaling.''

We got out our mini-stove and some delicious prote pellets. The Navy has such a rich imagination.

Sword's delight at hearing me didn't noticeably break out through the micro. His voice came over the trans scraped and cracky.

"Cass. I tried to leave you somewhere safe."

"I didn't promise to stay. You forgot to nail my foot to the floor. How do we meet?''

Deep-space silence. *"It's no use telling you you're making my job worse."*

"No. I got Moke and Yell. That's three extra soldiers. Quit patronizing me and give with the directions.''

A distant sigh. *"There's a possible base-site on the plain below here. Can't be sure, nothing's moving but Hall's trapped emissions. We came in behind the mountains to screen our approach and we daren't leave the ship until we're sure. Can't have you guys buzzing around attracting attention either. If you come, you come overland. There's roughly a hundred seventy miles between us."*

That made Yell a navigator. In terms of a planet it's right on the nose. "Yell?''

"Can do. We got planks. Gonna take us twenty hours min though, going don't look hot.''

"You just named what I had at the top of my birth-day list," Sword said on a heavy breath. *"Transport's going to be a problem and we're light on it, we were stretched for weight. Start coming. You're going to need all you've got, countryside's hell in gumshoes."*

"The picks shown?"

"If they had we'd be long gone. We're waiting for them to come and point the way. Make ground, guys, and watch how you go. There are parasites and bur-rowers and you'll need recyclers, air's oxy-nitro with nasty additives."

"We've met," I said. "They're yellow and wiggle."

"I was talking methane. Make it fast, we could run out of time." His voice lightened. *"Yell I can use."*

"Warm thanks from Moke and me. We'll be with you, just as soon as we've choked down our caviar."

"We've got prote pellets."

"Yeah," I said gloomily. "I know."

The air outside was wet and heavy. We had mud-shoes but they're awkward to walk in and by the time you've added mask and filters on top of a coolsuit you feel like a deepsea diver even without duck feet. Furry moss curled around our ankles and yellow stomachs glazed with sugar twisted towards us. Milling black specks whined at our facemasks.

We'd four planks, rolled into scrolls. Yell straight-ened one with a practiced snap and it ran out its two-meter length, inflated and hardened like a stiffjack. It hovered four feet above the mud, rocking gently.

"You can raise and lower 'em," he said. "Controls at the front. But don't raise it too high, they destabilize. Plus there isn't much room and we gotta get our gear on. I brought the smallest, the twelve-foot jobs have cargo-space but they're awkward over rough ground and you've a higher risk of showing on some wiseass's scope. These'll take us, but they're not too stable and anyone horses around's gonna end on the deck. I don't advise it, my meter says mudholes and you can't see 'em under this white stuff. And we gotta move fast. That complicates things.''

''You said twenty hours. Over a hundred seventy miles, that's less'n ten miles an hour.''

''A hundred seventy as the crow flies, doll. You gonna discover we ain't crows. And we're gonna have to stop and eat sometime or we'll be asleep on the plank and that's how you end in a mudhole. Be lucky to make ten miles per. Get packing, kids.''

There were cargo straps in back for lattices and food packs, which Yell rated basic. He let me keep my little laser so long as I didn't point it, this being something my Granny needs to tell me after ten years as a burglar. He had a thermal lance I last saw working on ceramic slung alongside and Moke was lying over a medium cutter with twelve-foot range and a beam cuts jigs in steel. They'd a job getting it strapped and balanced, Moke isn't heavy and it tended to pull his nose down, but they stuck at it. Yell figured it rated it. Me, I wondered when the grizzlies were coming because that's loaded-for-bear country. The fourth was cargo and Yell towed it himself on a magnetic link that made it waddle behind him like a wooden dachshund.

We must have spent an hour before we moved at all. The mudshoes got hooked at the nose, we snapped safety straps and convoyed out. I started flat on my face, got a crick in my back and tried to roll which very nearly ended me up underneath with my feet pointing at the sky. So I sat astride for a bit until I found a particularly large reversible belly trying to wrap itself around my ankle. I swear I could feel it digesting me through my suit. I pulled my feet up in a hurry and sat with my knees to my chest. Then I lay flat again.

"Knock it off, Cass, you're like a Mexican bean," Yell said from up front. He had the compass and was orienting through endless leathery stems, his knees clasped around the edge and his feet crossed behind him. He looked comfortable. I tried it. Guess it takes practice. A thousand years might do. Moke was lying easily over his cutter gazing thoughtfully into the mud but he doesn't count, he was probably planning shapes with kinks in them. When his muse has him by the short hairs he ain't responsible.

It was going to be a long twenty hours.

The country was nasty. All the vegetation was too mobile. While we traveled we smacked stems out of our gear. The suits being neutral they skipped us, but the moss seemed to function on touch and if you didn't keep moving from one foot to the other it climbed up your leg. It could have been harmless but I didn't feel like testing.

You could have followed our route by the furrow of bending leaves that tipped as we went, and since they had rainwater trapped between leaf and stalk it was like trucking under a waterfall. Now and then we'd meet a thicket of black stuff like blood pudding sprouting hairy tufts, and the hairs bent to follow us like they were tracking by radar. The black specks clouded with a static crackle and things you couldn't see scuttered under the moss. Not seeing them was the only plus I could think of.

At least we hadn't met large animals or anything looked intelligent.

"There may not be any," Moke said. "If Yell's right about salty seas, and he could be since they're small and landlocked, their life has to be highly specialized. The chemical overload could have happened before they'd a chance to develop complex forms.''

''The crawlers look complex enough for me.''

''They could be it,'' he said. ''Unless there's something on the steppe. It's the vegetation that's developed, and it hasn't much variety.''

''Or the flies.''

''You can't tell,'' Yeller said. ''Unless you got a microscope. You could bottle some for Retta.''

I called him several names and he grinned. From the expression of his mask.

None of us did much grinning, it was Machete Beach without machetes. We didn't want to mess the environment, attracts notice. Yell took first turn at forcing stems, then Moke spelled him. Then I volunteered. It was pride and I regretted it, damn stems were tough as rawhide and if you didn't keep your guard up they smacked like a lash. I'd aching arms and a whole zebra of weals before Yell came up front again.

He was right about the speed, too. We moved as fast as the plant-life would let us, which was often slow walk. Other times we met spaces of marsh with floating saucers as big as traxies swaying on threads overhead, masses of swollen pustules that looked parasitic dragging them down. Scarves of silky fur rooted in the stems blew out for yards on a breeze that smelled of sulfur. Bubbles of gas glooped up from below.

There'd been almost no light under the forest and we traveled on IR filters among drifts of steam. Rose-colored sunlight glistened off the marshes and columns of cloud spired over the mud. They burned yellow-green, drifting like they'd nowhere special to go. Sometimes they'd brush and run together in one high shooting flame.

"What's that?"

"Marsh-gas?" Moke said. "They're thickest where the bubbles are. Not alive."

"Then why are they moving against the wind?"

He didn't answer. Yell put speed on and we got out. I felt better when we had. The biggest stretch of bog spread out around an island of rock where blobs of jelly hung on the cliffs and cascades of fringe stirred from cracks. Yell pulled towards it.

"Chow-down."

"Don't think I wanta take my mask off."

"Neither do I, we'll put up a shelter. Gimme a hand, Moke, let's unload."

He'd picked a flat shelf under the cliff, clear of the water and away from the layers of fringe. When I got down crunchy bladdered stuff burst under me with a scatter of rude pops and a horrible stink. Yell laughed and threw the tent. I dumped it vengefully and switched in the inflator. It puffed and ticked but we finished with a pyramidal dome eight feet at the base, with atmosphere, that was plant-free. We'd a built-in scrubber across the lock to make sure.

We shed masks and flopped. It gave us a minute with a disposal-bottle each where we needn't fear for our virtue and the pleasure of a quiet surface. I'd a massive ache across my shoulders and my arms felt broken.

"How far we come?"

" 'Bout forty miles. Twenty minutes before we get back on the road. We'll need to rest oftener when we get tired."

"Yeah, right."

Moke set up the stove and we fixed ourselves another brew of hot prote. It was food. Yell put the billy back in the cookhole and measured brown powder.

"Here you are, Cass. Brings the dead to life."

I sat, creaking. Coffee. "Remind me to write you into my will, Yell. I'm gonna leave you my dearest possession."

"That yellow diamond as big as the Ritz?"

"Mokey. Every household should have one. You can have the diamond as well."

Moke swatted. "Wait until I write my will. I'm looking around for someone to leave you to."

"There's probably a law against it," Yell said amiably. "The Anti-Cass Leaving Law. Comes under the heading of non-assistance to persons in danger. What's that?"

A soft brushing on the transparent roof. We put our noses to the plastic and peered. The wavy fringes that had been ten yards off when Yell picked a place for the tent had lengthened until the tips were dragging across our wall. They fingered us slowly, feeling towards the lock.

"Yech," I said. I adore wildlife, it gives me hayfever wherever I meet it. Traveling here was just ducky. "I hope our damned suits are spore-proof. Those things look people-nivorous to me."

"We'll find out," Yell said cheerfully. "They may not like the taste of you either."

I wasn't ready to bet on that. They looked like they very easily might. Even Yeller looked more thoughtful than he was saying. Only Moke was happy. He had a slate in his hand and he was sketching like crazy.

Insanity can be comforting.

13

By the time we were repacked and moving it was evening and the terminator was coming to meet us. The shadows had grown darker with crimson halos. The jungle stayed the same but we came on more and more rock, some rising out of bog, some half-grown over by tides of triangle. The wavy fur got longer and thicker until it almost covered them.

We'd just crossed another swamp and were nosing westwards through stems towards a mound that made high spiky shapes on purple sky when Yell hauled his plank into reverse and came to a stop, rocking. His trailing dachshund ran on into him with a light thump and jumped back shuddering. Moke and me braked frantically. He turned us a blank mask and a flat hand.

"Watch it, there's stuff up ahead. My scope says movement and not crawlers. Big, fast and a lot of it. If we just found raspberry jellofish I'd rather go around, we ain't equipped for combat. Keep your voices down,

Evander thinks they don't hear us but that's an opinion.
Let's head north.''

Moke moved up and we clustered noses. ''I'd like
to look. We've never seen them just living.''

''Dammit, Moke, we got the lighthouse to look for.''

''Gotta say I met better moments for meditation.
Though I'm only the hired help.''

Mokey lives with people who don't understand him,
such as the whole human race. It's the penalty of genius.

''It isn't curiosity exactly, it's just trying to know
what's going on. We'll handle them better if we know
how they function. Aurelia's on my conscience, I'm
not going to forget her. But I need to see. A few
minutes, Yell, it could help in the end.''

Yeller sighed. ''Okay, boss. You and me? We better
leave the planks and go up on foot, Cass can keep an
eye on them. But make it fast. Won't help the kids if
they eat you.''

''Nuts to that. I went last time, I go again. Sorry,
Yell, but if we need a guard you're it. I'm getting clos-
est because I'm smallest, the leaves barely cover you.
And if the fucking toadstools eat you both I'm not
hanging around on my own, I'm allergic to crawlies.
If anyone can survive this place it's you, you've had
experience.'' I reached for my mudshoes.

Yell sighed again. ''I keep thinking I can tell her
something. Okay, get going, I'll come up slow behind
you. Don't let him go into a trance, Cass, we'll lose
time on the detour anyhow.''

''Okay.''

Moke was on the ground, duck-footing off into curly
growth. I grabbed Yell's scope and slithered after him.

There was movement all right, strong vibration and
enough to say a community. A lot of fast skittering

motion and some clumsy sliding, not more than five hundred yards away. If we'd kept going we'd have run slap into it. Moke hadn't waited, his lean shape was bent over in the leaves with his nose aiming like a pointer. I slid up to his shoulder and pointed too.

Two feet of stems separated us from the open at the base of the rocks. I guess it had a force-field because charred masses of white stuff were piled up like an earthwork and the surface under our feet writhed continuously like a big wrinkled pelt. That was useful because it stopped anyone seeing our personal waves.

The stuff that grew on the other side was suddenly different, emerald chunks with dark-red hollows in the dying light. They made concentric circles of lump from big in the center to rings of little ones around the edge. Maybe it was radial symmetry. Maybe it was cabbages. Maybe it was an optical illusion. What it looked like was crops. Some of the lumps were bigger than others as if maybe they got harvested now and then. Bare black mud showed between.

If we hadn't seen kraals from space it was because these guys didn't live in them. Or not here. Light pointed domes were balanced among the rocks. Where there was level space they'd used it, where there wasn't they'd built it, either by filling with glassy struts or cantilevering in layers along the face of the cliff. The houses were the pale plasticky stuff we'd seen in the camp, which explained why we hadn't detected industrial emissions or agglomerations of metal. The colors echoed the violet and crimson sky, or the black-green streaked white of the jungle. They just missed being invisible at a hundred paces. There might have been twenty, though we could only see the face nearest us.

"No roads," Moke whispered.

It figured. The movers were raspberries okay, maybe

as many as fifty, and they drifted up and down the cliff
like they were swimming. They weren't as big as our
eight, maybe five feet high to the edge of the cap. They
moved with the same looping swirl like a garland of
Disney ballerinas, identical in size and shape which
added to the cartoon look, as if they'd all been drawn
by the same artist.

They were a garland because they were coming
down the slope that way, a long twirling line, their
tentacles brushing the surface of the rock. They held
their tendrils raised in a spire above their caps and trailing threads touched their neighbors fore and aft. Since
they took the path of least resistance the line drifted in
curves, everyone exactly following its leader. The guy
at the front had to be lonely, he was getting the thinking to do.

"What they doing?"

He shook his head. "Going that way. What is it?"

The one building down at ground-level, a high beehive with a ribbed dome and sides cut away like a
country bandstand. It was about the same size, maybe
thirty feet across, with a low platform at the base.
Arched pillars supported the roof. Its pearly walls
gleamed with ceramic and looked rose and opal in the
sunset, burning against the black jungle like a party
lantern. There was some kind of shape under the center
of the dome that stood and waited, twirling.

"Hell. A thingummy. Toadstool-in-a-turnip-field.
Like the others. I betcha."

"Spins faster."

"Maybe they just weren't in last time."

He turned a featureless profile. "Telepathic plastic?"

"Maybe they push it. Could be an electrical field.
Dammit, maybe it's clockwork."

"Yeah, electrical, could be. Retta detected strong emanations." He turned back, absorbed.

I lifted my glasses. The ballet-corps weren't alone. Something else flumped clumsily alongside, skidding and tumbling from level to level. Low dumpy shapes that skittered sparks in the gathering darkness. The western sky was almost the color of clotted blood, high scarlet clouds on royal purple over our heads. The pulsing canopy of jungle was covered with crimson gloom. I twisted the sight and the shapes came into focus.

"Mokey?"

He reached. "I thought so."

The procession was mixed in with big vanillas, the ones with the thrashing hair that blew without wind. Their fringes whipped as they humped and the beads caught the light like sparkly crowns. Little nubby clumps hung on their skirts.

"They do get up and move."

"I don't think it's voluntary."

I took the glasses back. It was hard to see in the sunset but there could have been clear threads joining them and the ballet. If you looked hard and were Moke you might think they were on leash, dragged along by the scruff of the neck. I upped my input and got a flare of brilliance. The raspberries were as hot as linked braziers, they glowed in the dark. Their tendrils burned like flames. They probably lit a lot of the way for themselves. But some were carrying infra-red torches, too dim to show while there was sunlight but glaring like arcs now it was dark, and the place shone like a carnival.

The vanillas were getting dragged at speed and it looked like the biggest could nearly make it on their own. Their roots had grown to rudimentary tentacles as if they were imitating the mobiles but not quite well enough.

They weren't being led gently. The lashing threads snapped off nubbles at the cap and the floundering thrashers fell and thudded down the rock. A lot had lost chunks of cap and stem and the cliff-face was slimed with wet jelly. When a couple hesitated on a ledge the nearest ballerina snapped a tentacle and they overbalanced down and landed at the bottom in a smash of sludge. The line below picked up the beat and whipped the remains onto their roots.

"What's going on?" I whispered.

"Looks like they're going to the bandstand. A ritual?"

"They ain't nice to their dancing partners."

"Retta said they were insentient."

"Then why are they walking? She thought they might be borderline. Them things moves, Moke."

"Doesn't prove much. Vegetation's responsive even on Earth. Could be a sort of automatism."

He didn't sound convinced.

"You heard the story cabbages scream?"

"Hey," Yell whispered from behind. "You guys staying all night? Let's get the hell out before it gets darker. It's going to be fun enough navigating in the jungle without trying to grope past them without a scope. Come on."

He'd brought the planks in a waggling line. We waddled back and got aboard. I had to rip my legs free of a mound of clutching hair that had climbed to my waist. I spent the next few miles finding and shedding fresh bits. And it lay on me and wiggled while I ripped.

The sun went down and slaty vapor built over the mountains and loomed. One of the little fast moons showed an irregular bright blotch that changed shape almost visibly, not much bigger than a bright star. The dim atmosphere smothered all but the major stars and we could almost have been alone in the universe. The sky was pricked with sparse distant points.

Yell was right about the navigation, we were traveling on full filter and we could see the village torches blazing above the pinnacles long after we'd passed. If Moke's theory they saw our light as a blue-white glare worked we weren't getting to use much equipment. And those things gave out electrical fields, I'd a headache cut my skull in two.

"This got to be a civilian settlement? They don't look like scientists to me."

"How do scientific jellofish look?" Yell said sourly. "But from our own outpost planets I'd say they could be farmers. You plant a base, you bring in civilians and they found a society. That's how we do it."

"Then Sword and Hall really could be near the base," Moke said. "If there aren't many people they probably settle around the Navy or whatever it is runs the sci-station."

"If we're sure it's a sci-station."

"Think it's got to be. If they're bringing specimens back for examination either their big scientists are here already or they're about to arrive. Those guys don't look fitted out for lab-work."

"What the hell were they doing?"

Yell tried to scratch his scalp with a glove through his blue hood, which never works, it's frustrating. "If they're farmers . . ."

"They grow cabbages or something."

"Something. We don't know they eat them."

"Okay, whatever. They herd and cultivate insentients."

"They weren't just eating. The ones we saw in camp were broken off clean. None of that mess."

"That's what I'm trying to say," Yell said. "It wasn't a dinner-party. Farmers weed crops."

"But insentients are their own kind."

"They still eat 'em. We're particular what we eat. So we weed. I read once, people used to do it with their animals too. A cull. Weeding the unfit to keep the breeding-stock pure. Maybe they were weeding."

"But those looked like fit. They were moving by themselves. And they'd young."

"They may like 'em rooted. If you happened to eat cabbages you might object if they walked around the farmyard."

"You objected like mad to those little fern-stages that walked on the bed and rooted in your armpits," Moke said.

Fucking Virginity. "I remember. Clearly."

"And when you find a bad line you weed the young as well. Stops 'em spreading."

Cute idea. "Lovely people."

"If they really spread fast I imagine life's cheap," Mokey said.

"That's what Sword thought. They suicide if you catch them."

"Or maybe just die." Moke has his own talents, he reads faces through masks. "They're clones and telepathic. They got to be identical in everything. From the same seed, the same pile, the same life-history. And sharing minds. Supposing most of the group was killed. If they've a kind of telepathic group-mind, imagine losing it. All yourselves and your feelings suddenly cut off. They could just die. Of loss. The vanillas being insentient wouldn't suffer as much so they might survive longer, and that would be why there's more vanilla material. But Pete got a feeling off theirs, even the insentient. He said it was lonely.''

I shivered. It was a nasty idea. Brought back from the dead to a world where you were alone, and not even clever enough to know what hurt. "D'you think that's why they destroyed it?"

"If Pete who isn't telepathic felt it was suffering, for them it could have been shrieking its heart out. Maybe they stomped it to stop the noise."

"They're not exactly humane killers."

"Retta thought vanillas aren't exactly conscious."

"But if you can hear it yelling, what does conscious mean?"

"I don't know," Moke said after a pause. "It's not a human system, that's all you can say."

We were still driving through whippy stems but thick dark sky showed above our heads, with a second little moon climbing out of mist and the scarce stars glinting like candles far away. When I got leaves silhouetted in the scope they'd rolled up like sails, long drooping cones with dewdrops at the tips. The cloud above the peaks had expanded over half the sky and a warning flash flickered over the underside showing sagging bellies of vapor. Thunder rumbled. The flash lit another rock-island close in front.

"Marsh coming up," Yell said wearily. He'd been batting stems a long time. "Get some speed on."

"Yeah. We need it."

The gauzy marsh-plants had folded too, their pads curled into knots on the high stems. The breeze had dropped completely and their parasitic fur hung lank. Another sheet of light glistened off the water and stretches of mud. Two or three yellow-green gas-pillars drifted in the distance, moving sluggishly in random spirals. We headed out on the wet expanse, opening throttles.

We'd been sitting on planks for most of eight hours taking it in turns to whack trail and we were stiff and itchy. The heavy atmosphere had got heavier with night and it smelled of thunder even through a recycler. I'd lost the headache I'd got from the toadstools but a dull tightness behind the eyes was strain, or recycled air, or just traveling in red light in permanent filters. The sudden speed disturbed the vapors, making stems near us dip and curve. They were much too supple. Everything here moved too much.

Yell headed the line with his dachshund in tow, Moke at the tail and me between. My butt hurt and I was trying a new wiggle. We stayed in line to miss the stems, Yeller picking the way. I was watching his linked planks rising and falling when the hair rose down my back like all my fur was standing straight up. I glanced backwards and saw a column of light coming up behind, a dozen yards from my right elbow. Some kinda swamp gas, all right.

It was moving without wind and fast, closing with us in an unswerving line. It looked taller in the dark, or maybe it had grown, ten or twelve feet high. It burned vividly yellow, a slow granulated swirl spiring top to bottom inside as if some kind of life was peering out, poised with a kind of alertness. My hair was trying to rise under my hood. A bright wink caught my eye on the other side and I saw two or three more beyond Moke and others out among the stems. They seemed to rise higher as they got near us and they were really converging, centering in towards our planks. The shudder I had was nothing to do with superstition. It was the feeling you get when you touch a bare wire.

"Yell!" I yelped.

His head swiveled, and Moke's with it. Up ahead more and more lights were springing out of mud. Bubbles burst under us and a new one leapt in the air right between the dachshund and me. A flare of electricity ran over the plank with our humped gear piled on top and outlined it in fire. Something inside sizzled and sparks trailed off the edges of the tarp.

"Shit!" he said explosively. "Go around, Cass, and move. Don't touch that bastard. Then let's get the fuck out. Full speed and to hell with the emtrails. Go!"

I jinked right, managed to slide between the light in front and the one heading for my elbow and pulled into space. The plank brushed the skirt of the nearer and winced as if someone had leaned a heavy hand on its side. For a moment it stood almost on edge while I hung on with teeth and nails. There was a clatter from the pack on the back. If I hadn't had safety straps I'd have been underwater. I slid dangerously, lost a leg overboard, touched surface with one foot and got a distinct strong shock. I snatched it back with another yelp.

"Watch it, guys, the suckers are live."

"Tell me about it," Yell said. "Look up ahead."

When we started there'd been two or three random lights wandering in the distance. Now the whole place was alive and more were coming from all directions. The bog in front was a rippling wall of yellow-green fire.

"Fuck. Can we make the island?"

"We could. Question is, will it stop them?"

"I think so," Moke said. He was fumbling in front of him. "They're connected with the bubbles so I'd say they're confined to the marsh. But we can't spend the night here, we've traveling to do. Let me in front,

Yell, and watch my tail. I'm giving her full throttle, it could be bumpy.''

His plank swerved out into the yellow wall and I saw his narrow head outlined against it. He was still pulling at something under his chest. Then a clear blue-white line slashed across the dark, cutting stems and shriveling silk to glue, and touched the nearest pillar. Said pillar spurted suddenly as if somebody'd poured on gasoline, towered towards the sky and burst in a cloud of fiery smoke. The next, that had been coming up for another try at my arm, pulled suddenly back, spun on the spot and veered away.

''I thought so.'' He was adjusting for aperture and the light widened into a blinding fan. ''Get up on my sides if you can, it just feeds them at a distance but around twelve feet they overload. But they suck energy, my charge won't last with this drain, wasn't made for it. She's going to overheat and blow the battery. Full ahead, let's hit land quick.''

We leaned on our throttles and drew together in a tight triangle. The fanned cutter was carving the night, its way marked with spurting flame and gusts of smoke. The marsh was boiling around us, pillars rising and falling, some spiraling nearer, others veering further off. A crackle of scorched vegetation and the sizzle of sparks followed our trail.

A big swirling column rose suddenly out of the mud just under my nose and I pointed my laser into the middle and gave it full blast. Moke was right, it ate energy. I thought it was going to lap charge all night when it gave a kind of electric gasp and leapt twenty feet into the air. Hot fumes drifted sootily over my head.

''Next!'' I yelled.

It was maybe lucky we hit bank before one obliged

or I'd have had a mittful of exploding battery too. We shot out of marsh with a jerk like a bumper car and dived into jungle. A swathe of whiplash stalks fell in front like reaped wheat and Mokey cut the beam before we could do more damage. We found ourselves charging blind into darkness, stalks like bullwhips snapping at our faces.

"Cut drive!" Yell shouted.

The same idea'd been leaning on me and Moke reacted so fast his hand had been ready on his lever. I pulled into reverse just in time to keep the crash with the dachshund small and we hung, rocking. We were all breathing hard.

"Thanks, Moke. Said every household needs one."

"Greedy bastards, I've used enough charge for three hours' cutting. It wasn't exactly discreet. We burned a lot of marsh back there and we must've lit the night up like a thunderstorm."

"That's okay," Yell said. "A thunderstorm's exactly what we're getting. Maybe why they were so frisky. Speed this stuff grows I bet the traces've gone by morning. But I'm taking a minute off to get at the gear, I'd like the second cutter before we meet something really interesting."

"Be my guest."

We'd been too busy for a while to look at the sky but the wall of cloud now covered it from one horizon to the other and repeated sheets of lightning flowed across the clouds. The landscape strobed like a disco. Flaring slashes cut downwards now and then and the distant grumble had become a heavy crashing of thunder only a mile or two away that followed one explosion on top of another until the noise was continuous. A steel-blue flash cut the night in half almost on top of us and the detonation shook the ground.

"Gonna rain."

"You said it. Have a sheet." Yell was rummaging on his dachshund and he flung me a plastic cover, tailored to fit over plank and cargo. "It ain't the latest art but these things haven't the power to throw a field and run the engine at the same time. It'll stop your gear shorting out. Get under, this is coming sudden."

We pulled them over our heads and draped the skirts around. The plank sucked in and made a seal as soon as the cover settled.

"Wonder how the toadstools deal with this. They got IR vision, lightning got to burn their eyes out."

"Or what they use in place of."

"I bet they take shelter. It's why I figured no one would notice Moke's firework display. Okay, kids, move on. And stay away from peaks, it's a bad night to fry."

"They're all that."

"I'm worrying particular about this one."

The first gust of wind hit moments later and a fusillade of raindrops at the same time. We linked sleds before the rain got heavier and clung together through the cowering forest. The rolled sails of the triangles had folded down to lie doubled against their stalks and the whole writhing mass coiled up and sank into the ground as the storm got into gear. Hissing sheets of water slashed across the leaves and smacked us in the face.

The planks staggered and a solid river poured across the awning over my head. Moke and Yell were blurred silhouettes as chains of lightning ripped across the sky and crashed and thundered through the stems. Yell waved us urgently down and we crouched at ground level, our drive-units laboring, keeping up just enough way not to be blown off into the roaring waterfall that had just replaced the air supply.

The plants were prostrate, pressing themselves into the carpet of moss like soaked curls. The plain could have been lifeless. When the hail came we were flattened too, trying to pad ourselves against lumps of ice the size of tennis balls. The awning absorbed some of the energy but it was the soil-temperature saved us. It radiated so much warmth the lumps were almost melted before they hit ground, but what was left kept us crouched in humps with arms over our heads through half an ice-age.

By the time we uncoiled the squall had passed and there was steady rain driving under the wind like a shower of nails. The jungle was slowly beginning to lift itself up. We did the same and got under way.

It went on raining until dawn. When the first streaks of orange began to layer the east, the steely lines of water tapered off and the cloud-cover shredded and drifted into blue. Stalks unwound like springs and rose towards the light, the triangular sails heading for what they could grab of sky. When we came out into clear ground half an hour later the jungle behind was one horizon-wide convulsion, as if the skin of the planet had been struck with allergic spasms.

I felt pretty allergic myself.

The mountains looked painted on glass: black facets in front, dark blue behind, misty blue in the distance where they faded in mist. There were red reflections in the hollows. The layers went back as far as you could see to saw-edges on the horizon covered in pink sparkle like birthday icing. The jungle washed up to their feet, tried to climb over and gave up in stunted puddles among the rock-slides at the base. The nearest cliffs were furry with fringe that blew from the cracks like a pantomime dragon. A steady hot wind ran over the face but they blew more than they had to. We'd been climbing slowly for a while and we'd finally come out into the open.

"This is nice. How do we get up?"

"Vertically," Yell said, gazing at his compass. "Question is where."

"Haven't we a position?" Moke asked.

"Had. Can't see a thing down here and we can't ask

for a beacon, too dangerous. Once we get up we're into a maze, there're canyons in all directions. And planks don't fly. They climb and they crawl but the grav-units aren't strong enough to take them far off a surface. So we go up and down. Told you we weren't crows, Cass.''

I looked at the cliff. It was sheer and it went a long way up out of sight. Glassy silk floated like seaweed, reaching for us. The sun glittered off it and something slimier shone higher up saying more delights in the top storeys.

"So let's go up and down."

"We can go up, anyhow. Maybe I'll see better. Could squirt the guys at least. Rock blanks us here.''

Vertical meant vertical. The planks had a ridge near the tail that gave a toehold. The packs thunked backward as soon as we turned and I listened to the clattering noises of irreplaceable equipment getting beyond replacement. I'm used to vertical but it's the first time I spent an hour drifting up a faceless wall strapped to an ironing-board. Dumb hanks of transparent silk reached at my face and trailed away too slowly as we passed. The tips curled around my ankles and tried to hitch on the board and got chopped away by the exhaust, smoking. It was a new experience. I decided to keep it occasional.

The drive-units whistled softly with the strain and the cross-wind that ruffled the face whistled a different note at right-angles like the beginning of a flute concerto. It also got between the plank and the wall from time to time and gusted us further away. We were keeping a regular eighteen inches off with allowance for overhangs but Yell thought it was safe to four feet, but with changes in rock density he found conditions dangerous enough to make a detour. When he thought the cliff bulged too far we made sure and went around it.

We were coming up under a jellied-over hump when a gust caught the edge of my plank and gave a little twirl underneath. The plank swiveled, spun edge-on to the cliff and shaled across the current. I saw black rock vanishing in front of my nose as plank and me skidded six feet out into sky. The board buzzed, see-sawed once and dropped like a stone. I heard Moke shout above, like a distant seagull.

I hadn't even time to be afraid. I slammed the throttle full ahead and leaned my weight on the nose. For once in my life I wished I was heavier. The cliff came into focus, disappearing upwards like the shaft of an express elevator. The plank swung, hesitated, caught, slowed and came back into balance like a jerky pendulum. I swung in space watching fringe and plates of pale jelly oscillate in front of me, still slipping down slowly, like Alice. My long-time friend. There was absolutely no marmalade. Then the drive hummed angrily, took hold and started to pull. The drone died back to a quiet whistle.

The cliff began reeling backwards for the second time. I didn't look to see how near I'd been to the ground. I was halfway back up before I noticed I was shaking. Later still I found I'd torn my nails bloody. The hanging fur had done its growing trick and it crawled over my suit as I passed, wrapping around my legs, tips nuzzling the rims of my filters. I tore handfuls away, tough and supple as fishing line. It came out easily and drifted downwards, mermaid hair waving on the draft, its filaments reaching at the cracks as it passed. Where it touched it caught and began to grow.

A shadow turned into Yell, coming down backwards with his dachshund under him. His blue mask was stiff.

He grabbed for my strap and clipped it to his plank.

"I'm all right," I said, like a frog with a cold.

"Sure you are. It's your circus training."

"Don't try to be Sword, I get enough from the original."

"Wouldn't dream of it, princess. I just found out why he does it. It's a form of hysteria."

I choked and clung a minute to his hard waist. Moke was above and we linked straps, with a couple of yards between for maneuver. He reached out a hand, and took it back. You can't hold hands and steer. The cliff went on falling slowly.

The ridge had a great view if you like country. I prefer the kind comes in concrete with balconies. Slices of rock like broken glass rose in front, piled and scattered and cut with gullies full of red darkness. Yell was right, we needed wings. A minor grav-plank might get up and down it in a hundred years. The way we'd come a sea of jungle wavered off into distance. Northwest it straggled towards a flattened cone in a paler color that didn't writhe. It could have been grass. Or anything. Anthills. Landscape art. A pearly bump reflected light near the top, too far away to have a shape. Something big and polished, stuck like an oyster shell against the peak. The ridges slanted like they'd been cut with a cheese-wire. The rim we were on leaned north with a sharp overhang that didn't look good for getting down.

"That way," Yell said. "Look for a crossing. Stay linked, Sword'll be mad if I lose you."

We backed on the wind and let it carry us, grav-units hissing. We needed speed. The ridge was splintered with cracks grown with orange blisters and other nasties. We slid over most without dropping. Once or twice my nose ducked into a deeper hole and jerked up just before we fell head-first, and Moke's and Yell's linked boards swung inwards. When they weren't doing the same to me. It was seasick city. But we made ground. Problem was where next. The ridges unreeled into sky like a broken pavement, glittering with mica.

Maybe an angel was what we needed. It showed in a flash of light off the side of my eye that made me turn. A shape was outlined against the disk of the sun, balanced like a phoenix between fans of light that spread above and below it like wings. It had arms, legs, a human head. I jerked Yell's straps and he turned. By the time he and Moke had got into reverse I was on the ground running.

The sky-colored feet touched rock and took the couple of strides to meet me. I had to see him move to have cold in my gut and bright slashes under my belt-buckle. The height and length rose into the sky, angular and narrow. His head had the bend of a tall guy in a small guys' world. I caught my knees shaking, braced them and went the rest of the way slowly.

"Hall?"

"Cassie." Warm behind the mask. He held out blue arms. "You okay?"

"Betcha," I said to his chest. "Just ain't fliers. How's Sword?"

His arms tightened. "Fine. We're both fine." Hallway isn't a natural liar, he's one of the most transparently honest people I know. That lie was engraved on his voice like etching on glass. "Can't share my wings but I can make trail for you. Sword's watching the base and I came looking. Yell in charge?"

"You're kidding. Everyone thinks me'n Moke's excess baggage."

"You're never excess as a baggage, Cass. And Sword's anxious to see Moke. You know he'd rather neither of you were here."

"Tough shit. Don't you sorta show in that gear?"

"We hope not. We reckon so long's we keep sun-wards they won't see us, the light blinds them. It's why I came in from behind. I'm obvious to you because your sight's different."

"It's a theory."

"Worked up to date."

"You know there's Geeks in the jungle?"

"There are villages all over."

"You guys close?" Yell said over my shoulder. "Thought I saw you down the canyon."

"Right. If I stay near the rim I get a view. We aren't far. Sword's going to love the planks, we were worried about how to move people. Not sure how many there are. We've a couple of spare gravpacks but there are kids and we don't know what state they're in. Planks are slow but they carry weight. If we can get the prisoners away we can maybe hold out till the ship comes."

"You hope."

"We hope," he said gravely.

"Okay, maestro," Yell said. "Make us a route. Don't know about these guys but I've corns on my belly."

"Speak for yourself." Mine were all over. I'd a couple in places ain't yet been invented.

Hall kicked off into air and we followed below, wag-gling like a convoy of wooden ducks. The ridge rose and fell and the pale cone got closer. The sun threw our linked shadows in front, pointing to the distance. My belly rumbled.

Only part of it was hunger. Sword never sends a messenger if he can come himself, not to me. Never.

•　•　•

After a while the ridge dipped and melted into a mess of rock-falls and slopes of rubble that could have been volcanic. The cone in front looked like a weathered crater. It was gold-beige with vegetation but we were too far away to see what.

"What's that?"

Hall'd come down to give advice for the seventh or eighth time and he was hovering close to Yell's shoulder, his drive-units cutting horizontal swathes over heaps of cinders.

"What Sword wants Moke to look at. It's even bigger than it looks and only a couple of miles from the base and it's the one place in the neighborhood they've visited often enough to leave tracks."

Moke leaned his chin on his forearms and squinted. "It's big. Bigger than the last."

"You've seen another?"

"Something like it."

"That's what he wants. Conclusions."

"Uh-huh," our genius said informatively. And went on squinting.

It looked like a jumbo-sized roc's egg from a jumbo-sized roc, the kind used to swoop on Eastern cities in the old vids. Or one of Father Brown's jewels burning with strange fires that a hundred negroes couldn't carry, assuming his jewels were the size of a football-stadium. The dome threw off sunlight. It was pale and glossy, lit from inside like a lamp, a glowing pearl. There was something unclear around the bottom. If we'd seen one before it wasn't in the same league. The last had looked like a country bandstand. This was Sinbad territory. Family-size.

We watched it get bigger for half an hour without reading more off it except it was big. Then Hall turned abruptly inward to a shallow gully that formed an apron just below the cliff-edge, and the chameleoned hopship was glued to the back pretending to be stone. If you knew. I guess the rock had to be too hard to burrow in. Their tent was in front.

It was the same design as ours, a squared pyramid, small rainbows around it saying shield. They cut as we came up and we fell off and spraddled. I swear my knuckles were level with my ankles. I didn't figure the boys could be comfortable, the tent's eight-foot width's designed for people and neither of them's the right size. I crawled through the lock wondering if my pelvis was unhinged or it was only my spine was broken and landed on Sword.

He was lying diagonally across the floor, which was the only way he was getting in there, hood thrown back, a pair of glasses in his hand. When I fell in he managed not to drop them and drew his knees up. He rolled on his side, stiffly.

I thought at first he'd been too long on his belly. If he had, he'd been there as long as the guys in King Solomon's Mine. I hadn't seen him in five days. When people are close you don't see them change. Or he'd glazed and gone solid in the night. Whatever, before he left the ship I shared a bed with Lorn and now I was looking at Swordfish. Old model.

Only he wasn't in Face. No scars. Just bone jutting under skin that was nearly yellow and the cerosteel muscles standing out all over like an anatomical diagram. Ridges lifted the blue fabric, down arms and thighs, across his belly, cutting his shoulderblades. You could have used him to teach a medical class. His face was a skull with white lips over whiter teeth, drawn back as if there wasn't enough skin to go around. Only his eyes hadn't changed, though they were tired enough to be Moke's.

"Cass?" He reached an awkward hand. "I didn't want you to see this."

"It's mine, I got the right."

"Couldn't I have left you a little illusion?"

"You gotta be kidding. You expect me to spend the rest of my life remembering you passed your last three weeks seducing a slinky black navigator? This is one thing I can do she can't. Move over. Fuck illusions, I want you."

Okay, it's unfair. It took Yell two years to work monstrosity out of his system when he got back his beauty and he ain't totally over it, though Issa's got a rope on him. But I'm not in love with Yell. Cute though he is. Sword's mouth pulled together.

"You can't think I'd do that."

"Can't I?"

"Then I didn't." He smiled, a ghost from the past. "You're my absolutely terminal perverse bitch. Don't you know I can't forgive myself? I wanted a brat like normal people and bring it up in that stupid loft among the parakeets and live long enough to see it didn't join the Navy. Thought we could apprentice it to a sculptor, or something constructive. Hell, if it hadn't any talent it could fill in holes in the road."

"Like its daddy. I suppose you wanted a matching pair. Like Scotties. Black and white."

"Dammit, Alanna's a relic of my childhood. Tech with my unit when I was a pilot. Still a few of us around. We were talking. Involves making mouth-noises."

"Yeah, sure, I done it. You trying to say she didn't want to lay you?"

"No." The crease at his mouth deepened. "I'm not even saying I didn't want to lay her. I'm just saying we didn't."

"Goddammit, Sword. I wish you had."

His brows raised. "There's a reason?"

"Yes. This way . . ."

This way he'd told me he was dying. Twice in my life I've wanted to turn time back, when it's seemed something was so close, so almost within reach only the smallest twitch could grab and twist it and make it run backwards. Once when I saw Dosh burned in front of me, and once when I saw Sword vanish into an electrified floor. For a few seconds, as if I had it in my hands. But how can you twist twenty years?

I wondered if there'd been, any time since he was twelve years old, some moment, a handle you could turn and make things different. When his father sent him to military college? He'd agreed. He volunteered to have his heart cut out at fourteen. When Razor wanted him to have surgery and be normal? He'd refused. Without implants he wouldn't have been Swordfish. Before I met him. If it had happened I never would have. It hadn't and I had. And he was dying at my feet and I'd no handle even to pull at to try to make the universe give him back.

"I liked the stupid loft with parakeets."

"So did I."

We sat holding hands, crouched stiffly like very old people. It wasn't until Hall crawled in with a thermos-jug I saw Yell had got the other tent up and Moke was kneeling in the entrance looking across, his head lifted, the hood making his face a blank mask.

"I don't like it," Yeller said.

"It's now or never, they'll be here anytime."

"That's one thing. The other's Cass. Before you let her jive you, do I get to say she's on her knees?"

"I know," Sword said. "We're still going."

I knew that story. It was called Alanna and he had her to make up to me. I squeezed his hand.

"We got gravpacks. Ain't going to be tiring, be half an hour. I hurt too much to lie down anyhow."

"Ever fallen asleep on one?"

"Moke'll pinch me."

"I'll pinch them both. Come on, let's do it."

On his feet he moved with something like his old grace. He'd swallowed a handful of gels when he thought I wasn't looking and I didn't like to think what was in them, but I didn't hassle. Nothing was going to change much now. I took a nalgy with my prote myself to get my back straight and we crawled out into a dull midday.

The dome was at the highest point of the crater-rim, bulging on the sky. It looked unreal, like a ghost-egg. It was maybe heat made its outlines shimmer like reflections on water. Sword wanted Moke to see it quick. The ships couldn't be long now. They had to be uncommon slow to have taken this long. Unless they'd reasons I'd rather not think about.

Gravpacks are among things I haven't experienced, though I didn't tell Yell. Sword knew. He showed me controls.

"Just don't do cartwheels, Wonderwoman, they may not notice light-trails but they'll sure as hell see aerobatics. Take it gently. You okay, Moke?"

"Yep," Moke said, muffled. "Doing my slate up."

"Attaboy."

Rising was like going up in an elevator, in a flower of white glare that lighted the zenith and glazed the sky like the inside of a cup. The base they'd scoped was on the lower slopes and Sword figured if we got up fast we'd be in sun again, blurred out by brightness. Part of the reason he wanted there now was the sun overhead. Seemed to me we were using up a lot of faith. We straightened at altitude and hit a down-slant towards the dome.

From above it was a real roc's egg: round, white, reflecting. The eroded crater stretched south and west, its interior egg-shape inverted, a black bowl of sick forest. Below on the hillside maybe five miles away was what had brought our boys. An outline in disturbed soil, a circular track as big as a pad with trails leading off. Some of the clearest led up the mountain towards the egg. Others disappeared more faintly other ways and got lost in vegetation.

"What makes us think there's no one home?"

Sword's voice was inside my ear. "If they'd come we'd have seen, we've had them scoped. There's no life-sign, even insect. It's dead."

"Or it's going to be?" Moke diagnosed.

"I'd rather not. We aren't here."

"Okay, I'll just slate it."

The stuff underfoot was lichen, or maybe a mold. Yellow-brown like fine fur, a couple of inches high, covering everything. It fluffed gently like crushed velvet. Naturally it did it against the breeze. Tracks were worn in the nap, none coming from our side but a whole braid circling around from beyond as if the toadstools danced grand chains around the egg's outside. I could just see them, holding tentacles, their skirts jouncing, like dainty ladies doing a minuet. With spare trailing threads, lashing little nubblers to death with their pinkies in the air.

The dome was immense down here. We cut packs and slid up to it, keeping the mass between us and the base. Just the cap rose a hundred meters into the sky, a great translucent puffball, opal in the sun and dove-gray and purple in the shadow. The platform swelled twenty feet above our heads and circled for acres.

We took a hop of grav and ended on a surface as slick as a skating rink, clouded like chalky water and stained with colored streaks, depths fading into depths like it had no bottom.

"Lot of foundation," Moke said. "Wonder how deep?"

"Underground connection?" Sword asked, suddenly alert.

"Wouldn't like to say. Got to be set in a big hole. It's not just built, it's melted in the rock. Guess storm-winds get violent."

"So I hear. Yell says you got wet."

"Wettish. Interesting arches."

A Moke understatement. Our country bandstand wasn't just the great-great-grandbaby of this one, it was still in diapers. The arches were glass lace, pointed and carved in concentric rings that faded into the perspective. The distance was a glowing cave. Nothing as straight as a corridor, just diminishing rings offset to open on more archways inside. The stuff was the same as the hull of the dome but in duskier colors, deep pink fading to claret and sea-green and black-purple as you went towards the center. But it wasn't dark. The depths shone with undersea light like a big pearl shell. The red sun lit the outside columns in bright neon lines.

"No seams," Sword whispered. "It's why we wanted you to see it. How's it built, Genius?"

Moke's blue profile considered. "Evander says they secrete their plastic."

"It's bigger than the Spacedome, mec."

"I know." He turned his head. "Two methods, Cass. A lot of work over a short time or a little over a long one. From a lot of people with a little power each. You seen a kidney stone?''

"No. You don't need to show me."

"Same ribby look. Accretion. If your spit hardened, you'd only need to spit often. Every time you came past. All of you. It's how cairns are built."

"Symmetrical spitters."

"It was an example. How it's made. Carefully. Maybe by a lot of individual gum."

"Not exactly technological."

"I'd figured not. Great builders, but not by machinery."

"Then how did they get into space, Genius? You don't make ships by spitting. To my knowledge."

"They've big ideas," Moke said slowly. "Maybe they got past it. Had a technology once and now they haven't because they don't want it."

"Or it got past them," Sword said. "There's something limited in them. They reproduce, fight and die. So as to spread, to do the same again. They could be a technology in decline. I wonder why? Let's look inside."

I peered into the lace shell. "Lot of ground. Did we say half an hour?"

"It's our only chance, Cass."

The arches filled most of the space and the farther we went the better Moke's ideas looked. The pillars rose with the roof until they were high thin hoops, twisted pendants hanging like stalactites almost to the ground to fill the spaces. Every inch was shaped, patterned and streaked with color. It was all symmetrical, everything balanced but no pair of arches the same. The light was evenly dim, the floor evenly smooth. The hanging lacework hid the core in involved skeins until

I began to think there wasn't one. We looped and zig-zagged, noses inwards.

We must have played daisy-chains for a quarter of a mile before a brighter light showed ahead. Sword moved quickly in front, his disruptor in his hand. Even when he isn't thinking mayhem he likes to be sure. Nothing so mere as death has ever stopped him.

The arena opened out suddenly like the middle of a maze. We were under the highest part of the dome because fifty yards of unsupported shell soared over our heads letting dim red light through in a sudden douche like a second dawn. The center was exactly what you'd expect. But the biggest yet.

"Toadstool-in-a-turnip-field. Gnarly."

Moke tipped his head up and up. "They got to really see differently. Wonder what they look like to themselves? They're not like that to me even with filters."

"Doesn't have to be how they are," Sword said. "Just how they like to think it. Like commercial girls, all tits and fluff. Turnips are the opposite, they're simplified. Would you say?"

"Yeah. Not much more than knobs."

"Big knobs."

"But no drippy stuff."

"I guess it's idealized. But what does it say?"

We stood underneath and gawped. It was sixty feet high, it spired lazily fifteen feet above the ground and the whorled upper cap looked like the model of a brain. But not human, it was a perfect dome. It was covered with intertwined tentacles and the twisting filaments rose from among them. If you kept your eyes on it you could see the tentacles writhing slowly like a nest of snakes. In sugar-plum colors good enough to eat. The gingerbread house. All it was short of was an oven, and maybe they were outside trucking it in.

The garden below was clear greenish lumps that swelled out at the top, the barest sketch of toadstools. The floor under was one polished sweep like a frozen lake.

"Got technology when they want it."

"I guess. That's a grav-generator."

"Built in the floor and covered over. Like their ships. When they bother they're good."

"Not much room in here," I said. "It's full of dangle. Hall said there's villages all over. Paths come from everywhere too. Can't be meant just for the base? Unless the personnel's enormous."

"Don't think so. Routine sci-station. They could surprise us, but it's too big. Got to be for everyone. They compress, maybe."

"Haven't looked it," Moke said. "A lot got to stay outside. Among the pillars, or even out where the trails are. Could be why it's concentric, they add more when they can't get in. From the camp, they're hierarchical. Maybe the center's for big guys."

"That would figure. You slating, Mokey?"

"You betcha. But there's too much. Don't want to rush you, Sword, but we better get back. I'll look this over in camp. Can't think here, would take all day."

"Okay. Got an itch too. They've taken too long."

We scooted for the edge. I had the prickle in my neck as well, not the one says people behind you, something else. A nasty sort of scratchy prickle where I couldn't get at it, under my collar. We were in the outer layer of arches when we heard the rumble. Sword stiffened and held out a hand.

"Hell. We've missed them. Can't move until they've cleared the pad or they'll scope us. Stand still."

We stood. At least twenty minutes, while he waited stark as a mast, his blue-veiled head turned slightly towards the base. The rumble was followed by a long clear whistle, which dwindled. Then as far as I could tell it cut off. Sword went on standing. A long time later he turned and nodded.

"They've taken them down, but it was a fleet of lighters. Four or five. Let's go. And be careful."

We crept out onto yellow fur, my back bristling. Sword hovered up slowly then beckoned. We rose cautiously in the air and followed the sharp jerk of his thumb in a straight streak sunwards.

Maybe a mile out I risked a back glance and saw the base was closed. There had been ships, the black circles spaced over the pad said so. Yellow rings of nappy growth irised in as I looked.

"They've gone down."

"We'll find a way to go after them, Hall's working on it. Keep your head up, Cass, look forward. You'll veer if you turn."

I already had. There was water under my filters and something in my head that went around in syrupy circles like their nasty sugar toadstool. I'd taken a loop in the moment I hadn't been looking and had to put speed on to catch up. We cut blue air, a bloody glare in our faces, my eyes full of floating cobwebs, my back wanting to bend under the weight of the pack.

I guess it was mostly heat. We'd almost made the mountain when I blacked out. I felt vaguely for the lever in the dark and didn't know where it was. Razor's second law. Never go out on business in unfamiliar equipment. My fingers skidded over numb slickness and Sword's voice was shouting in my ear in the distance. I'd have liked to oblige but he was too far away.

I think he got a hand to me in the end. A hard violent bracelet that circled my wrist. And slipped.

I fell a hundred miles and ended with a sucking

squelch in a mattress that clung and gave and went
down and down. It got blacker and blacker.

"Thank God for recyclers," I mumbled. Or thought
I did. "You guys gonna hafta pull me out."

And ended nowhere.

There was light in my eyes. Much too much light. I thought for a moment I could see myself in a mirror, mouth wide open as if I was screaming and hair standing on end like a nest of snakes, blown about by a wind that twisted it in coils like the tentacles on the statue below. Then I saw the face was Sword's, so dark it could have been in negative, his irises as blinding as searchlights, the pupils like arc-lamps. His lips were moving as if he was trying to speak.

As I came around my ears did a pop and I could hear him. He was speaking, but so low and deep it shook the ground under the tent. His chest and shoulders were outlined against the glare and it seemed I could see his ribs through it and the ceramic and steel tubing of his metal heart pulsing inside. I thought the setting sun had to be behind him, though I wasn't sure how it had got there since the last time I'd seen it it hadn't been much after midday. The light sprayed and retreated in rainbow pulsations, layers of spectral color repeating the lines of his body, the bright fibers flashing and retracting in waves.

"Cass? It's okay, you're not hurt. Come on, try to sit up."

I lay still not quite knowing why I was shivering. I didn't want to put my hand into the rainbow brilliance that sprayed from his shoulder, it looked burning. And his voice was too black, too vibrating, too slow. I've been getting into trouble in Swordfish's company for more than ten years and what he does is yell at me. Sometimes he yells right out and sometimes he just freezes me to death but the one thing he's never done is make noises like seven pigeons playing subway, it's the worst sign ever.

"I died," I said.

"No, you didn't, Cass," Moke said, poking a face like a bronze hatchet over his shoulder. Heat like the heart of the sun radiated out of it, I could feel the blisters rising on my cheekbones. Light sprayed behind him too, it had to be an epidemic. His voice only shook the tent-ribs but the sky trembled. "Sword pulled you out. Hall's tested everything, it works. Get up. You can."

"If I didn't die, why isn't he yelling?"

Sword filled his lungs with turquoise fire, drawn out of the air at the four corners. A red flow of oxygen surged up from the floor and tried to replace it. "Get up, you miserable little pest, or I'm going to go find me a woman." The planet paused in its orbit. "With a sense of balance."

That was better but still wrong. He can rise to heights of evil irony unclimbed by man when I fuck up and that wasn't it. Not to mention the FX stuff which was repulsive and definitely a new trick. I sat anyhow. The light flared and steadied.

It wasn't sunlight, the blue globe with its spreading corona was still above us, barely fallen towards the mountains. There were too many rainbows. Hall and Yeller burned like dance-stars in neon halos, fine brilliant rays flowing out of them like wings. The chameleoned hopship on the other side of the wall was a blue-black dolphin with a vivid glow aft where her tubes were em-hot from landing. The rock wall behind her, where lines of fringe streamed on the level wind, flickered with colored lightnings as if they were made in optic fiber. My own hand burned like a lantern through my coolsuit.

"There's something wrong with the light," I said, sniveling a bit.

Sword's searchlight eyes hardened to diamond. "What?"

That's when I got it. "You can't see?"

"What?" he repeated, digging holes in my shoulder-bones.

I put my hands over my eyes. They were shaking. I had to hang on hard not to open my mouth and start making a noise like a fire-siren. It was maybe concussion. I knocked my head once when I was a kid and I saw a lot of stars for quite a long time. I'd an idea I'd taken a super-sized nosedive.

"What did I fall on?"

He shook me, his voice urgent. "Cassandra. What's wrong with the light?"

It was dark behind my fingers. Reassuring. Not a single rainbow. "What d'you see with concussion?"

"Blurring," Hall said on the other side, like the lower reaches of Charlie Mingus. "Bright flashes, maybe. What is it, Cass?"

I took a peek through a minor slit and closed it in a hurry. "You got halos."

Sword held me against a molten chest, his lips hot at my ear, his voice coded in the magma. "It's okay, Cass. You fell a hundred meters at min thrust but there was a bit of power under you and I got there before you hit. Some kind of plant-life swallowed the impulsion. You're just shaken, Hall's checked for bones and internal injuries. It could be a slight concussion. We got derms in the medpack for whatever the damage is. Don't panic."

I opened my fingers another crack, just to check. Right. His halo was as bright as the bare corona above him but his negative face wasn't blurred, you could have used it to make woodcuts. I've never seen anything clearer.

"Is it okay if I don't look at you?"

"Sure."

"Most natural thing in the world," Yell boomed like a gong. "Totally normal. Feel that way about him every day."

Swordfish omitted to answer, which ain't the guy I know.

"Try this," Hall's anxious double-bass arpeggioed over my head. I could feel my lips smoking. "Processed water. Lay her down, Sword, if she's concussed she's better flat."

"I'd rather sit." It didn't hurt, I just felt numb. Like bits of me were missing, everywhere they'd touched. "Ain't headache, it's the light-show." I raised my hands. I was interested in what was left of me. Nothing much above the neck, from inside. Someone's head was there, with ruffled hair stuck in spikes with icy gel that gummed my fingers and froze the prints off and clung in frosty lumps to the skin of my palms. It was

slick and adhesive at the same time, covering my face
and head like a plaskin mask. Like frozen Face. It was
in my ears, in the hollows of my face, over my lips,
under my collar. My eyelids were stiff with it. I crackled them up to stare at transparent goop. My belly took
one glance and got into heave mode. "What's this
stuff?"

"Nothing," Sword said, but I heard plates crack under the crust, fault-lines opening on seas of lava. "Just
jelly . . ."

"Jelly?" I was cracking too, wide open like a clam-
shell. I could feel the firehouse shriek bubbling in the
back of my throat. My voice came out like the Virgin
of the Sun-God, sparkling as sequins and wavering
over four octaves. "What happened?"

Bronze Mokey knelt and caught my wrists in hands
built around molten bones and outlined in islands of
scar and black labyrinths of callus. "There was gelatinous stuff in the cleft, Cass. Where you fell. It saved
your life, cushioned the shock and gave Sword time to
pull you out. Hall's checked, all the readings are negative. We thought we'd wiped it off but I guess it's
clung in the wiggly bits, you came around before we'd
finished. We didn't want to scare you by making a
folksong out of it. Maybe you got a drop in your eye.
Let me get a wipe and finish up."

He laid his flaming cheek against my mask. "Share
it." I heard the ice sizzle. "Look good if we're stuck
for life." I figured we pretty certainly were, I felt us
soldering, the slick web melting together like we'd only
one skin. His veins were running fire into my blood
and blood into his fire. I wondered why Sword didn't
mind more. "There're no allergens, Hall's checked.
Your shots would cover them anyhow."

"Yeah." I hung onto a little bright line of sanity at

the back of my skull. Moke's whitehot cheek was part of my head and we were stuck together for life. It might or might not look good, it was going to make eating a problem. And that could be the least of our troubles. "I fell into gelatin. I had a mask and a hood on. How'd it get up my nose?"

Ringing silence. Moke soldered both hands onto my shoulderblades and my suit shriveled.

"It sucked like a bog," Sword said from the center of a magnetic field that spun force-lines off each word as it left his black lips. "Your mask and hood got torn off as you sank. I fished, had to get them back before the air poisoned you. We were as fast as we could, Cass. I know you hate guck."

"It doesn't seem dangerous," Hallway throbbed earnestly. "I did all the tests."

"Yeah? Then why do you—"

I stopped. Because they didn't. Every trace of halo was gone. A red light shone from a dull sun overhead. Mokey lifted his face easily to look at me with green eyes so exhausted they were mostly pupil and Sword, yellow-white under hair that showed threads of gray, had both arms wrapped around me as if his back wasn't bent into a bow by strain his skeleton had got too worn to stand. My glove was common sky-blue, casting a purple shadow on his knee. I put it around his neck and took my own weight, which told me I'd bruised my ass and was going to regret it.

"Hell and damn, I hate guck. Will someone give me a towel to wipe my face?"

"Four," Hallway said.

I'd rinsed my eyes with drops from the medpack and had a prote sandwich. Two layers of prote with prote in them. We'd a mutual agreement not to have hysterics and everyone was chomping. Hall was also chipping the holo in.

"At least three picks in orbit I've got on the scanner, could be from Resurrection. It would be natural for some of them to head for main base after the kickup, they can't expect us to take it calmly. And a few here. At least one more darkside."

Three white blips strung across the starfield, twirling visibly. If the line was regular there could easily be another. Or more. A flick and the image changed dimensions. The projector focused and threw the yellow plain on the back of our retinas. Four medium beer-caps swirled in from the east against the rotation, braking, pulling vaporous contrails that were snatched into tatters by the hot wind. Their sides were still glowing from upper atmosphere. They weren't bothering to creep secretively. They did a graceful glide and came in for the pad. They'd grav-units. You don't get that movement any other way.

The pad's outlines had stopped being faint. A steady red blink rippled around it and it looked as if the whole mass plus its crushed velvet had risen to meet them. They hit the quarters in four ordered plops, neutralizing rotation, and smoking plush shrank away under their hulls. When the last was in place the lights cut out, the pad gave one quarter-turn and began to sink into the dirt. A wide round pit opened above it. The image blurred as Hall ran it forward, though the speeded image showed yellow fur groping the edges. Then it rose smoothly into place, heaved, settled and was solid as if it hadn't moved. Four diminishing rings marked the surface.

"How long did it stay down?" Sword asked.

"About twenty-five minutes. However long it took to get them unloaded, I suppose."

"Fast work."

"We knew they didn't stick to their chairs."

"Which way did they come?"

"Out-Arm. As we did."

"So they may or may not be the guys we're waiting for."

"Right."

"So we're going to have to go look at them."

"It seems indicated."

"Hey, guys," Yell said. "Assault ain't my thing, I was brought up a pilot. But I came to help. How're you getting down there?"

Hallway turned him a grave face. "We scoped it while we were waiting, same time I located the villages. We know where some shafts are."

"There had to be entrances," Sword said. "You can't raise and lower the pad whenever someone wants to walk around the homestead."

"Such as which captains got the habit," Yell agreed. "And?"

"We know two. A big one just down-cone from the pad, I'd say freight-elevator, would take ground vehicles. And a personnel-shaft around the other side, facing the forest. Haven't seen ground vehicles yet but we know the far one's personnel, we've seen them go out and in."

"How deep?"

Hall shook his head. "Hard to say. We scoped the upper shaft down three hundred meters and began to think we'd got to lava. It's hot in there. The other may be deeper. Figure we reached bedrock, but I wouldn't like to say it was the base of the galleries. Could as easily be the roof."

"Grav-unit country. See why you wanted planks."

"Should have brought 'em," Sword said. "Didn't

know what we might be facing."

"We'd an advantage," I said nastily. "We knew we'd be facing finding you. So when d'we start?"

"You don't, Cassandra. You fell in that jelly because you were finished, as Yell said. Hall and I . . ."

"They're all the same. Like Yell in the jungle. Women, children and Mokey last. We get to stay up here and eat the last bullet while you macho hunks go in and inflame the natives. The hell with you. You need me, same reason Yell did. I'm the smallest. I take the least room, use the least energy, leave the smallest emtrail. I'm also dispensable. Sis Aurelia needs you to take her home. I can't carry her, you can. Move over."

"For all the same reasons, you can't get her or anyone else to the entry if they're hurt and I can," Sword said with menace. "And among other things, I'm leading this expedition and I just said no. Argue and I slug you. I get to fall in the river, okay?"

He would bring that up.

"Who's on the plain?" Moke broke in. "I know you guys talk politics with breakfast but someone's in trouble."

We fell over each other reaching for glasses but I was the nearest. There was someone, and the someone was human. It's the only animal staggers on two feet, dropping to knees and knuckles. Until I got the bino focused and made it specific. Only one human animal staggers with its ass in the air, its naked skin streaked and patched with scarlet burn-scars, yellowed fangs bared to alien atmosphere. There was blood on his face.

"Drib, and he's done for. Sword . . ."

He was on his feet. "Hall—?"

"I'll come," Yell said. "He's the medic. Roll us a plank, Cass."

I scrambled for the exit hauling at my mask and

jerked my gear off the back. Another disastrous clatter. I was going to get old and wrinkled minus eyepaint like any other savage, my makeup was in there. I flicked the switch and the plank deflated and turned itself into a scroll as the guys crawled through dragging gravpacks. I threw it to Yell.

"Got something he can breathe through? His nose is special."

"Tell your granny," Sword snarled. "Keep the glass on us, Cass, and tell me if you see anything. We don't want a swarm of Geeks here, supposing they're behind him."

"Sure," I said to his departing emtrail. "What you going to do about it, put down weedkiller?"

"Correct. Got anti-Geek powder."

"Yeah. Right."

"We have," Hallway said mildly from inside. "Present from the Navy, though Retta's friend Jean was in on it. Messes their perceptions. Or that's the message."

"More experimental garbage. Hope someone means to pay us for testing it."

"They're honorable men. Who're your heirs and assigns?"

"Shut up, Mokey. You are. Who're yours?"

"Central College of Art and Design. At the moment."

I might have known.

The white fans of the gravpacks dwindled over folds of crater, a glitter of mirage mimicking them over the mountains. They weren't taking time for anything fancy. Like getting the sun behind them. I tracked to Dribble and found him flat and small, a little brown trophy spread across a big yellow rug trying to grow him under before he could move. He raised a bloody snout, looked at the sky and tried to brace a paw. It wobbled. His hearing's out of hume-normal too, he can hear gravpacks.

Blue for cool sounds great in theory but it shows up on yellow like an exercise in art. They'd have made a great kiddy-blanket. I could see them soaring in to land, Sword with a mask and what looked like a pale-blue tarpaulin, Yell snapping the plank rigid as he touched dirt. It flicked and expanded. Drib was wheezing with a noise like tearing canvas, I could hear him as soon as he got the mask on. Sword had an arm around him, making petting sounds. He had derms in his pouch, the tearing snorts eased. They got him on the plank and clipped straps and Yell spread the cooled cover over it.

"How we doing?" Sword's voice whispered.

I ran the glasses around the pad and the forest beyond. "Don't see nothing. 'S he all right?"

"Apart from no lungs left," Yell said. He sounded raw. *"We're coming back the long way."*

Drib coughed violently inside his tarp and managed a wheeze. *"I fine, Cass-Mama. I get kiss you now?"*

"I'll think about it, dogmeat. If you die on me, you don't."

"Hokay," he choked dutifully.

Sword made wide motions with something glittering as they rose. He held his end of the plank with his one free hand, it was taking Yell both. I remembered planks were helpless off solid surfaces, like mine plunging down the cliff. They took more care this time, angling sunwise, their white exhaust fans moving in balance.

"Uh-oh."

"Tell me. Can't look back, this thing's awkward to handle."

"Bandits at ground level, eleven o'clock."

"How many?"

"Three wreaths. Read maybe—wow!—gotta be twenty to a wreath, these guys is serious. You gonna find out if Jeannie's powder works."

"Not many for them, they work in chains. Keep me posted."

"Group minds," Moke said softly in the other ear. "Watch their coordination."

"You mind ass, boss, they sting to hellangone," Dribble wheezed.

"They haven't got you this time, pup. Just breathe."

Our boys'd made maybe a hundred meters and rising, their exhausts whiting out in sunlight. They'd drawn together with the plank in front to avoid a silhouette on the disk. Down on the crater-skirts wreaths of toadstools poured over the curve, the graceful ballerina motion covering terrain fast and with a directness said nothing wrong with their scopes. They were making straight for the place Drib had been lying, in converging lines like they meant to hold a maypole dance. From up here they had uniform *corps de ballet* colors, one line in mint green, one sugar mauve and the nearest pale pink. As usual the lines were identical. Their filaments minced with wincing delicacy just above fur-level.

"Don't fly, do they?" I whispered urgently. The leaders had picked up the fresh scent, maybe encouraged by blood, and flounced suddenly into the air. The whole line followed, springing in six-foot bounds.

"*No,*" Dribble managed in a croaky whistle. "*Air in frilly bits makes rise up, can't fly really. Get up real sharp slope, though, make holes in.*"

"*How high can they jump?*" Sword came back.

" 'S okay. Couple meters. Hope Hall's recording, they're coming to ground zero."

The explosion happened as I said it. The leaders swirled around the ruffle where Drib had fallen, circling to let the whole ballet in, and the wreaths knotted to stay close. I guess Sword didn't spare the dosage. The spinning ballet splashed out like an opening starshell and the fur rug was covered suddenly with jerking toadstools, buzzing like a smoked-out wasps' nest, mingling, staggering and cannoning off each other.

They didn't like contact. Where colors touched they sprang back as if they had repelling poles and bounced into others they liked even less. It was the study of atomic motion in gases, Lesson Two, back in the days when my mama made me go to school and I used to have to play this mess through my desk. But this gas was heating, it got more chaotic the longer it lasted.

Stammering caps wandered about the plain, spinning fitfully, but they didn't look happy alone. Some were wandering at random, others bouncing in stiff jerks on the tips of their tentacles. A few had keeled limply over and were sinking into rest-mode, their skirts spread, filaments coiled beneath.

I guess fur didn't agree with them. The ones that touched sank further and further, flattening in gasping pulsations, until there was a damp ring of collapsed jelly spread on the plush like a dropped candy-wrapper. The spiring tendrils wilted and fell, twitching feebly. Then the last gasp of air seemed to go out and the jelly began to steam off in the sun, quite fast. In a minute or two all that was left were soft transparent drifts like torn plaskin.

It was creepy how easily they disintegrated, as if there hadn't been much there to begin with. The ones that were left turned around and just plain ran away. It was pathetic and terrible. They didn't look like stinging toadstools any more. More like a first-year dance class

of little three-year-olds made a big public boob and
running to hide. I could see them gropingly hold out
shivering tendrils, reaching for others of their own
wreath, looking for something to clutch to.

"Looks like it works," Sword's normal voice said
over my head. I turned. The guys had touched down
and were letting the plank take its weight on the rock.
"Sorry, Cass. Nasty stuff. Stopped them looking,
though, rather they'd trouble down there than find us.
Can we get Drib inside?"

I took the front of the plank and steered it through
the tunnel. Hall was waiting to trip the cover. I was
careful with the kiss, his poor little skin hadn't much
surface. He was covered in allergic blisters clustered
so thick they ran into each other. The blood had come
from his nose and he was breathing through his mouth
like it took all his strength. He licked me feebly with
a tongue like dry leather.

"You horrible brat. Can't trust you anywhere."

Hallway was searching the inside of his thigh trying
to find a surface to stick derms on. Sword's set were
almost invisible under new blisters.

"I had to run, Cass-Mama. Once I eat way out of
cage, air hurt so bad I get out quick, hope it get better.
Not help really."

"Shut up."

I was dripping on his paw. The metallic shovel nails
were caked with blood, almost torn from the quick as
if he'd spent a long time digging through steel. I know
Drib's nails and they don't give easy. Mokey was
pressing a sponge-pad loaded with antallergen over his
skin trying to tame blisters and Hall had finished with
the derms and was using a squeeze-can to add stuff to
his air-supply. The tearing died down and he stopped
twitching and sneezed.

"You got maybe prote?" he asked. "Me not have nice prote sandwich in week."

"Damn." I wiped my nose on the back of my glove. "Do believe he don't mean to die after all. Wouldn't't've cried if I'd known."

"You always say you gonna celebrate," he said, with nearly normal smugness. "Know you not telling truth."

"Don't know what you brought it back for," I said to Sword. "It calls me names."

"Yeah, I know," he said. "His intelligence is one reason I value him."

I'd have kicked. But his face under the graying hair was the color of something died in the dark and his shoulders were bent. I tried not to let him see I saw it. He looked empty, as if he might dry out to a drift of film and blow away too. I didn't dare touch him. In case I made it happen.

"We in school when shield go down," Dribble said. The blisters were fading and his breathing was almost back to normal. It was only his choirboy flute came out hoarse, almost low enough to be adolescent. He was stuffing prote with a nuskinned paw. "Relia and Miz Beth, she teacher, they get kids under desks when wall fall and Geek things land on top. I try hit them but I said, they sting to hellangone, I get plenty stung, fall over an they grab off Relia an Miz Beth and kids. Two boy, two girl. Look for little Chans maybe, ready met 'em."

He paused to snuffle. It was a dry one since his glands weren't functional but the face he made was worse for having no tears.

"Real bad. Go like crazy, smash like want to flatten everything. Kids cry and try hide, they drag out and

smash with sting-things. You never heard like that, we
all choking, heads hurt, kids cry, Geek things hum and
hum like happy. Mister George was he-teacher he try
stop them, he bat them with wall piece, smash him too.
He fall down, all over blood, Miz Beth fall on floor
and they drag her out. Relia crying, scream for Sword,
I run after and they take me too. I bite but they poisonous, burn mouth. Got people already, four Marine
guys, two each he-she. Everybody choking, Marine
guys all blood.''

"Are they still alive?'' Sword asked intently.

"One guy, Marine, hurt too bad, die. They poke us
over and over, choose guys from bims, put in different
cage. Cage maybe insulated, head less bad after. Me
want to stay with Relia, I get stung again.'' He held
out an arm wealed over with red. "I try, boss.''

"Sure, pup. I know.''

"They take away dead guy. Other try stop, he stung
too. They less rough after camp, maybe find they kill
us. We got two boy-kid, girl-kid with Miz Beth and
Relia. We see them cage, like glass but cloudy, you
see through but not clear. They make air inside, throw
prote. Air bad and we all cough, why hurt guy die I
guess, none of us breathe good. Then they get better
and it come right but we all sick, Geek smell all over,
can't eat. Prote bad anyhow, none of us swallow. Then
they try more and it get better but nothing taste. Like
paper, but at least we breathe. When we too hungry we
eat paper. Everybody weak, me strongest, why I get
out.''

"But everyone else is still alive? They haven't tried
experimenting on any of you?''

Dribble shook his head. A little red dampness welled
in his eyes. "Do'n' know. One of girl-kid get take
away in night, we hear screaming. After that not hear

anything more. She not come back. Not know what do
with. Miz Beth she bout crazy, she an Relia try stop
them. They got less rough on bims, work out they not
so strong. She-Marine get stung, she got laser hid an
try use it, they sting real bad, we hear crying all night.
She kill some, I think. Jelly an stuff all over, real stunk
out, all bims sick, they come and clean. Since then they
leave us alone.''

"So who's left, Drib?"

"Me, one guy, two boy-kid, in other cage they got
two Marine bim, Relia, Miz Beth and other girl-kid.
They waiting something, they keep us real careful. Lot
of Geek come look through cage but not touch.'' He
looked at us with his reddened eyes, anguished human
hazel. "Bad guys, crazy somewhere. Two times they
have chasing. Big nubby things that move, with beads
on head? They chase all through ship, smash and
smash, smash right to pulp, go on smashing in heap.
Some big Geeks get smash same time, they lose mind,
can't stop. Green stuff all over, over hold, over cage,
over them, all full of it. They crazy guys. You help us
get away?''

"Why we're here. How'd you get out?"

"We know they land. Henry, is other guy, know
ship, he tell me what happen. When he say we down,
I eat cage. Henry help, he patch hole with all clothes
to keep air out while I run. Bad air real bad, burn me
inside. I run like hell, ships in big hole but passages
all over. Follow trails in sand an find tunnel up. Like
cero-coated, I tear nails on. Think they make stuff from
smashed green things, collect jelly careful when get
mind back. It turn hard. Passage go up not quite
straight, guess they float, stink all the way, I sick everywhere. Me, I gotta claw. Is deep down there, claw forever till I fall out top. Then run. I hope air better, isn't

much. Burn less but stink too.''

Sword leaned his jaw on his palm, his eyes distant. ''So it's a full mask job, and planks. Can these guys walk?''

''Not think so. Kids weak. Marine bim got stung, she sick, not know if she stand even, can't really see in bim-cage. Relia make sign to me, see she moving, but everyone move less and less. Lose hope, maybe.''

''Okay. We got to get down there. Can you guide us, pup?''

''I try,'' Dribble said. His burned and blistered hide quivered. ''They waiting for something. Not know what.''

''Not tonight,'' Hallway said swiftly. ''Kid can't stand himself. We've got to plan this, it's going to be complicated. Let's get some sleep or none of us is going anywhere.

Sword grunted. I thought he might stand up and yell Excelsior, it would have been in character. But he looked broken in two. He half-rose, then let go and slumped across the floor.

''You're right. Hope you're good at praying.''

''So do I,'' Hallway said.

Someone was muttering in my ear in a quiet little whisper. Seemed to have been going on for a while, all night maybe. I turned over, bumped Moke's hip and writhed around in my sleeping-bag. No use. I was hopelessly awake. I sat and looked around.

It was full dark, the thick intense dark of blotted moon and rare stars, covered with the slaty clouds that drift over at sundown. The cleft should have been black. It wasn't. I looked for the light and saw the tail of the hopship burning indigo, a sparkle of pale optic-fiber drifting above it like seaweed. That shifted me fast. If someone was warming the ship it was either Sword fixing to go Excelsior or we were in deep doo-doo.

My hand was lifted to shake Moke when something invisible pulled me back and something that wasn't a voice said: *don't do that.* I'd my mouth open to say **Why not** when I saw why not. The fucking halos were back. Muted by darkness, but a vivid fringe of luminous color that outlined Moke's and Yell's heads and burned out from my own bare hands. Not real color but something different. UV color, maybe, or X-ray color. It lit them without touching their pillows, cut off at the neck by the aluminum edge of the sleeping-bag. Mine ended at my sleeves but I'd the feeling if I thought about it harder it would stretch all over.

In the other tent two heads burned like moons through the layers of plastic. Two? I did a double-take. Sword was out after all. But he wasn't. His slack shape lay across the angle, Hall's and Dribble's breathing blowing over him like rainbow steam that filled the pyramid with light, but his glow was faint as cloud. The breath from his lips was pale vapor, the flame under his skin red and low like a lamp before the battery dies. My heart squeezed together as if it would stop.

—*It's no use, we can't do anything*, the voice that wasn't said. *There are things we can. Let's go.*

So who was I, Joan of fucking Arc? **Shut up,** I said crossly. I seemed to be hauling my coolsuit on anyway. *This is absolutely dumb, dumber than the average Cass. Sword's going to live till tomorrow just to kill me.*

—*Right,* the unvoice said. *He'll live until tomorrow. We got stuff to do tonight.*

—**Who the hell are you?** I said to the darkness. It paused weightily.

—*I am what I am. A lost traveler? Part of you, now.* Mama! *What does that mean?*

—*I was semi-sentient until you swallowed me, in stasis. Now we're one. We can use each other.*

—**I think I'm going to throw up.**

—*It won't get rid of me. I am you, no one can part us. We're wasting time. I can help you.*

—**You can help me to die of disgust.**

—*You're being childish. I'm not native here, I can't*

bond. *The protein disagrees with me. I've been stranded a long time. But I've ancient memories. Helping you is helping myself. I want what you want, I must. You're me. We have to go out. I can feel your people, they need you.*

—*Sure they do. What they need most is Sword.*

—*He can't help them. I can. I know these people, the ones you call Geeks, we've met before. They aren't bonders with my kind either. But I know how they function. Even in stasis I've been aware of their movements. Now we have a body I can take you around them. Trust me.*

—*Give me one good reason why I should.*

—*You have no choice. Neither of us has. And you don't have anyone else now. Without me, all any of you can do is die. Let's go.*

Oh, fuck. I was out of the tent and moving softly over the platform. *Why should you do anything?*

—*Because I need you, as you need me.*

—*Then can't you for Crissakes turn the lights down?*

—*You need light to see. So do I. Keep going.*

Sword's always slept like a cat but Hallway's ears are pretty sharp too. A pebble clicked under my feet and I stopped. Dribble and Hall murmured. Sword was as still as a carved tomb.

"Shit," I said. To myself. I crept toward the cliff-edge. Sense said, take a gravpack.

—*They'll see it,* the unvoice said. *Hallway never uses one at night, you need sunlight to screen your emissions. We can run instead. It's easy.*

Sure we can, I thought. *Easy as falling off a cliff.* I took a step and fell off the cliff.

I ought to have killed myself, the surface was sheer as a wall and I went down it practically in free fall.

My toes kept touching little bumps and crevices, outlined with floating hair that backed off when it saw me
coming like I was red-hot. I took a look and saw that
I was. Awake and moving I burned like a Japanese
lantern, lighting the cliff-face all around and the plain
beneath. The Dong with the luminous fucking nose,
only I was luminous all over.

They weren't going to see me, naturally. Just my
gravpack, if I'd had one.

—*Right. The pack's in their visual range, we aren't.*
But they're in ours. Run.

I ran. My feet touched the talus of scree under the
cliff so fast and light not a pebble shifted. But the
squirmy gel that grew among them did. Away. From
me. I could grow to like that. The plain flew up to meet
me and began to reel out behind, crawling fur that
burned yellow-white where my light touched and
fluffed away from every step in frantic circles like a
stone in a pond, cross-waves bursting where the rings
met. The plain was ruffling as far as I could see. Which
was practically forever. It was dark as pitch and I could
see everything, the plain below, the cliff behind, the
ring of the pad rushing up at us like it was outlined in
landing-beacons.

The hell with it. I get these dreams. Especially when
I'm over-tired. Except I didn't feel tired at all.

—*Look right.*

I did. The pad was five miles from our base and I'd
covered it in maybe ten minutes. The Ghost-Egg was
above on the rim, shining opal pink as a good pearl
should. On the lower slope of the cone, between it and
the pad but much nearer the pad, a smaller circle
glowed like a redhot manhole-cover.

—*Personnel-shaft. They haven't used it lately, it*
isn't time for the purge. Can't be long now, it's more

*than twenty days. They're usually regular, they must
have something special on hand.*

Like sacrificing prisoners.

*—Don't be romantic. They don't care about pris-
oners, what good would it do? They probably want to
cut them up, you would. This is social. Maybe they're
waiting for someone. They're hierarchical, didn't Moke
say so?*

Pair of wiseasses together. I was veering for the
manhole like a rocket, rooted fur trying to escape under
my feet.

—You really think this is a good idea?

—Yes.

—Figures. I stamped carefully around the glowing
circumference. ***Don't suppose you know the magic
words?***

—Open Sesame. What else?

Wiseasses. I must have put my foot on the right place
because the manhole was widening. Not upward like
Earthly ones but sinking into the dirt as the pad had
done. Then I guess it did a slide sideways. The hole
showed under, a polished surface reflecting my light. It
looked as if it went down to the center of the planet, and
maybe out the other side. A hot puff of air like the draft
from a furnace blew out and flamed off into atmosphere
above my head. The depths were red with heat.

—So now what? It looked as sheer as the sides of
a well. If it sloped the way Dribble said, the slope was
so slight I could scarcely see it curve away.

—So we go down, what else?

I stepped over the side and found my hind end on
the world's fastest fairground slide. I opened my mouth
to shriek and my jaw froze.

*—Don't do that, they hear at that range. Keep it
low.*

—Thanks. Is it okay if I groan deeply?

—Sure. Go ahead.

I decided not to bother. I concentrated instead on trying to dig my hands and feet in to brake against the gathering speed. It was too dark to see much but I'd the impression the redly glowing walls were flying past my face at what had to be sixty per and rising.

—Correct. Which is why you'd better stop that now before you lose your skin, not to mention your coolsuit. Haven't you heard of friction, dammit?

—Oh. But my hands had lifted already. ***Isn't there going to be a kind of mess at the bottom?***

—No. Trust me.

I couldn't see the slightest reason why I should, except I was slowing. The end of the tunnel was in sight around a long slow curve and I could see a sanded floor coming toward me at steadily decreasing velocity. By the time I hit it I was almost going backward. I landed on my points like Fonteyn being a swan and drifted into the alien base.

The corridor stretched into the distance not quite straight, its ends vanishing left and right into a perspective of red gloom. Like the arc of a circle. Radial symmetry, no doubt. Luminous braids of track twirled both ways, with a flourish at the bottom where I'd just landed.

—Interesting. I've never been here. Left or right, do you think?

—This may be news to you but I haven't either. If the bastard's really a circle it probably doesn't matter, we get to come back to the beginning.

—You could get dreadfully bored on the way, this circle's big. How about left, I think there's breathing.

—These guys breathe?

—Since they're mostly air, they have to. Why do you

think they collapse so easily?

—Fur. Disagreed with 'em.

—Alien protein. It disagreed with Dribble, too, but he has more flesh underneath, he soaked it up. Their integument's thin.

—Heard it was tough.

—Not to the local vegetable solvents. When it ruptures, their nervous systems are left lying in the grass, quite bare. Unpleasant, really.

—Take your word for it. I'll dispense with the diagram. Where you get all this stuff?

—I know what you know. I'm also finding out more and more of what they know. It's enlightening.

—Tell me about it.

I was dispensing with the queasiness in my stomach too, we didn't seem to have time for it. I was moving left over the twist of trails, not quite sure I'd actually decided. Worse than a neural-linked laser, except I've been there. But there was breathing, I could see it. The phosphorescent green air came drifting out of pointed arches opening on the corridor, from doorways offset along both sides, in pulsating gusts. I stopped at the nearest and looked.

A hall with sculpture and a second arch beyond, offset likewise so you couldn't see straight in. The phosphorescence was stronger here, with a scent. Like onions, but stronger. I was glad I had nose-filters or I might have had tears in my eyes.

—Sure hope I'm cooled.

—You're cooled. Take a look.

I'd moved in before I remembered the trouble Moke and me had with our tracks back on Resurrection. The damned sand was everywhere. Wall-to-wall desert, Navy issue. If I knew anything. And I hadn't a blower. I must have left footprints the length of the passage.

I glanced down and saw nothing. Only the luminous trails of the toadstool coming in and out, pausing in front of its private artwork, passing into its private room. If I thought about it I'd say my feet couldn't be touching the floor. I thought I'd rather not think about it. Maybe it was an optical illusion. Maybe human tracks didn't show in this light. It had to be hellish hot, the whole passage shone with volcanic convection.

The inner room was what we'd seen before, but occupied. The hollow in the floor had a collapsed dancer, its frilled skirts gracefully spread, coiled tentacles showing faintly through the translucent cap, filaments arranged on the sand in a radius of bright threads. The top of the cap was something I'd never seen before. It was a mass of slowly writhing worms heaped in a dome that had something of the look of an exposed brain, not human . . .

—*Yes, you did. Back at the temple. You thought they were idealized. Remember?*

—**That was Mokey.**

—*You always agree with him. But he wondered if they might be real and you see he was right. You just didn't see them.*

—**They come out at night.**

—*Nonsense. They're just the wrong wavelength, like your coolsuit. These people aren't too imaginative, they show what they see. That's what Moke thought. They like color and they show that as they see it too. Not as you do. I can't make you share, you wouldn't like their minds. In any case they'd know. Look closer.*

It had a general pale green, one of the mints. But it was like the ones we'd seen at the Resurrection base, the cap was shot with welling pulses of other colors, pearl and blue and rose.

—*Emotions. They dream. It's common to intelligence.*

—**Is it?**

—*Of course. You can't invent without some imagination. If you imagine, you dream.*

—**Do computers dream?**

—*If they're complex enough to count as intelligent. Look next door.*

—**Why in color?**

—*It's muttering. A form of communication they use outside the group-mind, like the sonics. I'd say having nightmares. That was a traumatic experience, your friend Sword has a talent for destruction. It lost part of itself and now it's grieving.*

—**He'd be gratified to hear it. They got to know we're here, the place ought to be crawling with guards.**

—*They've routine patrols. Avoid them, their electrical auras are dangerous when they're awake. As it happens they don't. They just can't imagine a solitary mind. When they're cut off from the group they go mad, as you saw. They can't exist alone. It's why they don't survive group destruction, the last few die. Half a dozen's their lower limit and then the mind's crippled. They took a long way around to avoid your ships and when they didn't see them they assumed they'd lost you. An expedition like yours is a mental impossibility. They believe Dribble self-destructed as they would have done and it was his protein that was lethal to them. They've noted you need care when dissecting humans. Look next door.*

—**Nice. And when do they start the dissection?**

—*Not for a couple of days. Their specialists aren't here, it's why they've been holding the purge off. Look next door, dammit. They're making themselves uncom-*

fortable for the big boys, it's social. As I said.

I moved over to the inmost doorway. The garden was inside the arch but it wasn't any way tranquil. I could see Toad might be having nightmares. The rows of little nubs were sitting demurely like lettuce waiting to be picked but the old wavers were rippling like an angry sea. Their flashing head-beads threw disco-reflections across the walls like the room was on fire and their caps were heaving and tossing. Several had torn their roots almost out of the bed and had pushed toward the front, shouldering smaller caps out of their way. There was something frantic in their motion, almost drunken. Like whatyoumacallits.

—*Maenads. Don't play stupid, it wastes time. Take your gloves off.*

Christ. Alien protein. **You want to see me go gazoo the way they did? I'm gonna look good splatted over the ceiling.**

—*You're being childish again. Take your gloves off. And your hood, spit's even better. Never mind the little ones, they aren't awake yet. The adults will have daughters, tonight. They split perpetually by parthenogenesis between fertilizations. Get moving, there's a lot to do. We want to touch them all if we can.*

—**Holy shit, there's got to be a million.**

—*There may be seventy mobiles, each with a garden. Less, they came out in force yesterday and every clone-group there lost members. The guard-group's intact and just became socially superior, but they were due for a fight. Eighty's about the upper limit before they explode if there are several clones involved. Hence the purge.*

—**I was talking about the fucking crawlers. There's a million right here.**

—*Then you'd better get started. We've your friends to contact. Work comes first.*

—Why? I want to see the guys, it's what we're here for.

—Let's do it my way. You may actually end by getting them out.

All the guys I know got attitude. I was shucking off gloves and hood while it lectured. While I lectured. I've a great imagination sometimes. The next minute I was up to my knees in the bed with armfuls of writhing jelly under my fingers, pressing hands and lips against slimy caps. They rolled and squirmed under me, fringes whipping at my face. All I needed was one of those in the eye. Oddly enough I didn't get it. They snuggled up like dogs, little nubs wriggling against my ankles.

—Okay, next.

—I was just getting friendly.

—We're not here to get friendly. Move on. A handful each will do, they're clones. If you get tired one might be enough, though I'd rather have a margin. Keep moving.

The arrangement was radial and symmetrical. I made the round of the quadrant and found them all asleep. If colors said something, a lot were having bad dreams. I'd been around maybe thirty gardens and had moved into the next sector before we met a patrol and I stepped in a doorway until they'd passed. They were mauves, a group of three, and I'll speak for their auras. They frizzled my hair at six feet.

I almost forgot to get my hood back before they got level and just had time to shove my hands behind me out of sight. If the owner of that cubicle had chosen that moment to waken we'd have had trouble. But I guess I was really cooled out. The patrol swirled past in a tippling of spires and a roiling of tentacles without pausing. I was lucky. They looked into doorways from time to time but they chose one three down.

—You may call it luck. I call it work. Let's go.

By the end I was jelly up to the elbows and my lips were hot. Stiffened plasticky stuff crackled between my fingers. Some of the apartments were empty, the construct broken, the floor smoothed out, the garden a bare cave with dried jelly splashed across the walls. A few were just unoccupied. I guess they belonged to the night-shift. Their partners were in.

—It's better than Postman's Knock. Do I get to hand out stamps next round?

—Stand still. We're coming to the hangar-deck, time to rest a minute.

—You won't have noticed but we've passed it at least five times already, this place is a rabbit-warren. With radial symmetry. I adore radial rabbits.

—I said rest, you're getting hysterical. Put your gloves on.

—Sword was wondering . . .

—How they fly space without technology. He's right, they had it, it's decayed. They're a very old society. Their telepathy's been developing for generations and a lot of their appliances aren't needed anymore. They don't need holo, for instance, they get too much of each others' visions.

—They have comm-links.

—Because they're only fully telepathic within the clone-group. Some of them can communicate partially across group barriers but the ability's disappearing. It happens when the groups are related and it's part of their decay that they're less and less so. They're jealous and very aggressive.

—We noticed.

—It's the way their biology's gone. They're extremely sensitive to alien protein and as they've moved into space they've become psychotic about it. They eat

each other, and increasingly only their own clone. They feel safe that way. Cultivation used to be general, now it's strictly for peasants.

*—**Eating people is wrong.***

—It's foolish, when it cuts down your gene-pool. Theirs is getting more and more restricted. Their society's based on war. They need the group to survive but they go berserk when there are too many minds in the same space. Another side-effect of telepathy. You aren't the only people who get headaches from alien auras. When the group gets too big they go mad and there's a slaughter. I think it's always been that way, but it used to be limited by their in-group tolerance.

*—**You mean family don't make their heads ache.***

—Basically. When the whole race was interrelated the slaughters were small and local. Now they're huge and universal. Since the remains of destroyed clone-groups die, their genetic diversity's dwindling all the time and their aggressivity's increasing.

*—**Driving each other insane.***

—And breeding to make up for it. I suppose their ideal would be a planet for every clone. But they're so competitive for power, every clone's also out to extinguish all the others and have the world to itself. They breed faster and kill each other faster all the time. Technology disappeared with civilized society. They're now an entirely warrior race who've only retained the tools they need. Ships, weapons, gravity devices, communications. Battle-computers. They've learned a lot from you. Sword said they weren't stupid.

*—**Just dumb.***

—Do you too have a civil war on, or did I imagine it? Shall we move out? We've around two hours left before sunrise. Just time to see your friends and get home.

• • •

The cages were in a store-room behind the hangar-deck, two big beehives of cloudy plastic with hoses and cables. A compressor thumped softly somewhere in the background. The nearer of the two showed a clear patch in the side where fresh plastic had been grafted recently. I pressed my nose to it.

"You Henry?"

The big guy inside with his arms behind his head got up and planted a black square hand flat on the wall. "That's me." The one who had wadded the hole with clothes while Drib ate out. He moved stiffly.

"You okay?"

"I could recover. Ain't got an army behind, have you?"

"Not right now, sorry. Just me and my dog. Or vice-versa. Can't even take you, you ain't cooled and you no idea what they got for elevators. Got friends outside, though. And my info is, the Geeks are staying quiet for a couple of days until their experts get in."

"Great. I'll remember that while they're carving."

"Don't be bitter."

—*But we can help.*

"But we can help." *We can?*

—*Tell him to keep his hand there.*

"Just keep your hand there." *What is this?*

My reflexes were getting weirder. I rose four feet into the air to the level of the big hand that faced me and slid my own smoothly through the plastic to make contact. He almost drew back, took a deep breath and stayed standing.

"Gucky, huh? Ignore the visions, I get 'em myself. It's the air or something. Pass me the kids next."

"You sure this gonna help?"

"No. Pass 'em anyway, if you think hopeful it may even work." *What may work?*

—*Just do it.*

He grunted and lifted a skinny brat with gaunt bones and scared huge eyes.

"Hi. Ain't a Chan, are you?"

Dumb nod.

"Know your grandma. Your sissy here?" I'd both hands through to the wrist, grasping fingers like shivering twigs.

Equally dumb shake.

"She's not?"

"Dunno." His liquid eyes were too scared to cry.

"We can't see," Henry said behind him. "Shapes, is all."

"His granny gonna be real pleased to see him. Next."

The next was sobbing fretfully and Henry had to take his wrist and hold it while I wrapped my paws around. He tried to grab away and Henry and I hung on together.

"Gucky, huh? It's okay, don't hurt. You doing okay with the kids, Sergeant." Stripes where his shirt had been.

"Got a pair of my own," he said tonelessly. "Did the dog-kid make it?"

"Why I'm here."

"Never thought he would. Gutsy bastard."

"Both. Listen, got me a laser. Small, old and the last guy tried to use one got hurt, but if I give it to you you use it like you had sense, huh? And when me or my mates come, think twice about shooting, we're human."

His eyes lit even through the plastic. "Just give."

"Last resort, right?"

"Yup. Kids first."

"Geeks first, dammit. We're trying to save the kids. See you."

"I hope."

I ran my hands over the wall like spreading butter. For some reason it closed right back up as if I'd never been in. The bims were next door, a flower-pattern of spread palms around white noses trying to see.

"Relia?"

Muted sob. "Cassie. I knew Mac would come, I've told and told them so. What's he doing?"

"Uh— He got held back. Hang in, kid, we'll fix it. Give me your hands."

"What does it do?"

"Uh—" Search me. "Helps. Hall's there too. There's no danger for a couple days." I hope. "Who you got with you?"

"Beth, Rosemary and Sarah Chan. And Margaret's hurt. She tried to stop them taking Becky." Another sob. "Do you know where she is?"

"No use dreaming, doll. Glad little Chan's there for her granny's sake. Tell her Bubba's next door. Next."

Beth, the schoolteacher. "Ain't gonna introduce you to Sword, he has a weakness for pretty black ladies."

Wan grin. "Maybe later."

"Not if I can help it. When we done the kid and Roz could a couple of you bring Margaret? Don't wanta come in, wall take too long to fix and it gonna show. You need time."

"For what?" she said softly.

"For this to take." Whatever it is.

"Margaret's badly burned. We're all shaky but they whipped her almost to death. It's going to hurt her."

"Gotta risk it, babe."

The little Chan looked at me with her brother's huge eyes, equally tearless and silent. Roz was a skinny blonde in rags of Marine uniform with a lash-mark on her cheek and scorched hair.

"Ain't good. If we lift Marg we kill her maybe."
She leaned her lips to the hole, coughing on the seep
of raw gases that passed my wrist. "Takes all she can
do not to cry, when she's here. But she's in and out.
We've no nalgies and she's delirious with pain. I
daren't."

—Patrol. Close it up quickly.

I dropped and shrank, pulling as far under hoses as
I could. Pinks this time, another trio, humming as they
circled around the cages.

*—Nervous. Since Dribble escaped they don't like to
come close, they're doubtful what these may be doing.
Margaret's near the wall in back. Ask them to move
her against the side.*

"Hey. Can you slide her to the edge here?"

Aurelia's face, a milky stain. "They didn't see you."

"This nutty color counts as cool. Sorry I ain't got
more. Thanks, guys, that'll do."

It didn't surprise me at all when I shoved my whole
head through the plastic like it was air and leaned my
palms on the floor. Margaret had been Beth's color
before she lost her uniform and most of her skin. Now
she was gray with a frightening bluish tinge between
areas of black-brown crust.

"Turn her head, Rosie? Can't come closer, hole
gonna show."

My mouth pressed down on her scabbed lips, bright
breath moving between us. Bims never switched me
on, it's one of my failings. *Hey!*

*—Think of it as mouth-to-mouth resuscitation. Stay
there, this is real work. Then move fast, there's a cross-
patrol coming.*

*—Thanks. **Gonna haveta practice sprint-starts,
with your timing. You coulda let me kiss Henry, he's
more my type.***

—Shut up and drop. Close the wall behind you or they'll choke.

—Tell your granny.

I lay on my belly trying not to pant, watching busy braids make outlines on the floor. Blue. They'd a fine variety on guard tonight.

—You weren't listening. They've averted a hive-war for a week or two only because your friends reduced their numbers, and they don't want to look bad in front of the Clans Major. That doesn't mean they trust each other.

—Don't suppose you know where the armory is?

—No. But there's something here I can show you.

—Bombs?

—At least technology. In here.

Med-lab by the look. Glittery things. Plastic polyhedrons strung on grav-beams down from the arched roof with stuff inside that sometimes shone and sometimes steamed. A whole honeycomb of plastic boxes in pink, green and mauve, stacked in a ranked pile. They were horribly small.

—I said they're mostly air. It's temporary, anyhow. They'll be consumed at the purge.

—Consumed?

—Eaten. By their clone-mates.

—That could be bad for their health.

—Incredibly. The remains are saturated with your exob's devil-dust.

—I'm not sure I want to see that again.

—I'm glad to hear it.

I laid my hands on the top layer. The plastic began to sag and melt. As it wasted it dripped on the layer below and carried infection with it. The thready stuff inside dissolved into goo and slumped down, layer by layer, into a shapeless heap like the stub of a candle.

—I guess we just upset them some more.

—Rank blasphemy. With luck they'll think it was alien protein.

—Wasn't it?

—After a fashion.

At which moment I got a good look at the jars. I guess jars. A string of threaded polyhedrons hanging the length of the arch from vault to floor. I looked inside the middle one then checked them up and down. Then I turned away, revolted, my belly clenched.

—If I'd seen those first, I mightn't have done that.

—I know.

I pressed my hands furiously on the necklace of hands and brains. It failed to melt.

—You and I better understand one another. I done your stuff, you do mine.

—I'm trying. There's no good reason for these to be contaminated, if they turn up missing there'll be hell to pay and more prisoners may be sacrificed. They're divided now between dissecting them all and trying to breed a pair for study. Her remains will dissolve when air next touches them. That should serve your purpose, they won't be studied. It's called discretion.

—Tell me about it.

—Sun's coming, let's go. They become active at dawn.

I made the circle to the foot of the shaft so fast the walls blurred around me. At the foot I paused. I don't know how Drib made it. It looked as sheer as a factory chimney and a whole lot higher. The perspective curved off slowly into red dark. I understood his nails.

—So climb.

I hopped on the rim and poked my fingers easily into the ceramic lining. It was as misty and malleable as the plastic of the cage. My toes made comfortable little steps and I was climbing like a squirrel, but a whole lot faster. Maybe halfway up it occurred to me I had to be leaving a track like the Abominable Snowman and I glanced back. The shaft below shone smooth and clear.

—*Concentrate, we haven't time for slipups.*

—**Ha.**

—*You're missing at camp. They'll be coming for you.*

—**Holy hell. Why didn't you say so?**

—*I just did.*

—**More ha.**

—*By the way, it might be better if we kept this private. Just for now. Hallway has his worries, and you don't want them thinking you're having more hallucinations. They might decide we're untrustworthy.*

—**They gotta think I'm crazy already. What the hell do I say?**

—*I'm sure you'll think of something. It'll come right in the end.*

I snarled. But I remembered those jars, the ones that wouldn't melt. I wasn't sure this relation was completely equal.

—*Don't worry, it will be. I said I need you. You haven't gone the whole way yet.*

And what did that mean? But answer came there none.

When I got on the plain I must have broken the sound-barrier. I did another squirrel-job over the rocks, soared into the air and landed at the tent gasping. And no, I don't know how I got over a couple hundred meters of sheer rock, some of it overhanging, without grav. Maybe I was turning into a goat. The first rim of sun was showing, red and dim, over the line of the forest as I crawled through the tunnel into a muddle of

Moke, Yell and Hallway, head to head like a convocation of ponies. They turned and stared.

"Hi, guys, you look worried. Just out taking a stroll. Natural function."

They looked at me, three strained faces, colors ranging from white through flush to furious.

Moke caught himself first. "Cass. You've been out with no mask on."

"Oh," I said, disconcerted. "Have I? Been practicing breathing. Can count up to nearly four hundred."

"We saw you coming," Hallway said tightly. "Over the edge. That blue shows. You took out a pack in the dark."

"Wrong. If I had you'd've seen it. You just seen me."

"You came over the rim," Yell said.

"Was leaning over. Told you."

I dropped on a pack and stared down at my hands. I wasn't sure whether to cry or not. I felt a bit like the little Chans, too dry inside to squeeze out tears.

"What's wrong, Cass?" Moke said in my ear, squatting.

"I'm waiting to grow green fur," I whimpered. "I've caught a fucking *symbiote*."

He looked earnestly into my face, as if he'd never seen it before. Maybe the fur was really there. "Oh," he said softly. "Is that what's doing it? Never mind, I promise to love you both."

"Dammit, Mokey," I said, and fell all over him. Seemed I'd water to spare after all.

Hallway had let it drop. He sat in a corner with his head in his hands. Yell was eyeing me speculatively. He's a spacer, and spacers go in for symbiotes. He didn't himself but half his friends did. I've never thought to ask what they're for, they make me nauseous.

"Hall, we got to do something quick. I got ideas."

"Forget it, Cass," he said wearily. "Unless you really were out on the plain with a pack."

"I never touched 'em, cross my heart."

"Then you're only guessing. We've all guessed. Try to stay close to camp, will you? Those things could tear you apart, and if they catch you they will. And if you get scoped we're all blown, and that's it for trying a rescue."

"They're waiting for their top brass to arrive. That gives us a couple of days, but we got to move. They'll be here day after tomorrow."

"It's a possible scenario. Sword and I calculated roughly the same."

"But we can't just sit here, the guys are expecting us to come for them."

"If they knew we were here, I expect they would be."

I opened my mouth, and my throat closed up. Moke's eye sparked, and steadied.

"Since they can't . . . We've four planks and four grav-packs for ourselves and maybe a dozen of them. Four of them children. Me, Moke and Yell—makes fourteen, fifteen guys to get out. Under fire. Even supposing we manage to get in. The best we can say is, we'll die quickly. Leaving you and Drib in charge of the ship, with your cover blown. Can you pilot that thing?"

"You know damn well I can't. I want to talk to Sword."

He looked at me in silence. "There was something queer on the scope last night," he said at last.

"Probably Cass's astral body," Yell said. His eyes were still narrowed.

"Up in orbit. Another blip."

"Uh-oh," I said. "I truly believed they weren't due for another two days." *Know it all, huh?* Maybe the bastard was imaginary after all.

"If it's alien, there ought to be a fleet," Moke said. "Since they move in groups. Did it look alien, Hall?"

"I don't know. Queer. Not the same shape, and sliding around. Moon-hopping. You won't see it now, it's behind one of the inners."

"Someone of ours?"

"If it is they aren't calling."

"Phantom," Yell said. "Told you it was an astral body."

"I don't know." Hallway sounded unhappy. "It's invisible now."

"Or evaporated. Could be an echo."

"Looked like a ship. Until it vanished."

"Uh-huh," Yell said. "You never know what echoes gonna do."

"Yeah," Hall muttered. He still looked bad. Zonked. Through the other wall Dribble was crouched in a miserable hump over Sword's body. Didn't look as if either one had moved since last night. I stood up.

"Well, if nobody here cares any more, I'll go hold a couple hands."

"Hey, Cassie," Hallway said. Half-hearted. Slapping people down isn't his style. "I didn't mean it like that. There are things we all want too badly."

"Sure, I know." I picked up a redundant mask before someone else worried about my sanity and started to pull it on.

Dribble's long howl of pain and grief cut across all of us. It had come through the fabric of two insulated tents but he's always had a voice like a dog-whistle. We whipped around. He was standing in the middle of the shaded plastic next door, his deformed head lifted to the sky, his shark mouth opened on another wail. He looked like the world's last wolf mourning its father.

Hallway tried to head me off at the tunnel but I was nearer and faster. I shot through before him and covered the space between tents faster than light. I didn't have to push through the neighboring lock to know. Drib turned me a face streaming with human tears, his shovel-nailed paws lifted as if he meant to gouge his own cheekbones.

"Cass-Mama, we come too slow. Sword dead."

Dead and through my heart. I fell on my knees by

his side. His hair, that had been sprinkled with gray yesterday, was ice-white, the stretched skin looking already mummified. I stared wildly around and found the mask still in my hand, I hadn't gotten around to putting it on. I touched his icy forehead. It felt as if he'd been dead for hours. I held my filters to his mouth to be sure. The lenses stayed clear. Not a mote of breath. The mechanical monster in his chest was still pulsing, I could hear its distant thud. But his ribs were still.

"Sword, you bastard. I forgive you any number of black navigators. You could have had them all. But I don't forgive you this."

Hallway was standing over me, long and helpless, his face milky. "Cass. I knew, I didn't want to tell you. He didn't want you to know."

"Know? For Christ's sake, how long has he been dead?"

"This minute, Mama," Dribble sobbed. "I sitting with, he breathe once and stop. Just this minute."

Hallway lowered his head. "He's been in a coma since last night. It could happen again, Cass. I mean, the breathe and stop. It's that infernal piece of machinery, it won't let him lie. Come away, please. It can only kill you by inches, watching. I've tried to make Drib go but he won't believe me. He's not alive, not really. Nothing will bring him back now. He's never going to open his eyes or know you. Please come."

—*You fucker. While I went out roaming. The last chance to speak to him while he knew me. And you told me he'd live.*

—*You needed the knowledge. You all did. What could you have done?*

—*Sat with him. Just sat. Shut up, dunghill, I got nothing to say. You cheated me.*

Silence. I laid my head on Sword's cold chest and

felt the damned tubes throb under my ear. His neck was icy too, his hands skeletal patterns cut in snow. I took one between mine and hung onto it.

"Cassie."

"Go away," I said. "Just go away."

They all did in the end. Hall managed to drag Dribble out, still whimpering, and left me alone with the end of ten years' imbecility. There may be stupider stories, I don't know one.

The red sun moved across the sky and changed the angles of the shadows. Sword lay like a marble crusader in his sky-colored suit and I sat over him in mine. I dripped his face wet with salt water and waited to see if either one of us would turn green. Like a public fountain. The tears left salt glaze on his skin and ran sideways down his cheekbones and wet the icy hair behind his ears. I felt like the spring of a well that would never run dry. I wiped my nose on my blue sleeve and darkened it with wet and the glaze grew deep, like the first beginnings of a stalagmite. King Solomon's Mine.

—The shield of Perseus, an unvoice said in my ear. It sounded like Moke's. When she saw her reflection it turned her to stone.

—*What?*

—Thinking.

—*The dumbest kid I've ever seen,* an echo whispered.

—Drib's next. Got to be. We could do it.

—*Mokey?*

—Um.

—*You too? You touched me. The bastard. Why didn't you tell them?*

—Same reason you didn't. Yell's guessed but

he doesn't care, Hall has too much to cope with already. I got to think.

—*It doesn't matter to me, now.*

The glaze on Sword's face was too thick to be salt, too transparent. I lifted my hand to wipe it clean and found it was sealed on his. Tears ran from my eyes in long strings like beads, threaded together, and dripped on his eyelids. His white mouth had parted. Not a dropped jaw, he still looked no more than marble. Another final sigh, one for each of us? A runnel of salt found its way to the fold by his mouth and brimmed over his lips onto his silent tongue.

—Turned to stone. Metamorphosis.

—*You could have kept me a last word.*

—But I knew you'd come. Why do you think I left the door open?

—As soon as they arrive. When they're all in the Egg. They'll be unguarded then, or almost. Even if . . .

—*Right from the first day. You were always . . .*

—In reverse. Need a diversion. The mirror of Perseus. I wonder . . .

—*Thou northern wind, and a few small drops . . .*

—*I've never taken it off. Look. Did you think . . .*

—Can be. Mirror. With Hall's help. If he . . .

—*As any maiden may, I'll . . .*

I stretched my spare hand to pick up his other and lay it on his chest with the first. They were bigger than mine. Ridiculous. Why guys are always breaking things, hands too big, bims have to work at them with their smaller fingers. My hands weren't nearly big enough to cover his. I shut my palms on them anyhow. The strings of beads were glass rods that joined us eye to eye. There was something strange and hollow in my spine, as if I'd become glass myself.

—Reverse. It's the answer. If only . . .

—*Waited so long, I knew you'd . . .*

—*A twelvemonth and a day.*

—Would need timing. Let's hope I . . .

—*But it was imagination, you know I wouldn't . . .*

Hollow.

—Three by then, should help. Now . . .

Glass.

—The shield of Perseus, the magic mirror . . .

—*Just got to be smartass. It's lucky I've never . . .*

—*Began to speak. Oh, who . . .*

—*You know I have.*

—Yes, that's it. And it will. So long as . . .

—*Of heaven, my dear, to kiss . . .*

—All of us, it's a psychosis.

Your lips of clay.

Voiceless whispers. I sat frozen, so cold I couldn't feel my hands or feet anymore. Maybe I couldn't feel anything.

The hush of material on plastic said someone had come in behind. Moke's hands slid around my glacier middle, warm and hard, and locked.

"You can't do it alone, Cass, there isn't enough of you. You'll kill yourself."

"Does it matter?"

"It does to me." He leaned his cheek against my neck. "Dammit, if I don't look after you, who will? There's enough of us both."

We sat together, his living warmth flowing through my skin into my frozen veins. Under us the pitiless thumping of that expensive miracle of steel and ceramic went on as if it was ticking out eternity.

"I hate it," I said, closing my hands hard on Sword's icy knuckles.

"I think he did, in the end. What a thing to carry with you as a memento mori."

"It's hideous, Moke."

"I know."

Under me something stirred. I stiffened, scared clear through.

"What?"

"Nothing. I thought . . ."

But it had. The endless metallic ticking had skipped, restarted and begun to fade. Tick. Pause. Tick. Pause. Tick. Long pause. Faint distant tick. A pause as long as the creation of the universe. The slightest low tick, far away.

His nuclear heart, made forever, had stopped.

Long purple shadows were stretching from the mountains onto the yellow plain when we staggered out. The cleft was dark, lit by a glow of reflected light that reddened the filaments blowing around the hopship and burned faintly on her camouflaged nose. Moke was holding me up. We covered the few strides like climbing a ladder and he helped me fall through the door.

Dribble was curled in a corner with his knees around his ears snuffling very softly as if he was afraid of being overheard. He crawled to lean his back against my shoulder. His human eyes were red and swollen.

"Cass-Mama, how we save Relia now Sword gone?"

"We'll save her, pup. Or maybe she'll save herself. Tough girl."

Hallway hadn't shed noticeable tears but his face was a frigid mask, his freckles staring on bleached skin. "What makes you think that, Cassandra? She's an aristocrat. A lady. She's never been involved in a fight in her life."

"That's where you and Sword were both wrong. I don't know how you got the brass to look down on her. Aurelia's Ari, right. She's Sword's sister and she got her guts where he got his. But while he's been running the Strip she's been helping Daddy run the DeLorn-McLaren empire. She was her Mama's social secretary. The guy who handled the Dips, the guy who worked in the school and tried to save kids. You don't understand Aris. They ride horses, God help us. They play golf. They grow disgusting green things and fertilize them by hand. They sail coronas and go Ringgliding. I bet she's tougher'n you are. Go jerk on your bootstraps. If you gonna marry her you'll need to."

His face rosed over. "Who said—?"

"Nobody need to. You got it writ on your forehead."

He looked down again at his big surgeon's hands. "Her father won't—"

"Don't mix his snobbery with yours He wouldn't have cared if I'd married Sword, and compared with me you're respectable. There any cold prote around here? I'm starving."

"I'm heating it," Yell said. "Take a bite out of this, kid, it'll put hair on your chest."

"Hair on my chest's what I've always wanted."

I took his silver flask anyhow. It might put hair on the inside of my belly, and God knew I needed it. He drew his hand back quickly.

"Christ, Cass, how'd you get so cold in this climate? You're like the Flying Dutchwoman, frost on every spar. Soup in three minutes."

I hiccuped and leaned on Moke's shoulder, an arm around Dribble's shivering neck. "How's your ghostblip, Hall?"

His brow furrowed. "Gone. Maybe it was an echo."

"Nasty things, echoes. Place is a regular mine of them." Had a bad case myself recently.

—*Happens with a group. Until it's under control.*

—**You mean Moke and me are turning into toadstools. We'll lose our minds shortly because there aren't enough of us.**

—*You need food.*

—**If Geeks can't survive in small groups, how did they manage on Resurrection? Eight had to be close to the limit. And they were different clones. While we're discussing it.**

—*Were we? Depends on the clone. These here are minors, young ones sent to settle an outpost. They come in groups of twenty, so their backup's poor. Your clones kept their brothers nearby. A major clone can have a thousand members and it's very strong, strong enough to support its members at a considerable distance so long as their brothers on the support-ships act as relays. The ones coming are Clans Major and they aren't easy. Their auras are multiplied by their active numbers.*

—**Great. You got any ideas about what to do with them?**

—*Moke has. Didn't you hear him?*

I remembered his voice, whispering. "Mokey . . ."

He tightened his arm around my waist. "We'll fix them, Cass."

"Is that a royal 'we'?"

"Nope. We wouldn't leave you out, you'd hate it."

"Oh," I said. With apprehension.

"What's that?" Yell was kneeling upright, gazing through plastic into the clotted sunset.

Hallway grabbed the glasses. A bright curving thread like a river of lava was wandering through the jungle under the leaves. It had to be hot because triangles were

curling and folding on each side into a blackened rim.
The scorched trail lengthened. Moke leaned over and
pointed. Others were spreading in from the south and
west. A faint gleam on the farthest horizon suggested
something even more distant on its way over the curve.
A wide band of premature night marked its path
through the forest like a brand-scar. Another bright
streak glimmered over the brow of the ridge to the east
and more wound under the setting disk beyond the
cone. Snail-trails that moved. Coming toward us. On
the cliff behind us a burning waterfall had begun to rill
down, following the line of least resistance in sinuous
curves.

"Torches, I think. Though a lot of the heat could
just be themselves, it's dark enough to show. Plant-life
doesn't like it. Looks like a migration of the outer villages."

Moke and I looked at each other.

"How far can they travel, Hall?"

"Surprisingly long distances on foot. They have to
move around a lot, there are discolored trails all over.
Speed the vegetation grows, they have to be used often."

"On tentacle," Yell said. "They move fast when
they want to. Anyone farside?"

"Could be another sci-station, we've seen vehicles."
He paused, his face tight. "Sword and I. If they're all
coming in you'll see them. They patrol occasionally.
Not often, they're confident. Wonder what's going
down?"

The lava was running together, flowing out onto the
plain, swirling in coils and settling in rings on the ruffled fur. Fairy rings. Like poisonous mushrooms. Each
group set itself to spiring and conical huts spun out
from under them, circles of luminous stuff that grew

hard as it cooled, developed points and turned into a forest of little scout-tents with what looked like a campfire in the middle. The fur was invisible in the dusk but I could feel it writhing, rippling in vortexes like raindrops in a pool.

—*The planet hates them.*

—*Because they burn? It digests them. Most of what you see's illusion. The vegetation's used to thunder, it regenerates quickly. We get rather a lot.*

—*You mean their fucking auras do the damage.*

—*That and their alien protein.*

—*How do they sleep on this stuff without getting digested, sand it over?*

—*Burn the floor clear, it's what you'd do. They probably sand it too.*

—*Come to think of it, where's the damn sand come from? Ain't seen no beaches to date.*

—*They secrete it. Weren't you told they have a silicious inner structure?*

—*So?*

—*So they have waste products. Like everyone else.*

—*And they sleep in it? Yech.*

—*It's quite clean. And very convenient.*

—*Sure it is. I always knew they were great guys really.*

"Have some more prote," Moke said peaceably. "Come on, Drib, you got to eat or you'll get sick."

Dribble shook his shark head, scattering salt like a wet dog. His ears drooped. "Not hungry."

"If we're going to save Relia you got to get better. Come on, have a bite. We need you."

The Mokey touch. Dribble looked pathetic but he took a mouthful to be nice. Half a minute later Yell refilled his bowl. Twice.

Outside, rings of light starred the plain like

something festive—a circus holo or nursery wallpaper. A soft high whistle said the first wreath of bottle-caps upsky was coming in to land. The pad was lit for them, throwing a bloodred wash across the yellow ripples. It gave them a nasty infected look as if the planet's own skin was inflamed. They all came in at once in perfect formation and skirled into a braid. The crews got down and wreathed to put up pup-tents and the pad took the ships below. Ten. The next ten came around half an hour later, just in time to meet the pad on its way back up. Half an hour after there were five, but bigger with jumbo-sized crews.

—*Senior clone. They grow more. The settlers are juveniles.*

—*I'd never have figured that out single-handed.*

—*These are from Hallway's other station. Geological unit, I think.*

—*I won't tell him. He's worried for my sanity already.*

—*Very wise.*

They made themselves a separate and more imposing camp nearer the shaft I'd used last night, with bigger huts and a showier bonfire. Showy enough to let us see it was some kind of stove that burned off the fur down to bare earth where they wanted to move. I guess their prote-problems were serious. We sat in a row with our noses against the tent-fabric watching the light-show, even Drib. Though he didn't stop snuffling big drops on my sleeve as he stared.

The burp of the trans took us by surprise. Hallway had been watching the aliens setting up camp on the plain, his face somber. More streams kept arriving but they were tailing off, looked as if all the nearby villages were in. He woke with a start and reached for it. He

caught the squirt and played it back into a set of rapidly
inserted beads.

"Hercules *to ground-base, do you copy? Approach-
ing cautiously, arrival-time ten hours approximately.
What's your status?"*

—*Stop them,* my head echoed explosively.

"Hall, no. They can only do damage." ·

He turned red eyes on me. "What's the use? Drib
says it's hard to get down, impossible up, even for him
and he's specialized. Sword might have done it. I'm a
man, Cassie. Just a Tech, not an aristocrat. I didn't get
to be hyped and die."

"Shit, Hall, you did it once. When Sword was a
boy."

"Once, for him. Yes. I owed him. And Razor backed
me. This time . . ."

"What about Aurelia?"

It was a low blow, I saw that. The red glazed over.
"We need backup, Cassie. With Sword's help—well,
I'd have risked it. But I've you and Drib to consider
as well now, and—hell. We'd never do it. Three
guys—okay, even if I let you and Drib join in—we
can't take that place by force. We need an army. And
if we try to take one they'll see us and kill the prisoners. We can't win. The best we can do is bomb them.
This time I agree with the Captain."

"This is Hercules," the trans repeated impatiently.
*"Ground base, are you receiving me? Is anyone there?
Come in, please."*

Moke put an urgent hand over the mike. "No. We
can get in there, I know the way. You've got to wait.
We'll have help."

"Like whose? I can't do it, Moke."

"Well, I can. If I have time. Tell them to hold off.

We can still save the guys, but not if *Hercules* comes busting in in the middle.''

"Please do it, Hall, we need a diversion. Mokey's working on it. We have till day after tomorrow, let us have tomorrow to work. We can get in there. We have to try. Please stop them." *Where are you?*

—Doing my best, dammit. What's the matter with the guy? Am I inaudible or something?

—*He didn't touch anyone, he isn't on the net.*

—Shit. Jump up and down on him.

"It's worth the try, Hall," Moke urged. "What we came for."

He looked at us in turn, his eyes weary and burned with grief. "I can't think straight. We've worked whole days straight through, it's what finished Sword, he wouldn't let go. I'd do anything for his sister. For him. For us both. But I don't see this, it's us against hundreds. What can we do?"

"This is Hercules. *Ground base, come in."*

There was a rustle at the doorway. Sword ducked through, made a lunge and took the mike from his hand.

"Hercules? Ground here, McLaren DeLorn. We have the situation under control but we need time. Essential you stand off until we can finalize things here. Do you read me? We need forty-eight hours. Alien ships expected from out-Arm and they have to pass. Have you got that? Forty-eight hours and let them pass, our survival depends on it. Acknowledge, please.''

Pause. The trans gave a relieved sigh. *"DeLorn. Glad to hear from you. Thought you guys were dead. What's your status?"*

"Stable. There are alien ships due in later, maybe forty-eight hours off. Prisoners are here and most are still alive. We're planning a rescue-attempt, getting it lined up, but we need their ships here to work our diversion. It's important they shouldn't be hindered. If they see you around, they're going to be worried and we could lose the prisoners. Will you stand off? We'll keep you updated on our status. Please copy.''

Hall was staring at him, his freckles standing out like splattered paint. His eyes were incredulous. ''Sword? You're dead.''

The evil Swordfish eye swiveled. Bright and clear. His hair was taking longer but the black was dominant. His grin was totally Sword normal. ''As they say, the announcement of my demise was premature. Stick around, we got to talk about it.'' He turned back to the trans. *''Hercules?''*

Empty crackling. Finally, *''Captain doesn't like it. They've enough picks there to cause us trouble already. Will you clarify?''*

Moke leaned over his shoulder. ''We need the aliens out of their base to reach the prisoners, they're well dug in. They've a festival planned for after the landing when we can hope the base will be nearly empty. It's then or never. We can't take the base by direct assault, there are too many. You have to stand off or we won't get the chance.''

''But we're going to need a fast pick-up immediately after,'' Sword added. ''Our entry's liable to put the cat among the pigeons. Tell the Captain you can help us, we'll stay in contact. But we need the time.''

The next pause was longer.

''Okay, the Captain agrees. But forty-eight hours is the limit, after that we're coming in bombing. Alert your people, we want you off before that. Acknowledge.'' Another little silence. *''I've a query from Evander. Did you ever meet up with Faber and Blaine?''*

Sword laughed. ''Since they've devoted their lives

to driving me crazy, how would I avoid it? Entire human mission present and correct, plus we've recovered my dog-kid. Hope to have the rest here, day after tomorrow. Thank Evander for her concern, it's appreciated. Captain's message received and acknowledged. We'll try to be ready for you. See you later, guys. Take care.''

The interspace hitch. "Hercules *to ground-base, I copy. Best of luck. Over and out.*''

"Yes, okay," Hallway said. "This I want to hear."

Sword took another swallow of delicious hot prote and patted Dribble's head. The little brute was slavering all over his knees like the Day the Earth Failed to Catch Fire. He was being elaborately relaxed.

"Well, it's kind of complex. Cass caught this alien protein . . .''

"Which brings the dead to life. She has a big future."

"Don't be half-witted, I wasn't very dead. If you're in doubt, try blowing my head off. Not that it isn't going to be harder, next time," he added, his eyes dreamy.

"What kind of alien protein?"

"A symbiote, like the lady said. But not the kind comes out in green fur."

"I suppose that's something. What *does* it do?"

"I don't know, Bro. What's the whole question. What *does* it do? One thing it's done, apart from reviving the moribund, is given Cass data. Which we're all going to use, if you ever mean to make an honest woman of my sister."

Hallway flushed under his freckles. "I'd never noticed Miss DeLorn needed it."

"You hadn't noticed she needed you? You have to

be the last. I'll leave the two of you to sort it out between you, after we have her. Right now it's the having
that's the problem. You'd better listen to Cass, she has
the dirt.''

"I'm listening," Hallway said grimly.

"There are eight of them left," I said. "Three kids.
Sorry, one got dissected. There was another guy who
died. One of the Marines, woman, is hurt bad, you
gonna have trouble with the transport. They're none of
them in good shape, the air and the prote disagree with
them. But at least one guy's competent and I left him
my laser. I'd say access is possible by grav-pack,
planks are more doubtful 'cause Drib's right, the shafts
are nearly vertical. Getting out's going to be the problem.''

"There is a freight-lift," Moke said unexpectedly.

I glanced at him, surprised. He lifted an eyebrow.

"I'd hoped there was," Sword said. "That would
solve it, if we can find it. Cass has passed on her symbiote to at least some of them so we could have co-
operation.''

"I don't know," I said doubtfully. "I can communicate with Moke. Less with you. Maybe it depends on
who gets it.''

"You've been linked to me for nearly thirty-six
hours, Cass," Moke said mildly. "Considering how
short a time Sword's had, I'd say you must have a
degree of empathy.''

Yell grinned. Hallway didn't. "And what exactly has
Cassandra in mind as a plan?''

"I haven't. Mokey has.''

"Try trusting the boy for once, guy. Been doing it
myself for years. What do we have on the ship in the
comm line? He's going to need it tomorrow. As are
you. And make him eat, Yell, will you? He just gave

me everything again. He does it at least once a year,
for exercise.''

Mokey looked thoughtful. He'd forgotten to swallow
again, which is the sure sign of an attack of muse. It's
why he needs Sword and me to live with when Yell's
out with Issa, if he doesn't have someone he's liable
to die of starvation.

"Right," he said vaguely. "I'll show you tomorrow.
I'm going to need you guys up in the Egg, you'll have
to figure how to get there. I'll tell you what we need
and Yell can help us pack it over. It's all in your line,
Hall, I'll fix my own. Cass and Sword are going to
help me."

Hallway shrugged. He was still pale. "Just give me
the list. Since we're dealing in miracles."

"Not miracles," Sword said patiently, "alien prote.
It's lucky we don't react the way Geeks do."

—*Hmm,* said my unvoice.

—**What the hell does "Hmm" mean?**

—*Hmm,* Sword echoed.

"Four packs," Hallway said doubtfully. "You and I can carry weight, and maybe Moke, but Cass won't get far with a load. And the units aren't made for more than one person."

"Plus the emissions. Plain's full and more coming from the outstations. We could meet flyboys and they'll be harder, especially if they come in sunwise. Nope. Two, you and Yell. He's had the practice and he's handy in a hotspot. You can carry most of it between you. We'll bring the rest."

"And how are you getting there?" He looked at Sword suspiciously.

"Oh." Sword has these casual moments. They send shivers up sensitive spines. "Why don't we meet you?"

"It's five miles."

"Then you'd better start packing."

"If you pass out again," Hall said flatly, "Moke and Cass can't carry you."

"I won't." Sword showed perfect enamel. "Let's go."

Hallway wrinkled his brow but he went back to hauling gear out of the hopper onto a sled. Yell caught it as it came down.

"Pass the cutter, boss-man. If you and Cass'll take the cams . . ."

"Yeah, sure," Moke said. It was his working voice, vague and preoccupied. "Don't know if we need the cutter. Don't want emissions, they're sensitive. And it could be wasted weight. Let's see what we can do without."

Sword squinted at it. "Big sucker."

"I know. But there's three of us. If we've really all day . . ."

"Cass had her arms around Drib last night."

"No," I said hastily. "He's a genetic mute already, complicates things. He can look after the trans, we don't want the Navy missing us and sending a couple destroyers in to look. I think all day. Or a lot of it."

"Okay. You're giving orders, guy."

"Never done this," Mokey said, mildly pleased. "Going to be an interesting problem."

That's what pleases Moke. The kind of problems other people don't start.

The plain was like a fairground. Or maybe one of those paintings of battlefields where the place is a nice even green with little round pavilions with pointy flags. Except ours was yellow and short on guys rubbing up shields. There was plenty of movement, though. Fairy rings of huts with toadstools spiring from one to the other. Visiting, maybe. They seemed to stretch as far

as you could see, right out of sight around the slope of
the crater. A design on a carpet.

—*You're sure they won't come up to the egg to do
some dusting?*

—*Yes. The gum's anti-static, it doesn't attract particles and the temple's out of bounds except for cere-
monies.*

—No engineers checking out the grav-units?
Sword said.

—*I believe there's a service-passage leading in below the platform. If someone comes through you'll see
them, but it's monitored from the base. They don't let
things go wrong in front of Clans Major.*

—I don't suppose they're monitoring now?

—*Not that I can detect.*

—You're always very sure.

—*I should be. I've been observing mentally since
the day they came.*

—*In stasis?* I asked.

—*Stasis prevents me from moving or developing. It
doesn't prevent me from being aware of the presence
of minds. I was aware of yours.*

—I scarcely care to ask if you encouraged Cassandra to fall in.

Silence. *She was exhausted.*

— I see. I was afraid maybe he did.

—*The installation was verified maybe a week ago,
though it didn't need it. They haven't your neurotic
doubts about technology. They're not likely to come
back before the ceremony next twenty-days.*

—Our doubts are rarely neurotic, Sword said.
Damn stuff goes wrong.

—*Then I expressed myself badly. It doesn't occur to
them it may go wrong, perhaps because they don't use
it much.*

—*That's really neurotic,* I said.

—*I suppose so. They see it as magic. The magic of the ancestors.*

—You mean they don't understand it. Mokey said.

—*They can repair it. The procedures are ritual. A new fault might bother them, it would be disorderly. They don't invent anything, either.*

—Hope you're right. We're depending on that, said Swordfish.

We were slipping down cliffs like water while we had this illuminating conversation. Hopping rocks heel and toe like something dreamed up on a midsummer night didn't seem to bother him. I guess he's spent so much of his life doing the impossible he takes it for granted. I don't, I was still terrified.

—*Awful lot of guys there.*

—And sprightly with it, Sword added.

—*Right. Sprighting around like all get out.*

—*That's exactly why you're getting across safely. Their movements are keeping the vegetation so disturbed they won't see your ripples.*

—Let's hope they don't look at the sky.

We all did, reflexively. Yell and Hallway with the grav-packs were loaded like donkeys and carrying a net of Hall's gear between them. You can miniaturize all you want but you can't get an effective properly shielded long-term battery with big output that goes in your pocket. They were keeping sunwards, but flying was risky. If anyone showed it was going to be them.

—How are the auroras in this part of the world? he asked.

—*Rare, in daylight. But meteorological phenomena take odd turns.*

—Fine.

I was getting used to the idea our sky-blue figures didn't show to toadstools but they sure as hell showed to me. Our shadows moved too in the rising daylight, but ruffled plush ran off in so many directions our outlines got lost in the waves. So far so good, as the guy said.

The yellow rug flowed past us, twitching fur flying under our feet, the nearest ring of tents rushing up like one of those tridee pictures where meteors crash on your head. Instant grue. Sword spun to miss the outer perimeter and did an incredible jink sideways as a medium-sized primrose with an electrical aura like a lighthouse swirled up from behind.

My own feet rose reflexively and carried me five yards into the air, right over the rainbow and into the middle of the camp. Spinning auras buzzed around me.

—Oh, God, Sword groaned. *Can't someone keep her in line?*

—*Wasn't my fault. Damn symb was showing off. Will somebody get me out of here?*

But I was on my own way out, leaping and swerving. A beehive dome passed under my bootsoles and I came out the other side to catch Moke and Sword between circles.

—*I thought it might be a good idea. You're most visible in the open. Try it yourselves, it distracts attention.*

—*It distracts mine, but I've a nervous disposition.*

—*Like his old man. Shaky as Mount Rushmore. Mount Rushmore hasn't lived ten years with you.* Moke glanced up. Oh. I was afraid of that.

We followed his pointed mask. The double white flare of gravpacks was cutting the sky to the east, headed for the blood-colored disk rising above the misty jungle on the first leg of a curve that would take them around the camp and into the Egg from the side. And the leading edge of the latest pack of beer-caps glinted off behind them, small sparkling hyphens just lifting out of vapor.

—*Damn. They're between our guys and the sun.*

—*Had to happen sometime.* Sword sounded philosophical. *Cover me, Mokey. Got another present from the Navy.*

—*I hope it isn't as destructive as the last.* Softhearted Moke.

But he moved up front to let Sword get into his kangaroo behind the cooled screen of the Moke back. That was a considerable bulge and I'd had my eye on it. I'd been betting on something sonic. What came out was a flare pistol.

—*They're going to believe in that the way I believe in the tooth fairy.*

—*In what? Don't move your hands or feet, Moke, this is fast and hot.*

—*Shift it, you guys, your shadows are showing.*

—*Ten seconds.*

He probably took fifteen. He dropped to a crouch to hold the fat barrel over his head and let go three fast shots at the zenith. They flashed up with a triple soft crump that would have had a human crowd stopped in their tracks. The mushrooms didn't even pause. Their voices came to us high and sweet, a crystal chime like glass plates tinkling far away. Then Sword was up and running, the pistol out of sight, and Moke and I were flying after him.

White sheet lightning broke over our heads, a soundless explosion of sky-wide brilliance that flattened our shadows and caught every toadstool in mid-twirl. We cowered instinctively, even me. And I'd known

something was on its way. My feet didn't, they kept
right on breaking the sound barrier like the Red Shoes,
with me inside trying to keep up. We slalomed through
vibrating auras in an ear-breaking twitter of cheeps,
their anxious filaments searching the sky.

Another sheet followed, and a third. We cowered
every time. By the time my vision came back to normal
we were most of the way over the plain and the sun
was ringed by a fantastic corona of solar rainbows that
arced across the visible sky and must have been in sight
almost to the poles.

—*Gee,* I said. *Could you do that again?*

—*Yes. But I'd rather not, natural phenomena
aren't normally as unnatural as all that.*

—Aren't they going to find this unusual?

—*You haven't got it, Mokey. They will but they
won't think it's technology because they aren't
technological. A society in decay. Believing in
magic because it's easier. They haven't been here
long. We've had the odd surprise ourselves on the
frontier.*

—*Some of you even thought it was magic.*

—*True. But as a race we know we're irrational.*

—*Only rationally.*

—*That's exactly what I mean.*

We dodged the last of the hut-rings and came out in
the clear zone leading up to the Egg. Sword's solar
effects were still in florescence and the big swirlers that
gyred around the pavilions all had their filaments
turned the one way. Away from us. We spurted into
the open and set off across before our flying shadows
and the rings of fur that avoided our feet could attract
attention. Their chiming voices ran up and down agi-
tated scales. But there was another sound coming from
the hives behind, one I'd been hearing without regis-

tering all the way. A sort of swift lilting chatter like a lot of very small voices trying themselves out in uncontrolled rilling at a slightly lower register. A sort of supersonic contralto.

—*They have overripe seed-bearers too.*

—*They gotta be going out of their minds.*

—*They're unhappy. They'll be relieved when the Clans Major arrive.*

—*Suppose the big guys haven't waited?*

—*It's more likely they have. Taking part in a big ceremonial. It impresses the populace. And they're celebrating a triumph.*

—Right, they put one over on the enemy.

—*The poor mutts. Gimme a hand, this cam's sticking in my belly.*

—I'm rather sorry for them myself.

—I'm sorry for anything comes in contact with humans.

—*You're sorry for everyone.*

—Somebody's got to be, with you guys.

—*Nice Mokey.*

We stood on the edge of the platform and looked over the country. The rainbows were fading slowly and the camp was getting back to routine, though there was still a lot of stretching and vibrating of tendrils among the toadstools. The personnel-shaft entrance was down and a group of pastel caps boiled out with glitter in their threads to scope the zenith.

—*What your emtrails like, Sword?*

—What? Freak thunderstorm, could happen to anyone.

The falling wings of two blue guys plus net caught up at the same moment. ''What the hell was that?'' Yell gasped, letting down his end of the glass of the bandstand. "Saved our asses, though. Saw those guys too late."

"A freak thunderstorm. Ask Swordfish." I hefted the cam over my shoulder. "Let's get in there, I feel nervous."

"Not as nervous as I felt when the sky went out. You couldn't yell 'Fore' or something next time, huh?"

"Find me a mountain and I'll practice yodeling."

"You got here fast," Hallway said. "I thought we'd be waiting."

"Yeah, we jogged," Sword said deadpan. He moved off into the arches and we followed, bumping and jangling. I hoped the jellyfish meant to stay away till curtain up.

"What is this?" Hallway asked as we passed through the labyrinth into the inner layers.

We'd last seen it in the afternoon. Now early sun fell on the eastern side leaving the west and apex in shadow. Lines of fire burned off the edges of the outer columns but the light in the depths was dim and the arches glowed with pulsing colors as if something alive was breathing inside. It was as solemn as a cathedral window. The rising curve of roof blazed between rings of lace, throwing opalescent light on the glass.

"A cult center?" Moke said mildly.

"A temple."

"You could probably say that."

"Hard to say how they see it," Sword remarked, even more mildly. "You can't guess how people so unlike us feel."

"It's where they worship the great god Me," I said violently. They all looked at me.

"A lot of religions start out automorphic," Sword

said. Milder and milder, it was sinister. "I mean the gods are people. It doesn't stop them rising to mysticism. The person turns into a symbol."

"I'm not sure these people have a Me," Mokey said, considering. "They have an Us, maybe. If the construct means anything religious I'd say it was a symbol of the group-as-personality. If you can make guesses, as Sword says."

"And we're here to profane it."

That explained the temperateness of the climate. Trust Hall to get bad feelings. It's the Luney in him.

Yell looked back over his shoulder. "I got an idea. Fuck 'em. They killed our kids. They broke down our chapel and tore the priest apart at the alter. I ain't religious much, but I got opinions. Like fuck 'em."

"They couldn't know what it was." That from Hallway.

"Didn't care, you ask me."

"You're a street pagan, Cass. I don't hold it against you, it's a kind of honesty, but you are."

"Thanks."

"But we don't have to descend to their level."

"But we do, Hall," Sword said. "I've never set up as a deliberate vandal"—this from one of the Galaxy's most destructive animals—"but we need a diversion, to get them away from the base while we get the prisoners out. I'd do it for that reason alone. My charity starts at home, roughly in the area of my sister, and Dribble, and Chan's children and whoever else of my kind's down there. And—"

"Buildings aren't the most important things people have," Moke finished. "The construct will hurt, I think, but it's minor. The big damage is done already."

Hallway stood still. "Like what?"

Sword caught his elbow. "Fuck it, do you care or

not? Come on, Teen. We've work to do.''

"Cassandra. It was you. What have you done?"

I got defensive, fast. "Listen, these guys are breeding themselves out of existence, their society's decaying, their gene-pool isn't worth a damn and they're going to overrun us before they extinct themselves just because they've no self-control. I'm on Sword's side. You didn't see the Marine who hasn't any skin left because she tried to stop them taking a kid away to dissect.'' And he didn't see what was left after they'd finished, either.

His blue mask looked at the floor. "They don't understand,'' he murmured stubbornly.

"I don't expect they do,'' Moke agreed, in the voice goes with his tomahawk face. Implacable. "But maybe they ought to.''

Never cross an idealist. They're kind of hard to rouse, but they're the world's nastiest beasties if you do. Nobody spreads fire and sword like a really sincere pacifist on the warpath. I could feel Swordfish slanting eyebrows behind his hood. Spreading fire and sword's his business but he does it professionally. Moke's always surprising both of us.

The center of the maze was in deep shadow with a luminous skin over our heads like the surface of water. Under it Super-Toad revolved in its turnip field like a marine jellyfish, its upper reaches drenched in showers of sparkle, the little crouching turnips humbly dull under its tips. The smallest of them was taller than I was. Hallway stopped again. I'd forgotten he'd never seen it.

"Right,'' Sword said. Pure battle-commander, he's had the practice. "If you get your gear over the humps there's space to screen you in the middle. Just don't for God's sake touch the thing, if we unbalance it I'm not Superman, I don't guarantee to pick it up.''

—He's as much chance as unbalancing the rock you're parked on. Don't worry about it.

—I hope not, Sword said. **We're going to climb all over it.**

—But I don't advise touching it grounded, it has a strong repellent charge. Watch yourselves.

''Hall, wear gloves.''

''Grandmother to you.''

Once he's started Hallway's professional. He and Yell grabbed the handles of their net and lofted it over the turnips into the center of the field. They kicked and floated a bit until he'd got it neutralized and then they squatted while he got his surgeon's gloves on.

''How is it?'' Sword called.

''Powerful, we're going to have to anchor our stuff down,'' his smothered voice came back. Sounded like he was in mid-operation already. ''Nice smooth floor, though. No difficulty with horizons.''

''Don't touch the tentacles, they kick like a mule. I'm not surprised this place is dust-free.''

''Uh-huh.''

A professional grunt. Busy. That left Sword, Moke and me. The Master of War grinned at us. **Okay, Babes, let's go.**

—How we get across there, fly? Hall and Yeller got the grav-packs.

—So fly.

—You forgot, **Cass,** Moke said.

I remembered one hard equatorial night's dream when I'd shoved my head and shoulders through a solid wall to lay my hands on people. Four feet up. **Yech. I hated that.**

—Then you're about to hate it some more. Up.

—That's my prince.

We rose lightly over the heads of the turnips and started for the summit. First ascent of the Big Toad. Yell raised a startled face for a moment, and went back to unloading. Maybe his friends' symbiotes did queer things too. Hallway kept his head grimly averted.

—*How do we do it?*

—*Molecular repulsion. Works better if you don't ask questions. Ever wondered how you manage to walk?*

—Have you wondered where our friend comes from? Moke remarked.

—*Out there. You wouldn't know it.*

—*I never bother to ask, Why me? No one ever answers.*

—*I told you, we need each other. Let's say, my last host died. Long ago. I've been in stasis a long time. My abilities are contingent.*

—On finding a suitable brain, I suppose, Moke supplied.

—*With a suitable nervous system, in suitable protein.*

—Does that mean there are more—hosts—out there?

—*Perhaps. I've lost touch. It was a very long time.*

—And what are our chances of getting rid of you?

—*When you've used me enough?* It sounded ironic. *Nil. We're one. Be grateful, I'm keeping you alive.*

—*I'm grateful,* Sword said. He sounded ironic too. *I just like to know my parameters.*

—*You'll discover them. In time.*

—Like molecular repulsion.

—*I find it hellish repulsive myself,* I said.

—Shut up and dig, or I'll repel you to the ceiling.

—*I bet Charming never said that to Cinderella.*

*—Yes, he did. They lived happily ever after,
didn't they?*

—I always wondered what that meant.

—It meant he was bigger.

—Phallocratic dogdirt.

—But tall with it.

That's true too. I peeled my gloves and scrunched
my knuckles. There was a hell of a lot of plastic under
us, it seemed to stretch for acres.

—You sure we can do this by hand, Mokey?
Sword asked.

—Yup. It's going to look like this.

—Oh. I looked at the graphic on the inside of my
eyes. *If you patent the process we can all become
millionaires and the slate industry'll go out of business.*

*—This will be news to you, but I'm a millionaire
already and the slate industry belongs to one of
my uncles. Neat trick, though.* Aristocratic trash.

—Always wondered how he saw things, I reflected
audibly.

—You should get it on tape, Moke.

—I'd rather get it in plastic. It's what I do.

In his case he's right. But it was one hell of a visual.
I started on the bit in front of me, waiting for it to bite.
It didn't. It smeared. Like spreading butter.

—Hey, I've done this before.

—That's how I knew it could be done, Moke said.

—So do it some more.

The stuff almost flowed, like it found our touch repulsive. The visual hung over it like a mold and it
seemed to run in on its own. Moke hung absently in
midair doing the twiddles in person. He's one hot twid-
dler.

"Yell, gonna need you here, we got to animate."

"Okay, boss. But don't know about you guys, I'm leaving emtrails all over. Can they see them?"

"Not where you are. And we haven't started on the garden. We don't leave trails, when we've finished nothing'll show anywhere."

The sun rose over the dome as the day went on, lighting the western arches and the huge opal roof, moving down the pillars toward the floor and touching the caps of the far-side turnips with green-gold reflections. An iris of concentrated fire spread over our heads.

"Be pretty here for a feast at midday," Yell said, glancing up. "What time we looking for action?"

"I'll be surprised if it's before twilight. That's when you saw the last one."

"They must have been showing initiative. Thought they were supposed to wait."

—*Desperation.*

—*Yeah, they looked desperate. Especially the vanillas.*

"Their vision's delicate," Moke said. "I imagine full sun's painful. Though they could have different timetables for social occasions."

"Whole point of ritual's repetition," Hall said from his surgery down below. "Isn't it?"

"Among humans."

"Unless it's Christmas," Yell said, passing tools. He was sitting astride a sheet of insulating foil on top of the cap, soldering reception-points. "Midday mass or something?"

—*Yeek.*

—*As far as I know it's a regular purge plus frills for the boss-men. They have high feast-days but I've no indication this is one.*

—*As far as you know.*

—Sometimes you just have to take a best guess.

—Where did I hear that last?

Mid-afternoon a frantic squeak cut into my head. Sword glanced up from the other side of the cap. *What?*

—Ships come in orbit, see on scope. Six big, move fast. I oughtta tell someone? Dribble had made it into the net.

—It's okay, pup, you just did. Don't panic, we'll handle it.

"Guess our bouquet of geniuses just got here," he called down. "Drib's seen them. Watch out for lighters landing, if they come in on grav you could get interference."

"Okay." Hallway didn't ask how we knew.

Mokey hadn't even looked up. He might have heard, but then he might not. When he's working you just can't tell.

The flare of landing passed over maybe two hours later and I turned and saw the ships come in. Five big transports, each large enough to be a troop-carrier. I saw them through plastic as insubstantial as mist that hazed the edges of my vision with pinky lace in backward layers against a sky like burning magnesium. I was beginning to wonder just how far this change was going to go.

—My God. There are a million.

—Only a handful. They're the Clans Major, they've the right to come in state.

Sword's articulated skeleton worked steadily on the other side of a transparent veil that was the cap, his even grin underlying concentrated lips. It was a weird effect, I could see the skeleton, the skin on top and the suit that covered them simultaneously and without the

least confusion. The one I looked at was a question of
focus.

He looked up and blinked. *Is that a parameter? I
hope these guys don't mean to cut up a prisoner
to while away the time.*

—*No. They'll want to look, but they won't begin
work until the purge is over. They're desperate, nobody
can concentrate for noise. I believed they'd wait, and
they have. Their gardens are the biggest and most developed, the whole base is going crazy.*

I seemed to hear it, a shrill glassy screaming like
every granule of rock on the plateau crying out together
in different tones at different wavelengths. Dissonant,
mindless. But with a growing pulsation beginning to
rhythm it underneath, working towards a maddening
beat.

—*They've let it go farther than usual, to the limit.
Couldn't be better. And your friends can protect themselves a little now, if they try.*

—*Is there any chance they can get out alone?*
Sword asked.

—*Not with that mesh of auras. And the children are
fragile, poisoned by bad food. You've got to go in for
them.*

—*So show us the way.*

—*It'll be open.*

"Are the prisoners safe?" Hallway asked tightly.

"We believe so. Hang in, guy."

His swift clever hands hadn't paused on the piece of
wiring he was fixing. Out on the pad the big ships had
been drawn down. I could see them falling into the
earth as a counterdraft of hot red air blasted out and
puffed in a swelling mushroom into the stratosphere.
A glitter of ice-germs crystallized and sprang across
the sky like a new galaxy, a nebula of thrown dust.

"Going to rain," Yell said.

"Quite hard," Sword agreed, admiring the pivoting joint of his wrist. "Could be a storm."

I was willing to bet on it.

We finished as the sun was falling, Yell and Hallway hopping the garden with their packs, the net folded, and Moke and I smoothing out traces where they'd hopped. Sword was collecting tools and checking connections up top. We'd all worked since dawn without a break and my belly was making noises. Nothing but changing sunlight had come into the dome, but the glassy shrilling below got less and less tolerable as it gathered into an endless beat like supersonic tomtoms.

Hall looked at us as we made the last hop and his face was impassive under the mask. He was sitting on something. Maybe Relia. Maybe his respect for other people's religions. Maybe us. He followed us out without speaking. Dribble was getting upset too, we could hear him squeaking and scratching himself back on the platform. Sword sent him a make-supper message. Nobody was going to be able to eat it when he was through but it shut down his jitters.

On the plain the yellow fur had had a nervous breakdown and died. Its withered corpse blew around in snuffy dust over scorched dirt. The dust couldn't agree with the toadstools either because they'd thrown up domes around their campsites, every ring shut inside its own bubble. We could hear the chittering through them. It made our journey home easier. Our two angels took off into sunset across the crater and the rest of us exercised leg-muscles over the ruins. It was a relief to run, I was cramped into knots.

When we drifted up the cliffside into shadow Dribble frisked out to meet us, dog tongue lolling, grinning as only a medium-sized shark can. His rump was doing its best to wag. It was brown again, the scars fading fast.

"I make you stew in pressure-can, I pour in vacuum," he squeaked proudly. "I know Cass-mama not eat otherwise. I make coffee in flask. You come back in now?"

Sword grinned at me. *Now you've got to.*

—Don't blame me if it gives me cramps.

We piled in and shed hoods and gloves, covering the floor with exhausted sprawl. I sniffed steam and decided to risk the bellyache. Yell and Hallway dropped like meteors out of the sun and slid over the rocky lip.

"Hey, come in," I yelled out of the tunnel. "We got food. White man share for small entry-fee."

Yell dumped his pack and kissed my cheek through the screen. "That do, or you want blood with it?"

"I'll settle for gravy. Come in, Hall, I feel like hugging everyone."

I did, too. I hadn't worked so hard since I grew into a lady, I ached all over and felt terrific. It was the disappearance of something. Maybe the Sword of Damocles.

He stiffarmed my charge with a flat glove. "I'm sorry, Cassandra, I'd rather not touch you."

"What?" I backed off, not believing it. Hell, I've known Hall almost as long as Sword and he's as good as my brother. "Okay, I'll wash. Right after supper."

He shook his head. "Not after supper, not ever." His honest eyes were troubled. "I'm sorry, Cass, it isn't personal. You didn't ask to fall into alien jelly. But I don't want to be mixed up with you and your symbiote, I've seen what it does."

"What does it do?" I said blankly. "It saved Sword's life."

"Did it?" His blue eyes were hard under sweated hair, his skin bad milk. "Is that really Sword? Or is it just some alien jelly moving my best friend's arms and legs and speaking with his voice?"

"Hall, you know it is. How could it not be? Sword's himself, you can't fake him."

"On the contrary. There's no way it can be. He's dead. I saw it, I tested. He was dead, so worn out he could never be put together. Not by me, not by the Navy doctors, not by the best specialist Razor could hire. Then he gets right up and comes in walking. Like he was when he was twenty. With all his color, smiling, running like a hurricane. The way you run. And the next I see he's floating in the air. I'm sorry, Cassandra, I don't recognize either one of you. And I won't touch you. Not now, not ever."

I backed away from him, seeing truth in his face. My own was breaking up. "I'll take a pan and eat next door," I mumbled. "Maybe un-Sword'll come with me."

"Cassie—"

I could see the hurt and it was real. But he couldn't touch me. And I couldn't stay and not be touchable. I grabbed the dish from Yell's hand and ran.

Sword came and sat with me after a while.

"It's okay," he said, putting his arm around me. "He's given so much for so long I can't grudge him. He gave me everything. I can forgive him in exchange."

"But he doesn't believe . . ."

"It's okay. He loves Relia and he'll marry her. That's what counts. It's all I want."

"The end of a life's friendship."

"We'll sort it out. The Moon's going to be the last to give in. You and I won't be welcome there, Cassie."

"It's as well I hate tunnels."

"Don't let it worry you. We'll go up any time you want."

"We will?"

"Sure. We can do anything, hadn't you noticed? They can't keep us out."

We sat in the growing darkness and looked out at the lights, while I leaned on his chest and wiped my face now and then with my sleeve. And listened to the steady beating of his heart under the bones of my temple. Sword's heart. His human heart.

The day felt like it was going on forever. I sat in our tent with Moke, and Hallway sat two walls away like something Rodin started to do and changed his mind about. He had his head in his hands as if it hurt. Sword sat on the floor opposite and talked plans as if nothing had happened. Like he wasn't some concoction of alien jelly. Like we all weren't, except Yell and Hallway. In anyone else it would have been spite, I could see Hall suffering through both walls. But the man just had his mind on the job. Yell shared our space and Drib shared theirs, and now and then one would carry food and messages between. But no sympathy.

—*Sword, you're a bastard.*
—*That's news?* he said.
—*You're hurting the guy.*
—*I can't help that, I'm in charge and I'm briefing. You guys get the Egg.*
—*Obviously. Do you want to liaise by radio ac-*

325

cording to regulations or shall we just talk?

—Spare me.

—*You're sure you're not really seven feet of alien jelly?*

—Wait until I've a free moment. I can show you things alien jelly never thought of.

—*I should hope not. It ought to have a little modest decency.*

—I wish you guys would shut up, Moke said. I know it's your after-breakfast scrap hour but I'm trying to calculate.

—*Is it only after breakfast? I've been here at least nine hours already.*

The patterned carpet below us was a ripple of uneasy movement. The ululations were so loud we could hear them on the mountain. Down where they were it had to be agonizing. Under and over and through them a shimmering vibration made the air and rock tremble, faintly, somewhere in their deep grain. I could almost see the wave-loops. They had a consistency and color, and interweaving of harmonic notes. The contralto pulsing made a dissonant counterpoint.

Urgent swirls broke out now and then among the wreaths, and died away in aimless coils. Groups spired off across the plain toward the personnel shafts that opened and closed like mouths and were swallowed, and more came up and went back to the huts. A layer of dirt floated above the ground, suspended, drifting around like smoke. It was like a hive getting ready to swarm.

—*They've respects to pay, it's a grand occasion. Some of them may never meet Clans Major again.* My private oracle.

—*I bet they're honored.*

—*Very probably. They're hierarchical. But they'd*

have to look as if they were anyway.

—Hey? A faint voice far away, like someone shouting from the bottom of a well. Is there somebody there? I keep hearing you. Who are you? Speak to me.

—*I'm Cassandra. Who are you?*

Pause. The voice seemed to collect its forces. Brady. Marine Sergeant Henry Brady. Was it you who came down? Where are you?

—*Hey, Henry. How are you guys?*

—Shaky. Very shaky. The big 'stools came last night and stood out here measuring us. They got auras like you never seen, like getting hit by a waterfall. The kids are at the end of their rope. You gotta help us. If you can. Otherwise me and Roz gonna try a breakout. The atmosphere down here's crazy, it's a madhouse, I think they're losing control. We're scared, doll.

—*No,* Sword's voice answered. *Keep still. They'll be leaving at twilight. Keep the kids quiet and don't do anything to stir the Geeks up. We want min guards. None would be ideal. Fake sick or something.*

—Don't need to fake, man. If you'll trade heads I'll have yours. But if we get sick they worry. Don't want 'em in, we're frazzled enough. I think Roz is on wave listening.

—*We're all listening,* a soft voice said. *Except Margaret, she's too weak. We need help to get out. Are there a lot of you? Three of us can carry ourselves but the children are frightened and Margaret's got to be lifted. I've a sense we're a long way down.*

—*Relia?*

—*Mac? You don't know how glad I am to hear you.*

—*Likewise, sis,* Sword said. *Stay cool, We'll get to you.*

—*At twilight?*

—*That's the message.*

—*How shall we know? We haven't known the time for days.*

—*You'll know. The whole pack's going to leave with the biggest noise yet. Hang in there.*

—*We'll expect you. How long?*

—*At least ten hours. It'll feel like a month but don't call too often, they could pick us up. We'll be in contact.*

—*Please come soon.*

—*Ten hours, kiddo.*

—*All our digitals have stopped.*

—It's the electrics, Henry said. You could run a power-station off these guys. Okay, people, radio silence. Hear from you, man.

—*Check. You'll know me.*

Hallway was still playing statue, his head still bent towards his knees, eyes turned on the floor. Maybe he was thinking about Aurelia. Maybe he was grieving for a brother who was only dead to him. Maybe I talk too much.

—*Shouldn't we tell Hall?*

—*He may not believe it. He's a scientist, Cass. He'll see for himself this evening.*

—*I guess we all will.*

A bigger than usual flurry had started among the nearer huts, three-quarters of a mile away. Sword grabbed the glasses. Skirls of dust rose above the tee-pees and something was struggling in the middle, sparks flying like a bonfire.

"What's going on?"

He handed me the binoculars. A wreath of medium-sized juveniles were lashing a bundle of the biggest vanillas I'd seen, green stumpy shapes that heaved and lumbered. They were obviously moving by themselves, in one big gelatinous lump like they were clumped for protection. Their sparkly beads tossed over humped caps and a continuous shrilling wavered up and down the scale in nerve-clawing frequencies. The raspberries looked as if they weren't destroying them, just slapping with their threads, trying to drive them back into a hut. The group swayed backward and forward, waving filaments outside, crystal strings whirling above. The vanillas were very high up, their caps lumpy, a kind of scuttering going on underneath.

"They're growing tentacles," Moke said softly. He didn't bother with the scope, his eyes were on me. I guess he'd taken to sharing my eyes, he has a visual mind. "And something else. Their caps aren't normal."

—Quite normal. But they don't often get to develop so far. Henry's right, the mobiles must be half-mad. Let's hope the Majors can keep them in check. This group's restraining itself but it's costing. Toward sundown things could get hectic.

—Thanks. We all feel better now.

"What's going on?" Hall called through the fabric. His voice was strained. He and Yell were beginning to be the only people not on-net. Difference was, I think Yell had figured it. Hall hadn't. Maybe he didn't want to.

"A scuffle," I yelled back. "The seed-bearers are getting lively."

"I wish they'd stop whatever it is, I've a devil of a headache."

It struck me that oddly enough, I hadn't. Again. I seemed to have become immune.

"Both sides shrieking their heads off. You using your resonator? Take a nalgy."

—*Only one side. The other's trying to go through ritual chants. The disturbance upsets them.*

"I wish you'd come take a look." He didn't want to use Sword's name. "That blip's back."

Yell and Sword both got up. Moke and I leaned on each other and used Sword.

"Uh-huh. Not one of theirs edge on?"

"I've been watching quarter of an hour. Profile's long, pointed. Theirs are moving too, looks like they're preparing something. All the ships in sight show movement. But this one's still moon-hopping. Thought I'd lost it, then it came back out by that minor irregular. Damn, it's gone."

"Yeah. Can't be serious, it's not big."

"You know of any Naval craft about?"

"Not unless *Hercules* sent an observer. I asked them not to."

"I wish they would," Hallway said. His voice was ragged. "We need them."

"We can't scare the Geeks, Teen. We've got to have the lot down here and occupied. It's one ship."

"If it is a ship," Yell said. "Said last time it might be an echo."

I could feel Sword considering. "Yeah, it could be an echo."

If he believed that I was a gilded crocodile.

The picks in orbit were getting their lighters ready for entry, because shortly afterwards the first flight ripped into atmosphere and whistled down. After that they arrived every hour throughout the day. The crews still up, if any, had to be the skeletons of skeletons. I wondered where they were putting them, down in the base. The last flight late afternoon got left on the pad. By then nothing in the Geek camp was civilized any more.

And the sun was falling.

We did the dust-slalom across a weirdly deserted plain as the shadows under the crater began to darken. The villages were quiet, movement battened down, though a teeth-drilling chatter bored on in the upper reaches of hearing. It was the quietest trip yet, nothing in sight.

Yell and Hallway had taken Dribble the long way around over the eroded bowl behind the Egg and the white trails of their packs had vanished below the skyline. Hall and Dribble had the nerviest part of the job, waiting by the shaft under the cone for the base to empty and hoping their suits were really cool. Moke and me waited for Yell to get over the rim and through the dust towards us.

"Okay?" Sword said. "Remember you're an artist, Moke, don't do anything I would. I want you guys alive. Don't know I can spare Yell either, now I've really tried his prote. If any of you figures out how to get ten guys, three children and a dog into two tents while you're waiting, send me a postcard. See you."

And he was gone.

"Acts real human sometimes, for alien jelly."

"Hall's sick, Cass. He loved Sword and he's known him most of his life. He saw him die. And Aurelia's in there. He can't even talk to her, he hasn't your senses."

"Won't have."

"He's a cool hand in a crisis," Yell said. "It'll be okay."

"I wish there were more than three. With one kid and the third that doesn't trust his leader."

"And one of them Swordfish," Moke said. "Come on, Andromeda. Let's go face the monster."

We walked into the dim cavern of the Egg, threading through pillars that seemed to have an inner glow as if the last of the sunset was trapped inside and burning quietly like a red-shaded lamp. Yell's padding soles echoed softly among the lace, running away in little rills of musical patter as the arches vibrated in unison. Moke and I drifted silently.

It was as we'd left it. Hallway's holo equipment was running without a sound, the images stirring in a slow liquid dance. Even close up it was hard to see the seams and we knew they were there. They'd have the show by torchlight.

"Give me a hand?" Yell said. He had the pack slung over a shoulder by half its harness, straps dangling. It was a weight he mightn't need, but we didn't know how hard getting out might be. " 'F I hop I leave an emtrail."

I glanced at Moke. I hadn't thought of that. Yell's as tall as Mokey but he carries more bone, before you count his gear.

"Yup," Moke said. "Hand each. Come on, Cass, it's confidence. Like riding a bike."

"I fall off bikes."

But I took an arm on principle and we rose easily over the field and made a soft landing in the grav-space beyond.

"Oops," Yell said. His voice spun off the roof in distorted ripples. We hadn't noticed sound effects in daylight, maybe it was something that came out at night. "Hall put a neut down around here someplace, stop us going through the roof while we worked. We better find it, or they going to see interesting shadows going up and down like plastic divers.''

''Here.'' Moke has an instinct for machines, call it brother-love. They're like Drib, he thinks they're people.

We got our feet on the neutralizer and had just about enough room to stand, the flat control-box of the holo gear molded onto the back of the innermost turnip showing a comforting red LED in front of us.

''Okay, guys,'' Yell said. ''Popcorn, ice-sticks, soda? It's showtime.''

We sat on the mat like the Three Wise Monkeys, knees drawn up to avoid the field, and watched the dome darken to full black. I could see the night through it, but it still hung like a translucent veil and the pillars kept their internal fire. They rippled a little from time to time, up and down, as if there was a real flame in there, burning. The Egg was silent. Moke and I squeezed hands. Yell's spine was solid against my shoulders. None of us spoke.

—*Here they come, lid's going down.* Sword on net from their place on the plain. *There have to be hundreds, gardens must be in full fecundation. Give them their show, kids, we need half an hour, probably longer.*

—There are guards, Henry's quiet growl said. Can see four from here. These guys talk to each other, even when they aren't here. I been hearing 'em. If we move they call the whole battalion.

—*It's taken care of, we hope. Biggest danger's if they panic. If there's a surge, cut your way out and take to the roof, their auras do the most damage. Keep a hold on the kids.*

—*We'll manage, Mac,* Aurelia said. The voices

came over loud and clear through Sword's conscious-
ness and I was getting to feel which of them was who.
**You're really coming? Margaret wants to get
up.**

*—Stop her, she'll need her energy later. Half an
hour, maybe. Got to let the shaft clear. They're
leaving now.*

I could see it as if I was there looking out of his
eyes. The open lid had sunk out of sight and the mouth
of the shaft was the head of a Roman candle spewing
colored lights. Then the wreaths got organized and began to twirl in braids and garlands. Dark clots blotted
the stream, blocking the tunnel now and then until they
were shot out like difficult corks and broke into lumpy
masses that dropped pieces as they fell. Whipping tentacles flashed like tinsel. Shards of jelly and gushes of
juice spurted behind them and an ear-breaking cataract
of shrieks mingled with the clear vibration of singing
raspberries. The vanillas' skirts dropped nodules of
half-formed young and the river of tentacles crushed
them in the dust until the plain was a mush of dead fur
and trampled jelly.

More lights began to show over the hump of the
cone. More garlands, there had to be whole clones
joined by their streamers. Bobbling caps staggered in
the middle with their roots scrabbling the dirt, and fell
over and got scummed to jelly under the mob. The air
hummed until the skin of the planet seemed ready to
crack and harsh ear-shredding squeals grated at right
angles. If you're a toadstool, ritual chanting could have
its problems.

—Thousands. Hallway's voice as heard by Sword
was white.

—Three or four. More the better if we want a

*good riot. Especially in an enclosed space. Let 'em
get in.*

Dribble said nothing but I could feel him shivering.

—*Know the way, pup?*

—**Think so. Must have leave smell.** Little bastard
pees wherever he goes.

—*Okay. Leave more as we go so we find our
way out.*

—**We come back same way?**

—*I want the freight elevator, it's over here. Take
too long to carry eight people up the shaft. We'll
need to get clear fast.*

—**I find it.**

—Think I've located the freight-shaft,
Henry said. He was husky. Been listening. Not
clear, but I've kind of pictures. I'll try to take
you.

—*Great. If we don't make it, take yourselves.*

—**We'll carry the kids,** Beth said. It felt
like Beth. **Me, Relia and Roz, one kid each.
Henry can probably manage Margaret. She
can't walk but she can hang on.**

—*Don't move yet, you may not have to. Give us
time.*

Time. The light of torches was coming up the slope,
streams converging from three or four directions. The
pillars shone. Rainbow glimmers ran through the shell
as if the plastic was in tune with the vibrations. The
lace pendants looked like they were moving, blowing
like cobwebs. I shivered.

''Pretty,'' Yell whispered.

Moke's face, gaunt under his mask, was enthralled.
Beautiful. I wonder if there's any way to imitate . . .
With preformed plastics you could just . . .

—*Martin, if you reach for a slate right this minute*

I'm going to kill you where you sit. Don't you know I'm scared silly?

He turned me a startled look and gave my hand a fresh squeeze. So'm I, Cass. Just reflecting.

"He's thinking about sculpture," Yell diagnosed. "Guy's consistent."

"It's the least you can say."

"Was trying for the least."

I hoped that didn't mean he was scared too. Me, I wasn't safe in my panties.

The torchlight wound in and out around the arches, they had to be coming from all sides. I glanced at Big Toad. It looked normal. To me. I hoped they thought the same. Then the first came out into the open and I cowered.

We'd never seen Clans Major. But Big Toad had a model, the first were fifteen feet high and looked like they were wearing coats of lightning. It took me a second to see it was their auras, so wide and bright they seemed to be twirling in bells of luminous glass. The edges of their fields trailed off in mist, but surprisingly sharp. As if the bell was slightly steamed up. The fields reached at least five feet each side of the cap and four above the apex and right to the floor as if they were slid. We weren't the only ones who didn't like them. The juveniles stayed a safe distance too, nobody fool enough to get closer than two yards. The guys who'd the honor of being nearest had to have headaches worse than death. Clumps of turnips floundered beside them, squealing so shrilly I put my hands over my ears and my head between my knees.

—Help. Do something.

Moke hastily switched in the resonator. Sorry. Better?

I lifted a careful nose. The guys were pale and Yell had a hand over his mouth.

"You okay, mec?"

He nodded, swallowing. "Noisy."

"Like killing the pig."

We were mouthing silently, though God knows we could've screamed like banshees and no one would have noticed. My ears had come right and the racket was only painful.

"Look at those," Moke whispered.

The major turnips were as major as their owners. The biggest was as tall as a juvenile and their screams were low enough to be human-audible. A few had tentacles fined and pointed until they were almost as long and delicate as the raspberries' and they scuttered just above the floor. Their caps had heavy developments of snake among the beads and the beads themselves were running together into long threads like stunted filaments. They used them to hold their nubbles on, some almost gathered into armfuls.

"Omigod. They're trying to protect them."

"You can't know that, Cass."

"I can feel it."

"No doubt they're the same race," Moke shaped. "Arrested development?"

—*I think the opposite,* Sword said in the depths. *They're advanced. They weed out the ones who turn sentient.*

I could feel him falling into the shaft, Dribble clutching his hand in a shovel-nailed paw and Hallway's blue-white reaction-trail drifting behind them.

—*There are more down there,* he said, *the ones they left. Almost every garden's moving.*

—*Shit. Are the vanillas dangerous too?*

—We're about to find out. They don't have auras.

—They're developing.

They were. Faint, but showing pale halos around the green caps. The nearest juveniles were pushing them away, lashing furiously at the halos that burned brightest.

—I don't think the raspberries like them.

—Could be their thoughts are critical.

—Sword—

—We have to save our own first, Cass. He's always understood me. *This has been going on for millennia. Maybe our ways look revolting to them.*

—They used to look pretty revolting to me.

—It's a question of distance.

His own had just narrowed to the shaft bottom, where an expanse of churned sand led off either way.

—Okay, Drib, make with the nose.

Snuffling pause. **Toad stink all over. This way.**

I'd have gone the other, but he was leading. They loped off down the corridor. I glimpsed shuffling gelatinous masses.

—Holy shit. When you said moving you meant it.

—Yeah, Sword said. *Big brothers haven't noticed yet. I think vanillas like us.*

—They wanted to do that to me, too.

The big shufflers were galumphing toward them, rubbing against their knees like dogs. Or that was how it looked. A flood of little nubbles crawled among the half-formed streamers, tumbling like puppies.

"What's going on?" Moke whispered.

"I don't know. I've never seen them move that young."

Yell was looking interrogative.

"The vanillas are moving in the shaft," Moke ex-

plained. "Including the babies. Or Cass thought so—
I'm not sure. I don't think the ones here can, they're
still vegetable. What did you do to the lot downstairs?"

"I touched them . . ."

"The Cassandra touch," Yell mouthed. "When do
we go?"

"Soon as Sword gets action."

Our congregation was still filing in. Moke's diag-
nosis was right, they filled as much of the dome as
they could and then piled around the edges. The huge
Majors filled the open space nearest Big Toad, maybe
sixteen gathered auras in a dense circle of changing
glare. The guys behind couldn't be seeing much but I
guess it's the price of rubbing auras with the mighty.
Juveniles and minor clans were packed in a boiling
mass behind, the Egg burning like a night at the opera.
The plastic had to be sensitive to them, the columns
had begun to fluoresce in the crackling charges and the
place might have been lit with neon.

The hum was getting louder and more regular,
maybe synchronizing frequencies, settling to a high
singing drone. The mass had slowed its rotation until
it was as slow as Old Toad, but Toad was doing the
opposite. Its spin speeded until it whizzed like a car-
ousel over our heads and the movement was squeezing
noise out of the cap. It started as a low whine, climbed
the scale as the construct speeded up and turned into a
drone of its own, high and clear, out-ringing the sound
of the audience.

"It's a musical top," Yell whispered. "Wonder if it
plays tunes?"

"It probably is. How're the guys?"

They were moving around one of the curved corridors, a rustling of tips following. When Sword glanced
back the passage was jammed as far as you could see

by a mass of mobile jelly, bead fringes whirling over their heads like summer lightning.

—**Nearly there,** Dribble snuffled. **Must meet guards soon.**

—*Action time,* Sword said.

Moke turned to me. "It's you, Cass."

"No."

Yell swung on the mat and grabbed my shoulders. "Cass, you got to. You're the only one who can."

"Why me?"

It's a useless question. I stood, took a couple of steps into the open and rose on the grav-field, drawn up in a spiral by Big Toad's currents. The pale roof swelled.

The vanillas were just being whipped into the arena in front of the rows, the first lashes falling on shrieking caps. Coiled tentacles gathered up armfuls of little nubbins into the shelter of parasols above. The drone was deafening. Hypnotizing themselves. They'd a wake-up coming.

I was cooled and the fast spin of the construct threw flashes of light that muddled my shadow, as good as invisible. The Majors screened me from the crowd behind, too busy chasing vanillas to look up. I angled in toward Toad's dome and found the standing-space Moke had left in the middle. It whirled me on my heels like a disco-dancer but the center was stable. I stayed upright. The whining skirts had to be heading for fifty. I lifted my arms.

Down in the labyrinth Sword came out in the lighter-bay and the first of the guards turned twirling toward him.

And Yell threw the switch on the projector.

The crowd spasmed in a single convulsion. Hall had been right to have doubts. I hadn't realized what sacrilege looks like. They stayed still for a long second-

count, even their spirals frozen. Then there was a wild
flare of auras and a long broken hoot of dismay. The
anguish came through even to me.

Toad had thinned and shrunk, slagged down toward
the size of a vanilla with a glittering bead-crown flashing around its cap. And the forest of nubby turnips had
begun to rise all around, taking shape and fining into
slender-tentacled floaters with snaky domes that
writhed slowly and tinsel filaments mixed into the
flashing beads. They grew and grew until they were
almost as tall as Toad itself, a grove of young trees
arching like willows, their tendrils curving, reaching
out to touch the shrunken mushroom as if they were
sorry for it, posturing like dancers. Mokey'd made
some good guesses, his new-look vanillas weren't too
different from the developing screamers on the floor.

—The shield of Perseus, his voice said below with
calm abstraction. Medusa petrified everyone, including finally herself. It's a psychosis. If you turn
everyone else to stone you end by becoming stone
yourself. But turn the process around and maybe
they'll melt. Called evolution.

The magic mirror. And I spun in the middle, the
virus made flesh.

—*You have to will it,* the unvoice said. *It's you, I
can't carry it alone. Why do you think Moke or Yeller
wouldn't do?*

It didn't need to tell me. I was the only goddamned
bim in the place and bad stuff is what bims are made
for. The guys stand back and philosophize and look
disapproving, but if it smells, call in a woman. It lets
them look at us from higher up, the second sex. I shut
my eyes and screwed my brain. *That* way, the one
where your hand disappears in another dimension. Into
shape. I could feel leaves and stems running along my

arms, curling up my thighs, spiraling into tendrils above my head. My spread fingers branched in handfuls of stalks that uncoiled into buds.

In the lighter-bay the guards were buzzing together, staggering, some spinning for the cages, some headed for the intruders and the half-seen movement behind. Our guys were defined by their shadows and Hall's footprints had made trails in the sand. Henry was using my laser on plastic, pushing terrified child-bodies through the hole. His own broadcasting-system was improving, I could see through several sets of alternative eyes. Up on Toad's cap what I couldn't see was the floor, I couldn't see anything but leaves.

I breathed in and flung out my hands. Persephone lives underground, mistress of death. But in spring she's the sower. Of seeds, of stars, of stone. The flowers opened. Lemon-peel bells with powdery stamens spraying their pollen in streams. That blew out in circles, scattering the crowd. Crimson pollen, red as blood. Mine. My own cells, flying in handfuls from the centers of flowers that had been my flesh, pouring over the big Majors, spilling beyond them, carried further and further by the wind of the panic that had gotten hold of everything in sight. And melding with what they touched. The shield of Perseus, magic mirror. Look in it and change.

An underground sea of heaving caps broke from the red-lit passage and fell on the panic-stricken raspberries among the lighters. They didn't know what was wrong. They'd gotten the disaster message from their brothers in the Egg without knowing what had happened. But then, none of them did. How could they? Watch out, guys, the aliens are coming. Homo sapiens sapiens, the one creature in the whole dumb universe who never cares what the hell he's playing with.

Hallway was clasping Aurelia and Sword was snapping planks into shape for Margaret and the shivering kids. Big Henry lifted Beth and Roz down, laser in hand. When they were lined up he got a thought and turned it on the ranks of lighters behind him. Fire and smoke blossomed. Sword shoved the planks into motion and Dribble led the way, away from the mess into the other half of the maze. Coughing and laughing and crying, the loaded planks followed, Hallway holding Aurelia's hand in the rear. The surge of vanillas was headed for the far entry carrying staggering guards with them.

A mass of chaos boiled beneath me. I caught one glimpse of it as I fell, voided, into the force-field, withered shreds of stalk drifting into air behind. And the power cut out leaving the slowing top to whine down, just in time for Moke, rising, to catch what was left of me and carry it to the floor.

Swordfish was jogging down a luminous corridor with a child in his arms, guiding a plank in front of him with Margaret clutching the edge. The rags of her uniform barely covered her and her skin was pied with evil marks but her eyes were alert. Roz held one side. In front of them Henry's broad back hid most of his but it looked like it had Beth and the other two kids astride. Boys, so Sword's was little Chan. Seeing through Sword's eyes I saw what he saw, which limited my vision. Hall and Aurelia seemed to be behind. A smell of metallic burning chased them. His sight was different from mine which figures, he has modified eyes still. The place looked bright and blue. The constructs in open archways shone out of the dark in pale relief as they passed. Timid green caps peeped around the edges, half-grown fringes following the strangers. Brave new world.

—Cass. Get up, you haven't time for a nervous breakdown.

I wasn't sure if the voice was his or Moke's but it was urgent.

—Come on, doll, I need you.

—**Freight elevator,** *Dribble squeaked ahead.* **You make it work?**

I was getting them all like a vid-show over the net plus a backwash of tension and fear, except Hall who showed through other people's eyes. He didn't know how completely he was left out.

"Put my sister down and work for your living, Teen," *Sword said inside my ears.* "Or why did the Navy buy you an electronics degree?"

"Don't be nasty, Mac," *Aurelia said. She'd a hope. He's been nasty as long as I've known him. She was standing almost straight, Hall had to be the only guy she'd met apart from her brother she'd had to look up at.*

"Suppose it uses a sense we haven't got?"

"There aren't any senses Teen hasn't got," *Sword said.* "Not around electrics. Elsewhere he can be as dumb as your average dweeboid."

Oh. I've rarely met him sour, but that tasted of lemons. Having your lifetime brother decide you're an alien could just be annoying even to him.

Hallway pushed past with his eyes down and walked into the circle. The arc nearest them was missing. All that showed inside was sanded flooring and an arched roof. He unhooked his scope.

"I think there's a plate. But Miss DeLorn could be right, it isn't hand-operated . . ."

"Obviously. They haven't any hands." *Something was getting to him. Sword isn't impatient. But the noise behind was climbing to a crest.* "They don't do mira-

cles of telekinesis, it's electrical. Get on with it, Hall, or I may decide to prove you right by dissolving into a puddle of green gloop. Then you can get the rest of the way out by yourselves.''

Hallway turned a hurting look. ''I'm trying.''

Henry had the planks rounded up and he and Roz leaned on the wall. There was sweat on their faces. I'd forgotten it was hot in there as the inside of a volcano.

''Better sit on the floor, no telling what parts of this move. It's okay, baby, I was lying. I can't really turn into gloop. Give your Uncle Hall a kick where he keeps his brains, it's the bit nearest you.''

The little Chan had a stranglehold where most people have their carotids, which made anything bizarre more normal than she imagined. Hall was on his knees by her feet but she didn't accept. She tightened her sleeper on the guy who never sleeps.

''Don't listen, honey. My brother's a tease.'' I know a million guys wouldn't put it like that. The kid wasn't listening. She stuck her thumb in her mouth. At seven it's a bad sign. ''He'll get you back to Grandma.''

Superman. Hah. The elevator jerked, suddenly dropped a couple of feet, caught itself and began to circle up into the shaft.

''And Uncle Hall's a genius, all you got to do is chew his butt a little.'' He put the kid on the floor so as to steady Margaret's plank. They were getting a spin on as the rise speeded. **Cassandra. You've got to get up, you guys need out, now.**

—Cass, please. Come on.

That was Moke, and anguished. I saw splintered visions of a disappearing passage with white faces in red light and his superimposed, blue-masked and bony, outlined against an aurora of disturbed electricity. I shook my head and tried to sit.

"There's my princess." Yell grabbed a wrist and hauled. "Let's go."

"What's going on?"

"Panic," Moke said. "If they aren't clone-brothers their auras clash when they run into each other. I'd say protocol says the big guys leave first but somebody forgot. And the big guys themselves aren't all the same clone."

"Couldn't make way if they wanted," Yell said. "Packed in like sardines. They're electrocuting each other, doll. Let's get out before they start on us."

Blue lightnings flickered around the outline of Big Toad overhead and the garden was fluorescing green and yellow under its holo icing. Looked like the finer detail was starting to melt, but Moke hadn't had time to work for eternity. I got up on shaky knees, then shakier feet. My hair stood up and tried to poke holes in my hood and a ripple of sparks ran up and down my suit like a collapsing power-station.

"I don't feel good."

"Don't blame you. Genius says we go through the roof. He ain't explained how we're getting up there, but hang onto Ole Yell and I'll make encouraging noises."

"We need Sword for Cass," Moke said. "It's blood-loss, I can't replace it by myself. Give me your other hand, Cass, we got to make a circuit."

I gave it to him.

—Think lift, Cassie. It's all you got to do. Just don't pass out again. Not until we're outside.

Yeah, sure. All I had to do. I looked up at the dome, about five miles above. Or three hundred feet, which came to roughly the same. Think lift. Right. Lift, abracadabra and shazam.

We lifted. Me, Moke and Yeller in a ring like a set

of cute little Girl Scouts playing posies. If we kept on this way our Leader would organize us in some wholesome campfire singing.

I wished the available campfire wasn't the roasting integuments of shriveled floaters, wailing and thrashing in the super-audible as their muddled auras flashed and shorted all over the floor. The nearer arches were mounded with crisped bodies and a lot of lacework was melting, dripping tears onto the caps below. Jostling green nubbles pressed inside the ring nearest Toad, which was sagging. Their half-sentient clone-mothers clung in a twisted wall trying to keep them inside. They were right. With any luck they'd survive and carry away what I'd spent my blood on. And with a little more the big Majors would do the same by sheer selfishness, they'd almost certainly made the open. You could see the molten paths where they'd done it.

—Look up.

I did. The roof was only a yard or two above our heads, milky nacre shot with fever-gleams. Yell clung onto our hands, his teeth closed. Dim starlight shone beyond like glowworms through water. It had to be a yard thick.

—A bit less, I think. Maybe two feet. Their building techniques are formidable.

—*That's what they are, Moke. I'm formidded.*

—Raise your hand, Cass.

—*I did want to go . . .*

"How do we get through?" Yell asked beside me. "We ain't got the cutter. Dumb . . ."

"Just put your hand up."

My fingers touched the ceiling. Which parted like mist, and re-formed behind me. Two feet could be right. There were maybe eight seconds when my face was completely inside and I'd abstract thoughts about suffocation. Then my hand and head were in air and the rest followed, to the waist, the thighs, the knees. Like Venus rising on a shell. With tritons.

We stood on the summit hand in hand and gazed over the plain. The wailing was no different out here. Or maybe it was. The northern personnel-shaft gaped open and a mob of shapes danced on the rim. They didn't seem to be wailing at all. They ululated, trilling like birds. Finding their rhythm.

"Vanillas."

"From below?"

"Got to be, the new ones aren't developed yet."

"A hard birth."

"Doesn't sound it."

—*Why should it?* my unvoice said. *They're too new-born to know disaster. All their problems are in the future. I hope they're going to be able to cope.*

—*A whole circle of ribs. An Adam-umbrella.*

—*An Eve circus. This'll shake their society all the way down.*

—*A Medusa psychosis. Didn't you say that, Mokey?*

—A cure for one. They were petrified, they've altered like Toad. Could be painful. They all saw themselves in the mirror.

—*They were psycho before.*

—*Then they had shock-treatment. Go home, Cassandra. You're through here.*

—*I'm waiting for my guy.* I spend my life on it.

—*He's waiting for you. Go home.*

The ground was opening under the cone and a blank pupil of darkness widened in the dust. The iris rose to fill it, a pale ring blotted with dark shapes. It settled and the planks moved out, bobbling on the night drafts, alien straight-walking striders guiding from behind.

"They made it," Yell said with exultation. "Let's go get 'em, kids. This looks like a ski-slope, I bet you can slide all the way."

He let go to demonstrate and vanished in the dark, his pack-straps trailing. Moke wrapped an arm around my waist to stop me collecting another bruise, my legs didn't work right. It was good as flying. When we hit dust Yell was on his grav and cutting a line towards the walkers and Sword was waving in the distance. Moke took my weight most of the way, until our other half offered a hand to share with his Chan baby. Nobody noticed but the new vanillas, and they looked at us with polite surprise. The same way they were looking at the rest of the universe.

We weren't the only people being born from the waves tonight. They were learning young the world's a surprising place. Surprises me pretty often, too.

It took a couple of gravpack trips to get the planks up top but the guys weren't giving a damn for pyrotechnics. They'd no reason, the plain was a desert of wailing crossed now and then by skirling wreaths of vanillas up from the depths, come to look at the free sky.

It was more worthwhile than usual if you like fireworks, the Clans Major weren't showing true grit. The first of the big transports came swirling up on a pillow of light as we reached the scree at the cliff bottom and four more followed in bursts behind. Then a popping of smaller caps shooting out in series, headed out for their orbiting picks and a quick getaway. There weren't as many as there had been. I recollected good ol' Henry putting in some work with a laser. Those on the plain would have done best if their crews had been able to get back to them, but it looked like they'd gone

for their baggage and there was a problem with the
lower personnel-shaft. The kind that shoots columns of
smoke and flames. By the time the limping raspberries
had draggled out by another way a couple of wandering
vanilla wreaths had found the ships and tried what
pushing did. They found out. The guys weren't going
far until they'd got themselves a crane.

—*These guys just don't have your education,*
Sword.

—*The other side of a group mind, Cinders. If*
one's brave they're all brave. If one knows, they
all know. If one panics . . .

—You can't blame them. Anyone would have
panicked in there.

—*Not what I meant, Moke. The pick crews*
above were sharing their riot, I hate to think what
it's done for discipline.

—*And they're short on technology. They need to*
catch up on their history. If they'd been familiar with
holovisual techniques they'd have known what you
were up to right away.

—*It's my little friends' experience with the Terran*
film industry. It's corrupted their minds.

He got an arm under me and the other under the
little Chan and glided the cliff like he was climbing
stairs. Beth waited at the top to make the kid collection.
Hallway was half inside the hopper pulling on a folded
lump that collapsed all over him and turned into a survival tent. He dove back in and began to grub for its
pressure-unit. He didn't ask Sword to help. Sword
leaned in anyway, turned it out from a tangle of cook-
ing-gear—they must have been living in there like a
litter of puppies—and squatted to meld it on a corner.
Hall spread the tent over a flat piece of rock and held
it straight as it inflated. They didn't look at each other.

Beth had shoved the kids through the nearest tunnel as if she'd the energy, which basically she hadn't being floppy at the knees, but she solved it by crawling. I hoped someone might give her a medal but they probably wouldn't bother. Her body-count didn't rate it. Aurelia and Henry were working at edging Margaret through the other without spilling her off her plank. Dribble was pulling from inside, I hoped she survived them.

I sat on a pile of rock and felt the sky turning around and around over my head like the Big Toad sagging on its spindle and saw bright trails disappear like bubbles at the zenith. I felt like the inside of my head was drifting after them, out into space, frothing like champagne as it went. Moke came and held my hands, which was useful. It stopped me floating.

—Cass, get a grip. You were a foot in the air.

—*Oh.* I giggled. *Felt like five thousand. Why isn't Sword thinking something useful?*

—You'll scare the kids, he said with despair. We've got to get them under shelter.

—*Quite right. Do you think Henry's cute?*

—I think Henry's married. Yell's cooking prote.

—*Yes. I'm glad we married Yell or we'd have to cook prote ourselves. I cook prote awful.* I found I'd started to cry. *Mokey, that was horrible.*

He looked down. You can't . . .

—*If you mention omelettes and eggs I'm going to fly into space and start a new career as a meteor.*

—I was going to say, always get things perfect. The riot was inevitable, Cass. Didn't you know?

—*No. Did you?*

—Yes. He laid his warm forehead in my lap, lank yellow hair over his eyes, his cheekbones sharp against my hand. Given what they are and the state they were in. They were crazy with killing fever before we came. I think the sentients must often kill each other when they lose control, and the Clans Major were the last straw. They had the strongest auras and they were nearest the horror. It was a powder-keg needing a spark. We made sparks. I hadn't foreseen the big transmitters, but I knew there had to be a mess.

—*They transmitted panic?*

—I'm sure they did. Or they mightn't have had to fight their way out.

—*They burned everything. Like maggots in an apple, all the way outside.*

—If you see most of your kind as un-people that happens, Cass. It spreads. From despising insentients to despising everyone.

—*But at least they believed the vanillas were insentient. It was a ritual cull, not a murder.*

—*No, they didn't,* the unvoice said. *They know which way's up, they're no stupider than you are. They've been killing seed-bearers on the verge of sentience for thousands of generations, ever since they began to mutate. The ritual was a considered holding-back of evolution, they can't bear change. They don't have to kill or eat vanillas, they don't have to have a runaway breeding program. The juveniles who haven't had time to grow gardens live perfectly well on vegetation. It's an insane idea of clone-purity.*

—We used them. Sword wouldn't think it was worth arguing about, he came to get our people. Their telepathy worked against them, the panic above confused the guards inside and it let him save the prisoners. We had to do it.

I shivered. *I hope nobody finds something they have to do to us.*

—Let's try not to make them.
—*Does that help?*
—Not often, he said.

The shelter was up and Hall was bracing struts from inside. Aurelia fell through the tunnel and lay on her back, spreading arms and legs like a starfish. The way she was shaped it was probably the first time in a couple of weeks. She made luxurious grunting noises, very like a bim.

"I want to hug someone. Mac, take that hood off and be hugged, you look like a Martian."

"No," Hallway said in a spurt, like a pistol-shot.

She sat up bewildered, her long hair broken out of its chignon and mussed around her face. She could have passed for beautiful. "He's my brother."

"Hall thinks I'm a monster from outer space, though I don't guarantee he's specific on Mars," Sword said lightly. He stretched his length through the lock and pressed a masked cheek on hers. "It's the atmosphere or something. Welcome to civilization. Let me pass you some prote."

She laughed. She sounded like she was effervescing nearly as bad as I was. "I don't know if I can stand the excitement of real Earth food. My head's floating."

"Then sit still and I'll get it, it may nail you down. Hug Hall while you're waiting, he's a bit disconsolate."

She looked haughtily through ten feet of cold air. "I'm not surprised. I thought he was your friend."

Hall folded suddenly on the floor and laid his head on his knees. He looked like something unloved and abandoned, a mechanical thing. Like a sentient crane or a rig-strider. His red hair was too bright for his suit, they looked artificially festive like a Bosch holiday. Aurelia arranged herself in the opposite corner being offended. After a moment's thought she untangled her hair and started making a rope, rather carefully. She didn't look like a lighthouse. She looked like a girl with all the hope in the world. Sword considered them as if they belonged in a microscope and went away.

"Mac," Aurelia called after him. "Why's Cassie sitting outside on a rock? She looks awfully ill. Bring her in where she can lie down."

Hallway lifted his head, his face desperate.

"She likes it out there," Sword said.

Aurelia ran a cold eye over both of them. She really had been Helen's social secretary. "I suppose she's a monster from outer space too." Hall half-lifted a hand and let it fall. "Bring her in anyway, Mac. If Mr. Hallweg feels unwell perhaps he'd better sit elsewhere."

Sword inspected both of them. "I shouldn't do that, sweetheart, the guy's liable to walk over a cliff and he hasn't my talents. Why don't you console him first and lecture him after, or vice-versa? He may see the error of his ways. I'll look after Cass."

Aurelia pointed her long straight nose in the air, but I've seen that expression on bims before. Provided he didn't walk over a cliff in the next five minutes, that's how long he was getting to find out how badly he needed her. Then she was going to fold neatly at the knees and have to be rescued. There are things you don't have to explain even to a lighthouse.

We left Beth and the kids in one hut, Roz, Margaret and Henry making like Marines in the other and Hallway and Dribble in the outer division of the shelter. The inner one was for when Aurelia was satisfied with Hall's state of contrition. Looked to me like he might or might not be contrite but he was going to catch up on tactful nothings of the sweet Lunar kind any time.

Moke and me retired to the hopper with the rest of the dropouts, namely Swordfish, and Yell came with us because he doesn't figure Moke can eat without him. Don't know what he thinks the guy did for his first twenty-five years but friendship's a beautiful thing.

When I saw the hopper I saw why the guys had been short of matériel, we just about got in so long as we made four-way spoons and if anyone wanted to turn he had to yell *Lee ho!* so we'd all do it at once. We absorbed prote soup with our knees to our chins while Sword leaned his elbow on my head, which was merely spite because there was plenty of room to wave it in the air if he'd wanted.

The trans in the tent was a slave of the hopper's, which I guess is obvious to normal people. I wasn't feeling too normal so I didn't find out until three in the morning when the bastard went off like a fire-alarm. Sword switched it in because he's the only guy long enough to reach with his butt jammed in the locker.

"This is Hercules. *Ground, are you receiving me? Come in please. Request status. Repeat, request status."*

"Hercules? Ground, we copy," Sword said before Hallway'd had time to untangle Aurelia. "Where've you guys been? I've had a beacon out for nearly six hours."

"You had an electrical disturbance in high atmosphere, we've been trying to raise you since eight SG. Is that DeLorn? How are you guys?"

"Crowded," Sword said. "We want to go home."

The voice changed, to brisk, female and human. *"Hector? Have you got them?"*

"Evander? How nice to hear a person. We lost two, I'm sorry. Specialist David McCoy, injured in action, a child who may have been Rebecca Garcia. They're

not sure, they were in shock. Private Margaret Aymon's injured. That's five adults, Brady, Aymon, and
Cord, my sister and Mem Brown, three kids and our
Drib. Both Chan brats and a boy, name's Nicky, wants
his daddy. When are you coming?''

*"You're stuck there for thirty-six hours, Mr. Am-
bassador sir. I'm sorry. I hope it isn't a problem? You
asked the Captain to stand off. With all the traffic in
and out of the system we've had to withdraw to stay
out of range. We can get you a pickaback day after
tomorrow. How are supplies?"*

"We've prote and prote," Sword said mournfully.

*"Great. It's marvelous for nervous stomachs, you
can't throw it up if you try. I hope you've our muti-
neers, the Captain's anxious to talk to them. In case
they're worried, Retta also wants to talk and she could
take precedence."*

"What, them worry? Never. Besides, you're holding
one of Moke's sculptures hostage. Give him three
minutes to organize and he'll be back to it like a homing whatsisname."

"Bird on the wing?" she suggested helpfully.

"I was thinking of something more rapacious. Like
a wolverine."

*"A wolverine on the wing. Yes, I like that. Listen,
DeLorn, seriously, what have you guys pulled? We've
been watching alien ships rush in and out of there like
a smoked-out wasps' nest for the last fourteen hours.
Their twitterings have varied from hysterical to plain
crazy and I've never seen them move faster."*

"Neither have we. Don't let it worry you, they've
gone. And there's no need to follow, they're headed
for home pastures. You did say thirty-six hours?"

*"That's what I said. Starting now. You'd better
make out a report for the Captain while you're waiting,*

he's going to have to explain this to the Navy. Maybe you could tell them Blaine was essential to saving the modesty of the female prisoners or something."

"And Moke and Yell were necessary to saving the modesty of Blaine. Yes, naturally. I thought it had to be something like that. Thanks for the hint."

She laughed. *"We want you back. See you, Hector. Give my love to Andromache."*

"Check and out."

"A—hh," he added, leaning luxuriously on all of my left elbow and quite a lot of one hipbone. "And nothing to do but sleep, and eat elaborate meals of gourmet prote. Prote soup. Prote pellets. Prote flakes. Prote coffee . . ."

"Spelled B-O-R-I-N-G," Yell said sourly. "You want to cook?"

"I may." Sword made a large gesture that almost broke the forward screen. "Prote bacon's one of my specialties."

And he went back to sleep right where he was. I kicked him furiously but he was unconscious. With determination. It's one of his talents.

A demonic noise was crashing through my sleep like the roaring of a waterfall. We'd had thunderstorms every night but this one was special. Maybe it really was a waterfall. Maybe our bit of platform was where it happened when they had one. I struggled out from under Sword's arm and found the whole mess stirring, limbs poking other people's faces in the dark.

—What is it?

"A ship," he said out loud. "Right on top of us. Christ! Where's the trans? Can't be *Hercules,* they haven't had time. This guy's either uncommonly lucky or out of his mind, they only just missed the cliff.

They're going to take us with them. What the hell?''

—*Geeks?*

—*That's a human lighter, Cass, I'd know the engine-note anywhere. All I don't know is whose.*

The thunder stopped in a crashing silence and a voice hailed outside. With a bullhorn, by the echo. "Up top, ahoy!"

There was something familiar about it. That went with tri-dee tattoos and long silver hair. Yell recognized it too, his ear-to-ear grin reflected in the light from the panel.

"Let me," he said, with a flourish nearly cost me an earlobe. "Issa?"

"Hi, Shorty," she yelled with metallic clarity. "Sorry to wake you but there's a Geek fleet maybe two hours out. Don't know about you but if I were me, which I am, I'd clear system. Get down here, I got transport. Only fast, we ain't a battleship. Like my armament's zero so all I can do is jump like a jackrabbit. Shake, it, kids, those guys are rolling."

Sword was on his feet. "On our way, Yell. Pick up everything, stores, clothes, bedding, whatever we could need in an empty hold with sick kids on our hands, and stick it aft." He reached for the trans. "Can you take fourteen, Iss?"

"Take forty if I gotta. This here's a haulage job. But you're right about the hold, five-star it ain't. Been trucking agri gear, place smells like the Haywain. Tarry, you know? We can bunk kids if there aren't many but you guys get floor."

"Can you get a hopper in your lighter-bay?"

"Only if I leave my lighter, which I wasn't fixing to. We got grab-gear, can haul her external."

"You could be grateful, I do have armaments.

Though I'd rather jump like a jack-rabbit. Be with you."

Moke was outside and I could hear him dimly yelling in tunnels. Confused voices answered in shades of bewilderment. A few moments later Hallway staggered to the port with pallor beneath his mask and leaned in.

"Sword? What's going on?"

"We identified your blip. The moon-hopper. She's sent her lighter, there are bandits coming."

"My God. Relia." He vanished.

"Okay, Cass, stick with the ship. I got to carry kids down the cliff and Yell'll need help with Margaret. I'll tell people to throw gear in as they come past, we can use it to pad Issa's plates. She could need the stores, too. Sling it all in the aft locker if you've time. Back soon's I can."

I sat in the dark by myself, shaking. *What do they want?*

Pause. Maybe it had gone. I sort of hoped it had gone. It had been okay while it lasted but I had the rest of my life to live. In which I'd rather be mostly alone except for persons of my choice such as Sword and Moke, and Yeller at mealtimes.

It hadn't gone.

—*Sorry, I just localized them. Under two hours, you'd better move. It's a cleanup expedition with sterilization equipment. Planet-busters.*

My heart did a flop. *What happens to the people? Theirs?*

—*Those that could leave have left already. The rest—didn't you hear Sword tell you they were kamikazes?*

—*The villagers, all those juveniles.*

—*Minor clans, not important.*

A jerk and squeeze in my chest. *All my young va-*

nillas? The new ones, who got their first look at the sky last night?

—*That's what they've come for. I imagine they, too, had their prime hanging off.*

—*All of them?*

—*They've come to sterilize,* it repeated patiently.

—Come on, Cass, you hate this place, Sword said in my inner ear. You've been hating it every second since you got here.

—*I do. I detest it. Those wriggly leaves that smack your face. The things in the marsh. All that hair that grows and swims. I hate it. But they've no right. It isn't theirs. They've no right.*

—They sterilized twelve of our planets, four of them populated, over seventy million people, he said gravely. You've never known just what we were fighting for. And we weren't a visitation of angels ourselves.

—*That's a reason?*

—No, of course not. None of it's a reason. They've no right at all. But how can we stop them?

—*My little vanillas that were just born.*

—It's shit, baby. But shit happens. Load me the aft locker. I want to save you, that's something I can do. Like Issa, she's been hanging around in case she had to save Yell. We're human, that's how we function. If I ever turn angel I'll warn you. You won't like me nearly so well.

—*I don't like you now.*

—That's my Cass. Tent coming over, watch your eyes on the ribs.

I caught it, weeping. And began to load it into the aft locker. I think the aft locker had the whole camp and maybe part of the platform when I'd finished. I hadn't the heart to stop and look.

Sword and I stuck with the hopship while the others packed into the lighter. Seemed I was needed. Seemed something someone needed me. We hung in magnetic grapples under the freighter and rattled, watching the planet turn through the haze of Issa's reaction-tubes. The haulship was a big slow lumberer with a lot of room for tractors and some for improvement but she shone with love. Or anyhow, someone had painted *Rainbird* and *Hampton-of-Argos* across her hull in letters that only looked ragged at closer than three miles, in a cheerful shade of chrome yellow. I'd thought it might be sentiment but Yell assured me across the trans that really they'd just got the paint cheap. Seemed to me if she was there at all, someone, such as Yell, must have been doing a little calling-out when the rest weren't looking, but Sword's always saying spacers are psycho. Iss is possibly more psycho than most, at least on the subject of Yeller.

Sword was in the pilot's couch in front and I was trying to fit on the jury straps they'd rigged for Hallway where the main gun-battery's supposed to go. The couch and the straps were both too big so I was glad we were grappled. I hoped Sword hadn't had any bright ideas on dogfighting in open space but unluckily it's what he was trained for. We passed the time with a discussion, that mostly started at ground-level when he reached for his helmet.

—*If you mean to plug that bastard into your central nervous system, I'm going to sit in the aft locker with the rest of the gear. I might get to not be sick.*

—*Okay, in that case I won't,* he said cheerfully. *We'll just drift on up in hope and charity and if I make a hole through Issa's hull we'll say sorry to the corpses after they're crated.*

At that point he put on the helmet, snapped enough jacks to run a factory and took off like an arrow. I tried not to fall through the seat, with only moderate success. Guess my hind end's sharper than Hallway's.

—*Yell doesn't do disgusting things when he's driving,* I yelled through the scream of departing atmosphere.

—*I'm unacquainted with the details of his sex-life but it looks colorful to me.* We shrieked in on the hull and snapped into the grapples. The lighter was behind us still laboring through the stratosphere and *Rainbird*'s crew must have been scared out of their panties. Being psycho, they got the magnets on before we drifted. Vague obscenities filtered out of the trans. *If you mean he doesn't plug himself in, he's a professional spacer and I'm a Naval killer-pilot. But he would too if you gave him a big enough ship, have you looked at his sockets?*

I had. They're flapped, but they come both sides of

his spinal column behind the neck plus both wrists and both ankles. I only run to one behind the ear, I'm wimpy. Sword's are among the things I don't care to think about. Hall once told me they blew all his motor control-centers last time the on-board computer shorted out. *Don't bother to hold any more conversation, you just killed me. Twenty gees is against my religion.*

—*Sorry. Hall objects to my flying too.*

The lighter had just about caught up and the guys with the bad vocabularies, whoever they were, were busy winching her into the bay. Issa got on the trans to swear a bit on her own. Sword at his control-panel seemed to be reflecting.

—*Yep, lady's right, I can see them. Nasty. She rates her ticket, keeps her lookouts right up to the job.*

—*Yell was with us.*

—*So he was.*

The hopship's viewplates didn't show anything but the hull above and cloud below, or vice-versa at this angle, but maybe her scope was different. I saw what it showed echoed in Sword's retinas, a half-moon of spindling bottle-caps that already had shape and motion.

—*They're horribly close.*

—*Very. Guess we spent a lot of time loading. Hope the guys can get some way on this thing, she doesn't look speedy.* Being hauled had to hurt his pride, he likes to do things himself. Preferably all of them. *Or invisible. Wouldn't like the Geeks to start out by sterilizing us.*

—*Lighter was slow, she was carrying weight. Apart from being short your gifts.*

—*Weight's what she's made for. Unfast by na-*

ture. I haven't the firepower to engage head-on without backup.

—I'm surprised we haven't heard from **Herc,** *I'd have thought she'd be yelling her head off.*

—She probably was, he said casually. *Hadn't time to listen, was using the trans for other business.*

—Don't you think we ought to call them?

—What for? She can't do anything. Unless you really want another of your conversations with that comm-tech.

—She may think we're dead.

—If we live through it, she'll learn better.

I wished that thought didn't make my hair prickle. Hallway's helmet was also too big and there was room inside for it to stand on end. I suspected it was taking advantage of that.

—So what are we doing, out here?

—Spiritual exercises. Shut up and pray.

If I knew him, he usually did his praying with his finger on a firing-button. Or in his current wired-in mode, maybe his finger had become the firing-button. Hall had been right about the neural effects, Swordfish and his ship were one. And since I was riding on his sensations I was part of both of them. The ship's skin felt like my own and *Rainbird*'s warming engine was heating my face. Sitting there naked in space waiting for the jellofish to catch us. I could feel the goose-bumps on my stern-plates.

—Shit, they really are rolling. Hope Iss gets all our guys out in time, her lock's bound to have a slow cycle too and they've a load with them. "Issa?" he said into the trans. "Could you guys stay in the lighter a while? She'll be okay now she's in the bay. You got to get this rig moving."

"She's gonna move. But I got to get on board

first, who the hell you think flies this heap? Bay doors closing. Stand by, my mate has orders to get way on the engines. Could get warmish out where you are.''

"Great, I love a hot climate.''

The blue haze deepened at *Rainbird*'s tail and charged particles streamed into space.

—*You think this is a healthy place to sit?*

—*No, but when did either of us do anything healthy?* Sword sounded uncannily relaxed, which is the worst of all bad signs. It's how he gets in the middle of a battle. *I can't shoot from inside and we're the only guys with a gun. I wouldn't mind a main cannon.*

—*Neither would I.*

—*Never mind, I've got you. If they get too close you can yell insults.*

—*Yeah,* I snarled. *They'll run for their lives.*

—*They would if they knew you.*

—*You could always try,* the unvoice said neutrally.

—*Shit, it's him again. I hoped he'd gone.*

—*Personally, I'd hoped he was an it. Or conceivably, if necessary, a she. I don't fancy male persons of foreign origin taking up residence in my Trojan woman. It's improper.*

—*Please don't be funny, Sword, I'm terrified.*

—*So'm I, Cinderella. I told you. Have to come home and change my panties every time.*

He was keeping our own engine on warmup, a faint excited vibration like a tremor in the blood. I could feel the hopship trying to get away, to blow the grapples and get out there and at them. It shivered like a dog on the end of its chain. The twirling bottle-tops swelled in the scope, every detail picked out now in bloody sunlight. Somewhere across *Rainbird*'s hull a heavy thunk came through the grapple-bars, jerking both of us in our seats, and the charged stream from her tail got longer and brighter. I knew she was really moving when the planet under my head began to shrink. Slowly. Very slowly. The ballooning warships were swelling fast.

—*Never seen a tailstream look this way. Pretty.*

—*That's because the bastards are invisible in space, at least to human eyes,* Sword said. *I guess our vision's changing. Interesting habits your friend has.*

—*No friend of mine.*

—*I rather hoped it was. We're going to need it.*

—*If we lived to have grandchildren, they'd probably like this.*

—*Let's be optimistic,* Sword said. *Maybe they'll be able to re-grow us from spores.*

—*They, who? Thought these guys were here to sterilize.*

—*So they are. Let's go talk to them.*

He slipped the grapples just as *Rainbird* picked up speed and the hopship fell away from her into space. I felt the broad gripping-arms slide over my back like claws and we were out, swimming in void. Like a fish. A very small fish. Sword gunned the engines and we arced out toward darkness.

"*Hey!*" Issa yelled over the trans. "*What you doing? Once we're in warp we can't come back for you. I'm going too fast to turn already. Told you, all I can do is jump.*"

"So can I," Sword said. "But don't worry, we'll catch you. I'm the sting in your tail, it's why I stayed out here. Beep me ten seconds before you go, I don't want to be inside your sphere of turbulence when you warp."

"Sword." The voice was Hallway's. *"You can't do it, you haven't the artillery. Come back, you'll kill both of you."*

"Did you set her up right, Teen? Were your hands clean?" His tone was lightly jeering.

"I always do," Hallway said bitterly.

"I been telling you that for thirteen years. Why do you believe it today, now you've decided I'm not human? This is the one time in my life it can't matter. Not to you, Teeny. Look after my sister. Cass is one of me."

So was Aurelia, I thought. Hall just didn't know it yet. Not so far on as us, but she would be. I'd touched her.

"Mac," Hallway said. His voice was desolate. *"I started protecting you when I was fourteen years old. I can't let go like that. Maybe you haven't been human for thirteen years. Maybe you weren't human before that. I don't know. I don't want you dead."*

"Got work to do, Hall. See you. Don't forget to beep me. I was figuring to be at the wedding. If I'm invited."

"You're invited. Get back here."

"Beep ten seconds before you jump, and don't fuck up. I mean ten on the nose."

"Check." Hallway always comes through in a crisis.

We leapt out of the flare of *Rainbird*'s motors and dived at the alien disks like a hungry piranha. Just one. With small sharp teeth.

—Like a cute little pussy-cat, Cindy. It's all you need. Ever get a faceful of claws?

The alien ships were almost on top of us, the planet tiny below. The nearest swooped up huge in the plate, its tremendous bulk gyrating. The group was spreading, spinning around to approach the target from different sides. A girdle to circle the equator, a couple splitting off for the poles. The one coming our way had broken rank, meaning they'd seen us. The edge of my vision showed *Rainbird* in our aft vidplate, pulling up from the plane of the ecliptic, heading outsystem, her cargo engines laboring. She wasn't going to make it. Not in time to warp safely. The spinning-top bearing down on us was fifty times her size and moving like a Chinese saucer. Its stationary rim bristled with gunports and a flat cylinder big as Issa's entire tail-section was slung below, held in a set of grapples that made *Rainbird*'s look like Lego.

—*What the hell's that?* I yelped.

—*Be reasonable, Cass, you don't think you bust planets with an itty-bitty stock-cube?*

—*It's not a question I got around to asking.*

—*If you were underneath it, you would. Be grateful we're in space, at least they can't drop it on us.*

—*They can blast Issa into vapor.*

—*Which would be impolite of them, she's a lady. Geeks just have no finer feelings. Have you heard of this trick? Patented by Sir Francis Drake, I understand.*

—*Don't know, what's its name?*

They'd seen *Rainbird* but maybe they weren't looking for Sword, whistling down at them out of her tail-blast. By the side of the warship our two-man hopper was like a mosquito taking on a whale.

—*Get under the fucker's guns,* he said, with the sweet young absence means concentration. As the bulking side swam toward us he slid sideways under her belly, the open pores of a row of gunports almost sweating up our nose, and we were running the breadth

of her underside, a scarred black plain seamed with
burns and studded with the nozzles of reaction-tubes
like grouped cooling-towers that spun away in a blur
of motion.

The enormous cylinder of the bomb stood above it
balanced on thick pillars that didn't look strong enough
to support its weight. Beyond, over my shoulder, the
planet was small and blue in the plate, violet atmosphere patterned with spirals, a couple of the small inland lake-seas sparkling through haze in reflected
sunlight. We couldn't see *Rainbird* anymore for the
mass that blanked out the stars under our feet. But I
could feel her running, the spinning warship dropping
down on her like a stone from a cliff.

—*And what's this game called?* I asked, in a very
small voice.

—*Rain-in-the-Face. Hang on, princess.*

He'd one medium forward laser and a couple of light
tail-guns and I was sitting where his cannon ought to
be. I took a deathgrip on the seat. The vast architecture
of the bomb flung itself on us and passed beneath, its
grappling struts flashing past our sides as long and wide
as a junction of fleetways. I almost expected to see
traffic. Then it was behind and leaning on our neck-
bones and Sword had both his thumbs down hard. A
line of blue-hot particles streamed from the swiveling
gunports, homing into the loom of the mass. We
flashed on by and arced away.

—*Acceleration,* he said coolly. And we zipped out
of the warship's shadow into sunlight and were whistling down towards atmosphere, while he hauled back
on the controls with the computer battling gravitational
forces. Our mini-minnow skipped the outer layers like
a flung stone, the glare of skin-heat raising blisters on
my left arm, and began her long backward curve to-

ward a pattern of stars that had just re-oriented to become sky.

The aft screen was glowing. And glowing.

—*Close your eyes,* Sword said sharply. "Iss?
Stand by for turbulence, there's going to be debris. In
particle form, I should think. In your place I'd reinforce
your field."

The triggered bomb lit the vidplates behind us like
the beginning of the universe and the whole sky dissolved in light. I put my hands over my closed eyes
and bent my head as far between my knees as the straps
would let me and saw the bones of my fingers outlined
across my eyeballs inside the lids with searing radiance
showing through. The hopper was picked up by a
tsunami as big as fifty Pacifics and flung out toward
reeling constellations, her stabilizers screeching, pin-
wheeling in an ocean of disturbed gravitation.

—*Evil things, bombs,* Sword said peaceably. *They
go off if you light them.*

He caught up the hopship's motion and edged her
nose into the arc. She came gradually about, the mad
gyrations of stars turning back to a regular circle. He
got back his gravity, turned into the rotation and pulled
her around in a shallow glide. Insane forces tore at our
skin and I could feel my cells trying to separate, held
together by a kind of desperate glue.

—*Now, where did we leave Issa?*

—*My God,* I choked. *Were these things made for
that?*

—*No, but this one seems to have survived it.*

Situation normal, white man crazy. *I can see why
they said this was a kid's job.*

—*You can?*

—*Sure. They're the only guys with imaginations
limited enough not to have a nervous breakdown.*

—They can't do it at all, Sword said. *This stuff needs an adult mind.* Rainbird's *still with us, anyhow. Shall we join the kiddies? I don't think these particular Geeks are going to want to chase her, she comes expensive. I said a good clawing would make them see reason.*

He turned quietly back on-course and aimed the hopper's nose at the stars. Spinning corks bobbled below, still spun by the blast. The planet's violet atmosphere was hazed with currents of dust.

—I didn't want to be the one who smashed it, I whimpered.

—You aren't. It's still there. Atmospheric disturbance. Storm season just came early this year.

"*Hey,* Swordfish." Issa sounded more metallic than the comm quite justified. Maybe she was shaken. "*Get your tail here. I'm laying twenty minutes to jump.*"

"Thank you, Raissa, but I asked for ten seconds. We'll catch you."

The planet grew smaller behind us. He was right about the Geek cleanup group, they'd concluded sweeping the cat wasn't part of their duties. I'd have said some of their ships were damaged, their maneuvers had a lumbering quality. They were still spacing out around the planet's poles and equator, but there was a gap left to fill where one of them had evaporated along with its bomb.

—It's a virtue of being small, Sword remarked. *The blast threw us farther but we didn't break up.*

—That's nice. Can I have a new neck? They're standing a long way out, if they're planet-busting.

—You'll never make Admiral. You saw that thing blow, and they're going to launch twenty. It's about what it takes for a mass this size. They take up position, hang off a safe distance, guide their

bombs in and set them off simultaneously on the edges of atmosphere. If it's properly coordinated the atmospheric gases ignite. World's biggest firework show.

—Sword, you're horrible.

—*I know. I've done my piece, now you get to do yours. The female of the species being what we know.*

—What?

—*You didn't think I brought you out here at danger to my personal life and limb just so I could listen to you bellyache, charming though that is?*

—It wouldn't have surprised me, you're endlessly perverse. I came to hold your hand, I was afraid it might be another suicide trip.

—*Me?* he said. *I just got through dying. That's my ration for the next six months. Did you really come to hold my hand?*

—Maybe I'll just sing Mozart's Requiem. Or dance on the seat.

—*Well, you can use your voice anyhow. This is where you shout insults.*

—Like, Swordfish-you-are-still-a-shit?

—*Not at me, imbecile, at them. Consult your oracle.*

—I'd rather consult a dictionary. Can I yell Bastards?

—*Yell what you like, only use the trans. I've taken my acquaintance's advice on frequency.*

—You got one too?

—*A little voice that murmurs in the night. Yes. Have you ever wondered how these guys reproduce?*

—No. I'd rather not think.

I looked at him with suspicion. All I could see was

the back of his helmet and that looked as innocent as an aluminum halo. Portending the worst.

—*So what does it do?*

—*Just shout,* the unvoice said. *I've picked you a frequency too. We should get there between us.*

I glanced in the forward plate. *Rainbird* was enlarging ahead, her tubes glowing blue, a regular pencil of drive stretching behind like the tail of a comet that trailed across half the system and curved toward the planet below, blown off-course by the solar wind. Our vision was getting all-hell specialized. I kind of wondered where it would stop. The planet with its speckling of shiny bottle-tops was a cobalt bead half-eclipsed in darkness, a bright line of atmosphere circling the limb at the dawn edge. I looked down at it. Brave new world. For half a day.

—*So shout.*

—*BASTARDS!*

The sound that came out of my mouth was so high I felt rather than heard it. I might have been broadcasting in X-ray. The trans vibrated with a tinny trill like a mechanical death-rattle. My throat opened on a bubble of pure high-frequency sonics and closed behind it, skinned. I thought I'd never speak again. I assumed the alien ships were receiving it, because I saw them stagger in the aft plate.

Sword swung the hopper on its axis and lit after *Rainbird* like the last train to San Fernando.

"Ten seconds," Issa said. Her voice was distorted, the yell must have done something to the mike. But she sounded jangled too. The blue pencil lengthened abruptly and veered into white, and beyond. *"Dammit, Sword, move your ass, you're right in my sphere. I'm gonna fucking erase you."* The bulk of the freighter grew in our foreplates, as a bright exhaust behind a

ring of darkness. *"Five. Four. Three . . ."*

A thread of linked pearls had abruptly sprung out around the outline of the planet, tiny spots of light that grew and brightened and became diamonds. And swelled, and touched at the edges. The entire globe was a distant light-bulb, a single sphere of piercing brightness. That blazed and opened out until it lit the space all around it in an expanding balloon of radiation.

"One. Mark. We're into warp . . ."

Our minnow flashed into a sphere of blurred-out stars and my stomach turned inside out. I'm not accustomed to going superlight at no seconds' notice in a ship the size of a one-man racing-yacht. Probably Sword's the only guy who is. He matched speeds at the instant of warp-out and we were standing abruptly on *Rainbird*'s badly-painted flank with her waiting grapples clanging on our hull. The flaw washed over us as we passed through together, and I made another hole in my seat. A second later the system was gone. I sat back panting.

In that instant of passing I had a distant fragmented mental vision of sky that burned weirdly through heavy cloud and a blast of hot wind that laid black-green forest flat like night. Plastic barnacles shivered on their rocks and a wreath of something mushroom-shaped and skirling flew over electric marshes, planing on the gale. Of course they all had my blood, a little infinitesimal part of me. I saw with their sight, for that one passing second. They were all singing like crystal angels.

Then it was dark and Sword was disconnecting his jacks in front of me.

—Hand that to a fourteen-year-old and see who has the nervous breakdown, he said.

"Are you nuts or something?" the trans shrieked furiously. I sympathized, he often makes me feel the same way myself. The guy with the nervous breakdown's usually me. *"I thought you were both fucking dead. How'm I supposed to explain that to Mokey? Don't ever do it again."*

"I hope not to have to," Sword said humbly. "That was absolutely my last appearance as Meany, the Terror of Space. Cass and I want to commune with nature a little, we'll join you later."

"The fuck you will. If you're figuring to walk around over my hull and into my lighter-bay in warp-mode you can just forget it. The sucker's sealed. You're both stuck there until we meet up with Hercules."

"On an exclusive diet of cold prote? You're a fierce hard woman. I'm not sure you aren't worse than Cass."

"Thanks," I said.

He grinned and stretched. *Well, as I was saying. All we have to do now is . . .*

—Don't. Look what happened last time you said something. What the hell happened back there?

—It's called a chain reaction. You wouldn't know, you didn't stay at school long enough. That shout of yours kind of set off the bombs before the ships had time to get into position. Much too far out. But they ignited each other. Made quite a bang. Poor Toad. Should have known better than get mixed up with you. Of course it did give the atmosphere a shaking, bound to. We doubt if it's fatal. Radiation belts are going to be hairy for a while. That could be good, it should deter the bad guys from coming to investigate. And by the time they do . . .

—By the time they do? I said coldly.

—Your little bloodloss problem should be mak-

ing itself felt back home. In thousands. Cheep. Sentient vanillas all over the furniture. Reminds me, I'm hungry.

—*You're monstrous.*

—*So you keep telling me. It doesn't seem to stop you misbehaving,* he said contentedly. *Why don't we eat?*

There was a bump somewhere behind the couch, and a sound of scrabbling.

''What?'' I mumbled blurrily.

—Hi. Did you know you'd all the bedding in your aft locker? Issa's crew's friendly, but their deck-plates are like paving-stones. We've corns on our behinds.

—*Mokey?* He was bending into the aft equipment-space with only his bony rear sticking out, but I'd know it anywhere. It looked perfectly solid. *How did you get in?*

—*Martin,* Sword growled. *You're practicing long-range molecular dispersion, it's anti-social. Couldn't you at least knock or something? Cassandra and I were having a private conversation.*

—*My God. You mean he came through the wall.*

—Through both of them, actually, yours and ours. It's a little bit dicey in the middle, the part that's in hyper, but if you hold your breath you hardly notice.

—*You guys have done this stuff before,* Sword said. *Right through the roof of the Egg, carrying Yell with you. Wondered where you were going to end up. I'd hoped it wouldn't be in my bedroom.*

—*That was two feet.*

—It's the same principle. You're growing up, or hadn't you noticed?

—Sword, this stuff scares me.

—Scares me, too, baby, but it's a bit late to think of that now.

—We never really had the choice, did we? Moke said, emerging with blankets. Since we seem to be stuck with it, we may as well use it. Especially since we got crying children up there.

—You're breaking my heart, Mokey. If I were free, I'd be only too anxious to come and help you. But since it isn't Thursday till tomorrow . . .

—Are you sure? Moke said. I thought today was Tuesday.

—I just unilaterally declared it Wednesday, Go tell Relia she can't have Cass as a bridesmaid, she isn't maidenly enough. She'll have to be madam of honor or something. I'll buy her a gilt G-string for the occasion, for decency. Oh, and remind Sissy to give Hall a kiss or he won't turn into a frog like the rest of us. They could find that disconcerting on their wedding-night.

—I think she already did, Moke said. Forgot herself for a minute. She was rather upset, she'd been meaning to give him the option.

—She's never had any sense, Sword said despairingly *He might have taken it.*

—Not a chance. Anyway, he'd decided to swallow you so he'd nothing to lose, had he?

—When you guys have finished, I said, *I've news for you. I just unilaterally declared it Friday, permanently, and you can both go away. I'm never going to speak to either one of you again.*

—Thought Sword claimed you weren't speaking, Moke said with innocence. Couldn't hear anything but heavy breathing myself. Thought it was him being strong and silent again . . .

I furiously thought molecular dispersion. Nothing much happened. I tried it again with a hop at the ceiling and a disagreeable shiver. Several breaths of disturbed air swished past my ears. Plus something vaporous, maybe hull-plates, in multiplicate. Whatever, I swam up through them and came out two feet above worn rubber. I know, because I fell straight down onto it and bruised my behind in a new place.

"Shit," I said. It had a gucky feel and a warm noisy smell. From the décor it looked like Issa's control-deck. Three different astounded faces turned around forward from where a set of navigational holos were making expanding rings through a dark-blue starfield.

"Serves you right," I said grumpily. "Shouldn't have tried to shut us out."

And I got up from the floor and wandered aft, trying to look as if I knew where I was going.

—*You might have warned me,* I complained internally. *This is turning out painful.*

—*You'll learn to control your directions in time,* it said. *Did you have to jump three decks first try?*

—*How was I to know? I just took a little hop through the bulkhead. You aren't supposed to be able to do that.*

It didn't deign to answer, but I thought it sniggered.

—*Try down here,* Sword's voice said, from too close at hand. *Always knew your sense of direction was inadequate. I found this unused cabin with a long bunk, I heard they had a Luney navigator. Doesn't seem to be in.*

—*Then he, she or it is going to regret that.*

It was entirely like him to get there first. And, naturally, to leave Moke molecularly dispersing the aft locker single-handed. But I went and found him anyway. There was more room inside to get back to where we had been than in the hopper, it was nearly luxurious. Moke could always get Henry to help, the whole crew had to be catching us up. After all, it had only taken me three days to displace through three decks and fall on my butt. There's nothing like progress.

We met the first of *Hercules'* picks maybe fourteen hours later and told them they could go home. They weren't especially grateful, and showed signs of not believing us. Issa radioed them holos of the explosion and they ended by turning reluctantly back. I was relieved by that, the last thing those vanillas needed was the kind of help *Herc* had on offer. I got the idea the crew was miffed the Geeks had got to make the big bang first, they'd been hoping to do it themselves. Also, they took *Rainbird* as an insult to the honor of the Navy, which was more understandable but not to Issa.

"You mean you'd rather they were dead according to regulations," she said ferociously.

"Civil craft are specifically excluded from the battle-zone. You're in infringement of Code 143/Z3-92 and I'll have to report it to the Admiral . . ."

"Horsewater."

"He will, actually," Sword said cheerfully. "It's in the manual. But I shouldn't worry, when I knew her her vocabulary was nearly as bad as yours."

Issa made a snarling noise and dropped something that sounded like linked saucepans onto the mike. You could hear the pick's comm-techs cowering two decks down.

"A-aah," I said. "All the pleasures of a return to civilization."

"Shut up and have some fake steak," Yell said. He'd found a decent old-fashioned hotstove someplace in the storeroom and was massacring our rations.

"Will I be able to tell it from the real thing?"

"If you aren't blind, senseless and short of a nose, yes."

"Great. I finally feel at home."

"But you got to pay for it."

"Yeller. Don't tell me Mokey's welshed on your salary."

He looked at me fixedly and his normally friendly eyes were cold and concentrated. "This isn't Moke, Cass, it's you. I've a good idea what you got, and I want a piece of it."

"Dammit, Yell. The fucking thing seems to be incurable and we don't know exactly what it does. But you've seen some."

"Right. That's why I want it, and why everyone I know's going to want it too. Not to mention Iss. We need that thing, Cassandra. Give. You owe me."

"I know I do. But I didn't know what I was falling into. Maybe you should wait and find out."

"I'll risk it," he said.

I hung around his neck long enough to feel two sets of disturbed vibes shaped like Sword and Moke, but I didn't care. He's tasty.

And we headed on out toward *Hercules*.

The Captain took one look at the pride of Issa's heart and had a fight with his better feelings that showed behind his face like a Punch and Judy show, but the forces of right came out on top and he welcomed her aboard. He was the only one. Her crew was one beautiful black male, lightly symbed with gold spots that had a tendency to go powdery in the center when he saw pretty guys, one female Luney who topped Hallway and had to go through hatches bent double and a round-faced lardy type of indeterminate sex who turned out to be she, the mate and the other guy with a ticket. The Navy cringed and gave them room, then the Dips got in the act and did likewise. Except Chan, who kissed everyone loud and hard in public, and a company of Marines who organized a bash that went on all night until the Officer of the Watch looked in and said tiredly they could stop now, it was tomorrow. They cheered loudly and began again. We started the new day thirty hours later with a set of very second-hand heads.

We'd have gone another fifteen rounds if they'd let us alone but somebody with mean ideas detailed the Marines to alien-attack drill and removed Margaret and Roz to the infirmary so the party came to a reluctant end. Henry was nursing both Chan children, who'd developed a reflex not to let go that was going to need help from the psych department if they were ever to see their parents again, and Chan herself was draped over a couch like a neat small cat. I wasn't sure if she was asleep, unconscious or foxing. In any case Issa and company felt better and decided not to clean out their hold onto the chessboard. Since it was still extremely agricultural this probably improved Navy–Merchant Service relations.

Evander got Moke and me as we were escaping to the Ambassadorial Suite to stick our headaches in the jackoo and dragged us to the Comm lab.

"Okay, I want the story. So does the Captain. Mr. DeLorn's concocting some sort of untruth this moment, I understand."

"Don't blame him too much, he can't drink without anti-alk pills and I think he'd OD'd, he's semi-conscious."

She fixed me with a steely eye. "If I hadn't heard

he can't drink without anti-alk I'd have attributed his state to quite another cause. Or he's playing Hamlet, which isn't impossible.''

I thought so too. I didn't tell her that.

"But talk to me. Dammit, Blaine, it's important. What did you guys do there? What was so important we weren't to raze the place, and in the end the Geeks came and did it for us? Don't tell me you took a fancy to the scenery.''

"Actually she did," Moke said. "She got real upset about it.''

"And you stood and cheered. How like you.'' Ironic Evander. Moke looked innocent.

"It was very nasty scenery."

"Which isn't going to stop him basing his next five inspirations on it.''

He looked at me with a mild eye, not too much redder than usual. "There was a violent genetic mutation happening when we got there. Seemed better to let it run. If *Hercules* had interfered they wouldn't have taken it home.''

"Alien prote," I contributed. "Disagreed with them.''

"How? Retta's going to want detail, I hope you took samples.''

"Only what's on our boots. There's probably quite a lot, especially in the hopper. And the folds of the tent-fabric.''

"Which you've been using to sleep on." She sighed. "That's what comes of leaving it to amateurs, they've no sense of priorities. It's all right, Andromache, I realize you didn't go there as a scientific expedition. But Retta did hope . . .''

"We think the vanillas went sentient. Sort of caught up on their evolution, you know? The raspberries were upset. That's why they tried to burn the place . . ."

"Tried?"

"Burned. The place. With their settlers and everything. In case they were infected."

"Beastly things. Sentient vanillas is what they deserve."

"Oh, I think they've got them. There was a kind of panic and they ran like rabbits but I think they took it with them. Like a plague, sort of? We think the war may be over."

"Trouble at home," Mokey said. "We thought it might be a good idea to just let it spread."

"You sure you guys haven't been practicing genocide while we weren't looking? Hector's capable. It's a disease of heroes."

"He's not," I protested. "Anyhow, it wasn't him, he was sick himself . . ."

"That's another thing I'd noticed. He was rumored to be dying. He seems to have changed his mind."

"Was the climate. Had a sort of crisis and pulled out of it. Maybe all that oxy and stuff."

"I think you'd better see a doctor. All of you."

—*Help.*

—It's all right, Moke said reassuringly. It can fox a scope.

—*What about Sword? He'd a mechanical heart last time around, aren't they going to notice?*

—They didn't look, remember? He wrecks the machinery.

"You can't autodoc Sword, he wrecks the machinery." In haste. "Admiral Brand had to get him a dispensation, he cost too much. All that cerosteel. I expect you could try out his bloodpressure or something . . ."

"They aren't genocided," Moke said with decision. "They did their best to genocide each other but I don't think they made it. We could wait and see.''

Evander looked at us with exasperation. ''There's something you aren't telling, I can feel it. But we'll wait and see. What else can we do? Those kids are in remarkable health, after what they went through.''

''Apart from the trauma.''

''What trauma? They adore Sergeant Brady, he plays with them. Ask Chan. She says she's going to have to adopt him. Little Nicky Ruggieri's learned to read in the past ten days, and his father's been losing his mind for three years waiting for him to grow old enough to be processed for dyslexia. I'm having you all scanned, don't think I'm not.''

—*She's such a nice lady, it's a shame to lie to her.*

—Can't help it, Moke said. Do you want to spend the rest of your life in the zoo? ''Sure,'' he said, with a nice smile. ''We're in line already.''

They scanned us. Up, down and sideways. Except Sword, who's known to wreck the machinery. Then they started on a mind-scan even he couldn't get out of. They plugged us all into a kind of Iron Maiden with knobs inside and dug holes in our heads. They called it debriefing. I sat with my eyes unsocketed, which is truly disgusting, while some guy who thought I was hypnotized asked me dumb questions and my unvoice played him dumb answers.

We sat in a tidy row and watched from the hillside as the vanillas went crazy all on their own, and the Egg boiled over from inside and the big bottle-caps bubbled into space. Sword, romantically pale, fainted gracefully (I could feel him liking that) *and arose like the Phoenix reborn, untouched by human hand, especially mine. We filed out on the fur in masks and grav-packs and processed solemnly down the shaft the raspberries had thoughtfully vacated, and we led the*

*prisoners out by the hand while the Geeks wandered
the wide Gromboolian plain in ever-decreasing circles
without noticing.* If he believed that, he'd believe anything.

He believed it. After all, his equipment told him it
was true. And real, gen, hi-tech equipment can't be
wrong. Can it?

Moke got bored in the middle and said plaintively,
I wish you guys would stop laughing like macaws
and give me a hand, I've work to do and Henry's
flagging.

We looked in our heads and he was. He was managing the big cutter under Moke's directions and Roz was
polishing behind him with a heat-wand. They were both
using a lot of symbiotic energy, but they were both
sweating. The cero chimney was the length of the
lighter-bay and rising. The translucent children laughed
and raised wreaths of linked hands. That's the Moke I
know. We all leaned hard and helped them. It distracted
our attention, but the scope didn't even blink.

They found what they deserved, which was zilch.
Retta got enough alien bacteria and several kinds of
mold out of the baggage to keep her slightly happy,
and since the planet was officially a blast-zone there
wasn't any point investigating the biosphere anyway.
They'd get a surprise if they ever went back.

They put our eyes in, let us out of the Maiden and
handed all of us official certificates mentioning us in
dispatches. It didn't make much difference to us civilians but the Marines got up-graded, Sword was cited
for another medal and so was Hall, which had to be
exciting, he hadn't had one, and Issa and her crew fell
about. Though I think it spoiled their reputations in the
spaceyards.

And a while passed and nothing happened, except

we got nearer Earth, and the remains of the alien fleet pulled up stakes one morning and lit out for home and silence descended. The war was over.

Next thing, they let us go home ourselves.

Luna was quiet. We passed through Liberty Port without being noticed and took a subway. Yell was fixing transport for Moke's candle, which rated space-freight by that time and was getting hauled back to Earth on its own, all three thousand feet and penalties never thought of if it broke up in atmosphere. It wasn't going to, it was rocket-tube material through and through with a mixture of Moke special that was secret. We bucked peaceably through galleries and stopped off for the seventeen varieties of Moon-coffee at the concourse at Lunaport and hauled our asses onto the shuttle without getting a second glance from anyone. And watched Earth come up to meet us, big and blue, a glass-alley marbled with white swirls, gilded rime speckling its nightside, as if nothing had ever happened.

Ashton lay in eerie silence. When we left, the sonic batteries were howling from the mountains and the

coastal platforms were answering with snail-trails of
fire that covered the sky with phosphorescent smears
while life cowered below trying not to be noticed.
There were powdered rings out in the 'burbs now that
looked like Razor'd been doing some heavy reasoning
with House people since we saw him last, but the radiation count was within limits and the sky wasn't
much more garish than usual. A yellow gantry here and
there said someone was rebuilding.

The Internat was thinly busy with guys in suits carrying briefcases, starting out for journeys of immense
importance on other bits of Terran dryland where
they'd exchange credit and credits and gain and lose
each other's faces, and they managed to look as if it
mattered. They passed their eyes quickly over our
stained blues and hurried away, fearing we'd knives up
our sleeves. For one time in my life I hadn't. And I
didn't even feel bare.

We crunched the ramp towards the belts where traxies still rose and fell over shivered towers and found
the City fathers hadn't got around to replacing the
safety barriers, which were in shards under our boots.
The belts were running but not too many citizens ran
with them. Those that were still in residence were taking a pause before they came out, to be sure the glass
rain had really stopped falling. Some flossier boutiques
had timidly begun to uncover their windows and lay
out displays. The Strip, never much alive in daylight,
looked bleached and shrunken like it had run in the
wash. We crossed paths with a couple of skaters who
looked at Sword's height with four nervous eyes and
took the long way around.

Gordon's windows were bravely untaped and the
geraniums in his boxes newly replanted. There wasn't
a breadline, which was either good news or bad. We

filed in and found him behind his counter unpacking bagels.

"Hi."

He looked at us with solemn eyes. "You got back."

"Mostly. We got back, we eat bread, we drink beer. Preferably yours. How are the 'keets?"

He shook his head with disbelief. "I have new stock. A gift. There's an urgent message for Moke, and two people want you upstairs."

"Gift?"

—*My old man,* Sword said, not without pride. *Always pays the family debts.*

—*In 'keets?*

—*In everything. What's the message?*

Mokey took it, nervous, and ripped. Hampton-of-Argos. He smiled. "They want Sword's statue after all. Guess the war got over and needs memorialized."

"Wait till they see the new one."

"That's for here. Right in the center, where you can see it from everywhere. Going to be the tallest thing around, with a beacon you'll see out of atmosphere. The Childermass candle."

—*I owe it,* he added.

—*Sure you do, Moke. You're going to give it to the City for free.*

—How did you know?

—*I been trying to keep your books balanced for three years. How wouldn't I?*

"I'll be glad to see the last one go," Gordon said. "No offense. It's beautiful, but I got to dislike the way it sang when the guns were running. Got in your blood."

"All they got to do is not play guns at it. Maybe it's quiet in Hampton-of-Argos. What does it do when birds tweetle?"

"Answers," Moke said peaceably. "Makes a cute sort of ting. New one's going to shine. Who's upstairs?"

Gordon looked uncomfortable. "People."

—*Uh-oh,* Sword said. *That means my family. Smells like Hall and Relia.*

The yard had its summer show of roses and hanging begonias, with hollyhocks getting ready to tower behind. The cages had been remade in white-coated mesh with a few modest paradiddles and parakeets fresh from the lab. Our door had a fresh coat of paint, to hide the crack it hadn't before. In chrome yellow. The season's color. Gordon'd done the winow-frames white. The batten blinds were shut.

Sword looked inquiring and led the way. My own vibes said internal passion upstairs. The door was unlocked and the living-room smelled new paint. Someone had put our covers through the cleaner. Hallway and Aurelia were sitting side by side on the couch with their knees together trying to look as if they weren't holding hands, and they got disorganized when we interrupted. If they hadn't felt us coming, the passion must have been intense.

We hadn't seen either of them for a while, they'd spent a lot of time having intellectual conversations in corners of the hold followed by ditto in the Dip's mess. When *Hercules* docked they'd evaporated into the wide closed spaces of the Moon, we deduced looking for Hallway's family. Hall had been very quiet. Coming to terms, maybe. He could have been ashamed. Sword hadn't gone near him. Now they were definitively in the same place he stood still.

"Hi, guys," Sword said. "You didn't have to bribe Gordon to shut it, we're almost related. And anyhow, we felt you. Have a drink. If there is any."

"Sure there is," I said. "Yell cabled ahead, you think he has no sense of priorities."

"Great. So sit, place is clean. We haven't had time to touch it yet."

Hall went on standing. "You promised to come to our wedding."

"Right. My brother's marrying my sister. I'll stand at the back and cheer."

"I'd rather you stood at the front and held the ring."

"The Cathedral probably has a regulation about aliens from outer space within the precincts," Sword said easily. "Against City ordinances. You better check."

Hallway's face was stretched on its bones. "I've never known you be vindictive, Mac. I was wrong, isn't that enough? I told you back there when you decided to kill yourself one more time. I've been looking after you since I was fourteen, it's too late to change. I had to watch you die, then I saw you get back up again. Not natural. Has anything you've ever done been natural? Dammit, bro, I didn't want to lose you. And now I have it too. My kind don't choose this stuff easily. This time I hadn't the choice, but it made no difference. I couldn't have let you and Relia handle it alone."

"What about Cass?"

He smiled faintly. "Cass has been living with weird shit since she was a baby. It's easy for her. What do you expect from Razor's daughter?"

Sword sighed. "I know. You've spent your life for my sake. Debts paid. If you ever owed them. You can do as you like now. I'm glad Relia picked you, you're the guy I'd have wanted."

"Okay, pay back. Do something for me."

"Name it."

"I just did." They matched eyes. Hallway was taller.

When he stood up straight, as he was doing. "Be my best man and stop giving me a hard time."

"Done."

"And give me some skin."

Sword gazed at his hand. It looked like a hand, unnaturally long like the rest. "If you want it."

"Don't fuck around. I said things haven't changed."

"They've changed, Hall."

"Not between you and me."

The shake turned into an embrace. Hallway's eyes were red. "Damn you. And Relia wants Cass to hold her train."

"I hope it's a long one," I said. "If it's long enough they may think we're a perspective effect."

Aurelia exploded in a gurgle. I hadn't known she could laugh. She still looked like a lighthouse, but the kind they steer by twenty miles out at sea. You could have harnessed her wattage to run half the City.

"Please, Cassie. I don't care if they think we look stupid, my family's been this way all my life. It's our wedding and we don't care. We come this size. The little Chans are carrying flowers and they're even smaller, you'll look charming."

True love's an awesome thing, it can convince you of anything.

"Whatever you say. I have to warn you, your brother's plans include a gilt G-string. I hope it matches your color-scheme."

"Dammit, Cass." Hall turned pale eyes down. "You wanted to hug me. Now's your chance to stand on my foot."

"Is that a challenge?"

He bent. I didn't stand on his foot, though I could feel Sword waiting. I happen to like Hall.

"I'll make the jewelry," Moke said with enthusiasm. "I can see Aurelia in a pointed crown. Like the Snow-Queen."

"And my G-string. Sword promised."

"Kill her," Sword said. "She'll wear a dress with a high neck and flowers like a human and no one'll know the difference. If she opens her mouth, tread on her. Relia, pet, you got my best friend. Be kind to him."

I remembered Hallway once saying the same thing to me. They were a lot alike.

"So how about these drinks? If you aren't moving I'll make them myself."

Sword headed for the bar and Moke for a corner with a slate in his hand. I could see a light of hope in his eye. If there's one thing he hates it's velvet formals. He'd rather meet an alien toadstool any day. I gave Aurelia my sweetest smile.

"Can Martin carry flowers too? He looks cute with a basket."

"No," she protested. "He's Lars's groomsman. We were taking it for granted."

They're a lot alike too. I smiled at him smugly.

—*Now you get to look dumb like the rest of us.*

—No, I don't, he said with serenity. I'm doing the floral arrangements and Relia's ring. I've never worked in stage design.

Sword rattled bottles so I wouldn't know he was laughing like a drain. There are times you wonder why guys live so long. I guess a lot are like him, too tall to throttle.

It happened in the Cathedral, to the strains of the Wedding March plus the sound of competing scandal-vids having yelping hysterics. The DeLorns were there dwarfing the pillars, Sword with his medals jangling like a soup-kitchen, his father in orange and purple

sashes and Helen not quite in a shred of silk by Par-
meggiano that shouldn't have been allowed. I began to
think there might be something to be said for being a
millionaire.

The Hallwegs dwarfed the DeLorns. They'd all red
hair and freckles and included a surprisingly goodlook-
ing sister hardly shorter than Hall and two small neph-
ews bigger than Moke. Nobody laughed audibly.
Maybe the smell of money got in their throats. United
Space marrying the Moon has to be nearly as pacific
as ether.

Everyone was holographed from every conceivable
angle, especially Aurelia, who looked virginal, and
Helen, who didn't. Sword looked like Sword, which is
to say the guys who came to interview him didn't stay
long.

"And when do you and the Lady Cassandra mean
to tie the sacred knot, Colonel?" a reckless bim in
sapphire crushed velvet cooed, shoving a mike in his
face. She was possibly just ignorant. Or she may have
been blinded by medals.

"Cass and I cut the Gordian knot last year," he said
in the mild tone sends rational people looking for sand-
bags. "We're now going to settle down and have one-
and-a-half children, who will be semi-legitimate."

The lady laughed on a little descending scale. It got
tremulous towards the bottom, maybe she'd noticed his
teeth. "One-and-a-half?"

"The other one-and-a-half are Moke's. We're
having one mine, one his and one gene-spliced. We
confidently expect it to be a genius. We shall ensure
their survival by hiring a nursemaid."

At which point the lady gave a nervous titter and
left. I was surprised she'd stayed so long.

"I suppose you're serious?" his father said grimly over my head.

"Perfectly."

"Then I'm going to have to give Cassandra her wedding necklace for her birthday."

"She won't hold it against you. She likes bright things that glitter."

"Right. Guess I picked you up on an off-day."

"Is he always as bad as this?"

"Yes," I said.

"No," Sword said simultaneously.

"He gets worse in the presence of the media," I allowed. "He isn't used to being visible, it bugs him."

"Then he'd better start getting used to it. He's my heir and I want him at board-meetings. Steve Morland's taking over some of our subsidiaries and I've a place for my son-in-law. I want my son on show too."

He and Razor. I could see those two evil old men getting along.

"And what would you like me to do with the Strip?" Sword asked politely.

"What your stepfather did. Delegate," his father snapped. "There's also the question of the Governing Council . . ."

"How about our Mr. Steele?"

—*Who?*

—*Gordon,* Sword said with patience. "We need to call in the Gooders. He's highly thought of."

—*But who's going to bake the bread?*

—*Don't be selfish, Cass. The world's full of bakers.*

—*Not like Gordon.*

—*Why don't you go talk to the nice lady about Moke's candle, he's sinking.*

I shot a terrified look over my shoulder and saw it

was true. I left at a run. I could still hear Cameron DeLorn in the distance trying to beat Swordfish into a plowshare. I wished him luck.

Dribble was doubled on the steps behind a sheaf of regal lilies, running like a waterfall. Someone had put him in white wetlook leather so it didn't make too much difference but his nose and eyes could have been used as a fog-warning.

"Hey, there," Moke said, dropping onto the stone.

"Pup, you're making a puddle. Relia wanted you to come behind and throw things. You know, rice and stuff."

He lifted a desolate snout and wailed.

"I not come near Relia. Me spoil pretty dress. Me bad ugly dog, spoil all pretty people holos. Hide here." He sneezed. "This flowers give hay-fever. Not-happy."

"Hey, Drib. You don't got to look this way. You can look any way you want." Another joy of our new condition.

"Me need nose," he sobbed. "Me Sword dog-person."

"You can be Sword's dog-person and beautiful too," Moke said. "Nobody said you got to have a snout. Things've changed, Drib. I'll make you a face."

"Surgeon make me face already one time. Work good, feel bad." He turned red tearful eyes on each of us. "I got do all over?"

"Things changed," Moke repeated. "I'll design you a real handsome face and you can make it yourself, we'll show you how. Then you needn't look up any more skirts, you can have a lady of your own. And your kids needn't be ugly either, they can make their faces too. I'll fix you some pictures. You can show me how you'd like to look.''

''Me go on be able to smell?''

''You go on be able to real stink, Rover. Man told you. You ever know Mokey lie? Now wipe your nose and come throw rice or Relia's gonna be disappointed. She asked you special.''

He broke off a lily and took a bite. ''Me choose any face at all?''

''Yeah, but look at Moke's designs first, you could look silly as Cleopatra. Boy got taste. Come on.''

We hit out for the aisle, where guests were trailing Shirohito raggage on the slabs. Dribble pattered sedately between us on his hind paws, pollen on his muzzle, a half-eaten lily in his hand. He looked emblematic, like Pierrot in love. Several vidmen turned him startled stares and began winding. He didn't notice. Aurelia led him to the stairs and posed him among the Families as if she'd never seen millionaire thread-estate in her life. Her own dress got wet, but only in patches. He came out on her feet with the lily behind his ear. It was a real pretty effect.

The wedding of the year, in fact.

The party came much later, in the Park. Part of it was the Governing Council, which now had Gordon on it. Part of it was just the Strip discovering no one was sitting on its head any more. Guys dressed as birds and bees zipped around, on and off skates, and spacers floated around dressed as spacers, which ain't distinguishable from other people pretending to be someone else. There were a lot of masks, which any psychologist, professional or home-made, will tell you lets guys behave worse than usual without feeling bad in the morning. On the Strip very few of them feel bad in the

morning anyhow unless they really hung one on last
night but that's probably another cup of Schadenfreude.

It was dark and the walkways over east were back
in full action, rumbling through the canyons in ribbons
of light. Traxies zipped over and under. The river was
lined with yellow necklaces. Moke's Candle rose out
of the jungle of towers like a corn-stalk, a topless nee-
dle pointing at the stars, a fountain of children flowing
upwards into the sky. The nav beacons that studded its
height were swallowed in the glow that burned through
its ceramic and the beam from the tip was lost in cloud.
But you could see it from out of atmosphere. You could
see it from the Moon. You would probably be able to
see it from Resurrection when my vanillas finally res-
urrected it. It was over two miles high in its final version, including the lower buttresses, and fifty thousand
people had worked on it. Every face was Moke's own
design. When it was finished, half the city slept for a
week. So did Moke, but he was the one woke still tired
with his eyes full of fresh visions.

We walked on a hillside among bushes watching
copts running in and out of daytime-only pads and kids
making a fire in a trash-eater, which was jerking all its
claws frantically trying to put it out before its brain
overheated, and a whole crew of guys feeding their
noses at a candy stall. Someone else had a medium-
sized orgy going in a stand of rhododendrons, which
looked to reach mass any time and go critical. There
was a general heaving of vegetation that invited you
not to look and see what was in there. Sword scanned
it over with a paternal eye.

"I like peacetime. Quiet and normal. Relaxing."

"You don't think you ought to maybe make a bit of
law and order, allowing this is your turf?"

"No, why?"

I shrugged. "Suit yourself. I guess someone else'll call in the fire department."

"It's what they're there for."

"That is public property."

"I know. It's time they did. Now they know what happens to their taxes they can stop their own kids burning 'em down. My guys got work to do."

I wondered what. I could see three from here and it looked to me what they were working at was the orgy. They were putting a lot of enthusiasm in, too. When it went crit they were going to hit sky among the first.

"We had a war, Cass. Now we're getting around to a peace. You got to let people celebrate. We can be serious later."

"Sure. How's the Serious Crime Squad?"

"You mean Hilt. Patrolling. He'll probably slap a couple of wrists before breakfast, it's what he's paid for."

"And what's his boss doing?"

"Walking in the Park and looking at the lights," Sword said peacefully. "Not being dead."

"Lot to be said for it," Moke agreed.

We walked. I trailed pearly silks and my birthday necklace, in real solidified carbon. My hair wasn't long enough to pagoda but you could lacquer a crest and I had. It all made an agreeable crissing on the grass and twinkled a little, starrily, in the copt headlights. Sword's shiny leather loomed almost as tall as Mokey's candle and his gauze overshirt was strictly for kicks. He wasn't having anyone think he was serious. Not tonight. Moke had a jean vest against the dew, which is how he likes it. His pants had a seat in them, which is how I like it. The grass smelled grassy and the rhododendrons rustled, some by themselves. The dome hummed to itself and parted in a blue slit to let in a late-homing shuttle headed for the Internat beacons.

The leaves opened in front of us and a pair of guys in liquid silver came out, their long-toed shoes slapping on the path and the high antennae that topped their insect masks nodding in the night breeze. One had the pointed probe and rolled tongue of a butterfly, the other the blank winking facets of compound eyes that ate up most of his head and left the front an unfeatured plate. They both wore silver gloves that wafted festive streamers past their elbows. The butterfly raised something shiny and metallic.

"You DeLorn?"

"I'm Swordfish," Sword said gently.

The silver glove leveled towards his face. "A gift from Sheikh Jizman. On behalf of House, everywhere."

Sword stood still, his hands empty. The flash of the laser lit his black hair and brown skin, an even shine of teeth. He was smiling. It caught him between the eyes and bored his skull through, the angled beam threading him like a bead. I saw it spill out the other side, hardly scattered, a string that swung him from the dark sky. We all stood frozen in that moment of threading, as if we'd been standing there forever and would always, a perpetual tableau.

Then the butterfly grunted on an odd high note and let the laser fall. The butt glowed dully in the dark and he clasped one hand in the other, a burned smell rising from his glove. The tube clattered on the path. Bluebottle had already backed away.

Sword went on standing still, his eyes reflective. He slowly raised a hand to his smooth brow and rubbed his palm over it, like he was removing a casual smut or a little rime. When he brought it down his fingers were loosely closed, as if he held something alive inside, maybe a bug or a grasshopper that might fly away. He extended his arm, palm up under the cupped fingers. They recoiled. The bluebottle had drawn his own gun and was standing with it, at a loss, not knowing what he could do. The butterfly still clasped his glove. His breath whistled. Moke and I watched, interested.

Sword's smile was still gentle. He beckoned with his other hand, to come closer. The two guys stood paralyzed. The lifted hand was almost in their faces.

His fingers opened slowly, as if to let out something fragile and precious. A ray of unbearable luminescence flashed from between them. A piece of the sun was lying on his palm, the smallest gem of intolerable light. That began to swell as the enclosing fingers let it go, into a sphere, a widening globe that blazed out like flashpowder. The whole Park stood outlined in a flare of white brilliance. That lasted a second. All our eyes blinked.

When we got our sight back the silver insects had gone. And their lasers, and their shoes, and all the shrubbery over a thirty-yard radius. It was lucky we'd been alone.

"Dangerous thing, radiation," Sword said with calm regret. "Blows up in your face."

Moke and I nodded seriously. We went on down to join the party, where the orgy was welling visibly and the trash-eater had just joined its ancestors with an evil ozone smell. A crowd of masked dancers grabbed our arms with happy yells and invited us on in. They thought fireworks were a great idea.

It was only later we heard Sheik Jizman's house and grounds had vaporized in the night with everyone in them. But of course Sword hadn't wanted to make a mess of the Park and you got to molecularly disperse

somewhere. If there was a day of national mourning I
didn't hear about it.

*—We're monsters. I'm not sure we aren't too dan-
gerous to live.*

We stood on top of the hill looking down on the
space below where the fireworks were in full display.
They were nice fireworks. There wasn't necessarily
much powder in them, a lot of people had begun to
improvise.

*—That could have been true a month or so ago.
Back then I think Hall was right not to want to touch
us. Now it's too late. Hadn't you noticed? It's catching. I did ask you how you thought this thing multiplied. Thousands of people are like us already.
Everyone on the ship. Everyone in the family.
Everyone who helped Moke. Before long, maybe
just everyone. Period. And half of them don't even
know it yet. They do things. Without knowing why
or how. Wait until their kids grow up.*

—I don't know what we are, Moke said dreamily.
But I think it's going to be interesting to find out. I
wouldn't be surprised if it doesn't know either.
Probably it makes something different with each
intelligence it touches. So many things I hadn't
imagined.

—Everyone?

*—Yes. Everyone. It isn't going to be simple.
When was it ever? But I agree it's going to be interesting.*

—It. It used us.

—And we've used it. Up to date.

*—So when do we pay? It turned the Geeks upside
down.*

—Maybe they'll be better upside down, Mokey

said. Did you know it's how a lot of artists like to see the world? Gives you new perspectives.

—*I'd like to know where it really came from,* Sword said. *And what it wants. It's got very quiet lately. Had any conversations recently, Cass?*

—*Not now. I think it was lonely. Maybe now we all talk all the time it just likes to listen.*

—It came from very far out, long ago, Moke said. Alien.

—*And it can cross space.*

—It could. Until it lost its intelligence and couldn't get back out.

—*Until us.*

—*Maybe it needs a host with imagination. If it can cross space . . . There wasn't any sign of a ship near it.*

—And it knows dreams. Moke's face was vacant in the light of the latest starburst, his eyes full of opening flowers.

—*What see, mec?*

—Right there, in the space where they're dancing. Something lacy, only strong enough to jump on. Preformed plastics. A frozen waterfall with arches, pouring down. It could even move in fixed patterns. Open, with a lot of air in it. In clear colors, really high. Could fix it so people could climb up and sit. They'll fly, later, maybe. The kids'll want to . . . Got to talk to Yell about materials.

—*Dreams.* Sword leaned around to take my free hand. *Right now I got the Strip to run. And . . .*

—And I want to build a waterfall. Can't we just live a bit and build things?

Sword gazed up at the constellations above.

—*For now.*

Mokey followed his gaze. Right. For now.

—*Yeah,* I said, looking after both of them. *For now.*

For now. Because, what will any of us be tomorrow? This guy's stopped talking. Does that mean it's satisfied with my dreams, our dreams, our human chatter? Or does it mean to turn us into something we don't know, like it did with the toadstools?

Whatever we are, we aren't human anymore. Not the way we were yesterday. If there are fights and conflicts up there among the Geeks, we've got it coming too. How long before people begin to notice we aren't normal? Before they try to keep us out of their own spaces, without knowing it's too late already? Before normal starts to be us?

Or does it really matter? Aren't we going to change anyhow, just as the Geeks would have if they hadn't tried to hold off evolution? Maybe tomorrow we'll be humans and it's the ones left behind, if there are any, who'll be the un-men. The poor Neanderthals, sitting in the alley when the train left for elsewhen.

Who knows? I don't. Maybe our psychosis has blown up in our faces. If this is insanity, watch out, universe. If it's a growth-hormone it could take us where we've never been. If it wants our dreams it'll find we've plenty to share. Some of them nightmares, but that's how it comes. Take it or leave it, baby.

Whatever it is, yeah, right, it's going to be interesting. It's all in how you look in the mirror. Like the Gorgon. If she hadn't got tied up in her hair—

On the other side's Wonderland.

I'm all for stepping through. Only not today. I got stuff to do, too. But I'll have time tomorrow. All the time in the world.

Don't bother to call me, I can't say I'll be here. This exchange is closed.

. . . *message ends message ends message ends* . . .

SEAN STEWART

"...definitely follows his own drummer."
—Ursula K. Le Guin

__RESURRECTION MAN   0-441-00121-1/$11.00

"Stewart has written a book in which magic returns to the modern world...distinctive and original...powerful."
—Neal Stephenson, bestselling author of Snow Crash

In Dante's world, magic exists in the form of psychic angels and deadly mythical creatures—though both are shunned by society. After experiencing a disturbing vision of his own death, Dante must confront his own angelic powers, as well as the secrets buried in his family's history.

An Ace Trade Paperback

__NOBODY'S SON   0-441-00128-9/$5.50

"A superlative work..."—The Edmonton Journal

"Takes fantasy fiction beyond the quest tale into a larger, darker, more affecting landscape..."—Robert Charles Wilson

Shielder's Mark, a commoner's son, breaks Red Keep's thousand-year spell, bringing salvation to his kingdom and glory for himself. But when the politics at the king's court grow divisive, Shielder's Mark must learn to carry the many burdens of a hero along with the title.

__PASSION PLAY   0-441-65241-7/$4.50

"Dark and nastily believable...Sean Stewart [is] a talent to watch."—William Gibson

The redemption presidency has transformed America. Adulterers are stoned. Executions are televised. But sin still exists. And so does murder.